EGMONT PRESS: ETHICAL PUBLISHING

Egmont Press is about turning writers into successful authors and children into passionate readers – producing books that enrich and entertain. As a responsible children's publisher, we go even further, considering the world in which our consumers are growing up.

Safety First
Naturally, all of our books meet legal safety requirements. But we go further than this; every book with play value is tested to the highest standards – if it fails, it's back to the drawing-board.

Made Fairly
We are working to ensure that the workers involved in our supply chain – the people that make our books – are treated with fairness and respect.

Responsible Forestry
We are committed to ensuring all our papers come from environmentally and socially responsible forest sources.

For more information, please visit our website at
www.egmont.co.uk/ethicalpublishing

The Water Weavers

Kai Meyer

Volume 3 of 3
Translated by Anthea Bell

EGMONT

EGMONT

We bring stories to life

First published in Great Britain 2007
by Egmont UK Limited
239 Kensington High Street, London W8 6SA

First published in Germany 2004
under the title *Die Wasserweber*
by Loewe Verlag GmbH, Bindlach, Germany

Die Wasserweber text copyright © 2004 Kai Meyer
English translation copyright © 2007 Anthea Bell

The moral rights of the author and the translator have been asserted

ISBN 978 1 4052 1637 1

1 3 5 7 9 10 8 6 4 2

A CIP catalogue record for this title is available from the British Library

Typeset by Avon DataSet Ltd, Bidford on Avon, Warwickshire
Printed and bound in Great Britain by the CPI Group

CONTENTS

THE DREAMING WORM   1

THE FLYING RAYS   23

IN THE WHIRLPOOL   41

ON THE VERGE OF WAR   59

THE BATTLE FOR THE ANCHOR   75

THE HAND OF THE MAELSTROM   94

AINA   115

THE SECOND WAVE   134

THE KOBALIN PATH   151

FIERY RAIN   174

THE WEIGHT OF DEEP WATER   195

TWO GIANTS   212

THE CANNIBAL FLEET   228

A CONVERSATION IN THE DEPTHS   249

TYRONE   274

THE RIFT   298

WHEN GODS WEEP   319

THE OLD RAY   334

WHERE ALL MAGIC FADES   349

DOWNFALL   375

WHERE IS JOLLY?   391

MAGIC YARN   408

THE NEW WORLD   422

Other books by Kai Meyer

The Wave Runners

The Shell Magicians

The Flowing Queen

The Stone Light

The Glass Word

www.kaimeyer.com

THE DREAMING WORM

On the morning of her last day in Aelenium, Jolly went to see the Hexhermetic Shipworm.

His house in the poets' quarter of the starfish city was narrow, just wide enough for a low door and a window side by side. As usual in Aelenium, it had no right angles and hardly a single straight wall. The buildings of the city were made of corals that had a look of ivory, many of them left as they had grown naturally, others worked by stonemasons and artists.

'It's me,' she called out as she passed the guard and opened the door. 'Jolly.'

She hadn't expected any answer, and she didn't get one. She knew about the Worm's condition. If it had changed someone would have told her.

Jolly closed the door behind her. What she had to tell the Hexhermetic Shipworm was no business of the guard's, and she was also afraid Munk might have followed her, stealing into the house unnoticed. The last thing she wanted was to have him listening in on her conversation with the Shipworm.

This was her goodbye, and hers alone.

She climbed the irregular stairs to the upper floor and the largest room in the house, where the Worm hung dreaming in his cocoon.

Much of the room with its high ceiling was full of the fine, gossamer-like threads secreted by the Worm's motionless body – the only sign that he was still alive.

A few days ago, when it first became clear that he was beginning to pupate, Jolly had asked if he could be moved to her own room in the palace. But Forefather and the Ghost-Trader had said no, giving no reason for their decision.

Jolly hadn't really been surprised. As everyone kept telling her and Munk, they were the two most important people in Aelenium. No unauthorised person was allowed too close to them, and it would be the same for whatever might emerge from the cocoon when the Worm had finished pupating. *If* anything emerged.

'Hello, Worm.'

Jolly stopped in front of the billowing silken threads. The attic windows had been covered with translucent fabric, partly to shield the Worm from any prying eyes in the buildings opposite, but also in case hungry seagulls saw the defenceless cocoon. Only the palaces of the governors of Aelenium had glazed windows. Ordinary people's houses had wooden shutters to keep out the wind and weather – and the light as well. The fabric that had been stretched over the attic windows instead of shutters made the radiance falling in milky, blurring the edges of the shadows. There was no sharp distinction between light and dark anywhere in the room; everything merged and mingled.

'Hello,' said Jolly again. The sight of that eerie thicket of silk troubled her more than she had expected. Buenaventure the pit bull man came twice a day to make sure all was well here. He had told her about his visits, but this was the first time she had seen for herself how far advanced the Worm's pupation was.

The silk threads were woven into an enormous network that stretched from the floor to the sloping ceiling – not unlike a cobweb, but much more densely spun and without any obvious pattern. The ghostly thicket of threads was several feet thick now, and a denser oval shape hung in the middle of it – the Worm's cocoon. It seemed to be hovering. The threads holding it above the floor at shoulder height were almost invisible.

3

The Hexhermetic Shipworm himself could no longer be seen inside the cocoon. He was hidden by a dense layer of silk, and only a weak pulsation showed that he was still alive.

'That's rather . . . impressive,' said Jolly uncertainly. The sight seemed to slow her words as if her mouth too was filled with the silken web. 'I hope you're all right in there.'

The Worm did not reply. Buenaventure had warned her that conversations with him were a one-sided business these days, but the pit bull man was convinced that the Worm could hear them all the same. Jolly wasn't quite so sure.

'You gave us all a fright,' she said. 'You might at least have warned us something like this would happen. I mean, none of us knows much about Hexhermetic Shipworms.' She sighed, and cautiously put out a hand to touch the outer threads of the web. Its surface billowed like a curtain, as if a breath of air had passed over her fingertips.

'I came to say goodbye.' She withdrew her hand and awkwardly tucked her thumb into her belt. 'Munk and I are leaving. For the Rift. Here in Aelenium they hope we'll manage to seal the source of the Maelstrom, all of them: the nobles, Captain d'Artois, the Ghost-Trader, Forefather. And . . . oh, I don't know. Munk is good at shell magic. Perhaps he really will do it.' She paused for a moment, and

4

then went on. 'I'm not as good at it myself yet, even if no one says so. At least, not to my face. I'm not even half as clever with the shells as Munk. He . . . well, you know what he's like. So ambitious, as if some idea obsessed him. And he's still furious with me for turning shell magic against him on the *Carfax*. But did he leave me any choice?'

She began pacing up and down in front of the web. She'd rather have been having this conversation with someone who could give her advice. But even though her other friends were here with her in Aelenium – Soledad the pirate princess, Captain Walker and his best friend Buenaventure, the giant with the face of a dog – none of them could really put themselves in her position.

Except perhaps Griffin. But Griffin had vanished. His sea horse had come back to Aelenium alone. At the thought of him Jolly felt herself go weak at the knees. Before they could give way she sat down cross-legged, rather awkwardly. It was too late to hold back the tears running down her cheeks.

'No one can tell me what's happened to Griffin. They all say he's dead, but he can't be. Griffin mustn't be dead. They're just saying so, don't you think? I mean, he *can't* . . . oh, this is such nonsense, right? As if there were rules and regulations for such things.' She shook her head. 'But I believe he's still alive, I really do.'

The cocoon at the heart of the web went on pulsating, unmoved. At every faint movement in and out, a wave ran through the silk like a deep breath.

'What will you be like when you come out of there?' she asked. 'Do you know yourself? How about the Wisdom of the Worms now?'

She noticed that as she talked she was clutching her knees so hard that it hurt. Annoyed with herself, she let go of them.

'Forefather and the Ghost-Trader keep whispering together from morning to night. They say the attack on Aelenium is coming any time now. And this morning they made up their minds.'

She pushed a strand of hair back from her face. 'We're setting out,' she said, sounding exhausted. 'Our training is over. I think Munk and I can't do half what we're *supposed* to do yet, but there just isn't any more time. Within two or three days at the latest Tyrone's fleet will be here, and the Deep Tribes will probably attack at the same time or even earlier. No one knows how long the soldiers can defend Aelenium. Perhaps a few days. Perhaps only a few hours.'

Once again time passed as she said nothing, just stared thoughtfully at the floorboards in front of her. She was imagining what would happen when the servants of the

Maelstrom reached the city. The Maelstrom, that huge whirlpool raging in the open seas on the horizon, had gained control over the kobalins. Thousands of them were making for Aelenium in teeming armies. And the feared cannibal king Tyrone with his fleet would also fight on the Maelstrom's side.

Sooner or later Aelenium would have to surrender. That is, unless she and Munk could defeat the Maelstrom first. But for that very reason the battle for the starfish city was intended to give the two of them the time they needed. Dozens, perhaps hundreds, would give their lives to gain valuable hours and minutes for the two polliwiggles trying to enclose the Maelstrom inside its shell deep on the sea-bed.

And despite everything else – the disappearance of Griffin, Munk's ambition, her fear of the monstrous whirlpool bringing all this evil to Aelenium and the Caribbean – that was what troubled Jolly most: the thought that people would die in support of her and Munk. Because they were the only hope for Aelenium.

'I don't deserve to be trusted so much,' she whispered despairingly. 'They must know that, don't they? They must know I'm sure to disappoint them.'

She simply wasn't ready yet. Perhaps she never would be.

But that made no difference, and hadn't for a long time; they had to set out, that was decided.

She had protested, rebelled against the decision – in vain.

The Rift awaited her.

Her fate.

Jolly got to her feet, blew a kiss in the direction of the cocoon at the heart of the web, and wiped away her tears.

'The flying rays are ready to start,' she said. 'Captain d'Artois will escort us to the Maelstrom, and the Ghost-Trader will go that far with us too.' She smiled wearily. 'And Soledad. You know her – she absolutely insisted on coming as far as possible, and no one dares to object.'

She pulled herself together. 'Goodbye,' she said sadly. 'Whatever you may be when you come out of this thing – goodbye.'

With that she turned, left the high-ceilinged room, and slowly went down the steep stairs. The guard at the door looked at her wide-eyed when he saw that she had been crying. But he didn't speak to her, and she was thankful for that.

'The whale's under attack!'

Griffin jumped. He lowered the hammer he had just raised to knock a nail in and took his eyes off the roughly made wooden chair on the floor in front of him. Number twenty-eight. He'd been counting. Twenty-eight chairs for Ebenezer's Floating Tavern – the first ever tavern inside the belly of a giant whale.

'Harpoons, Griffin! They're throwing harpoons at Jasconius!'

'Who are?'

'Who? Kobalins, of course!' The former monk had appeared in the doorway and was waving his arms about.

When the giant whale had swallowed Griffin days ago he'd thought he was staring certain death in the face. Astonishingly, however, he had found himself still alive in the creature's belly, where Ebenezer met him.

Griffin felt sure that the monk's long years of isolation down here must have turned his wits. His plan to open a tavern in the monster's belly was proof of it. In aid of this crazy plan Griffin was spending his time down here making chairs and tables. Ebenezer had threatened not to come anywhere near land until he'd finished his work.

'Harpoons, Griffin!' repeated the monk, very upset. 'The kobalins have harpoons!'

He paced up and down the wood-panelled room in agitation. The gigantic animal's dark stomach cavity lay out there beyond the open door. But here, on this side of the magical doorway, they might have been in a room in a gentleman's country house: a very pleasant, very comfortable residence.

'How many kobalins are there?' asked Griffin.

'How would I know? Ever heard of a whale who could count?'

Griffin opened his mouth for a sharp retort, but at that moment a deafening noise filled the dark grotto of the whale's belly. Something shot towards the open door like a wall of shadow, accompanied by a rushing and roaring as if someone had torn a hole in the whale's side.

'A tidal wave!' shouted Griffin, and they both raced forward, flung themselves at the door and leaned all their weight on it together.

The wave, as high as a house, crashed against it, sweeping the man, the boy and the door itself aside. Water poured into the room, swirled over the wooden floor, and tossed tools and finished chairs around, breaking some of them against the walls. Griffin and Ebenezer both yelled with pain when their heads and backs knocked into the corners and wooden edges of the furniture.

The tidal wave ebbed away just as quickly as it had flowed in, and was not followed by a second one. Water began swiftly seeping out through the cracks between the floorboards. When Griffin struggled to his feet, groaning, there was only a film of moisture left over everything – but it was enough to make him slip. With a fierce pirate curse, Griffin sailed backwards to land on his rear end, and in his pain and rage he could have flung all the stupid chairs he had been so carefully making around him.

Ebenezer was wheezing. He sat on the floor, propped against the wall, and listened to the whale's voice. He claimed that he and Jasconius understood each other through the power of thought alone, and by now Griffin had come to believe there was something in it.

'He's swallowed them!' Ebenezer suddenly gasped. 'Griffin, he's swallowed the kobalins!' His eyes went to the open door in alarm, searching the splashing, gurgling darkness outside.

'How many?' asked Griffin, and with one bound he was on his feet again.

Ebenezer groaned. 'Not many. But they won't have drowned. Unless he squashed a few of them.'

Griffin hurried over to a chest where Ebenezer kept some of the weapons that had ended up in the belly of the whale over the years. Jasconius had swallowed whole cargoes of swords, daggers, springlock pistols and rifles. Unfortunately guns were not much use inside the whale – the gunpowder got wet, and then it was impossible to fire them. In addition there was too much danger of missing your target and injuring the creature's gastric wall.

Griffin took a sword from the chest, balanced it in his hand to test it, and stuck a long knife in his belt. Ebenezer looked away from the door and back at Griffin. 'You're not really going out there, are you?'

'Got any better ideas?'

The monk was torn both ways. 'Jasconius has never swallowed a kobalin before. They've always kept well out of his way.'

Griffin picked up a lantern by its handle and made his way past Ebenezer and through the door. 'You stay here and bolt the door. I'll see what I can do.'

'We could both of us hide.'

'And what about your tavern? Anyway, we'd have to come out soon to look for food. The provisions in the kitchen here won't last forever.'

Ebenezer nodded, but without much conviction. Unexpectedly, Griffin was moved by the older man's concern for him. Up till now he'd thought of himself as a prisoner of the whale and its tenant, fit only to make chairs and tables for the tavern of Ebenezer's deranged imagination. But now he realised that the monk liked him, and it wasn't impossible that he felt the same about the old man. Ebenezer was certainly a little odd – in fact downright eccentric – but he had a good heart.

'I'll be back soon.' Griffin said that more to himself than Ebenezer. The words made him sound braver than he really felt. His voice was shaking, as Ebenezer himself must surely notice.

Kobalins armed with harpoons. Even if they had lost their weapons as they fell into the throat of the whale, that didn't make them any less dangerous. Their long claws and sharp teeth were as deadly as knives.

Griffin stepped out of the light of the room and, carrying his lantern, slowly went down the hill on which the door stood. He looked watchfully around, taking care to appear determined. Kobalins like no prey better than a victim in mortal terror, when it's easier for them to attack without warning.

Behind him, Ebenezer closed the door. Griffin heard the bolt snap into place. The light around him was cut off and replaced only faintly by the weaker beam of the lantern, which cast a circle of light about three yards wide. Beyond the circle lay darkness.

There were gurgling and splashing everywhere as water dripped off parts of wrecks and trickled away into the spongy surface underfoot. Those sounds could hardly be distinguished from the hissing kobalin language.

With the crook of his elbow, Griffin nervously pushed several braids back from his face. He wore his fair hair in dozens of them. It was the way slaves who had been transported from Africa to the New World did their hair, and the style was seldom seen on a white man in the Caribbean, so Griffin was particularly proud of it.

He had just reached the foot of the hill when he heard a hissing from the darkness to his right.

He raised his sword, and something shot towards him as fast as if it had been fired from a catapult – a rake-thin body with scaly skin. The light of the lantern broke on the scales in oily rainbow colours. The kobalin's hands with their long claws were spread wide, and its mouth gaped like a shark's jaws.

Griffin let himself drop, at the same time thrusting upwards with his blade. Steel cut through tough skin and muscular flesh, there was a screech, the body disappeared somewhere in the shadows and then stopped moving. A long-drawn-out slurping sound told Griffin that it was sinking into the sludge inside the whale's belly.

Well, that was easy, he thought, and hauled himself up again. His blade was shimmering with an oily gleam. That first kobalin might have mistaken him for a confused, starving, shipwrecked sailor – but its companions had due warning now.

He just wished he knew how many he had to deal with.

His outstretched hand held the lantern above his head. He heard a rustling somewhere ahead of him, followed by the swift splish-splash of hurrying feet.

One at least, thought Griffin. Probably two or three. With luck no more.

Something struck him in the back and sent him stumbling forward. He cried out, stepped into a dip between the fragments of wrecked ships, and fell forward. Only a moment later did he realise that the fall had saved his life. A claw punched through the air above his head, and would very likely have broken his neck.

As it was, he rolled over on his back and brought his spine up against something hard. The lantern slipped out of his hand and sank into the sludge only a foot away.

By the last of its light, Griffin saw his adversaries. Two of them. Their pinched, wrinkled skin surrounded their open mouths in a grimace like some extra but unfinished touch – as if the creator of the kobalins had concentrated on those gigantic maws and sharp rows of teeth, but had skimped on the other features. Like a child who loses

15

interest in a piece of clay and finishes kneading his work listlessly.

Griffin struck out blindly above him with his sword in the dark, at the same time trying to use his left hand to help him up. But his fingers sank in the black mud with a sound like a smacking kiss. He struck again, but missed. Instead, he felt something grab his right ankle in the dark and pull it – something just outside his reach. A second hand grasped his other leg, and now the creatures began tugging in opposite directions.

They're going to tear me apart! The thought flashed through Griffin's mind in the fraction of a second. Without stopping to think, he brought his torso up fast and struck out desperately above his splayed legs and towards his feet. The sudden movement sent appalling pain stabbing through his back.

At last – his blade met something! There was a slicing sound, followed by frantic kobalin screeches. His left ankle was free. But the strength of the creature on his right dragged him on, away from the wounded kobalin.

Kobalins are mean-minded, malicious beings, but they are also stupid and in a way childish. If they can kill an adversary slowly and painfully, they prefer that to dealing with him quickly – not because they enjoy his torment in itself but because killing is like a game to them, and the longer it goes on the more fun they get out of it.

That worked in Griffin's favour now. They could easily have killed him in the dark, but the onslaught he feared didn't come.

Griffin tried to kick away the claws holding his leg. No use. The creature's long fingers held it as firmly as a clamp. Now the kobalin hauled him away through the sludge, across puddles and holes full of mud, over hard wooden edges and bones that broke under him to cut at his clothing and his hair. Once he felt as if his face was being dragged through grass – until he realised that his head was lying on the matted skin of a dead lion.

The screams of the wounded kobalin behind him died down, ended in sobbing and stertorous rattling, and then stopped.

Suddenly Griffin's leg was free.

Darkness like some kind of soft wadding surrounded him on all sides.

Squelching footsteps to his right.

Before he could jump up, claws grabbed his braids and pushed the back of his head down in the mud again. But still the kobalin didn't kill Griffin. It reached out and tore the sword from its victim. Before Griffin knew it he had been disarmed. Steel clattered somewhere in the distance – the kobalin had thrown the blade away.

Stupid, thought Griffin. Kobalins really are as stupid as they come! Not that it was any help to him.

He braced the muscles of his neck and throat, rested his weight on his arms, and suddenly leaped up. There was a terrible jerk as he tore away, and as he screamed he realised that he had lost some scraps of his scalp and at least one or two little braids – left behind in his adversary's claws. But he was free.

Somehow or other he got to his feet, while muscular kobalin arms snapped at the empty air like a pair of scissors behind him.

This time Griffin did not prepare to fight. He'd learned his lesson. He ran for it, almost blind in the darkness. Suddenly he saw a narrow strip of light, behind jetsam from wrecks that looked like mighty skeletons. Ebenezer had opened the magic door: a beacon in the dark to help Griffin get his bearings. The monk must have realised that his lantern had gone out and knew that Griffin needed something to show him the way.

'There's one of them still alive!' shouted Griffin in the direction of the door, gasping. 'At least one.'

If there was any answer, it was lost in the squelching and

splashing of his footsteps. The kobalin was racing after him, but it too became entangled in parts of wrecks and long tendrils of seaweed. Griffin heard a shrill cackle behind him. Did kobalins laugh? Or was it calling up other survivors of its own kind?

Griffin ran. Stumbled. Fell over. Jumped up again and raced on.

He reached the foot of the hill. The door on top of it stood wide open. Flickering light poured down the slope and the rough and ready wooden steps. The doorway stood isolated on the highest point of the rise, just a frame with an oak door in it, and except for the brightness there was nothing to show that anything might be behind it. Certainly not rooms, for the hill was visible and empty on the other side of the door. All the same, the light of the great fire on the hearth inside fell through the doorway.

Where was Ebenezer?

Griffin was now scrambling up the steps on all fours. His boots were full of mud, and he was afraid of slipping if he didn't use his hands to help support him. Looking over his shoulder, he saw the kobalin barely six feet behind – also on all fours, although it looked perfectly natural in that position. The light flooding out of the door bathed it in a scaly shimmer, an iridescent play of colour. Even as it climbed it was waving its claws, trying to seize Griffin's legs, feeling, snapping, hissing.

'Griffin!' It was Ebenezer's voice. 'Stay where you are!'

Stay where he was? Not likely!

'Watch out!'

Something large flew over him, just a hair's breadth overhead. It missed him only because it made him pause after all. Instead it struck the kobalin.

There was a hollow, metallic sound, and then the creature fell backwards down the steps, finally losing its hold, and disappeared into the depths below. Griffin swung round and saw it land on the very edge of the light coming from the doorway, jammed between two beams and half buried under a huge round object almost its own size.

Ebenezer's globe! The monk must have rolled it out of the back room, picked it up in both hands and flung it at the door.

Trembling, the kobalin reached out one claw, and then turned limp. Its grasping fingers met the globe, tried to find something to hold on to for the last time, and then slid away with a shrill squeal. The malice in its burning eyes went out. A broken yardarm had pierced its body from behind as it fell.

Ebenezer's hands found Griffin and helped him up.

'Was that all of them?'

'I think so . . . yes.'

'Are you hurt?'

'Yes. No. Not really.' He felt as if every word he spoke had to dig its way out through his aching head. Dizziness threatened to cloud his mind. 'Just a few scratches, that's all.'

Ebenezer dragged him through the doorway and into the light. Once he was on the floorboards Griffin's knees gave way, and he had to support himself on his arms.

'No kobalins have ever attacked Jasconius before!' said the monk as Griffin looked up at him. 'The Deep Tribes wouldn't have dared do such a thing in the old days.'

Griffin was fighting for air. 'I told you the kobalins were going to war. You wouldn't believe me. That won't be the last time they attack. The Maelstrom has forced the kobalins to serve it, and they aren't stopping short at the whale or much greater forces. They're going to destroy everything.'

Ebenezer took a few hesitant paces around the room and then stopped. 'I can't let this kind of thing happen again,' he said, as if talking to himself. His features hardened as he turned to Griffin. 'And I *won't* let it happen again either.' There was a new note of decision and gravity in his voice. 'Looks like we'll have to change our plans.'

'*Our* plans?'

Slowly, Ebenezer nodded: it looked as if his head were heavier than usual, and his words suddenly had more weight too. 'The tavern will have to wait. We're going to deal with this bunch of devils first.'

Griffin swallowed. Then the corners of his mouth twitched in something like a smile.

'Do you mean . . .' he began.

'We'll help your friends against these plaguy creatures,' Ebenezer interrupted as firmly as a sea captain ordering his crew to set a new course. 'Jasconius will take us to Aelenium by the fastest way he knows.'

THE FLYING RAYS

The cone of the coral mountain that towered above Aelenium had been hollowed out at the very top to make stables for the flying rays. The steep peak, with dozens of waterfalls cascading down it to be lost in channels and pools in the depths below, looked as if its natural summit had been levelled long ago, and today a broad, unfenced platform stood there. At its centre gaped a circular opening fifty paces wide, through which the rays flew in and out of their retreat.

It wasn't the first time Jolly had been up here – Captain d'Artois had taken her and Munk to the stables with him once before – but the sight of all the pits where the flying rays rested, fitted around the walls of the great hollow space, still struck her as both impressive and unsettling.

The hall around them was roofed, so that light (and sometimes rain) came in only through the large central opening. Although flying rays do not live in the water they like a damp atmosphere, and rainwater was channelled down to their pits to collect there. The strange beasts lay flat in their moist coral pits most of the time, apparently sleeping until someone roused them to go riding out.

There hadn't been time for Jolly to learn much more about these amazing creatures, and she regarded them with wary respect. Unlike the hippocamps, which for all their differences were not unlike horses in some ways – not just in appearance, even more so in their behaviour – she felt ill at ease with the rays. Lying outspread on the floor of their pits, they appeared heavy and lethargic, but when they rose in the air they had a breathtaking majesty. They were slow – the sea horses moved much faster through the water – yet they had enormous strength. Every ray could carry three riders, even more if necessary. And a blow from their pointed tails would kill a man instantly.

Two rays were ready to leave when Jolly and Munk entered their quarters. The animals lay spread out side by side, not in their pits but in the middle of the circle of light where it fell through the roof opening into the hall. The captain was waiting beside one of them.

Jolly glanced over her shoulder, looked straight into Captain Walker's gloomy face and had to smile for the first time that day. He, Buenaventure and the princess were right behind her, looking ready to put a knife to the throat of anyone who came a step too close to her. Jolly felt deep affection for the three who had meant so much to her during these last few weeks: they had been her friends, companions, and often protectors too.

However, they were not alone in coming to see the polliwiggles off. A large company was following them on their way to the rays' stables, including Count Aristotle and the members of the Council in their magnificent robes, cloaks and silken scarves.

Jolly did not particularly like most of those men and women; she thought them arrogant, spoilt and ungrateful. It was true that they all appreciated what Jolly and Munk were ready to do, yet most of them didn't hide the fact that they considered the venture the polliwiggles' duty – as if the two young people were obliged to sacrifice themselves for Aelenium, whatever Jolly and Munk themselves might think.

However, Jolly had stopped bothering about that long ago. She had other anxieties now. The Maelstrom. And the masters of the Mare Tenebrosum, those powers from another, unimaginable world that had made the gigantic whirlpool in the first place. Originally the Maelstrom had been intended to serve its masters as their gateway to this world, but it had closed itself to its creators and was now imposing its own rule of terror.

Jolly went up to Captain d'Artois. Out of the corner of her eye she saw the one-eyed Ghost-Trader in his dark robe take Munk aside and talk to him. The fair-haired boy kept nodding.

It was only natural for those two to look at the journey ahead of the polliwiggles in the same way. They had known each other for years, and all that time, without the boy's knowledge, the Ghost-Trader had been preparing Munk for this mission.

'Ready?' asked Soledad.

Jolly half turned to the pirate princess. In spite of their age difference, Soledad had been a true friend to her here in Aelenium and earlier. 'No,' she said.

The princess smiled sadly. 'Believe me, I'd go if I could.'

'Munk and I will manage.'

'I know.'

Neither of them sounded particularly sure of it, but there was nothing else to say now.

Walker moved away from the others and touched Jolly's arm. He seemed to feel even uneasier near the flying rays than she did. 'Look after yourself,' was all he said, but his expression was grim with anxiety. 'Good luck.'

'Oh, we won't need that. I mean, we're polliwiggles.'

He stared at her in alarm for a moment before her irony got through to him. Then he laughed, forgot how close they were to the flying creatures, and leaned forward far enough to give Jolly a last hug. 'Make sure you're back soon to get on my nerves again, right?'

She couldn't say anything, just nodded and waved to Buenaventure, who had been standing there all this time with his brows raised. You could never tell, with him, whether that meant anxiety, or scepticism, or was just natural to his dog's face. He scratched behind his left ear – making himself look even more dog-like, although he did it with a human hand – then put his head on one side, and he really might have been about to utter a howl of pain any moment.

Jolly lowered her eyes. She wasn't going to burst into tears now, not here and not in front of the members of the Council. The captain seemed to guess what was going on in her mind. He quickly took the reins, climbed into the saddle, and signed to Jolly and Soledad to get up behind him. While the Ghost-Trader and Munk mounted the other ray, their own was already waking from its trance. The first movements rippled through the creature's outspread wings.

A moment later it was carrying them up in the air with

gentle, undulating wing-beats. Jolly felt the creature's heart pulsing under her, very calm and gentle, and every time it pulsed she felt a little more composed.

Sighing, she took a deep breath, and glanced down. The second ray was just rising from the floor too, flying through the roof of the great hall and out into the open.

Walker and Buenaventure stood side by side to see them off, their faces showing how anxious and helpless they felt. The members of the Council waved enthusiastically, but Jolly ignored them. Munk, however, waved back in a casual, almost lordly way, like a king taking leave of his subjects. He had assumed many such mannerisms over the last few weeks. He liked the nobles of Aelenium to pay court to him. Didn't he realise that they'd forget him just as readily as they had welcomed him in the first place? If the polliwiggles' mission failed, they would be just two more victims of a hopeless war.

'Captain d'Artois?' Jolly leaned closer to him as the ray flew over the edge of the platform, and the precipitous coral slope lay below them.

'Yes?'

'If Aelenium survives . . . I mean, if the Maelstrom is defeated but I don't come back, could you do something for me?'

He nodded gravely, without looking round at her. 'If I survive myself – yes, of course.'

'Could you find Griffin for me and tell him . . .' She stopped, thought, and then plucked up courage. 'Could you tell him that I'm very fond of him? Much fonder than he probably thinks.'

'I'll be happy to do it.'

'Tell him I've thought of him often these last few days. I'd have liked to see him again before we set out.'

'I can understand that.'

Jolly was about to add something, but then told herself she was sure d'Artois had understood what she meant. If he really did meet Griffin, he would find the right words.

She looked back one last time. The ramparts around the city were clearly visible from the air. There were two of them, one at the foot of the coral mountain, built across the arms of the giant starfish shape on which Aelenium rose. The second barricade was higher up in the maze of streets, only a little way above the poets' quarter. If that second barricade fell the city was lost. Then the inhabitants would have to defend themselves in house-to-house fighting, and it would be just a question of time before the kobalins, cannibals and pirates overran the last positions they held.

Heavy at heart, Jolly turned her eyes away and looked

ahead. The rays were carrying them towards the wall of mist that surrounded Aelenium on all sides. A moment later the creatures plunged into the vapours and flew through the highest level of the mist. Up here it was like flying over clouds, grey and white cotton-wool clouds stretching down below as if they could easily catch anyone who fell from the saddle now. Tentacles of vapour reached out for the rays. Now and then their bellies touched the mist or their wings passed through it.

Jolly cleared her throat. 'May I ask you something else, Captain d'Artois?'

'Go ahead.'

'Is there someone . . . I mean, do you have someone waiting for you down there? Someone you're doing all this for?'

D'Artois' neck muscles suddenly stood out distinctly, and he braced his back. 'I'm fighting for . . .' He stopped. Perhaps he had been going to say 'for all the people of Aelenium', and then realised at the last moment how empty the words would sound. 'My wife is dead,' he said after a short pause. 'She died when the kobalins attacked the northern arm of the starfish. She was riding one of the hippocamps that they pulled down into the sea.'

Jolly's throat felt drier than ever. 'I'm sorry.'

D'Artois seemed to be concentrating entirely on guiding

the ray again. But she saw that the knuckles of his fingers were white as he grasped the reins. He was breathing deeply, as if that could free him from his sad memories.

Soledad put a hand on Jolly's shoulder, only for a moment, and then clung to the saddle again; she was not enjoying this flight.

'Everyone here has made sacrifices,' she whispered in Jolly's ear. 'Munk has lost his parents, you've lost Captain Bannon, I've lost my father. The soldiers are no exception.'

Jolly knew that, but still it was good to hear Soledad say so. In her own fear and uncertainty, she was in danger of forgetting that others too had to live with loss and grief. She was only one of many. Nothing special, as she had kept telling herself, even when Forefather and the Ghost-Trader tried to convince her that she was.

She was only a girl.

Somehow or other she found that a more reassuring thought than all the talk of polliwiggle gifts and shell magic. If she and Munk really did manage to overcome the Maelstrom, it wouldn't be because they were different from other people. If they defeated it, it would be because they hadn't forgotten what they were. Who they were.

And that was something worth fighting for.

*

'Can you see anything?'

The whale was drifting on the waves with his mouth open. Ebenezer stood between two teeth, holding tight with one hand and bending far enough forward to look out and up past the animal's gums. The sky was deep blue, like the inside of a jewel. Flocks of seagulls circled above the whale; they followed him wherever he went in the seven seas. If he surfaced they pecked seaweed and small shellfish off his back.

Griffin was perched high up on the whale's head. It had been a laborious and alarming climb up the tunnel of the oesophagus into the creature's mouth. From there he had jumped into the water, and the whale had dived down to come up again just below him, lifting Griffin to his back.

'Griffin!' called Ebenezer, down in the jaws of Jasconius. 'Tell us, can you see the mist?'

Griffin shaded his eyes with both hands, but the brightness still dazzled him. He gazed intently in all directions, searching for the wall of mist that hid Aelenium. Jasconius might be very intelligent for a sea-monster, but his sense of direction left a lot to be desired.

Anyway, how would a whale know about the points of the compass? Or degrees of longitude and latitude?

'I can't see anything!' Griffin shouted back. 'It's all so bright!'

'Wait a moment longer,' replied Ebenezer, trying to make himself heard above the crash of the waves against the mighty pillars of the teeth in the whale's open mouth. The monster's gums rose above him like a black dome. 'You'll soon get used to it again.'

It wasn't easy to keep steady on the smooth surface of the whale. Griffin had taken off his boots so as not to injure the animal's skin. Barefoot, he was crouching on the highest point of the mighty body that reached away under him like the hull of a capsized boat, black as tar and covered with thousands of tiny shrimps and shells.

Only now could Griffin see how enormous the whale really was. He suspected that his body must measure more than twice the length of a four-master – not including the gigantic tail-fin.

Griffin looked through the swooping flock of gulls to the horizon. The more his eyes got used to daylight again, the bluer and brighter the sky seemed; it was as if ink were being poured into infinity from somewhere beyond the sea.

But still he couldn't see any mist. Couldn't Ebenezer have told him earlier that Jasconius chose which way to swim, although the monk could guide the whale roughly one way or another? Last night, when Ebenezer took him up through the whale's oesophagus into his mouth for the first time, Griffin had checked their course by the stars. After that they had dived down to continue the journey. To make sure, however, Griffin had insisted on looking for their destination once more, in daylight. They might be closer to Aelenium than they thought, and he didn't want to risk missing the starfish city.

But apart from the gulls, the dazzling brightness and the black monster beneath him he couldn't see anything. No mist anywhere. Perhaps he was still too close to the surface. Not for nothing was the look-out always posted up in the crow's-nest on the highest mast of a ship. If he'd been able to fly like the gulls, then perhaps –

A frightful sound made him jump. A jet of water as tall as a tower shot up from an opening in Jasconius's back only about ten paces away from him, to the accompaniment of a roaring and rattling so loud that it hurt his ears. Seconds later Griffin's clothes, which had only just dried in the sun, were soaking wet again. The great mass of water almost washed him off the whale's back.

Cursing, he lay flat on his stomach and tried to hold on while the last fountain from inside the monster fell on him. He closed his eyes to protect them from the salt water, pressing his cheek firmly against the whale's skin.

'Griffin?' called Ebenezer from down below. 'Everything all right?'

Groaning, Griffin struggled up. 'Why didn't you tell me he does that?'

'I thought you knew about whales.'

Sighing, Griffin shook his head, rubbed the water off his face and looked at the opening in Jasconius's back. The jet of water had been at least ten times as tall as a man. The pressure necessary to send such masses of water so high must be enormous.

'Griffin?'

'Wait. Just a moment.' A crazy idea was taking shape in his mind. A *really* crazy idea.

'Ebenezer,' he finally called, 'how often does Jasconius do it?'

'Oh, I can ask him to stop for a while.'

'No, no . . . quite the opposite!'

'Too hot for you up there, is it?' Ebenezer sounded concerned. He seemed to think Griffin had suffered sunstroke on the whale's unprotected back.

'I just want to try something.'

'Try what?'

'Can you ask him to do it again? Blow out all that water, I mean.'

35

'Yes, of course.'

'Will he do it to order?'

Down in the whale's mouth, Ebenezer said nothing for a moment. Griffin was glad he didn't have to look him in the face just now.

'Probably,' replied the monk after a while. He sounded sceptical.

Griffin shooed away a seagull that took him for an outsize hermit crab and went over to the opening. Once he was close to it he saw that the edges had come together again. He took a deep breath. If he wanted to get higher up to look for Aelenium, he must try it.

Suppose the water pressure was too strong and broke all his bones?

He hesitated once more, briefly, then climbed on top of the opening. It looked like a gigantic compressed mouth that might open under him at any time. Griffin spent a moment or so choosing the best position and finally knelt down, legs and knees close together, hands clasped in front of him.

'Ebenezer? Now!'

'What the devil are you doing up there?'

'Just tell him.'

The monk hesitated. 'Think yourself lucky I can't get

'up aloft to knock some sense into you, my boy.'

Griffin grinned. 'Think you could, old man?'

'The hand of a saint is guided by the will of God, don't forget that. Including when it's tanning a loud-mouth's hide.'

'Who says so?'

'A saint, obviously.'

'Oh, get on with it, Ebenezer! We're in a hurry.'

Griffin was expecting more protests. Instead he felt movement in the whale's muscles beneath his knees and feet. He prepared himself and braced his whole body, afraid that any moment now he would be hit by a hammer of water so fast that he might not even feel the impact when he fell into the sea.

'Tell him to take it slowly,' he was beginning to say – and then he was suddenly picked up as if by a giant's hand, so gently that Jasconius might have been trying to hold a fragile piece of china in the air.

In his amazement Griffin uttered a yelp of jubilation which Ebenezer, down in the mouth of the whale, misinterpreted.

'Are you dying?' he shouted through the roaring of the water.

'After you, Ebenezer.'

Now Griffin concentrated entirely on balancing himself on the rising column of water. He spread his arms and relaxed slightly to offer a larger surface to its pressure. Everything went better than he had feared. Swaying, rocking, and with his stomach rumbling uncomfortably, he was raised aloft by the jet of salt water with more delicacy than he would ever have thought a monstrous creature like Jasconius could show.

'This is great!' he shouted, laughing.

He was rising first five, then ten paces up in the air above the whale's back. In the end he was high above the surface of the sea. Gulls scattered, screeching, indignant at this invasion of their domain. Water was spraying all around Griffin, but he still managed to look north, south, east and west.

And he could see the mist. A grey streak as if someone had outlined the horizon with lead. Far off, but they could certainly reach it within a day, perhaps faster if Jasconius made haste.

Almost as soon as he had seen the mist the pressure lessened, and the jet of water beneath him gradually died away. Griffin sank as if on a flying carpet, and was brought down almost tenderly over the opening on the whale's back.

Slightly dizzy but relieved, he slid along the curve of the

whale's body on the seat of his trousers and splashed into the water. After swimming a few strokes he was level with Jasconius's enormous eye. It was observing him with interest. Griffin was about to swim on, but then he trod water and turned to that great black eye, which was at least twice his own size.

This was the first time he had been able to look directly at the whale. The curved surface of the eye reflected him — it was as if his likeness were caught in a dark glass globe. But there was more than curiosity in the creature's gaze. A touch of melancholy?

Griffin drifted beside Jasconius's eye until Ebenezer called anxiously to him. Even then he couldn't tear himself away from the sight at once. He had never seen anything more beautiful. And the sight also filled him with a strange kind of grief, as if it expressed something of the great whale's centuries of loneliness. What was going on in his skull? What did he think about the tiny creatures living inside him? Was he glad to have a little company after so long?

He heard a deep note, almost like the sound of a trumpet — the whale's voice. It was a warm, friendly sound, and suddenly Griffin had to smile at the whale's eye and wave to him. It was a wonderful, bewildering moment. Only then did he turn away, heavy at heart, as if there were something else the whale had wanted to tell him, a thousand stories out of a time span of a thousand years.

Ebenezer reached out both hands and helped him to climb back into the whale's throat.

Griffin pointed out of the jaws of Jasconius into the open air. 'That way,' he said, and he and the monk hugged each other with relief. They set off quickly back to the stomach cavity of the whale and the door at the top of the hill of debris.

Behind them, Jasconius closed his mouth and waited until they had reached the magic rooms. Then he went down below the surface and, with mighty strokes of his flippers and tail-fin, swam towards the starfish city.

IN THE WHIRLPOOL

Jolly didn't know how long they had been travelling when Captain d'Artois turned his head to look at them, and pointed forward without a word. She craned her neck and narrowed her eyes, trying to make something out in the dazzling sunlight. But taking in the entire distant spectacle at a single glance was impossible. She had to turn her head to look from end to end of it.

'It's so *big*,' she whispered.

Far, far away the line of the sea dissolved into grey vapour, not unlike the wall of mist round Aelenium, but far higher and unimaginably wide. The water below them was churned up, but there was none of the turbulence of a coming storm about it, and there was almost no wind at all. The further ahead Jolly looked, the more clearly she could see that they were already over the outer rim of a titanic whirlpool: the sea was moving in a broad, curving course from west to east, in a pattern like the rings in a felled tree trunk. And it was very gradually leading down.

Again and again, jets of spray as tall as towers rose to the sky, apparently for no reason, since there were no reefs or sandbanks on which waves could break. The surface was raging and roaring, and here and there the waves seemed to have a will of their own, for they turned on each other as if other waves beneath them were resisting the fierce current. Streaks of foam lay on the water like skin on boiled milk, and here the sea was so rough and scarred that it no longer reflected the blue of the sky. The endless expanses below them had changed colour to a purple that was almost black, as if the turbulent water were washing up darkness from the depths, like camouflage fluid ejected by ten thousand inkfish.

'It will get much worse when we fly closer,' said d'Artois. His voice was rough and husky.

'Is that what you're going to do?' asked Soledad. 'Fly over the Maelstrom?'

The mere idea made Jolly shudder.

'No, of course not. That would be far too dangerous. But I thought it would be as well for us all to see just what we're dealing with. *Maelstrom* is only a word. But what's down there is . . .' He shook his head, as if he could think of no term for it. 'An abyss between worlds, says the One-Eyed Man. Looks more like the *end* of the world to me.'

He was right. If Jolly hadn't known better she would have been sure they had reached the far side of the ocean, where long ago people had believed the water poured over a cliff at the very edge of the disc of the world. Her foster father Bannon had told her that the world was a globe, and you never came to anything like the end of it. But the sight of the Maelstrom was enough to convince anyone of the opposite.

Jolly felt dreadfully small, far too tiny to oppose such a force of nature. Mile after mile of boiling sea stretched away down there, and that was certainly nothing by comparison with what awaited her at the centre of all this chaos. In the Rift, at the heart of the Maelstrom.

D'Artois gave a sign to the soldier flying the second ray, and immediately both animals turned to trace a wide curve in the air.

'Now we're flying back to where the sea isn't quite so rough,' he explained over his shoulder. 'It's important for you two to be able to dive straight down without getting caught by the current.'

'But we'll have to come closer to the Maelstrom anyway,' Jolly pointed out. 'Sooner or later we're bound to feel the current.'

'Not necessarily. A Maelstrom is funnel-shaped. Up here it may be fifty miles wide, but it narrows as it goes down. You'll be able to walk over the sea-bed and under its outer areas unharmed.' He paused for a moment. 'The One-Eyed Man says that at its centre, where it springs from a mighty shell at the very bottom of the Rift, the Maelstrom is no broader than a tower.'

Jolly looked across at the Ghost-Trader, or the One-Eyed Man, as d'Artois called him. The Trader was talking earnestly to Munk, but over this distance she couldn't hear what he was saying. Presumably his instructions were much the same as the captain's.

'How many miles will we have to go?' asked Jolly.

'If we bring you down on the outer rim of the Maelstrom. . . well, about twenty or thirty. I can't say exactly, because it's been growing larger every day. We've given up measuring it.'

Thirty miles, thought Jolly, shaken. The Rift itself apparently lay at a depth of thirty thousand feet, so Forefather had said. And were they to go all that way without any help at all? They couldn't even take a compass, for the water pressure would destroy the glass at once.

'Don't forget that you mustn't move far from the sea-bed,' d'Artois repeated. It was a point that the Ghost-Trader and Forefather had already hammered home. 'The Maelstrom will be looking for enemies approaching, and the One-Eyed Man says that as long as you stay close to the bottom it won't detect you. In fact it will be best if you walk. Swim only in an emergency.' He shook his head, as if tired of repeating rules that he himself didn't understand. 'You're to watch out for strong currents, changes of pressure, and so on. Any of that could be a sign that the Maelstrom is reaching out for you.'

Jolly nodded, bemused. She had heard all this hundreds of times over the last few days. But hearing it explained now by someone like d'Artois, who didn't take magic for granted, made the terrors ahead seem even more real and threatening.

Soledad had said hardly anything for the last few minutes, and she still remained silent. Jolly knew that the princess felt guilty, thinking of the burden the polliwiggles must bear, and her inability to do anything or devise any better solution made her angry with her own helplessness.

The flying rays were now bearing south again, where the sea was not so rough. During the flight they had already seen armies of kobalins in the depths below, dark swarms of them teeming like ants and moving towards Aelenium below the surface of the waves. Kobalins as far as the eye could see. Once they had flown over a region where it was raining dead fish from a clear sky, and they had all known there must be a creature of the Maelstrom somewhere below them, a monstrosity like the Acherus that killed Munk's parents. Perhaps they had even passed close to the kobalin commander, a being that none of them had ever seen, although Jolly had twice been almost within touching distance: once on the open sea during the voyage to Tortuga, again with Griffin on the shape-shifter's island. On both occasions, dead fish had come raining down close to the unseen creature.

The waves below them were gradually growing calmer, and finally d'Artois gave another signal to the second ray. The animals slowed their flight and began circling. Jolly looked over her shoulder. The streak of vapour on the horizon was still in sight, but the arms of the Maelstrom did not reach as far as this. The kobalins too had passed this place some time ago, so at least that gave her and Munk a chance of getting to the bottom of the sea without meeting them.

'D'Artois!' Soledad suddenly called. 'Look ahead there!'

'I can see it,' murmured the captain.

Glancing south, Jolly realised what they both meant. Something dark was approaching on the water, moving as swiftly as if it were flying over the surface.

'Is that a sea horse?' she asked.

'Whoever's on it must be riding at a punishing pace to go so fast,' replied d'Artois, frowning.

'A servant of the Maelstrom?' Soledad said what they were all thinking.

D'Artois whistled towards the second ray, but its riders had already seen the dot in the distance for themselves. The captain took a small crossbow from its holster on his saddle and bent it expertly with one hand. An old-fashioned weapon like this was easier to handle on the back of a ray than a pistol that had to be loaded and made ready to fire.

Soon the new arrival was so close that there could be no more doubt about its outline. It was indeed a sea horse. But its rider wore a motley assortment of piratical clothing, not a leather uniform like the guardsmen of Aelenium.

'Who the devil is that?' asked Soledad. Judging by her tone of voice, she would very much have liked to have a weapon in her own hand.

'I know that animal,' said d'Artois a moment later. 'It's Matador.'

Jolly trembled, she missed a breath and her heartbeat faltered. 'Griffin's sea horse?'

The captain nodded.

Then the rider raised an arm and waved excitedly to

them, and although his voice couldn't be heard above the rushing of the rays' wings and the distant roar of the Maelstrom, and his face was still no larger than a pinhead, Jolly knew who it was.

'That's Griffin!' Her voice broke, and then rose with excitement. 'Go down, d'Artois! Please – go lower!'

Still circling, the ray flew lower. When it was four or five times the height of a man above the water, Jolly could see Griffin's blond braids and then his smile. Now he was waving with such exuberance that for a moment she thought he might be a hallucination conjured up by her wishful thinking.

'Griffin!' she called, waving back. And more quietly, she whispered into the wind, 'Oh, Griffin, thank God!'

She ignored all the others now: Munk's stony face as he looked across at her; the Ghost-Trader's anxious frown; d'Artois as he uttered a warning; Soledad's good-natured murmur. She swiftly undid the strap holding her in place, stood up straight in the saddle, took a couple of steps over the ray's soft wing – and dived head first into the water.

Her companions' cries of alarm died away as her face and hands came up again through the surface in a swirl of spray and dancing air bubbles. For a moment or so she had been unable to hear anything but gurgling, roaring sounds, then she turned underwater and brought her head up above the surface. Griffin steered Matador her way, reined in the sea horse a pace or two from her, quickly undid the buckles of the belt on his saddle and jumped into the water to join her. One powerful stroke brought him swimming up beside her, and then they embraced and kissed, feeling as if the Maelstrom and the kobalins and the whole world around them had dissolved into thin air.

'I followed the ship,' he said breathlessly, water still lapping against his face. 'When you left Aelenium . . . in the *Carfax* . . .' He gasped for air. 'And I was almost too late again . . . you'd just left on the rays.'

She kissed him once more, harder this time, and they were both in danger of sinking because in their delight they simply forgot to swim. It had almost slipped Jolly's mind that, unlike her, Griffin couldn't breathe underwater.

D'Artois' ray was now circling low above the surface. The crests of the waves were licking at the animal's belly. Jolly saw Soledad smiling with satisfaction, which for some reason seemed to her extraordinarily generous and understanding, considering the situation. For the first time she was really aware how fond she was of the princess.

Not far away, something splashed into the water, and then Munk emerged from the waves beside them.

'Hello, Griffin,' he said, spitting out salt water. He was smiling, if a little grimly.

'Munk.' Griffin nodded to him, turned to Jolly once more and gave her a kiss – much too briefly. Then he let go of her. She knew why. He didn't want to widen the gulf that, by no wish of his own, he had opened up between her and Munk. Not in view of what lay ahead of them.

The Ghost-Trader's ray too was close to the surface now. The animals were circling around the two boys and the girl in the water, while Matador swam through the waves a little way off. As the rays beat their wings, cool air blew into the faces of the three young people. Perhaps that was why Jolly was shivering. Or was it the certainty that this was goodbye?

For now the moment she had feared for weeks had come: in a few minutes' time she would be alone with Munk, down in the depths. Just the two of them, with no one else to turn to.

Griffin gave her an encouraging smile, but she saw through the brave face he was putting on. He wasn't concerned about the Maelstrom or Aelenium or even the fate of the world – he just wanted her to come back to him safely. And it was in that moment, in those few seconds of intense emotion, she made up her mind that his wish would come true. Whatever happened, she wasn't giving up. She would do whatever had to be done – and then she would come back to Griffin.

'Jolly, Munk – watch out!'

Rucksacks of oiled leather fell from the rays into the water. Jolly and Munk picked them up and buckled them on tightly. Griffin helped her, and Munk too accepted his aid after hesitating only briefly. There were waterproof cans of salted meat in the rucksacks, fruit and raw vegetables, pieces of coconut – food that could be unpacked below the surface without spoiling or getting immediately soaked with salt water. When the polliwiggles talked or ate down in the sea no water passed their lips, although that made drinking fresh water more difficult. The rucksacks also contained bottles with corked, narrow necks, through which they could suck the water as if through a straw. They had practised all these things, like so much else; their mission wouldn't fail for any reason so trivial as difficulty in eating and drinking.

'And remember,' called the Ghost-Trader as they made ready to dive, 'always stay close to the sea-bed. Don't let yourselves be tempted to swim across difficult terrain. The Maelstrom will be sending out currents in all directions, and if it meets with unexpected resistance it will find you.'

'How does the Ghost-Trader know these things?' murmured Griffin.

Jolly took his hand underwater. 'I think he's seen it all before, back when the first polliwiggles defeated the Maelstrom in the Rift and shut it up in its shell.'

'But that was thousands of years ago!'

Jolly nodded. She had no time to tell him all that she had seen and learned since they last met, and just said, 'Ask Soledad. She knows all about it.'

He looked uncertainly at her, and then nodded back.

The Ghost-Trader's voice interrupted them, like a hand pushing them apart. 'It's time to go!' he called down from the back of his ray.

'Yes,' said Munk, looking askance at the two of them.

Jolly tried to read his eyes, but he quickly turned away. She looked at Griffin, kissed him one last time, and then let go of his hand.

'Goodbye,' she said, wishing she could think of something better, something to express all she felt for him.

'Good luck,' said Griffin. 'Come back soon, both of you.' He swam over to Munk and shook his hand under the water. 'Look after yourselves.'

Munk gave him a brief nod.

Jolly looked from Soledad to d'Artois and the Ghost-

Trader, and back to Griffin. Then the shadows of the flying rays passed over her head.

A moment later, when the sun shone down on the place where the polliwiggles had just been drifting in the water, they had both disappeared.

The sensation wasn't new any more, and had nothing intriguing about it. Keeping their arms and legs close together, Jolly and Munk sank into the depths, unaffected by water pressure that would have killed anyone else in a minute or so. Their polliwiggle vision let them see several hundred yards ahead, but down here there was nothing to be seen.

They fell through nowhere, grey and yet more grey, for polliwiggle vision drained everything of most of its colour, making it pale and dull and ugly – even if there *had* been anything for them to see. But there was nothing around them except for empty water, with swarms of tiny particles hovering in it now and then. No fish. No sign of life. The army of kobalins had driven all living things from this part of the sea.

'Do you think there are any of them still left here?' Jolly asked. 'Kobalins, I mean.'

Munk shrugged as they went on going down. 'Could be.

But that wouldn't really make much sense. They'll be needed more in Aelenium than out here.'

Jolly thought of what the Ghost-Trader had said about currents helping the Maelstrom to track them down. Once they had reached the sea-bed they might be safe, but what about now, while they were still going down? Weren't they helpless, at the mercy of any of the Maelstrom's currents searching these waters?

She quickly put that thought out of her mind, and concentrated on finding something to look at in her surroundings. But there was only Munk, descending level with her. She didn't even really feel as if she were sinking, since the water offered them no perceptible resistance, and there was nothing in sight to help them to estimate their speed. Were they going down slowly or at break-neck tempo?

During their training in the waters around Aelenium, the underwater city had always been close, with its sharp, jagged coral formations under the giant starfish. The sight had made it easier to take their bearings. But there was nothing like that out here.

Jolly's despondency grew. It was harder and harder to bear, and she could tell that Munk was feeling the same. His features were set as if he himself was absorbed in his own dismal thoughts. After a while she took his hand as they went deeper down, side by side. He responded to the gesture so gratefully that for the first time she felt some hope he might forget their quarrel and be his old self again, the same likeable, cheerful Munk she had met back on his parents' island, where she had shown him how to fire a cannon, and he had dreamed of being a pirate.

The last few weeks had changed him, making him grimmer, more reserved and inscrutable. But perhaps all that was passing off and they could be friends again. Down here they had to rely on one another, and there would be times when they had to turn to each other for encouragement and comfort. How could they do that if Munk was still hating her for falling in love with Griffin and not him?

Jolly lost all sense of time as they sank further and further into the abyss. Once something moved on the periphery of her field of vision, perhaps a fish. Not big enough for a kobalin, thank heaven.

They might have been moving through the water for an hour now, even several hours, and most of the time they said nothing. Both avoided mentioning their quarrel. Sooner or later, Jolly knew, they'd have to talk about it. There was no point in pretending it hadn't happened. And though she couldn't forgive him for it, she understood how he felt. He'd been so self-centred; there'd been such anger in him, so much wounded vanity.

At last, after half an eternity, they saw the bed of the sea below them. Jagged rocks rose from the darkness to meet them, looking for a moment like hooded figures. Shapeless stone structures reached for them as if with bony fingers. These cliffs rose from a dark grey, rocky floor, a plain leading gently downwards – down to the Rift.

Thirty miles, thought Jolly, as an icy chill went through her. She felt sick.

'That place ahead there looks good,' said Munk.

'Call that good?' she asked sarcastically, but next moment she was sorry. Now who was trying to pick a quarrel?

The place that Munk was pointing to lay a little further north – assuming north was really where the sea-bed fell away. All they knew was that the Rift was the deepest place anywhere in the seven seas, or at least so Forefather had said.

They moved sideways, swimming swiftly, and let themselves sink to the bottom. Both wore sandals with stout soles which offered hardly any resistance to the water, but would protect them from the rough floor of the sea if it resembled land above the water in any way. But who knew whether everything might not look quite different in a place like this? Did any of the laws of the surface still hold good here?

Shivering, Jolly realised that they were the first people ever to go so far into the ocean deeps. Or no, not the very first – several thousand years ago other polliwiggles had set out to defeat the Maelstrom when it first tried to break down the borders of the Mare Tenebrosum. The polliwiggles, so the story went, had shut it up in the great shell in the Rift, and there it stayed until, fourteen years ago, it had managed to escape from its prison. Soon after that more polliwiggles had been born, but all except two had died later. Only Jolly and Munk were left. Now it was their duty to trace the way of those first polliwiggles and overcome the Maelstrom.

The seascape down here was imposing in its absolute bleakness. The ground looked like a mixture of cold lava and ashes baked solid. There were no plants anywhere; Forefather said none could grow at such depths. Not even lichens covered the rock; all was bleak and bare as the peaks of the volcanic islands that Jolly had seen on her voyages with Bannon. No fish came into view either, although Jolly couldn't shake off the feeling that they were being watched from cracks and crevices in the porous surface of the rocks. There must be life down here, and with a shudder she thought of all the tales of giant krakens and the other creatures said to live at the very bottom of the sea.

The needles of rock around them rose higher and became even more bizarre. Some looked as if black clinker had been piled up in layers while it was still half fluid and left to solidify. Others had such sharp edges that it hurt just to look at them. Quite a number were like grotesque, distorted bodies leaning over the two of them like giants, baring teeth of dark stone. Those on the very edge of their field of vision in particular seemed to be moving if you didn't look straight at them.

Jolly bit her lower lip, hoping the pain would take her mind off her fears. It didn't help, and no wonder. She adjusted her rucksack, checked all the buckles and straps, and then turned to Munk.

'Let's go,' she said, drawing more salt water into her lungs with a deep breath.

'Yes,' he said quietly. 'We'd better be on our way.'

ON THE VERGE OF WAR

When Griffin returned to Aelenium he saw how the city had changed within a few days.

The coral mountain was bristling with weapons and engines of war. The many markets still to be found in the maze of streets only a week or two ago had gone. Instead of storytellers, there were stacks of sandbags and crates of weapons. Soldiers were patrolling the poets' quarter just below the second defensive wall, and there were no longer any public lectures, readings or song recitals here either.

At first sight it looked as if the ordinary citizens of Aelenium had dissolved into thin air. Almost everyone out and about in the narrow coral alleyways wore uniform. But when Griffin looked more closely he saw that many civilians had exchanged their everyday clothes for guardsmen's leather outfits.

In the city squares and parks, masters-at-arms were

training them in the basic techniques of fighting with swords and pistols. Only too soon it became obvious that the people of Aelenium were not natural warriors. Most of those not responsible for supplying the city's needs as traders, fishermen or servants worked in the library – and none of them really had any skill with weapons, although the Council had begun giving civilians regular training years ago.

It had long been known that the Maelstrom was arming for war, but now it was painfully clear that any preparations for defence had been inadequate. Count Aristotle and the other nobles of the city had been a little too ready to assume that the polliwiggles could be found and sent into action against the Maelstrom in good time.

Griffin had rubbed Matador down, and asked the grooms to tend the animal with special care after their strenuous ride. The sea horse too faced worse yet to come. Griffin wasn't sure when they would go into action – but when they did, fighting the kobalins in the water was going to be tough.

Walker and Buenaventure, who had greeted him and Soledad on their arrival, had gone off again in a hurry to help reinforce the lower rampart, the defensive wall above the piers. More and more wooden beams, sandbags and chunks of coral from the underwater city were being brought up to the barricades to deter the kobalins – although no one was sure which enemy represented the greater danger: the Deep Tribes or Tyrone the cannibal king and his fleet.

D'Artois, the Ghost-Trader and the Council themselves seemed undecided. The kobalins were indeed terrible creatures, with claws and murderous shark-like jaws. But their element was water, and no one yet knew how well they would fight on land. On the other hand Tyrone's cannibals and pirates were normal human beings, and very numerous: perfect allies for the Maelstrom in hand-to-hand street fighting.

However, Tyrone and his fleet were still fiercely embattled at sea in the waters to the west of the Lesser Antilles. The Antilles captains who had ruled those regions for years felt that the cannibal king had betrayed them, and had sworn revenge. That could only be useful to the defenders of Aelenium. Not only would Tyrone be considerably weakened – and with him, the Maelstrom – he would also lose valuable time. What had been planned as a surprise attack on the starfish city had become a predictable campaign for which the people of Aelenium could plan.

Griffin found his way through the streets and up steep

flights of steps, passing both the defensive ramparts and several smaller barricades. There were uniformed soldiers everywhere – most of them men, but with some women among them who were ready to fight for the city. Many soldiers had formed troops and were marching in good order; others, if not so well disciplined, were building up the ramparts or being given final instructions.

The Ghost-Trader had disappeared soon after they returned to Aelenium without saying goodbye. He had last been seen at Forefather's side, and when Griffin asked d'Artois about it the captain confirmed that the two wise men had withdrawn to the library together. 'None of my business,' the captain had growled, joining his troops to supervise preparations for the defence of the city and discuss final points of strategy.

Griffin wondered what Forefather and the Ghost-Trader had to discuss up in the library. Soledad, low-voiced, had told him about the Water Weavers whom Jolly had met when the *Carfax* went down, and what those three mysterious women at the bottom of the sea had said to her. Although Soledad wasn't sure what to make of it, Griffin couldn't believe that Jolly had been hallucinating. Perhaps Aelenium really was a place to which the old gods had withdrawn before they were forgotten and died. And perhaps Forefather really had been the creator god himself, the first deity, and had made this world.

Griffin thought all this as incredible as Soledad did. But much of it fitted the picture, beginning with the mere existence of a city like Aelenium, not to mention the Ghost-Trader's strange abilities and what Captain d'Artois had once told him about Forefather. He was the soul of the city, the captain had said, and maybe it was more than just a hackneyed phrase.

Griffin took the last few steps to the square outside the palace. The sentries who usually guarded the gateway had been withdrawn, since danger threatened not here, high above the water, but further down on the shores of the starfish city.

He met hardly anyone in the palace itself. Most of the women and children were hiding in shelters deep in the heart of Aelenium. There were no servants in the corridors, and the guest quarters were empty. An oppressive atmosphere lay over the abandoned passageways and halls. More than once, Griffin thought he heard someone following him, but then he decided it was only the echo of his own footsteps.

He passed his bedroom without changing his piratical costume for a new leather uniform. He had chosen what he wore now from among the debris in the belly of the whale: a pair of leather trousers, a black shirt, and a waistcoat on which someone had sewn a bent Spanish gold doubloon over the wearer's heart as a good luck charm.

He stopped outside Jolly's door. It hurt to imagine her still waiting for him on the other side of it – quite apart from the fact, he thought with a melancholy grin, that it certainly wasn't like Jolly to wait for *anyone*.

The door was not locked; he could easily get in. Her bedclothes were crumpled.

'Looks like Jolly had nightmares on her last night in Aelenium,' said a voice behind him.

Griffin spun round. 'So I *did* hear footsteps.'

Laughing, Soledad shook her head. 'Not mine, that's for sure. No one hears me if I don't want to be heard.' It sounded a little boastful, but Griffin knew the princess was telling the truth. Even if she was just walking along behind you, there was something supple and cat-like about her movements.

Suppressing a sigh, he turned to the deserted room again. 'I think Jolly often had bad dreams – not just last night.'

It was a strange moment as the two of them stood there, staring at the untidy bedclothes and thinking of Jolly.

Griffin cleared his throat. 'We're talking about her as if she'll never come back.'

'She will come back.'

'Yes,' he replied quietly. 'Yes. She will.'

'You don't go on a journey like that without going over it a hundred times in your head,' said Soledad. 'In your dreams too, whether you like it or not.'

Griffin shuddered at the thought of the terrors Jolly might have imagined, and the idea of what really awaited her down there made him shiver even more. His imagination was running to visions of dreadful monsters before he thought of a much more likely horror: sheer loneliness down in the black wilderness of the deep sea.

Soledad seemed to be thinking the same. 'I believe it's not the Maelstrom that frightened her most.' She turned and looked at him until he returned her gaze. 'I think it's Munk, don't you?'

'Yes,' he said. 'Yes, I do.'

'Will he be a danger to her down there?'

Griffin was surprised that Soledad had thought of that. Until now he had supposed he was the only one who saw Munk as a threat to Jolly. 'I wish I knew.'

'They almost fought that night on the *Carfax*. He wanted to make her stay in Aelenium.' Soledad's eyes looked more shadowed than usual. It made him uneasy to see her like that, perhaps because he had hoped she could dispel his own secret fears. Instead, she was merely confirming them.

'Why did you come here?' she asked. 'To her room, I mean.'

He hesitated. 'For the same reason as you, I expect. To feel near her. To say goodbye.'

She went past him to one of the arched windows. The room was very high and narrow, almost like the inside of a tower. Many of the rooms in Aelenium were of odd dimensions, showing that in the first place the city had not been built, but had grown.

Griffin followed the princess and looked out over the steep slopes of the city, the maze of streets and rooftops running down to the arms of the starfish and so to the water. Not much longer now and nothing here would be the same. Death and destruction would come to the city. The idea went to his heart. For the first time he felt really close to this strange place, and something like a sense of responsibility stirred in him. If Jolly was ready to sacrifice herself for Aelenium, he must bring himself to do the same.

'What will you do now?' asked Soledad, as if she had just been asking herself the same question and had already found the answer.

'Fight,' he said. 'Like Jolly.'

She nodded in silence.

'What about you?'

Soledad shrugged her shoulders. 'The idiots here won't let me ride a flying ray because I'm a woman. And still no one seems to know if they're going to take the sea horses into action against the kobalins.'

He nodded.

'So I'm going with the divers,' she went on. 'I've had them show me how these last few days. I went down to the anchor chain. The kobalins will try cutting it, to tear Aelenium away from the sea-bed.'

'If they really do that no one will be able to stop them. The divers can't reach the bottom here, it's too deep.'

'Surely we're not just going to stand by and watch, all the same.'

He sadly shook his head. 'It's madness to try fighting the kobalins in their own element.'

'We have to do something.' The corners of her mouth twitched slightly, but it didn't turn into a smile. 'What about you?'

'D'Artois has me assigned to the Flying Ray Guard.'

Unexpectedly, the princess went up to him and hugged him. 'Then look after yourself, Griffin. When Jolly comes back don't let it be me who has to tell her the kobalins tore you to pieces.'

He hugged her back, and blushed when she dropped a kiss on his forehead.

'I'm leaving you alone up here now, so give Jolly my love when you think of her.' With a twinkle in her eye, she went out into the corridor and closed the door.

Griffin stared at it for a moment longer and then turned to the window, heavy at heart. Flying rays were circling majestically above the mist.

It was Soledad's ninth dive, but she had been told that the sense of being trapped in the diving suits didn't wear off even at your fiftieth time. The oxygen from the aerated stone resting in a metal container under her chin enabled her to breathe through tubes for fifteen to twenty minutes, but the air very quickly turned thin and musty.

Soledad had never seen anything like these aerated stones before her arrival in the starfish city, and she wondered where they came from. The other divers didn't seem to know either. They told Soledad that the stones were kept in a cave near the heart of the city and carefully guarded. Once all the air in a stone was exhausted, it took several hours to dry out completely and absorb more oxygen. As there were only a few hundred stones, stocks would inevitably run low during the battle for Aelenium if the underwater fighting went on too long.

Soledad and a handful of other divers were to guard the furrowed underside of one of the starfish arms. The princess had managed to sleep for a few hours to recoup her strength for the next few days. She was going to need it. Although the sun was shining on the water up above, it was very dark down here, with a faint light only where the mighty anchor chain emerged from a complicated tangle of steel and branched coral. Shafts had been driven through the arms of the starfish, and torches were regularly placed inside them above water level. Yellow light fell through the openings in the shafts, but was soon lost in the depths. The light was just enough to let you see and face attackers – it would be too dim for reading a book, for instance. The murky water was going to make fighting down here even more difficult.

The anchor chain was so broad that it would have taken twenty men to encircle one of its mighty links with their outstretched arms. Next to those rusty links a human being looked as forlorn as a fish. Tangled waterweeds drifted on invisible currents, surrounding the metal here and there like dense undergrowth.

Every time Soledad looked down past the chain at the depths below she felt dizzy. Its endless line, just visible on the edge of the light from the torch shafts, sank right down into darkness, but the idea that it went on all the way to the bottom of the sea turned her stomach. Although she was under the water she felt something like vertigo. So much emptiness below her, such a great void.

Walker had protested when she told him she was going to join the divers, but she wasn't about to let anyone change her mind, not even him. Soledad knew what she was letting herself in for. She could have taken the easy option to fight on the barricades, and no one would have thought any worse of her for that. But not for nothing was she her father's daughter, future empress of all the pirates between Tortuga and New Providence, and she wasn't about to stand by and watch the kobalins streaming on to land. She wanted to do something to keep away those creatures of the Maelstrom — and as quickly as possible.

All the divers had now reached the network of metal struts and branching corals with the chain in the middle of it, fastened by mighty rings to the lower side of the arm of the starfish. Here, where the anchor chain joined the city, it was at its most vulnerable.

It was beyond the kobalins, who had neither explosives nor heavy tools, to destroy the metal, but their claws were sharp enough to dig the anchoring point up here right out of the coral. That was the main reason why their attack on the chain was expected at its upper end, not down below close to the anchor itself.

The torch shafts stood around the anchoring point in a wide circle, giving the strange place something of the look of a prehistoric temple – an improbable sanctuary that was surrounded by a ring of pillars of light.

The troops that Soledad and the others were relieving returned to the surface. Soledad watched their clumsy figures swim past the shimmering pillars and disappear into the darkness beyond. In spite of her companions she felt alarmingly lost, and she shuddered when she thought of Jolly, who must now be feeling the same, but a hundred times more strongly. She wished she could have found the right words to express her admiration for Jolly's courage before she set out.

Soledad and the other divers dispersed in the maze of branching coral and metal bars. Most of them perched on crossbars to save their strength for the coming battle. Little oxygen bubbles danced around their heads like swarms of silver insects.

The thin air was already draining Soledad's stamina. She tried to breathe more slowly and deliberately. Loosening one of the two small crossbows she carried at her belt, she bent it with the help of a crank, took one of the bolts out of the ammunition belt across her breast and slotted it into the device, ready to fire. Underwater a bolt scoring a hit didn't strike with anything like the same force as on the surface, but it would still go through a skinny kobalin body at a distance of ten paces. Pistols couldn't be fired down here, of course, but like the others Soledad was armed with several daggers. Slender stilettos had proved the most useful weapon in close combat. Their only disadvantage was that you had to let your adversary get close – not a pleasant idea when you thought of kobalin claws. They all hoped to keep their enemies at bay with the crossbow bolts.

Most of the divers had spent hours practising shooting underwater. Soledad was amazed by the accuracy of these men's aim in spite of the difficult conditions. She wished she could have said the same of herself.

So there they sat, crossbows in both hands, waiting. After about twenty minutes even those with the greatest stamina had to change their aerated stones, and then they went on waiting, silent and motionless, watching the darkness beyond the pillars of light.

It wasn't Soledad who sighted the first kobalin, but a man crouching on a blunted coral outcrop a little way from her. Out of the corner of her eye, she saw him begin to move excitedly, and despite all their practice it looked clumsy.

The warning was passed on very fast, in sign language, and immediately two dozen crossbow bolts were ready to aim into the darkness.

At first it was only a handful of kobalins, then more and more. Thin, spindly figures with limbs much too long for them came gliding through the darkness. Creatures with teeth bared and eyes narrowed. The light of the torch shafts was refracted in those eyes as if they had caught fire.

Xander, leader of the divers' squad, pulled hard on a narrow chain leading up through one of the torch shafts, to set an alarm bell ringing somewhere on the surface.

Overcoming her alarm, Soledad took aim, and fired her first bolt into the darkness. Did the kobalin scream when she hit it? If so, human ears couldn't pick up the sound. A cloud of dark blood engulfed the dying creature, making visibility even worse.

Now bolts were flying through the water everywhere. Most of them met their mark. The first wave of attackers hesitated, and then retreated. Soon the only kobalins still inside the circle of pillars of light were motionless corpses, drifting empty-eyed in the void like ashes above a fire.

Soledad didn't stop to think. She moved automatically. Her breath came faster, using up much more of the precious oxygen from her aerated stone now. But she kept herself

73

under control, reloaded both crossbows, and resisted the temptation to change her stone ahead of time – that would have been wasteful and too time-consuming.

Gritting her teeth, she stared into the darkness, past the drifting bodies in the clouds of blood that billowed around them.

She thought of Walker. She thought of Jolly.

Then they came again, and Soledad stopped thinking of anything. The creatures avoided the pillars of light as if they feared the brightness. They came gliding up from all directions, swimming with grotesque but rapid strokes.

Soledad killed two with bolts from her crossbow before a third reached her.

Claws flashed, and then steel.

The battle for Aelenium had begun.

THE BATTLE FOR
THE ANCHOR

Griffin had joined Ebenezer and Jasconius on the pier when the alarm bells sounded. Only one at first, then more and more, until finally all Aelenium was echoing to the sound of bells. Their peals raced at the speed of a stormy wind over the rooftops of the starfish city, ran up and down slopes, broke against filigree towers, richly ornamented facades, and the plain roofs of the lower quarter.

'Take care of yourself,' Ebenezer told Griffin as he said goodbye, holding him close with his broad arms. 'Remember, I'll be needing you yet for –'

'The first Floating Tavern ever in the belly of a whale.' Griffin smiled and clapped him on the back. 'I'll remember.'

Ebenezer let go of him. 'Jasconius and I will take up our position down here.'

'You be careful out in the water.' Griffin was worried about Jasconius and the monk. The waters around Aelenium would soon be swarming with kobalins. Human beings could escape from them on land, at least for a while, but the whale would be at their mercy. Griffin felt very guilty for bringing Jasconius and Ebenezer here in the first place. If anything happened to the two of them, it would be his fault.

'I know what you're thinking.' The monk waved dismissively. 'Jasconius and I have seen worse in our time.'

He stepped aside and studied Jasconius. The giant whale was drifting like a floating mountain beside the pier at the end of one of the starfish arms. His left eye was looking straight over the side of the pier, and seemed to meet Griffin's gaze. Once again the boy felt sadness when he looked into the depths of that eye. The whale was not a happy creature. It was a heart-rending sight.

Ignoring the alarm bells summoning him and everyone else to their positions, he hurried over to Jasconius. He stopped at the side of the pier, reached out his right arm, leaned far enough forward to touch the whale's skin, and laid the palm of his hand on its smooth surface only a few feet from the huge, melancholy eye.

'Good luck,' he whispered, so softly that not even

Ebenezer could hear it. 'I hope everything you want comes true for you.'

He surprised himself; the words had emerged from his mind without asking his permission first.

A low droning emerged from the whale's half-open mouth, rather like the sound you make by blowing across the open neck of a bottle. Jasconius's voice. He too was saying goodbye.

Griffin had to turn away to keep the tears from coming to his eyes. He pulled himself together and began moving off at a run. 'See you soon,' he called, without looking back at Ebenezer and the whale again.

He ran as fast as he could along the shore of the starfish arm to his ray, which was waiting for him at one of the lower positions, wings outspread. D'Artois had moved all the animals who were going into action during the first waves of attack away from their main stables, bringing them closer to the shore as a short cut.

'About time too, Griffin,' Rorrick greeted him. He was an experienced guardsman, and Captain d'Artois had assigned Griffin to his troop. Rorrick was a red-headed man of about forty who claimed to be able to hit any point in the water from the swaying back of a flying ray, without fail. If the kobalins ventured to show their ugly faces above the waves – and no one doubted that any more – it was his task to fire at them from the rays and, with luck, keep them from coming on land.

He had a large moustache, as fiery as the unruly shock of hair on his head, and his fingers were the longest Griffin had ever seen on any man. He used them to handle his weapons as sensitively as if they were musical instruments, and if he lacked patience in dealing with the rays and hippocamps he made up for it with his sure aim and incredible sense of balance. Griffin had already gone on some practice flights with him, learning to adjust to the marksman. He knew when he had to keep low on the ray, or when he must slow its wing-beats to give Rorrick a better view. The man was twice Griffin's age but never made him feel inferior.

Griffin returned Rorrick's greeting and swung himself into the saddle, bending forward to the creature's head, whispered a few encouraging words to it and took the reins. Around them other rays were taking off powerfully, never more than a handful of them at a time so that the animals wouldn't get in each other's way. Griffin and Rorrick were among the last to leave.

Swarms of rays were streaming from gaps and openings among the rooftops everywhere. They emerged above the slopes like black plumes of smoke, before drifting apart and fanning out in the air. As they did so they made ring-shaped formations to circle the city in opposite directions.

There were three such rings of rays in the air now. The furthest out were hovering close to the wall of mist, the next were halfway between the mist and the shores of the city, the third above the arms of the starfish itself. At the last minute d'Artois had decided not to send in the sea horses, although against the express wish of the Council.

'I won't send the hippocamps to certain death,' he had told the Council members. 'They have no chance out there in the water. The kobalins will attack them from below, and we won't be able to get at the kobalins with our own weapons.' No doubt he was remembering the death of his wife, dragged down into the depths by kobalins together with the sea horse she was riding.

Some of the noblemen of the Council had objected, but d'Artois had simply turned away and left them, saying he must get on with the defence of the city.

Griffin glanced through the air at d'Artois. The captain had picked him and Rorrick for his own team, as if he wanted to make sure that Griffin would be near him during the battle.

Griffin wasn't used to riding the rays yet; he found it much easier to ride Matador. And it was easier to relate to a hippocamp than a ray; the airborne black giants were too large, too majestic for that, almost remote in their silent elegance. Humans could admire them or fear them, but never felt really close to them – apart from those who tended them up in their stables. The grooms were terrified for their charges, and hours ago had begged every rider not to let any of them come to harm. Again, it was clear that everyone had something to lose in this battle. Some feared for their lives, others for the future of the world, others again for what was closest to their hearts: the rays, the sea horses, even the chickens that roamed freely in the city streets if they couldn't all be rounded up.

The wings of the rays raised an immensely strong wind as they took off. Those riders still on the ground had to brace themselves against the violent gusts if they were not to be plucked from their saddles. But at last they were all in the air, and soon every ray had taken up its position in one of the three defensive rings.

'Why isn't it raining dead fish?' shouted Rorrick through the roar of the wind in their faces.

'It only does that when the kobalin commander is close,' replied Griffin over his shoulder. 'The creature's still probably outside the mist. Or not close enough to the surface.'

'I thought kobalins obeyed only their chieftains?'

'Yes, that's right. But the chieftains in turn obey the orders of a being acting as deputy to the Maelstrom.'

'Some say you and the polliwiggle saw it.'

'We didn't actually see it,' said Griffin. 'I don't think anyone has done that. Or at least no human being. We only know that it's around when dead fish rain down from the sky.' He thought for a moment, and added, 'If you ask me, we ought to be grateful for every minute it *doesn't* turn up here.'

'Oh, it will,' said Rorrick, resigned. 'You can be sure it will if it's as powerful as you say.'

Griffin looked intently down from the heights. They were in the inner ring of rays, about ten paces from the surface of the water.

'Kobalins!' cried Rorrick suddenly, hoarse-voiced. 'Down there in the water!'

Griffin heard guns being cocked behind him as the marksmen made their weapons ready. Three of his rifles were at rest in firmly fixed holsters fitted to the saddle of the ray and pointing backwards, like a triple cannon. Unlike Griffin, Rorrick was not secured by belts, for he must be able to turn quickly in the saddle if necessary, so as to fire both behind and in front of him. Every movement made a

81

difference, no gesture was wasted. The movements of a marksman's hands had something almost mathematical about them, for he was estimating distances, angles and percussive force in his head the whole time. It was not unlike being one of the gunners manning the cannon on a pirate ship.

'Do you see them?' asked Rorrick.

Griffin steered the flying giant into a gentle diagonal, while keeping it in the same circuit as the rays flew around the city. 'Yes. There they go.'

Dark patches were now scurrying beneath the surface of the water, difficult to make out in the flickering light on the waves. Now Griffin understood why the kobalins were attacking before sunset and not at night, which he had supposed much more likely: they had been waiting for the sun to stand low enough in the sky. Its light was breaking on the crests of waves now, glittering and flashing, and it dazzled the marksmen riding the rays. The kobalins must expect it to give them a greater advantage than an attack in darkness.

Rorrick swore. But as Griffin was still wondering whether the marksman would be able to hit anything at all in these conditions, the first shot was already whipping through the air. The wind of its passing blew the smell of gunpowder and some of the noise of the shot backwards, away from Griffin.

The marksmen on the other rays opened fire too. Soon the surface of the sea seemed to be boiling under the flurry of shots, and the waves were pitted with countless pockmarks. The first kobalin corpses were drifting on the surface, while here and there thin, shimmering arms broke through the waves, aimed lances or harpoons and flung them at the rays. In the course of his first three circuits of the starfish city, Griffin saw only one ray fall: as it hit the surface its rider and marksman were torn from their saddles at once and dragged down into the depths. The kobalins set about the ray itself like a swarm of ants. Within moments it sank in the waves, buried under scrabbling bodies.

Griffin shuddered with horror, but then he was past the scene of the crash and had to attend to his own task. Rorrick called out instructions, telling him where to take the ray, and Griffin made haste to do everything his marksman wanted. Once he ducked down beneath a kobalin harpoon; another time a lance slid off the ray's wing, but left only a shallow scratch behind.

During every circuit he looked down in concern at Jasconius, who had now moved away from the pier and was forging strongly ahead, a mighty shadow below the surface.

When Griffin saw him down there for the first time he was amazed by the giant whale's mobility, and at the same time deeply concerned to see the crowd of dark shapes gathering around him. On his second circuit, however, the whale had far fewer opponents, and on the third circuit he saw that the kobalins were keeping a cautious distance from the titanic creature raging in their midst. All the same, Griffin was under no illusion: if the Deep Tribes concentrated part of their forces on a deliberate attack on Jasconius, he wouldn't be able to hold out against them forever.

When the rays crossed the part of the starfish arm where the anchor chain was fixed, Griffin noticed particularly dense kobalin swarms. Shuddering, he thought of Soledad, who must be down there somewhere. So long as the kobalins didn't come on land – and so far they had made no move to do so – the waters around the chain were the most dangerous place in the entire battle. The princess must be out of her mind to have let anyone send her there. But at the same time he admired her courage. If anyone really deserved to lead the pirates of the Caribbean, it was Soledad. Perhaps she still thought she had to prove it.

The next harpoons were flashing around his ray in the air like steel lightning. All his dreadful visions of Soledad's battle in the depths faded; he had his hands full keeping the ray under control.

He heard a gurgling cry behind him.

'Rorrick?' Griffin glanced over his shoulder.

He looked into the marksman's lifeless eyes. The man sat swaying in his saddle, pierced by a kobalin lance.

Griffin cried out with horror and rage, but when he tried to reach behind him with one hand and hold his companion in place, the ray bucked and Rorrick lost his balance. The body slid off, tearing one of the ammunition holders away with it, and fell to the depths.

Dazed, Griffin looked away as the dead man hit the waves and was drawn down into the depths by a dozen arms ending in long claws.

By the time Griffin lost his marksman, Soledad was no longer fighting for the anchor chain or the future of the starfish city. She was fighting for sheer survival.

All around her was chaos: kobalins, dead divers, rags of marksmen's uniforms, dark red clouds of blood that made it even harder to put up any defence against the attack.

The kobalins had just broken through the columns of light that were the torch shafts in a mighty attacking wave. Like a noose of lances and claws and snapping jaws, their ring was tightening around the defenders of the anchor chain. Within one or two minutes their numbers were halved, although about a dozen were still fighting desperately against the onslaught of the Deep Tribes.

Soledad had a handful of bolts left, but there was no opportunity to reload her two crossbows. A kobalin shot towards her through a cloud of blood, claws outstretched, fangs bared. Soledad kicked out to rise in the water, and at the same time felt her oxygen thinning. It was high time to change her aerated stone, but the attacker gave her no chance to do it. Somehow she managed to avoid its first attack and put the body of another kobalin between her and her adversary. For a moment the creature's attention was diverted, and it sniffed at the corpse like a hungry wolf, but without taking its eyes off Soledad. Hands shaking, she reloaded one of the crossbows – and was just in time to take aim as the kobalin pushed the other, dead monster aside and shot towards her with a fluid movement.

The bolt hit its mark. But the kobalin had been swimming strongly enough to come close to Soledad in its death throes. It hit and kicked out in its agony, its claws whirring in front of her face like scissor blades, and nearly tore the diving helmet off her head. She managed to pull both her legs out and kick it powerfully away. Moments later it had already disappeared behind a wall of murky water.

Soledad was drifting through dense, dark mist. She couldn't see much further than two arm's lengths ahead of her. That was a hindrance, but also protected her from the malicious eyes of the kobalins. All the same, she swam on upwards, even at the risk of leaving the murk and becoming visible to her enemies again.

Suddenly her head met with resistance. For a moment she was seized by panic and struck out, fearing a new attack. But then she saw that it was only one of the cross-struts of the labyrinthine iron and coral structure to which the anchor chain was fastened. Very close to her, brightness shone from one of the torch shafts set under the starfish arm.

She froze as several outlines swam past. Kobalins in search of adversaries. But the creatures didn't notice her; perhaps all the blood in the water blunted their sense of smell.

Soledad hauled herself further up into the tangle of struts. Once she saw a second diver. She gave him a brief wave, and pointed up, but she couldn't tell whether he had seen her. He too was hiding among the struts, obviously on the point of giving in.

She paused for a moment, forced herself to keep calm, and changed her aerated stone before lack of oxygen did the kobalin's work for it. Then she went on. The light was brighter now, and bathed her surroundings in a red glow with paler and darker streaks passing through it.

She was aware that she was coming close to the real target of the kobalin attack, the upper end of the anchor chain. If she was unlucky it would already be surrounded by warriors of the Deep Tribes trying to destroy its mounting.

Her fears were confirmed when the vapours grew less dense, showing her the chain itself. Dozens of kobalins were clambering on the mighty iron links like monkeys, using drifting curtains of seaweed and mussel colonies as handholds and scrambling up the chain itself as if it were a ladder leading from the bottom of the sea to Aelenium. Yet something prevented them from going the last part of the way. Now Soledad saw three or four divers entrenched up there, receiving every kobalin that approached with a steel bolt.

Soledad silently wished them luck and changed direction. There was no way she could get past the kobalins and join her comrades. She must find another way to reach safety.

Once again she looked across at the torch-lit shaft, and wondered where it led. To the interior of the starfish city, anyway, that was certain. She had never yet been in any of the shafts herself, but she knew that spiral staircases wound their way up inside their walls. It was from these staircases that the many torches in their holders were regularly changed. She could have tried rising to the surface through one of the shafts and then going on up the steps. But the gates to the shafts were barricaded to keep any kobalins from getting into the city that way. And presumably there were gratings, probably below the waterline too.

Soledad was thinking feverishly, at the same time looking out for more kobalins, when a mighty outline suddenly broke through the murky waters ahead of her.

At first sight she thought it must be another of the Maelstrom's monstrosities, a gigantic creature from the maw of the sea come to help the kobalins as they destroyed the chain.

But it was Jasconius.

The Man in the Whale and his titanic friend were coming to the aid of the divers defending the chain.

The whale swam through the middle of the crowd of kobalins, flinging the attackers aside with mighty blows from his tail-fin. Even Soledad, who was some way off, felt the current, was thrown against a strut, and cried out in pain inside her diving helmet. When she opened her eyes again, she saw that panic was breaking out among the kobalins. The whale's mighty skull was ramming them, breaking every bone in their bodies. His fins smashed them like insects. A giant of the sea, he moved with incredible agility, his speed giving the lie to his ponderous appearance. The kobalins would hardly have expected such a fierce attack.

Soledad weighed up her chances. Her only possibility of flight now was past the chain towards the underwater city. She didn't know whether or not there was a way to climb up from there to the city above, but she had no choice.

The term 'underwater city' was misleading, for the part of Aelenium under the sea was by no means a city. The gigantic starfish shape on which Aelenium stood had two mountainous outcrops, one above and one below the surface. While the upper part had been developed over aeons into something like the shape of a human settlement, with houses and towers and palaces hewn from the coral, the formations on the underside had been left untouched. Caverns and tunnels there were still as chance had created them; coral branches grew extravagantly in all directions, and the surface was covered with sharp ridges, spikes and points that could cost careless divers their lives.

The way to the riven, furrowed side of the coral was fairly clear; Soledad could reach it unhindered if Jasconius diverted the attention of the kobalin shoals a little longer. But fear made her hesitate – she knew what she was letting herself in for. She might lose her way hopelessly among the maze of coral branches and grottoes while the air she was breathing ran out, and still she might not even be near the surface.

Her glance fell on a crowd of kobalins that had left the anchor chain to get to safety, out of reach of Jasconius's deadly blows.

Suddenly, one of the kobalins raised an arm and pointed to her. Immediately ten or eleven of them began moving. She supposed they had been ordered not to leave any human beings alive in the water.

She cursed the indecision that might now cost her her life, pushed off, and swam rapidly towards the slope of the coral. A little way beneath it one of countless openings gaped, wide enough for a small ship to steer its way through. She dived past the coral edges and sharp corners and found herself in darkness. There was no source of light here apart from the faint glimmer falling in through the entrance, and she wished desperately that she shared Jolly and Munk's polliwiggle ability to see and find their way underwater. She herself had to depend on the faint light from outside and her sense of touch.

Panic-stricken, she looked around for her pursuers. The kobalins shot towards the opening, ready to follow her into the coral mountain. Soledad swam faster, using up far too much air now. The rugged wall of the cavern towered ahead of her. There was no way out.

Then everything around her went dark.

It took her a moment to work out what had happened. A black shape had pushed in front of the opening, plunging the grotto into total darkness. Jasconius!

It gave her a chance to escape deeper into the cave, although she couldn't see her hand before her face. But the shock left her feeling paralysed there in the water. Transfixed, she looked back at the opening. When the whale moved to show the way into the cavern again, Soledad's pursuers were drifting in the water, smashed and lifeless.

Moments later she came to her senses and suppressed the instinct to swim back to the light and open water. With a heavy heart, she left the brightness behind her.

But in the faint light she now saw a second cleft, right at the back of the cave. In her terror she had failed to notice it a few minutes ago. If she was lucky – *very* lucky – she would come upon one of the routes marked by divers on their patrols through the underwater city. Xander had told her that the ways where a diver could pass had signs along them, luminous stones. They didn't give enough light to see by, but were bright enough to be reasonably good markers.

If you could find them And if you knew how to read them in the right order.

Soledad plunged through the opening, going deeper into the interior of the underwater city. All was pitch dark around her.

Outside, Jasconius took on another troop of kobalins, smashed the bones of some of them and crushed others in his jaws.

Soledad stopped only for a moment to take the last aerated stone out of her bag and place it in the container under her chin. Then, groping her way forward, she set out in search of a route leading to the surface.

THE HAND OF THE MAELSTROM

'I wish we could simply swim across,' said Munk, looking gloomily at the labyrinth of crevices opening up ahead of them in the rock.

In silence, Jolly nodded. It might perhaps be more sensible to ignore the Ghost-Trader's warning and take the quickest way. So far they hadn't seen any indication that the Maelstrom was looking for them at all. Perhaps it had simply *overlooked* them.

Munk looked at her inquiringly. 'What do you think?'

She shrugged her shoulders, unable to take her eyes off the maze of crevices and ravines. From up here, the rugged chasms looked like black lightning flashes frozen rigid, touching and crossing and forming a sea of rocky islands.

They were standing on the edge of a narrow plateau that

reared up like a jutting nose from the slope down which they had been climbing for the last few hours. Both of them found walking difficult on the soft ground beneath their feet. The floor of it might be rock, but grey sand as fine as dust had settled in many places, and their feet sank in with every step they took, sometimes up to the ankles. It was like walking over a carpet made of flour, and to make matters worse it rose in swirling clouds at the slightest touch, hiding the view ahead. From a distance it must look as if they were pulling a cloud of smoke along after them.

But if that cloud didn't give them away, why would anyone notice if they swam for a while instead of taking the laborious way through the labyrinth on foot?

At first they had both done their best not to admit to each other that their feet hurt and they were getting cramp in their legs. But after the first few hours they had come to the tacit agreement that it was stupid to be so tough and grim about it. Now they were both freely cursing the difficult path, the poor visibility, and the generally miserable state they were in.

Their polliwiggle vision reached about two hundred feet ahead here, but the last part of that distance was dim and blurred. The rocky labyrinth at the foot of the slope stretched much further; they couldn't see where it ended, for the black chasms disappeared into the dark like a river delta flowing into a shadowy ocean.

The depressing sight suddenly robbed Jolly of all the courage she had felt earlier in their journey. At first the inevitability of their fate had driven her on, even given her new strength. She had thought nothing could be worse than the wilderness they found when they reached the bottom of the sea – until this rocky desert emerged from the darkness ahead of them. The dismal sight instantly destroyed all Jolly's hopes of ever reaching the Rift in time. They would stumble around in these ravines until their meagre provisions ran out. Aelenium would fall. The Maelstrom would reach the city, and then –

'Jolly.'

She jumped. 'Yes – what?'

'I asked what you thought. Shall we swim?'

She took a deep breath, felt the water stream through her air passages, and finally nodded. 'Otherwise we'll never do it.'

One last moment of hesitation, and then they moved towards the edge of the rock together. They did not sink down but kept moving on into the void ahead, swimming slowly. It still felt strange to be hovering in an element that they perceived as no more than ordinary water. Only in

Aelenium had Jolly learned that she could not only walk on the surface of the sea but also survive under it. To her, it was more like air – after all, she was breathing it, and it didn't prevent her from either hearing or talking.

Still hesitant, they glided further down until they could almost touch the summits of the rocky towers rising between the clefts. They felt fairly safe above the rock plateaux on the peaks, but whenever they found themselves passing over another ravine or crevice they shivered. They could see to the bottom of these clefts, which meant that the chasms were seldom more than five hundred feet deep. As there was no source of light here, and polliwiggle vision showed everything uniformly, there were no shadows either. But even that fact didn't make their route across the labyrinth any less eerie. There were hundreds of overhanging ledges, and anything might lurk hidden under them. Or in the countless caverns and holes in the rock walls.

Although they had still seen no sign of life, Jolly couldn't shake off a feeling that they were being watched. No one knew for certain whether kobalins could go down as far as these regions – for if Forefather was right, they were far more than twenty thousand feet below the surface of the sea. The Rift itself went a good deal deeper. There must, after all, be some reason why the kobalins were known as the Deep Tribes.

The slope down which they had climbed was lost in the darkness behind them now, and all around them, whichever way they looked, was this great expanse of crevices and clefts. Most of the time they were silent, though occasionally one of them warned the other if they were moving too far away from the plateaux on top of the towers of rock. In spite of everything they bore the Ghost-Trader's warning in mind, and tried never to rise far above the rock below them. If something *was* approaching, they would notice it in good time and could always seek refuge in the ravines.

Always supposing that 'something' didn't have eyes that could see better than theirs, and hadn't spotted them long before.

'Doesn't look as if this ever comes to an end,' said Munk. He too was getting gloomier and gloomier in this vast labyrinth of rock.

'No,' Jolly murmured in reply. 'And suppose we're swimming round in circles?'

Munk stopped moving his arms and legs for a moment, but then got himself under control again. 'That's impossible.'

'Oh yes?'

He mumbled something that she didn't catch, and said nothing for the next few minutes.

Suddenly Jolly heaved a sigh of relief. 'Munk!' she cried, pointing down. 'Look at that!'

He followed her gaze down into the ravine below them, but shook his head. 'I can't see anything.'

'Exactly.'

'What do you mean, exactly?'

'We can't see the bottom any more! The clefts are getting deeper. That means we're still going downhill, even if the tops of the rocks seem to stay on the same level. But in fact they're *rising*, while the bottom of the sea is still sinking.'

He thought about this for a moment and then agreed with her. A smile of relief played around the corners of his mouth, though it did little to brighten his face. Down here, even pleasure was swallowed up by the ever-present grey.

Jolly thought they ought really to feel reassured, but her heart was still racing. What wouldn't she have given for a compass! Instead they must rely on the vague hope that all downward slopes here really did lead to the Rift. She could only hope that the Rift was indeed the deepest place in these regions of the sea-bed. If not, then they had their bearings hopelessly wrong.

Once again a long time passed, and neither of the two said anything. Jolly noticed that sometimes Munk paused as he swam and ran one hand over the bag at his belt where he kept his shells, as if he might gain new strength that way. Secretly, she tried to do the same, but touching her own bag of shells had no effect at all. Perhaps it was because she had never built up such a close relationship as Munk with the shells and their magic.

'Get down!' he suddenly cried, and instantly sank deeper.

Jolly paused, hovered on the spot for a moment, and then followed him into the shelter of a rock. She had seen it too at the very last moment, just before she dived down behind the rock.

Several points of light had appeared in the darkness in front of them.

'Are those . . . are they eyes?' she asked hoarsely.

Munk's own voice was husky. 'No idea.'

They scarcely dared to raise their heads above the edge of the rock, but finally they ventured to do it.

The points of light had come closer. At first there were six or seven, but the longer they looked the more there were – almost as if they were looking at a starry sky, discovering new constellations every minute.

'If they *are* eyes,' whispered Jolly tonelessly, 'there's a lot of them.'

'Spiders have lots of eyes.'

'Oh, thank you, Munk! Thank you very much *indeed*!'

Once he would have smiled. Not now. He didn't even look at her. Instead, he hovered where he was, level with the top of the rock and staring intently over it.

'It's a shoal of fish,' he said after a while.

The bright dots were indeed tiny fish with bodies that gave off a constant light. None of them seemed any bigger than Jolly's thumb.

'Let's go down deeper,' she said.

Munk nodded, but he didn't move. He was still peering over the rock, fascinated. The light from the fish was reflected in his eyes, making them flicker wildly in a way that disturbed Jolly almost more than the strange shoal now swimming towards them.

She took Munk's hand and pulled him away with her.

'Hey!' he cried, but he did not resist. The flickering in his eyes seemed to last a moment longer before it finally died away. For a moment or so it had been as if the glow of the fish were caught inside his skull and looking out through his eyes.

They lost height quickly. The abyss must be much deeper than Jolly had assumed, for they still couldn't see the bottom.

'Jolly!'

'What?' she asked in annoyance, and then she saw what he meant for herself.

He needn't have bothered to answer. 'They're following us.'

The shoal shot across the edge of the rock, moved sideways with an undulating movement and streamed on down, straight after Jolly and Munk.

The two polliwiggles were racing headlong downwards now, speeding on as they swam strongly. The walls of rock shot past them on both sides. Now and then they had to avoid rocky outcrops and stony spurs, but they kept up their breakneck speed.

The fish were faster.

Light flooded over them, white and glassy like the radiance of a full moon rising. As if it were a single vast life form, not a teeming mass consisting of hundreds of tiny creatures, the luminous shoal seemed to embrace them.

Jolly swore. Munk shouted something like, 'Keep away from me!' and began flailing wildly around him.

The touch on her cheek felt like the most delicate of kisses. It was almost as if the little fish wanted to sniff her face or explore it with other senses. Jolly was startled when more of the fish nuzzled her hands and rubbed against her clothes. She had feared bites, and certainly pain. But all she felt was this tender exploration of her body.

Before they set out they had been given thin, dark, close-fitting leather clothing, oiled on the outside to make moving through the depths easier. Its other advantage was that it didn't become sodden with water. It was a little like the guardsmen's uniforms, although without the coral and shell studs or other reinforcements. The suits were in two pieces with a broad belt, plain and unadorned, and so dark that they were also good camouflage.

A fine sort of camouflage, though, if the very first living creatures they met unerringly made for them.

Munk was still striking out with both arms, unsuccessfully. Any moment now they must surely reach the bottom of the ravine, a narrow strip of debris covered by the ever-present dust at the bottom of the deep sea.

Jolly was first to come down on the sea-bed, surrounded by the cloud of luminous fish. She had turned and was moving on her feet again. Unlike Munk she had given up defending herself. The fish covered almost her whole body. Her arms and legs had fish clinging all over them, and there must be ten or twenty even on her face. She fought off her sense of panic and, with some difficulty, kept herself under control.

The fish had attached themselves to her by their tiny mouths, but they still didn't bite, nor did they give any other sign of thinking that Jolly and Munk were a tasty supper.

'Munk, keep still!' she called. The fish on her face bobbed

and swayed as she moved her lips. The light radiating from the little creatures was amazing, although not bright enough to dazzle her.

'Munk!' she called again. 'They won't hurt us!'

He froze in mid-movement, as if she had slapped him in the face as he performed his frantic St Vitus' dance. Hard as he had tried to defend himself, the fish were clinging to him all over, not at all impressed by his flailing and kicking.

'They're harmless,' said Jolly gently, and couldn't help giggling when one of the fish nudged the end of her nose and stayed there, clinging on with its mouth.

'I don't know what there is to laugh about!' said Munk angrily, but he seemed to be gradually calming down. He was a strange picture, standing against the rock wall a few steps away from her – a clumsy figure made of pure light, as if someone had cut the outline of a human being out of black paper and was holding the hole in it up to daylight.

'Perhaps they're spies or something.' Munk was obviously trying hard not to open his mouth too wide as he spoke, probably for fear one of the fish might slip in.

'Spies of the Maelstrom?' Jolly felt a moment's alarm. But then she told herself that the Maelstrom wouldn't be sending out spies, it would send assassins to kill them outright. It would have sent kobalins, or monsters like the Acherus, not these pretty little luminous fish.

She tried to push off from the ground and float over to Munk, but she couldn't do it. Something made her feet stick to the ground like a nail clinging to a magnet.

'They've caught us!' Now she did feel something like panic again, and quickly fought the sensation off, if with only moderate success.

Munk was going to say something, and then he froze. 'Do you hear that?' he asked after a brief pause.

At first she thought the sound was made by the fish somehow: a dull droning and rumbling that seemed to come from all sides. But it was quite different from the noises she had heard in the waters below Aelenium, which were teeming with fish.

Munk looked up. The top of the rock wall above was too high for them to be able to see anything; polliwiggle vision didn't reach so far.

'Munk!'

The movement of his head traced a curve of light as the fish on it spun round in Jolly's direction.

She pointed to the ground. 'Look at that.'

The layer of dust on the rocks was moving, undulating almost imperceptibly up and down. Now Jolly felt it in her legs too. The entire sea-bed was vibrating, only very slightly but all the time.

'An earthquake!' cried Munk, instinctively pressing back against the rock wall. Luminous fish swirled out from behind his back and clung to other parts of him to avoid being crushed.

Jolly listened intently. The rumbling was growing louder and coming closer. Faster and faster now. The dust vibrated more strongly. Her greatest fear was of rock fragments coming loose overhead. Was that why the fish were holding them down on the bottom of the ravine? So that the quake would bury them?

The dull droning was now swelling to a volume that drowned out Munk's voice. Jolly saw his mouth moving, but she couldn't hear what he said. Her glance went to the rocks above.

Something was happening up there.

It looked as if the darkness itself had begun to undulate. Jolly couldn't make out what it was. The water? Or churned-up dust? The blackness above her seemed to be boiling just on the outer edge of her field of vision. Now sand began trickling down. Presumably it was just a question of time before larger stones would fall.

The noise became deafening. Jolly was going to press her

hands to her ears before she noticed that fish had already pushed inside them, muting the sound. So in reality the droning and rumbling must be much louder.

Munk began hitting out frantically again. Jolly herself lost her self-control and tried to brush the fish off, unsure again whether the creatures were trying to help her or to leave her at the mercy of the falling rocks here.

Something charged away over the ravine. Like a stormy wind – or like a mighty hand – it swept over the rocks and shook everything around them. Only gradually did it fade away. Fine curtains of dust were still drifting down, but the noise died away. The ground below their feet felt steady. The quake was over.

Then there was silence.

As if at an unspoken command, all the fish suddenly let go of the two polliwiggles and scattered. For a moment Jolly and Munk were caught in a shining, whirling chaos, then the shoal rose from the bottom of the ravine, pulsating, and shot up in a cloudy formation. At high speed, the very last of the fish had disappeared beyond the edge of the rock.

Jolly fell to her knees and rubbed her eyes. In the sudden dim light, she felt for a moment as if she had gone blind. Munk took two or three stumbling steps, then leaned against the rock face again, breathing heavily.

'What the devil was that?' He sounded hoarse, as if he really had swallowed one of the fish, but it was only the terror that had brought his heart into his mouth.

'How should I know?' Jolly struggled up, leaned one hand against a rock, and tried to think clearly. She gradually got her ideas into some kind of order, but she still had difficulty in working out a reasonable explanation for what had just happened.

Something had thundered away over the rocks above. The fish had protected them from it by keeping them down at the bottom of the ravine, and they had been saved from whatever it was.

'Was *that* it?' asked Munk.

She was tempted to say *I don't know*, but then nodded. 'The Ghost-Trader spoke of currents, and –'

'Currents?' He clenched his fists and helplessly struck the stone behind him. 'That was . . . oh, I don't know, more like a tidal wave!'

'At least it isn't being particularly careful. So we may get enough warning next time.' She tried taking off from the ground, and easily floated a few paces further up. 'What puzzles me much more is what –'

Munk finished the sentence. 'What *they* were.'

'Exactly.'

'Not normal fish, were they?'

She shook her head, because with the best will in the world she couldn't answer that question. All she could think of was that some power might be coming to their aid down here. The Water Weavers? But when Jolly had met the three strange old women it hadn't seemed as if they were going to intervene in events themselves.

She would have liked to talk to Munk about it, and that, as she knew very well, would have been only fair – but something stopped her. She had told Soledad about the Weavers, but she hadn't told the Trader, and she still didn't know why not. Perhaps it was because the Weavers had told her things about Aelenium and the Ghost-Trader that he hadn't thought worth mentioning himself. That he had once been a god, for instance; who Forefather and the other founders of the starfish city were; the fact that the masters of the Mare Tenebrosum might not be monsters of pure evil after all, but were just claiming for themselves what Forefather had demanded so long ago, nothing less than a whole world.

Perhaps it was a mistake to hide what the Weavers had told her from Munk. On the other hand, Munk had known the Ghost-Trader for a very long time, and the two of them occupied the same square on the chessboard in Jolly's head, so to speak. Anything she was keeping from the Trader had better be kept from Munk too.

If he sensed what was going on inside her head, he didn't comment. Like her, he pushed off from the sea-bed, and together they swam up, very fast at first, then more cautiously, in case the power of the Maelstrom rolled over the rocky seascape again.

Once at the top of the ravine they saw that not much had changed, except that most of the dusty sand which had previously covered the rocky towers had been washed down into the crevices between them. Their surfaces looked cleaner now, some of them scoured smooth. With a shudder, Jolly wondered what would have happened if they had been caught in this chaos. Would swirling sand have torn the flesh from their bones?

'Do we swim or do we walk?' asked Munk as they cautiously stayed close to one edge of the ravine, ready to dive rapidly if they had to.

Jolly looked down. The bottom of the ravine was lost in darkness again, as if a deep black river ran down there. Then she looked the way the current of the Maelstrom had roared by. Nothing suggested the threat of danger there. She imagined the principle of it all as something like a stone thrown into the water: the Maelstrom was sending waves out like ripples, moving away in all directions and finally dying down. If they were unlucky enough to be caught in one of those ripples it would probably kill them, but at the very least it would tell the Maelstrom they were here.

'We'll swim,' she said, answering Munk's question. 'What else can we do? We have no time to lose.'

He nodded, but didn't look entirely convinced. His mind, like her own, must be haunted by visions of horror.

'We must just watch out,' she said, shrugging her shoulders, and she tried to seem as relaxed as possible. A glance his way was enough to show that he didn't for a moment believe in her composure.

He took a deep breath and moved away. Keeping even lower than before, they skimmed the rocky plateaux.

After a while – it seemed to them like many hours – they decided to stop for a rest in a cavern in the upper part of a rock face. It wasn't really a cave, just a recess providing makeshift shelter, but not deep enough to conceal anything unexpected inside it. Such as a giant kraken asleep there.

They laboriously ate some of their waterproofed food, drank even more laboriously from the sucking tubes of their bottles, and finally rested for a little while. Neither of them intended to go to sleep, but when sleep came after all it was the kind that leaves you even more exhausted when you wake: a sleep deep enough for bad dreams, but not so sound that it brings new strength.

When they set out once more they were both too tired to talk. Day and night did not exist on the sea-bed, and as there was nothing else to help them tell the time – no sun, no stars, not even the ebb and flow of tides – they soon lost any sense of how long they had been on the march.

At last they reached the end of the rocky labyrinth. A wide plain opened out ahead of them, sloping gently away to the very limit of polliwiggle vision.

Jolly and Munk glided steeply down from the last plateau, and when they looked back over their shoulders a little later the rocks rose behind them like a forest of petrified giant trees. It was a majestic and deeply frightening sight. If they had really gone through it all on foot, following the Trader's advice, they would have been hopelessly lost in such a maze.

That was a scary idea, but it also gave Jolly new confidence. Obviously acting on their own initiative and taking their own decisions weren't really so bad. At least, they had turned out all right so far.

The plain soon ended, leading into a collection of strangely shaped rocks. Deep fissures seemed to be stretching out to them like petrified hands.

'A coral reef!' exclaimed Munk.

'Looks like . . .' Jolly hesitated. 'Looks more like fragments of a giant coral!' On a sudden impulse, she pushed off from the ground and floated upwards.

The view from above was like a slap in the face.

Suddenly Munk was beside her.

'They're ruins,' she whispered. 'Ruins of a sunken coral city.'

Spellbound, Munk nodded. 'Like Aelenium,' he said hoarsely.

The remains of separate buildings could be clearly distinguished: structures grown from the coral that someone had hollowed out and reshaped; gigantic splinters with flights of steps carved into them; broken towers that had smashed like porcelain on impact with the sea-bed; roofs and even the facade of a palace lying flat, like a collapsed house of cards.

Munk was pale as a ghost.

Suddenly he raised his arm, pointed down, and froze. 'Jolly!'

'What?'

'Something moved down there!'

Her eyes followed the direction of his outstretched finger to the gloomy coral mountains. There was nothing to be seen in the smashed and splintered confusion. The sight was like a pile of broken shards immensely magnified.

'What was it, then?' Her tongue felt swollen. 'A fish – or something bigger?'

Munk cleared his throat and then, frowning, met her gaze.

'A human being,' he said. 'A girl.'

AINA

'A girl?' Jolly stared at Munk as if he had told her he felt like going to pick a bunch of flowers. 'Here?'

He nodded uncomfortably. 'I saw her. Down there.'

Jolly scrutinised him for a moment longer, then looked the way he was pointing, down into the ruined landscape of the submerged coral city. It was an eerie sight, filling her field of vision. Deposits of sand and colonies of shells had settled on the shattered ruins, although not enough of them to distort the shapes lying below entirely.

When and why had the city sunk, she wondered? Who had destroyed it?

And above all, why had no one mentioned it to them?

The place to which Munk was pointing lay bleak and forbidding beyond the eternal veil of grey that polliwiggle vision cast over the sea-bed. It was a sandy aisle between two towering ruins, one a shapeless block with many hollows and crevices, the other evidently once part of a palace, for she could see carved pillars and a number of rooms. The building had broken apart on impact, so that you could see into the open rooms as if they were a doll's house. They were empty and encrusted with shells; any furniture must have crumbled to dust aeons ago.

'There's no one there,' said Jolly.

'She *was* there, believe me!' Munk gave up trying to convince Jolly, and spread his arms. They had risen high above the ruins to get a better view of the shattered city. Now he moved down again, making straight for the aisle.

'Munk, wait!'

'You don't believe me.'

'Yes, I do, but we must be careful.'

He floated on the spot and turned to her. In spite of the ever-present grey, she thought his face was flushed with excitement. 'If it really was a girl, Jolly, then she must be a polliwiggle. Just like us.'

She nodded, bemused. If by any chance he hadn't been mistaken, that was the only explanation.

A third polliwiggle.

And where there was a third there might be more. Heaven knew how many.

'I don't like this,' she said, but she followed as he turned and went on moving down. They were about fifteen paces above the floor of the aisle now, and already too close to those oppressive ruins for Jolly's liking. Her own choice would have been to steer clear of them. Going the long way round might ultimately save time if any danger lurked there.

And she could positively taste menace in the water. It was as if all her senses were shouting a desperate warning. But there was no stopping Munk now. Jolly was amazed and alarmed to see him risking their whole mission so irresponsibly.

'Suppose it was a kobalin?' she said.

He didn't even turn to look at her. 'I can tell a girl from a kobalin, thank you.'

Munk was the first to reach the bottom. Clouds of dust swirled up as he landed on the sea-bed and looked around.

Jolly hovered in the water above him, letting her own gaze wander. Even less than the cross-section through the rooms of the palace rising on their right did she like the shapeless coral monster to their left. White plants had colonised the hollows in it – so plants *did* grow here – drifting in invisible currents like the fingers of corpses, alternately seeming to beckon and dismiss them.

'Which way did she go?' asked Jolly.

'That way.' Munk pointed along the aisle.

Good, she thought, at least he doesn't want to search the caves and ravines. The plants waving in the water looked doughy, like the bloated flesh of a drowned body. Jolly heard them as they touched each other with a slurping, lip-smacking sound, as if something was hiding behind them and greedily devouring its prey.

The surrounding mountains of rubble grew taller and taller as they approached the part of the ruins that looked as if it had once been the city centre. Clearly the coral city hadn't been destroyed while it was still above the surface, or at least not entirely. It had broken into hundreds of pieces, but some of its original structure still showed. The city must have been created much like Aelenium around a kind of mountainous cone, although Jolly saw nothing like a fragmented gigantic starfish shape anywhere. If there had ever been one, what remained was buried under the rest of the rubble.

'What do you think?' asked Munk suddenly, still looking keenly in all directions.

'About the girl?'

'About the city.'

'I'd like to know why no one ever thought it necessary to mention it.' She looked at him askance. 'Or did Forefather tell you about it? When I wasn't there?'

He shook his head, grave-faced. 'No, he didn't.' Was he feeling a spark of distrust for his teacher for the first time? Maybe disappointment? Of the two polliwiggles, Munk had always been greedier for knowledge than she was, and had spent far more time with Forefather than the impatient, rebellious Jolly.

He hesitated for a moment, and then went on, 'Do you think maybe Forefather and the others don't know about it?'

'Oh, come on!' She snorted with derision. 'Of course he knows about it. And you can be sure he didn't simply forget to tell us.'

'Then perhaps he wanted us to find the city for ourselves.'

'Oh yes?' You make it so easy for yourself, she thought, shaking her head.

'Perhaps he believed it had all disappeared long long ago. I mean, he may know a lot, but he's never been down here.'

Or not in the last million years. She thought of what the Water Weavers had said. If Forefather had really created everything, why was he so helpless today, nothing but an old man hiding in a city floating on the sea? It was hard to imagine that he had once had the power to create a whole world out of nothing. Even harder to think of such power now vegetating in a frail body, waiting for an end that might never come. If Aelenium fell, would Forefather die with the city? *Could* he die? The Water Weavers had said that many of the old gods were dead, but Forefather was the first, the origin of everything. Other laws might apply to him. Or no laws at all.

'Jolly.' Munk's whisper brought her out of her thoughts. 'Up ahead there. Do you see that?'

She slowly nodded, but it was only with difficulty that she uttered the words. 'You were right.'

'I told you so.'

On the path ahead, on the grey sand covering the floor of the aisle, stood a girl. Not ten paces away from them. In spite of the currents her hair wasn't moving; instead, it fell smoothly over her shoulders, clinging to her back all the way down to her hips.

'I am Aina,' she said. 'Welcome to the threshold of the Rift.'

'Who are you?' asked Jolly when they were quite close to the girl.

Aina looked like one of the Caribbean islanders. In sunlight her body would have been a beautiful light brown colour, but down here it was dark grey like charred wood. Not even that, however, could keep Jolly from seeing how beautiful she was.

There was no doubt at all that Munk had noticed too, for he was staring at Aina as if he'd never seen anything like her in his life before. Jolly herself was pretty, but she freely admitted that no one she knew could compete with Aina's beauty. Her figure was delicate, almost vulnerable, and her eyes large and dark, nearly black, as if their pupils filled the entire iris. Unlike most of the islanders, she had a small pointed nose. Like Jolly and Munk, she was not affected by the icy cold of the deep sea, for she wore no clothes at all, but she seemed to feel no modesty.

'Munk!' said Jolly.

Rather stunned, he tore his eyes away from the strange girl. 'Er . . . yes?'

'Don't stare at her like that.'

'I wasn't.'

Jolly's question still hadn't been answered, so she tried again. 'Who are you? What are you doing down here?'

'I was hiding from you.' Aina spoke their own language better than Jolly had ever heard one of the islanders speak it before.

'Why?' asked Munk, a little more composed now.

'I wasn't sure what you were. Who you were. There are others down here who aren't human beings.'

'Kobalins?'

For a moment the girl looked at them blankly. Then a smile crossed her face. 'Is that what you say? We used to call them claw-men.'

'Are there any here?' asked Jolly cautiously, although she wasn't too seriously alarmed. She had never taken her eyes off the crevices and caverns around them, and had seen no indication of any kobalins lying in wait.

'Many of them have left,' said Aina, shaking her head gently. 'The Maelstrom sent them away.'

To Aelenium, thought Jolly without any real relief. Had the battle already begun? Or was it all over by now?

'How long have you been down here?' asked Munk. 'And who sent you?'

Jolly thought she detected a slight note of jealousy in his voice. Was he afraid that Forefather might have sent other polliwiggles before them? And did that make him feel – well, what? As if he'd been passed over? As if he wasn't so *important* any more?

'We came down here a long time ago,' said Aina. 'Unimaginably long ago.'

Jolly pounced on the word. 'We?'

'I and the others who are like you.'

'What, more polliwiggles?'

'If that is your word for us, yes.'

The whole thing was getting increasingly mysterious. And then it suddenly dawned on Jolly. 'You're one of the polliwiggles from *last time?*'

Munk gave her a sidelong and glowering look of surprise. 'That's impossible,' he whispered grimly.

'Oh yes?' she replied in the same tone.

'From last time,' repeated Aina sadly, and her gaze was turned on distances that Jolly didn't even dare to imagine. 'It's all so long ago.'

How long ago might it have been that the Maelstrom was conquered for the first time and imprisoned in the Rift? She had only ever heard talk of thousands of years. Not even Forefather or Count Aristotle had said anything more definite about the time of the first war against the powers of the Mare Tenebrosum, it lay so unimaginably far back in the past.

But Aina looked no older than fifteen.

Jolly felt weak at the knees, and for a moment she had difficulty keeping on her feet. If Aina could live so long, what did that mean for other polliwiggles? For herself?

Awkwardly, she cleared her throat. 'Aina,' she said, 'are you one of those who fought the Maelstrom so long ago? Did you help to shut it up in the shell at the bottom of the Rift?'

The ghost of a smile passed over the island girl's regular features. 'I have seen the Maelstrom,' she said haltingly. 'I know the way.'

Munk seemed to have made up his mind simply to ignore Jolly's suspicions. 'Then you can show us the quickest way to get there.'

Jolly nudged him in the ribs with her elbow. 'Munk, for heaven's sake . . . !'

He swung round, and for a moment it looked as if the conflict that had been fermenting between them for so long was going to be decided here and now, in the ruins of a forgotten coral city, many thousand feet under the sea and before the eyes of this mysterious girl. For a second or so it seemed as if Munk was going to attack Jolly, not with the aid of shell magic or any other trick, but with his bare hands.

He thinks I'm unnecessary, thought Jolly suddenly. He thinks I'm only in his way. He thinks I'm no use down here anyway because he's much more powerful than I am.

And the worst of it is, she thought, that he's right. I *am* unnecessary.

No sooner had she formed the thought in her mind than she contradicted herself: no, I'm not. If he's going to trust the first weird being to come along so blindly and let the fate of the whole world slip out of his hands, it's just as well

I'm with him. If only to keep an eye on him. Him and what he does, and his stupid carelessness.

He needs me, thought Jolly. He doesn't know it, won't admit it – but he depends on me. And I depend on him if I want to get out of here alive.

'I can take you to the Maelstrom,' said Aina, but it didn't sound like confirmation of what Munk had said, more of an idea that had only just occurred to her. 'I can help you. But will you help me too?'

Help you to do what? Jolly wondered. But Munk had already spoken up. 'Of course,' he said.

'I'll explain,' said Aina. Her eyes were so large and dark. Jolly tried to read what was in them, but she couldn't make anything out there.

The girl looked searchingly around. 'Not here, though. It's too dangerous.'

'So?' asked Jolly distrustfully, and earned a sidelong glowering look from Munk. But she was not to be deterred. 'If you're one of the polliwiggles from all that time ago, you must have escaped from the Maelstrom, right? And you were in flight when you crossed our path. Rather a strange coincidence, isn't it?'

Aina looked at Munk for help.

'Jolly,' he said sharply. But he wasn't entirely dazzled,

and he turned back to Aina. 'Do you have any kind of . . . well, proof of what you're saying?'

Thank heavens, thought Jolly, greatly relieved.

'Proof?' Aina's eyes opened wide with alarm. 'Look at me – I don't even have any clothes!'

The little cow, thought Jolly.

Munk looked at Jolly. 'She's right there.'

'Oh, Munk, you can't mean this seriously!'

Aina frowned. She clearly felt uncomfortable to be in the firing line of their quarrel, and she was quick to intervene. 'Please listen to me and then make up your own minds.' She fell silent for a moment, looking anxiously at the great slopes of ruins to the left and right of the aisle.

Munk went up to her. 'Don't worry.' His voice sounded gentle and soothing. 'We'll look for somewhere to hide. Some place where we can't be found so easily. And then you can tell us all about it.'

'I've seen a place like that,' said Aina. 'A little further down. There's an overhanging ledge. I stopped to rest under it.'

Jolly looked thoughtfully from one to another of them. She still couldn't shake off her distrust of the girl, but she had to admit that it was only fair to give Aina a hearing. And she really didn't look like much of a danger. In fact, quite the opposite; Jolly felt Aina's vulnerability arousing her own pity.

After a brief moment of hesitation, she followed Aina and Munk downhill along the aisle. Now they could see tiny living beings here and there among the ruins of the city, transparent shrimps and blind creatures like cockroaches moving clumsily along. Obviously the deep sea wasn't as dead as they had first thought. There was further evidence of that in the shape of the ugly albino plants drifting everywhere among the ruins, fishing invisible nutrients out of the water with their blunt growths.

The aisle grew broader, and came to a bottomless ravine between mighty broken fragments. They swam across the ravine and reached a kind of plateau where a gigantic piece of coral had broken off, leaving a smooth top. Rubble lay all around.

'The place is over there.' Aina pointed across the strange plateau to where more coral mountains towered up on the very limits of their polliwiggle vision.

'This place is too open,' Jolly told Munk. 'If one of those currents comes along we won't have any shelter.'

He agreed with her, if reluctantly, so they skirted the plateau in the shelter of the heaps of rubble. Aina did not object. She even seemed a little alarmed to realise that she had already crossed that wide open space once.

At last they reached the place that the mysterious girl meant. Jolly had to admit that it was a good hiding place. Not a perfect one. Not an absolutely secure one. But somewhere they could take refuge for the moment.

It was a tower standing almost upright. Its top half had fallen when the city hit the floor of the sea, and a funnel-shaped slope of fragments had formed on the inside. There were no plants and no tiny shrimps here. But its great advantage was that other fragments had fallen to cover the opening, making a kind of roof. There were two ways in: the old door to the tower and a window opening further up. If necessary they could easily swim up to that opening.

'Looks good,' said Munk when they had made themselves reasonably comfortable on the heaps of coral.

'An hour's rest,' said Jolly. 'No more. We don't have much time.'

He nodded, and they both turned to Aina, who was kneeling very close to them with her hands clasped and resting on her thighs. Her long hair fell to her lap.

'It's strange,' Aina began. She seemed to be looking inward, seeing memories. 'It's so long ago now, but I can remember it all as if it were only a few years in the past.' She fell silent for a moment before going on. 'We'd been sent to close the Maelstrom. There were three of us, two boys and a girl. We were good friends.'

Jolly and Munk exchanged a brief glance, almost feeling ashamed of themselves.

'And we did it. We confined the Maelstrom, but we were left there too.'

'In the shell?' asked Munk, with a groan.

'Yes. You see, the Maelstrom wasn't dead. It wasn't even sleeping. It was simply shut up all that time, and we were shut up with it.'

There were any number of questions on the tip of Jolly's tongue, but she hesitated. Her pity for Aina was gradually turning to genuine sympathy. She tried to imagine what it must be like to be shut up in a small space with your worst enemy for thousands of years.

'What did it do to you?' Munk asked.

'At first we resisted. All three of us were powerful shell magicians, and in the beginning we could prevent it from doing anything to us. It even looked as if we could keep it away forever. But the Maelstrom had one advantage over us: it had all the time and patience in the world. It wasn't strong enough to break the shell magic itself, but it didn't mind waiting. A time must come when we weren't on our guard so much, and it did. When the years had worn us down it struck unexpectedly. And after that we were at its mercy.' Aina was shifting uneasily back and forth on her knees. It was a wonder the sharp edges of the coral didn't cut her skin. 'First it tortured us. Then, when the pain could grow no worse, it suddenly left us alone. It simply lost interest in hurting us. Perhaps we just weren't important enough for it to bother with us any more, because it must already have begun planning its return. We were only its past, and now it wanted the future. It separated us from each other, and it must have hoped we'd die of boredom. Or lose our minds.'

Jolly couldn't utter a sound. She felt ashamed of having distrusted Aina so much at first. Had the girl suffered what was now to be their own fate? Eternal imprisonment with the Maelstrom? Was that why Forefather had said he didn't know what really awaited them at the end of their journey into the Rift?

Munk put out a hand to touch Aina. Very cautiously, just a light touch on her arm. Perhaps he wanted to be sure that they weren't merely dreaming her into existence, that their fears hadn't somehow taken shape as a warning to them.

His hand went right through Aina's arm. It met with no resistance.

Gasping, Munk flinched back. Jolly leaped to her feet.

But the girl just looked sadly up at them without moving.

'I'm fading away,' said Aina.

Munk stumbled to his feet too. 'She's a ghost,' he whispered in a toneless voice.

'No.' For the first time Aina spoke energetically, as if all her grief and pain had suddenly left her. 'Not a ghost! I'm myself. I'm Aina. And I'm alive.'

There was a spark in her eyes that hadn't been there before. 'Perhaps this will be enough to prove that I'm telling you the truth.' After a moment's silence she went on more calmly. 'I want you to believe me. Since I escaped the spell of the Maelstrom I've been losing . . . losing substance. I'm fading away, and the further I get from the Rift the faster I fade. Perhaps because I ought not really to exist at all in the world and the time out there.'

That was madness – yet it also sounded so plausible that this time Jolly was the first to overcome her suspicions. Poor thing, she thought sympathetically.

'Why didn't the others escape with you?' she asked. 'Your friends.'

'I don't even know if they're still alive. The Maelstrom separated us. I haven't seen them for ages and ages. But I can sense them. Do you think that sounds crazy?'

Instinctively, they both shook their heads. Whatever

their own troubled relationship just now, they were still polliwiggles. Aina was right: there was an invisible, intangible link between polliwiggles.

'Will you help me?' Aina's eyes were shining. 'Will you help me to free them?'

Munk looked at Jolly. 'What do you say?'

She nodded. 'We'll try.'

Munk sounded almost hesitant when he turned back to Aina. 'Right, that's agreed. We'll help you if you help us. You know the way.'

Jolly looked into his face. It was closed to her, as so often recently. She didn't understand him. He had just been on the point of quarrelling with her because he wanted to stand by Aina. But now it was as if *she* had to convince *him*, not the other way around. Was it because he was disappointed to find that, after Jolly, here was a second girl he couldn't really approach?

She gave up the attempt to understand him for now. Matters were confusing enough without trying to think herself into a boy's mind.

'So we'll go on together?' asked Aina hopefully, through the black curtain of hair that kept falling over her face. It looked a little like strands of dark waterweeds.

Jolly nodded. So did Munk.

They sat there in silence in their hiding place, all of them deep in their own thoughts. And although a great many questions were still going through Jolly's mind, she was reluctant to put them into words. Did she really want to know any more about what the girl had been through? Or would the answers be worse than any uncertainty?

After a while she fell into an uneasy sleep, perhaps for several hours, and when she woke up Aina was still with them, sitting above them in the window of the ruined tower with her knees drawn up, lost in thought as she looked out at the black depths of the sea.

THE SECOND WAVE

'Buenaventure! Here they come!'

The pit bull man didn't look up when Walker pointed to the water on the other side of the rampart. With his keen dog-like senses, he had scented the kobalins not far from the shore before anyone else could see them.

The rays were still flying around the city in three great circles, but soon their part in the operation would be over, as d'Artois and the other commanders must be aware. It had been clear from the start that they couldn't hold off the armies of the Maelstrom from the air forever.

That task now fell to the men and women on shore, the defenders of the outer rampart. Most of them froze with horror when the first kobalins clambered up on land.

Thin, almost skeletal bodies with arms much too long for them; pinched, ugly faces with receding foreheads, eyes like dark slits and mouths so large that they could dive through

134

shoals of fish with their jaws open and swallow dozens of their prey at once; scaly skin shimmering in all the hues of the rainbow, a captivating play of colour in bizarre contrast to the creatures' otherwise hideous appearance; and not least claws as sharp as knives on their bony fingers. Some of them held weapons: primitive harpoons with many barbs, rusty swords gleaned from the sea-bed, and now and then a dagger that had once belonged to a shipwrecked sailor.

The kobalins made their way out of the water in an oily, shimmering wave, as if the foam itself were lifting them up: creatures not made to leave the sea, yet now they were venturing on land. Buenaventure could almost have admired them for their resolve – if he hadn't been certain that they were acting not of their own free will, but at the urging of their chieftains and driven on by threats. And those chieftains in their own turn were ruled by their lord and master, who himself obeyed the Maelstrom.

Buenaventure and Walker, with many others, were manning a line of defence on the northern side of Aelenium: a rampart twice the height of a man, made of pieces of coral from the underwater city and reinforced by sandbags, wooden beams, even furniture brought along by the inhabitants of nearby houses. To right and left of the rampart rose the walls of a broad alley. All the roads leading down to the sea had been closed off with similar barricades.

The first rank of defenders was waiting for the kobalins on top of the rampart, armed with loaded rifles and spring-lock pistols. At a word of command and at almost the same time, they fired on the attackers.

The noise hurt Buenaventure's ears and the gun-smoke stung his eyes. As the swathes of smoke dispersed he saw that the front line of kobalins had gone down, many of them dead, others injured and still screeching. More of them crowded up behind, clambering heedlessly over the fallen – they had no choice, for behind them more and more warriors of the Deep Tribes were rising from the surf, an incredible tide of bodies and claws and bared fangs.

While the marksmen on the rampart jumped down to reload their firearms Walker, Buenaventure and a number of others quickly took their places. The pit bull man was holding his sword with its broad, serrated blade in his right hand – it was a weapon that had served him well in the mines of Antigua – and in his left he had a dagger large enough to be a sword in any ordinary man's hands.

Buenaventure exchanged a short glance with his friend – it was the best they could do to wish each other good luck. Then, side by side, they flung themselves into battle as they had done countless times before. Yet they had never before had to face enemies like these. They were used to skirmishing on land and on board ship, often enough against a force of Spanish soldiers who outnumbered them and had better weapons; they had fought in the alleys of Tortuga and New Providence, in the great prison rebellion of Caracas, and the burning tobacco plantations of Jamaica. Down in the mines of Antigua Buenaventure had more than once found himself in desperate situations, yet in spite of it all he had always survived.

It might well be different today.

He struck out with the ferocity of a dervish, mowing down two or even three kobalins with a single sword-thrust, avoiding their barbed harpoons and their claws, breaking one creature's dry neck here, kicking another back into the advancing hordes there. At the same time he kept an eye on Walker, who was his equal in swordplay but didn't have his immense strength; as always, Buenaventure would come to his friend's aid if he was hard pressed.

The plan had been to fight in good order, but after the first clash with the enemy all such ideas dissolved. Everyone fought as best he could, always hoping to be a little faster and more unpredictable than the enemy. Fighting in the thick of a battle is not an elegant business, whatever historians may say, but cruel and brutal.

The kobalins had no physical stamina; their advantage was their sheer mass. If one died, two more took its place. If one was wounded and fell, those coming up behind took no notice of it but jumped, climbed and crawled on over their comrade, trampling many of their own warriors to death and filling the hearts of the defenders with horror at their cold-blooded cruelty.

Buenaventure had stopped counting how many he had struck down, but gradually he was driving a broad wedge into the tide of attackers. After a while his opponents were fewer, as if more and more of them were avoiding him and turning against Walker and his companions instead. Buenaventure had time to get his breath back, and in that short breathing space he understood what the kobalins' supposed tactics were: none at all! They were following no strategy, no well-honed plan of battle. And it wasn't the will to conquer driving them against the enemy ramparts but blind panic. Whatever their leaders had threatened if they were defeated, it must be far worse than death by the sword.

Buenaventure spotted one of their chieftains down by the water. It wore a headdress made of a shark's skull fitted over its head like a helmet; its hideous face looked out between the open jaws. It had fixed the arms of an octopus to both sides, hanging down from its head like braids. The chieftain was screeching and gesticulating excitedly, and the dangling octopus arms whirled frantically every time it moved its head.

With a single bound, Buenaventure leaped off the top of the defensive rampart to land among the squealing, roaring, iridescent mass of kobalins. He heard Walker calling behind him, and cursed, but he had no time to look round. Once again he struck out with both his blades, the short, straight dagger and the curved, serrated sword, and both bit into fishy kobalin flesh, sowing death among the enemy ranks. He was not proud of his many small victories, and felt no triumph when the kobalins flinched back and fled before him. It was all just the means to an end, steps on the way to his goal.

And his goal was the chieftain.

The kobalin with the shark's head, screaming out orders, saw the fate approaching it when it paused briefly and lowered its arms. For a moment it looked almost taken aback, eye slits widening to reveal fish-like pupils the size of coins. Then it called up its troops in the strange excited, jabbering kobalin language.

Too late.

Buenaventure reached it along a path of lifeless kobalins. The avenue that the pit bull man had carved open had already closed again a few paces behind him. Yet no one dared attack his back. Instead, the kobalins stormed on up the rampart, where they were received by the blades of the defenders, but themselves won skirmish after skirmish.

Buenaventure had eyes only for the chieftain. The creature was baring its teeth, and now the pit bull man saw the barbaric purpose of the shark's-head helmet: an extra pair of jaws around the kobalin's head, it doubled the terrifying sight of the creature's own dreadful fangs. The chieftain might well have put any other opponent to flight in that way. But not a veteran of the mines of Antigua.

The pit bull man's sword came down, cut through the lifeless octopus arms, split the jaws of the shark's skull, and beheaded the chieftain with a single stroke.

A shrill whimpering and lamenting rose, and the wave of attackers hesitated. The death of the chieftain did not decide the battle, wasn't even the fraction of a victory. Yet it gave the defenders of the northern ramparts a moment's respite.

The kobalins withdrew. Those that had only just emerged from the water slipped beneath the waves again. Others turned and plunged back into the surf. And many who were not quick enough to join the receding tide of their brothers were killed by the men and women on the ramparts.

A moment's breathing space, no more. It wouldn't be

long before another chieftain replaced the fallen kobalin, intimidated the attacking forces once more and re-grouped them for another assault. But for that brief moment, fighting on this part of the outer rampart died down.

Walker jumped off the barricade, struck down a few stragglers, and ran towards Buenaventure. He met his comrade with a torrent of mingled curses and cries of delight, and they went back to the rampart together, gathered their forces, cleaned their wounds, and waited for the next wave of attackers.

They knew it was coming when the first dead fish rained down from the evening sky, sparkling silver, as if the stars themselves were falling into the sea.

Griffin clung to the reins of the flying ray. His shock at the marksman's death had affected him so much that he almost fell out of the ring formation of the Ray Guard. But then he got himself and his mount under control again, and for a few seconds he was too busy steering the ray back into its orbit to think of Rorrick.

Only when their flight had stabilised again did the certain knowledge that his marksman was dead hit him once more. He saw Rorrick still sitting behind him, could even feel him, although the body had disappeared under the waves long ago. Then the thought of Rorrick's last seconds blotted out that image – the lance, then his fall.

Griffin's muscles were tensed, his knuckles white, as if they would burst through the skin at any moment. A thousand thoughts shot through his head. Fear of a second lance. Despair when he realised that they were fighting in vain. And above all the thought that he was to blame for Rorrick's fate.

If he had made the ray fly faster; if he had flown higher or lower; if he had noticed where in the water most lances were thrown from – then Rorrick might still be alive. But he hadn't done any of those things. And Rorrick was dead.

He felt like simply giving up. He was a pirate, not a soldier. He had often fought – if not as often as he had once liked to claim – and he had seen men die and ships sink. But this was different. This was war. Not a skirmish at sea, not an attack on sluggish, slow-moving merchant galleons.

War, he thought again. And all of a sudden the idea of killing and being killed had nothing daring about it any more, most certainly nothing heroic. At such moments it didn't matter who felt they were in the right or why, who was merely forced to fight and who was following a noble ideal.

We're all going to die, he thought. And then, unexpectedly, he found himself in a prosaic frame of mind that alarmed him almost more than his earlier despair.

All of us, he thought. Every one of us.

Jolly too.

He took his hand off the reins to rub his eyes until they hurt, and fiery wheels were going round behind his eyelids. Only then did a little reason return.

'Griffin!'

D'Artois' voice made him look to his right. The captain had brought his ray up beside Griffin. The wings of the two creatures were almost touching, and the abyss yawned between them.

'Griffin, you must go back to the shore. There are more marksmen waiting there. You can't give up now!' The captain's expression was deadly serious, and his cheek muscles were working grimly. 'Do it, Griffin! Now!'

Griffin nodded jerkily, then brought his ray some six feet lower in the air and turned it. It broke away from the circle and inwards, turning in a tight angle that seemed too sharp for such a large animal, and flew towards the coral slopes of Aelenium. Below it, in the water between two arms of the starfish, the waves appeared to be boiling, while thin kobalin hands thrust up everywhere through the sea and flung lances at the sky. None of them came close enough to Griffin to be any danger to him.

The place from which Griffin had taken off lay on the opposite side of the city. He had the choice of flying round the slopes with their gables and towers, or climbing in the air and flying over them. He decided on the second option.

The ray shot across the buildings in the ravines of the city, over narrow streets and steep gables, the tops of towers with battlements of branching coral, the broad roofs of the palaces. Griffin saw the libraries beneath him to his right, and the poet's quarter where the Hexhermetic Shipworm was still dreaming in his silky cocoon. Further away he saw the lower defensive rampart, just above the arms of the starfish where they merged with the massive cone of the coral mountain. Walker and Buenaventure were fighting somewhere down there, but he couldn't make them out at this distance.

To the north, beyond the city, far away across the water and above the wall of mist, black smoke was rising, and now and then the booming echo of cannon thundering in the distance reached Aelenium. The pirate captains of the Lesser Antilles were locked in battle with the cannibal king and his fleet. The outcome still seemed to be undecided.

And Griffin saw something else as he flew past, up in the city centre where the highest towers stood. He was too shaken by Rorrick's death to identify this complex of buildings at first glance, but then he recognised it: the library where Forefather's rooms lay, the most sacred temple of knowledge in the starfish city.

On a semicircular balcony with bizarre coral outcrops pointing in all directions like petrified arms, two men were watching the battle.

Forefather and the Ghost-Trader.

They stood side by side and motionless; they did not look at each other, but out at the rings of the Ray Guard riders circling the cone of the mountain in opposite directions. There were flashes and the sound of gunshots from among the flying shoals as the marksmen fired down at the water, where the kobalins replied to their attacks with a hail of black harpoons from below.

The Trader had brought his hands out from under his dark robe and was clutching the rim of the balustrade. Forefather was leaning on his stick, which towered above him. Griffin could see that their lips were moving, but the noise of battle and the rushing of the rays' wings drowned out their words.

The ray carried him past the balustrade barely a stone's throw from those two mysterious figures. Griffin sensed a prickling on his skin, a tingling and itching of the kind you may sense on a ship coming too close to a violent storm.

Like an invisible discharge of electricity, he felt a sudden certainty that the fate of Aelenium, perhaps of the whole world, was being decided on this balcony for good or ill.

All of a sudden the battle wasn't nearly so important, certainly not crucial. It was being fought only to gain time. Time for Jolly and Munk, but perhaps for something else as well.

He shuddered as he tried to think what that might be. His powers of imagination failed him, and he was almost glad of it.

The balcony where Forefather and the Ghost-Trader stood was left behind him. He wasn't even sure if they had noticed the solitary rider who had broken away from the ring formation of rays passing close to them.

Griffin shook himself. His head cleared again, and he looked for his landing place among the maze of alleyways. What was he fighting for? At least he had an answer to *that* question.

Certainly not for Aelenium. Not even for himself.

First and foremost, he was fighting for Jolly.

Up by the balustrade, high above the turmoil of battle, Forefather's hands clutched his long staff more firmly. The backs of his hands, freckled with liver spots, were tensed, and it seemed to the Ghost-Trader that he could hear the old man's knuckles crack.

On a coral ledge above them the two black parrots, Hugh and Moe, sat perfectly still. Two pairs of differently coloured eyes looked down into the depths without emotion.

'We can't wait any longer,' said Forefather in a hoarse voice. After their long and sometimes heated conversation it was even huskier than usual. 'You must do what has to be done.'

'Not until the second rampart falls,' the Ghost-Trader contradicted him. 'I've said so many times, and I'll say it again: the danger is too great. And the price . . .' Shaking his head gloomily, he let the word die away before he went on. 'The price could be higher than we can imagine.'

'But against that we must set the deaths of hundreds. And perhaps final ruin.'

'Either course of action can bring that. Let's not argue about it any more, old friend. I've made my decision. So far they're holding the first rampart. After that we still have the second. And only then . . .' Once again he broke off.

'You still place all your hopes on the polliwiggles.' Forefather looked at him with eyes that had seen aeons pass as a mortal sees the seasons come and go.

'And why not?'

Forefather shook his old head. 'What makes you so certain that you'll stake everything on them?'

'There *is* no certainty, I know that.' The Ghost-Trader hesitated. 'But I know the boy. He has the power that's needed.'

'But does he have the sense of responsibility and wisdom such a task calls for?'

'That's why Jolly is with him.'

'She's still a child herself.'

The one-eyed man smiled sadly as he looked at Forefather. Up on the ledge, both parrots put their heads on one side. '*Still* a child, you said, not *only* a child. And you know why. You can tell the difference for yourself.'

'But you too know what happened long ago. We both saw it, just as we are seeing it today. We stood by and watched, and there was nothing we could do to alter it.' He sighed. 'Even then we were too weak.'

'We are wiser today.'

'Are we?' Forefather gave a hoarse chuckle. 'I'm older than you, but even I am still waiting for the wisdom of old age. I'm beginning to give up hope of ever finding it.'

The Ghost-Trader smiled again. 'At least you've learned the pig-headedness of old age.'

'If I were as pig-headed as you think, I'd force you to do

148

what must be done. Instead I'm trying to convince you it's right, and I have to watch myself failing.'

All at once the Trader was in deadly earnest. 'It's no good. Not yet. Only when there is no other way out at all.'

'You and I have seen so many die. So much wasted life all down the ages.'

Above the water, the riders of the rays were forming into a single broad ring flying closer to the slopes of the city now. They had given up trying to clear the water of kobalins all the way to the wall of mist. Instead, they were concentrating on the shore and the wave of attackers rolling towards it from the sea.

'It's raining dead fish to the north,' said Forefather, pointing to the sparkling in the air against the misty background. The evening sun was bathing the rim of the swathes of vapour in a red-gold sunset glow, and in front of them fell something that from a distance looked like a rain of sparks.

'Then it is here,' said the Ghost-Trader. 'It is late in coming.'

'Not late enough.'

'No, indeed.'

Once again the old man turned to the Trader. 'You can turn the dying into stories, my friend. But more stories are told about the two of us than anyone could ever collect or write down. Doesn't that mean that we ourselves, in a way, have been dead a long time?'

The Ghost-Trader thought about it, and then nodded. 'Perhaps we just didn't notice before.'

THE KOBALIN PATH

Not much further now to the centre of the earth, thought Jolly dismally. She felt as if she and Munk had been walking through the darkness for a lifetime already.

Aina had led them out of the ruins of the submerged coral city and further down the slope. Two or three times they had come to the edge of a dark abyss where they had to dive past walls of rock. And still they were going on down.

Once Aina warned them against taking the direct way past a row of strange rocky stacks with what looked like black smoke rising from their peaks. It was boiling water mingled with ash from deep inside the earth.

'Underwater volcanoes,' Aina explained, adding that all kinds of creatures had settled in the warm waters around the craters.

It soon turned out that she had been right to warn them, for in the distance, on the rim of her polliwiggle vision,

Jolly saw mighty shapes swirling around the stacks. The creatures were like white-skinned moray eels with gigantic mouths and a single luminous antenna, a disgusting sight, between their half-blind eyes. The polliwiggles would probably have fallen victim to them if Aina hadn't led them round the craters in a wide curve. She kept urging them to hurry, particularly when they had to make such detours.

She didn't say so openly, but she seemed very anxious about the friends she had left behind in the clutches of the Maelstrom. Perhaps she blamed herself for what had happened.

More than once Jolly tried to imagine how Aina had felt when she set off for the Maelstrom so long ago. Had she accepted her destiny as willingly as Munk? Or had she felt like Jolly?

They left the rocky stacks and warm waters behind. Aina went ahead, followed by Munk and Jolly, who kept an eye on the crags of the rocky land on both sides of them.

'Aren't you afraid?' Jolly suddenly asked the strange girl.

'Of the Maelstrom? Of course. I –'

'No, that's not what I mean. If we really succeed in destroying it and rescuing your friends . . . you'll come back to the surface with us, won't you?'

Aina hesitated. Then she slowly nodded.

'Well, the world today is quite different from the world in your time. Everything's changed.'

'Not people,' said Aina, and there was bitterness around the corners of her mouth. 'Human beings never change.'

Jolly exchanged a glance with Munk. 'What do you mean?'

The girl did not reply at once, but seemed to be thinking. It was as if a wall had suddenly come between her and her memories, and she had to overcome it. 'Human beings were not good to me. They were afraid because I wasn't like them. I and the others could do things that –'

'That they couldn't do.' Munk finished her sentence for her.

Jolly's feelings wavered between agreement and surprise. She knew what it meant to be different. But wasn't that really just a question of the people you mixed with? The pirates on board the *Maid Maddy* had been outcasts themselves, social pariahs – and they had accepted Jolly for what she was.

Munk's resentment, on the other hand, was obviously for the people of Aelenium. Yes, he had enjoyed being revered as a saviour. But perhaps their admiration had just been a mask hiding their fear of the polliwiggles. Suddenly that idea didn't seem to Jolly so very far-fetched. Perhaps Munk had seen through them much sooner than she did, and now he shared Aina's dislike.

'They beat and kicked me,' said the girl, without looking round. She sounded very downcast, as if that time were not a thousand years but only a few days ago. 'At first it was just mockery, then they did it in fear. And in the end they tortured me. My own family threw me out.'

Lost in thought, Jolly nodded. Bannon and his crew had been her family, and they too had betrayed her. Back then, Aina must have felt as hurt and desperate as Jolly had.

The longer she listened to the girl, the more ironic it seemed to her that the three of them had been chosen to save the human race. Young people who would have met with dislike or at the best arrogance from the inhabitants of Port Royal or Havana.

'But you came down here to destroy the Maelstrom,' Jolly reminded Aina.

Aina gave her a long look. 'Where else could I have gone?'

And then they were silent again.

The appearance of Aina had taken Jolly's mind off her depression at the sight of this wilderness, but now their grey, dismal surroundings were getting to her again.

'Doesn't the Maelstrom have you followed?' she suddenly asked, looking at Aina, just to hear a voice again.

'Of course. It's looking for me.'

'The current?' asked Munk. 'A seeking current?'

Aina nodded. 'I'm sorry,' she said. 'You felt it too, didn't you?'

Jolly frowned. 'We thought it was looking for *us*.'

'No,' said Aina. 'I don't think it knows you're here yet.'

Was this girl really more important to the Maelstrom than Munk and Jolly? Perhaps it didn't fear the two of them at all, perhaps it was perfectly indifferent to them, knowing they couldn't hurt it. Unseen by anyone, Jolly clenched one fist. She would rather have gone on believing that the current *had* been searching for them. At least until this moment she had felt the Maelstrom took them seriously. But now their mission seemed even more hopeless. Sometimes it was an advantage to feel fear.

The slope ahead of them was overgrown now with something that at first sight resembled the pale worm-like plants among the ruins of the coral city. The growths here were very similar, but much larger. It wasn't long before the drifting worms were above their heads, waving like gigantic arms and legs on joints that someone had buried in the ground. They stood side by side in broad clumps, but in between there were many aisles along which the three of them could easily walk. Munk suggested swimming over this bizarre forest, but Aina wouldn't agree. They were too close to the Rift, she said.

She seemed about to add something else, but then thought better of it.

'How much further is it?' asked Jolly.

'Not far now. We've come over half the way already.'

How long had they been on the move? Jolly didn't know. The lack of any sense of time down here was troubling her more and more.

'Careful!' Aina stopped.

Jolly and Munk stayed where they were, staring intently first at the girl, then at their dark surroundings.

'What's the matter?'

'There's something here.' Aina's eyes wandered over the wall of plants rocking silently back and forth. Back and forth again and again, stirred by invisible currents.

Jolly looked at Munk, but he just shrugged his shoulders very slightly. Neither of them had noticed anything.

'Get off the path,' whispered Aina, taking off from the sea-bed with a swift swimming stroke and gliding between the flexible stems. 'Quick!'

'Path?' Baffled, Munk looked at the ground. The way through the plants didn't look deliberately laid out as a path. Jolly signalled silently to him that she hadn't the faintest idea what the girl was talking about. Nonetheless, they quickly followed Aina through the clumps of waterweed. The white, spongy texture of the growths felt unpleasant, much more organic than Jolly liked.

'Is this really a path you've been leading us along?' asked Munk in a strained voice.

Aina nodded. 'One of the claw-men's paths,' she whispered, but immediately put her forefinger to her lips to tell him not to ask any more questions.

They waited, anxious and motionless, as the plants moved gently over their bodies as if investigating the three intruders.

In the silence, Jolly hear a soft rustling sound – the plant stems rubbing against each other. Once she had picked up the rustling it came from all directions at once, until the noise drowned out even the hammering of her heart.

Three kobalins were making their way along the path, their shoulders bent. Their bodies were short and very stocky, and they had shorter and far more muscular legs than the kobalins on the shape-shifter's island. Their noses had developed nostrils the size of clenched fists. But they had no eyes – only slight hollows below their angular cheekbones to show where their ancestors had once had eye sockets. Like all the animals and plants down here, they were the translucent white colour of fresh coconut milk.

Jolly's stomach muscles tensed. She prayed that a

particularly strong current would close the plant stems in front of her before one of those creatures picked up her scent.

Munk took her hand. She nearly squeaked in alarm. His fingers closed so tightly around hers that it almost hurt, but she understood him only too well.

Aina did not move. Her gaze was fixed on the creatures passing by not five paces away from them. The girl's face wore an expression of deep concern.

Jolly stopped breathing. It was a strange feeling when the water stopped flowing through her lungs and gradually warmed up. But breathing out just now seemed to her too dangerous.

One of the kobalins halted.

It's picked up our scent, thought Jolly. It can feel that we're here.

The rims of the huge nostrils widened and then drew together again. At the same time it opened and closed its mouth full of teeth, as if trying to taste something in the water.

Us, thought Jolly, with a chilly feeling. It's tasting *us*!

The other two kobalins stopped too. Jolly noticed that none of the three had webbed fingers and toes. Instead their feet were extremely broad and large, almost as if this particular kobalin species couldn't move from the sea-bed.

Of course! It was obvious: white skin, no eyes, their bent

posture – everything suggested that these beings had spent their whole lives down here, after being exposed to massive water pressure for countless generations.

Now they were sniffing at their surroundings, nostrils quivering, while their mouths made smacking sounds. They're going to find us – the thought flashed through Jolly's mind. There's no way they can fail to find us.

The kobalins hissed a few times and then went on, following the path in the direction from which Jolly and the others had just come.

The polliwiggles stayed in their hiding place for some time before Aina finally sighed in relief and gave the all-clear. 'We're safe,' she said. 'For now, at least.'

'What kind of kobalins were those?' asked Munk as they made their way through the stems and out into the open.

'They live down here.' Aina looked in all directions again, to make sure they were safe, and then came down with both feet in the dust. 'They're different from the ones you know, aren't they? There aren't many of them left, but they're just as dangerous as the tribes higher up. However, at least they can't swim, or not very well anyway.'

'Could they have been looking for you?' asked Jolly. 'Maybe the Maelstrom sent them.'

Aina went on going downhill. 'Either that – or . . .'

'Or?'

'They're probably just hunting because they're hungry.' After a moment she added, 'You decide which you'd rather.'

Jolly swallowed and said nothing.

'But they can't eat *you*,' Munk told Aina, and Jolly was annoyed with herself for not thinking of that too. 'You don't have a solid body.'

Aina made a face, distorting her pretty features, and then shrugged. 'But that's no help to you two, is it? Two polliwiggles wouldn't be a bad catch.'

Jolly felt almost painful nausea rising in her.

They went on even more watchfully than before. Soon the trail of the kobalins disappeared from sight; the dust had wiped out the tracks left by the creatures.

The forest of deep-sea growths ended at the edge of a high plateau. The abyss below was black, surging and indistinct.

'Hear that?' said Aina.

Jolly and Munk moved together in alarm, but the girl made a reassuring gesture. 'Just listen,' she said in a whisper.

They did, although hesitantly, and it was a moment before Jolly understood what Aina meant. A distant rushing and roaring came from the darkness ahead of them, like the sound of a mighty waterfall or a tidal wave.

'Seeking currents?' asked Munk.

'No,' said Aina, shuddering. 'That's *it*.'

'The Maelstrom?' Jolly strained her ears even harder. Yes, that was how it would sound if unimaginably great masses of water were being sucked down into the depths as they rotated and were then spewed out again. The distant, resonant noise seemed to take hold of her and shake her thoroughly. Jolly trembled, as if a mighty voice were coming from the indistinct raging and roaring to intimidate her.

To her surprise she saw Munk crouch down on the edge of the plateau and take his shells out of the bag at his belt. With practised moves, he laid them out in the dust in front of him.

'What are you doing?' asked Jolly.

'Setting out the shells.'

'I can see that! But why now?' Had something escaped her? Had he noticed some danger that she herself didn't yet see? As if of its own accord, her hand went to the shells in the bag that she herself was wearing.

Munk didn't look up. His fingers moved the shells within the circle they formed, sorted out some, replaced them by others or changed the order of arrangement, as if he were after some particular combination. 'Forefather said we should try to find out how the shells react close to the Maelstrom. If they act differently from usual. It was important, he said.' He stooped for a moment, looked at the circle of shells, and then glanced up at Jolly. 'You couldn't have known that; you weren't there at the time.'

She thought of imitating him and taking out her own shells, but then decided not to; she wasn't going to give him the pleasure of triumphing over her.

'What do they say?' asked Aina, turning to Munk.

Say? Jolly thought.

Smiling, Munk looked up at Aina, obviously pleased to be with someone who clearly knew more than Jolly about shell magic. 'They're speaking to me, but only indistinctly. It's more like a . . . well, something like a dragging movement. They want us to go on. It's as if something were attracting them.'

Jolly stared at him. Her fingers dug into the bag at her belt.

'I brought my own shells away from the Maelstrom with me,' said Aina. 'I thought I might be able to help the others with them somehow. But I didn't set them out.' She hesitated. 'I was afraid it might be able to find me more easily if I did.'

Munk picked implications up quickly now. 'They must

be very old shells if you brought them down here with you all that time ago.'

Age meant power, Jolly had learned that much about the shells. The longer a shell had been lying in the sea, the greater the magic in it.

In the darkness, Aina was gazing towards the other side of the abyss. Her voice sounded almost melancholy. 'They were trapped in the Rift with me the whole time. Along with my friends – and the Maelstrom.'

'I could use them,' said Munk with unconcealed eagerness. 'I could try pitting them against the Maelstrom. They would be much more powerful than my own.' As if to lend his words more weight, he carelessly swept the shells he had only just set out so carefully into a heap and put them back into their bag, together with some of the sand that was trickling through his fingers.

Aina shook her head sadly. 'That's no good,' she said. 'I don't have them any more.'

Munk raised a hand as if to touch and comfort her, and then remembered that she had no solid body.

Jolly frowned. She was feeling more and more left out. Something that she couldn't understand was going on between Munk and Aina. Even casual gestures seemed to her like secret signals. And weren't they exchanging furtive glances?

I'm getting persecution mania, she thought, and remembered moments in her earlier life, lonely night watches on the deck of the *Maid Maddy* when her mind had played very similar tricks on her: movements in the dark, shadows stealing over the deck, figures hiding behind masts – all of them conjured up by her imagination, but no less frightening for that.

None of them said anything for a moment. Then Munk suddenly rose to his feet. His eyes were flashing. 'We'll go and look for Aina's shells,' he said firmly. 'We'll find them, and then we'll rescue her friends.' A radiant smile spread over his face, as if the battle against the Maelstrom was already won.

Aina frowned, and then glanced at Jolly as if asking her approval. 'Munk may be right. We could look for them and then use them,' she said cautiously.

Munk too suddenly seemed to remember Jolly. Almost impatiently, he turned to her. 'Well, what do you think?'

Are you really interested? she wondered, but she said, 'Sounds like a sensible idea.' There was no point in discussing their feelings at a moment like this. She had to trust Munk's greater experience in shell magic . . . she only hoped he knew what he was doing.

Munk turned on his heel. 'Good,' he said. 'Then let's start looking.'

'They ought to be around,' said Aina, after they had reached the foot of the precipice and found themselves on another crumbling slope of rocky debris. 'I left them somewhere here.' She looked anxiously towards the Maelstrom. 'But we must hurry.'

'Did you bury them?' asked Jolly, with a doubtful look at the debris underfoot.

'I put a stone over them, one about this size.' She made a circular movement with both hands. There were at least a thousand such stones in sight.

Munk's cheek muscles were working. 'I hope they're not broken.' His eyes were already searching the rocky slope.

Jolly shook her head, sighed softly, and set out in search of a stone the size that Aina had shown them. By tacit agreement they were all searching separately, picking up stones and looking under them. Munk went about it eagerly. Finally he opened the bag at his belt again, placed several shells on the palm of his left hand and let the pull of the magic guide him. His shells led him to the part of the rocky slope that Aina was already searching. She seemed to be frantic, and not as sure of herself as she had been a few minutes ago.

Jolly had just rolled another stone aside, without

success, when Aina called, 'Here! I think this is it.'

When Jolly looked, Aina was putting her hand into a crevice behind a piece of rock the size of a human head. Her features brightened. 'I've got it!'

Munk put his own shells back in their bag and set off to join her, but Jolly arrived beside Aina first. The girl was holding a single shell, larger than any of Jolly's or Munk's, and sprinkled with an interesting pale and dark pattern. In daylight it would probably be multi-coloured, iridescent, a wonderful sight.

'Only one?' Munk didn't take any trouble to conceal his disappointment.

Aina nodded shyly. 'The others broke under the stone. But this one will be quite enough. It was the most powerful of them all anyway.'

Jolly saw that Munk was looking past Aina into the crevice. Was he really so obsessed by the magic that this one shell wasn't enough for him? But Jolly had to admit that even she could feel the powerful tingling it gave off in the girl's hand, almost a sense of warmth that Aina was transferring to her and presumably Munk too.

'May I hold it?' asked Munk.

Aina smiled. 'It's yours if you want it.'

'You bet I do!' Almost reverently, he took the shell – it

was the shape of a snail-shell – and weighed it cautiously in his hand. His fingers were shaking. 'It could have been made for me!' Then he gave a start and smiled guiltily at Aina. 'Sorry. I didn't mean it that way.'

She waved his apology away. 'Your power over the shells is greater than mine. I can feel it.'

'Or mine,' added Jolly. She too was tempted to put out her hand for Aina's gift.

Munk could see the wish in her eyes, and for a moment it seemed as if he were going to move the shell out of her reach. But then he offered it to her. 'Here, you hold it.'

Jolly took the shell between her thumb and forefinger, raised it to eye-level and examined it. The strange tingling was no stronger, which might show that the shell itself had already decided on its new owner. It was fist-sized, convoluted and hollow, with an opening on one side and a spiral point on the other. Something made her want to hold it to her ear and listen, as she had often done with seashells when she was a child. But for some reason or other the thought also made her shudder. She didn't like the idea that the shell might really be able to speak to her.

Partly reluctant, partly relieved, she handed it back to Munk, who took it quickly, almost as if afraid that Jolly might yet change her mind.

'I hope you can do more with it than I could,' said Aina. 'It may be our only chance against the Maelstrom.'

Munk was still staring at the shell in his hand, but Jolly looked at the girl they had met on the sea-bed. 'If your body isn't solid, how can you pick up stones? And shells?'

Aina shrugged her shoulders. 'The further I went from the Maelstrom the less substance I had. And perhaps it's the other way around too.' Seeing that Jolly wasn't satisfied, she added, 'I don't know the answer either. I didn't make the rules.'

Jolly watched her walk away, not sure what to make of this. But then she followed the other girl.

'Are you coming, Munk?'

When she looked round for him, he had his ear to the opening of the shell and was listening. Their glances met, and he nodded. But suddenly she wasn't sure whether the nod was meant for her or for the shell that might be whispering to him.

The attack came by surprise and without any warning.

At the end of the slope, beyond a barrier of rock needles and angular blocks of stone, they had come to the edge of a plain of white sand. Aina had warned them not to go across this wide sandy expanse, and to step only on the grey slabs of rock to be seen coming up through the dust in many places if you looked more closely.

'Quicksand,' she had explained, looking down and wrapping her arms tightly around her upper body, as if she were shivering. 'One of us was almost drawn down into it once.'

Drawn down. The phrase echoed on in Jolly's mind. Down where? Even deeper into the centre of the world? *Could* there be a deeper place than this? Instinctively she looked up to where the surface of the sea must be, somewhere many thousands of leagues above them. Darkness stretched overhead like a dome of black velvet. By a small stretch of the imagination Jolly could have persuaded herself that she was standing under a night sky. Except that there were no stars here. No sense of infinity. Only a frightening weight pressing heavily down on her mind, her thoughts, her courage.

The kobalins attacked just as Munk had asked, 'How much further to the Rift now?' and Aina had replied, with an enigmatic smile, 'Can't you feel it? We'll soon be right in the middle of it.'

Ahead of them, the blurred horizon on the edge of their field of vision began to shift as a long line of several kobalins emerged from the darkness, their bodies as white as the sand on the plain. Their eyeless faces were turned towards the three polliwiggles, their coarse hands, with claws like sword-blades, dangled almost to the ground. Even their joints were sharper and more angular than in human beings, and Jolly found herself wondering whether they used their knees and elbows as weapons.

'Get back!' she cried, as the kobalins came out of the darkness.

Aina stood there as if rooted to the spot. But Munk's right hand fumbled with the catch of the bag at his belt which now also contained the large shell.

'Let them come,' he said softly.

'Munk!' shouted Jolly. 'For heaven's sake, get out of here!'

But he did not move from where he stood. The shells from the bag seemed to slip into his hand of their own accord, and before Jolly knew it he was crouching down on a rocky slab and laying out the shells. He placed Aina's gift in the middle, where it rose high above all the other shells like the tower of a strange fairy-tale palace with a swirling pointed roof.

'I have to find out how powerful it is,' he murmured.

The kobalins were coming closer, following the course of the stepping stones. Jolly didn't stop to count them, but she guessed there were at least ten. Maybe more.

'Munk, stop it! There are too many!' But Munk wasn't listening to her. Aina was standing close to him, and they were both looking at the kobalins.

A pale glow came from the opening of the large shell. The circle filled with light as the largest, brightest pearl that Jolly had ever seen rose from it and hovered above the shells, at the very centre of the circle. It was not the same as usual: until now, the magic powers of all the shells had concentrated to come together in a magical globe. But this time it seemed as if the other shells were enticing a pearl that had been there all the time out of the large one. The result might look the same – a glowing pearl hovering at the heart of the shell circle – but it was different. Jolly could feel that, and she didn't like it.

Something was happening to the water around them. It looked as if it were freezing into long strands as thick as a finger, undulating over the sea-bed like snakes.

The veins of magic, thought Jolly. The pearl was tapping the power of the Water Weavers! That must increase its own strength many times over.

Like a star, the now visible veins of water reached out in all directions from where the polliwiggles stood. Somewhere in the darkness the ends of the veins suddenly seemed to rise and move upwards, until they encircled the three companions like the cup of a flower. Then a hard, abrupt pulsing moved through the snaking, watery wall in a wave of pressure that seemed to come from all sides at once. The veins of water met above their heads in something that looked like a braid of translucent strands as broad as a tree trunk. It began swinging like a whip, and then swept in a wide curve into the row of kobalins a hundred or a hundred and fifty paces from the polliwiggles.

It was as if a giant's sword had cut the creatures down.

Before they even guessed what was coming towards them, the whip of water struck and crushed them. It all happened so fast that Jolly saw no details – she was aware of the death of the kobalins only moments later, when the horizon at the limit of her polliwiggle vision was suddenly empty and lifeless again.

The power of shell magic had turned the kobalins to dust, scattering their particles in all directions like fine ash. Nothing was left of them; even their footprints were wiped away and the sand left smooth again.

On impact – or a split second later – the strands of water themselves had dissolved once more, leaving nothing to show that they had ever been there. The pearl was gone too. Munk had shut it up in its shell with a movement of his hand, as was necessary if its magic was not to get out of control.

Jolly fought off a sudden desire to vomit, swallowed convulsively, and got herself under control again with difficulty. Her legs felt weak, but she stood where she was and stared mutely at Munk, who was still crouching motionless in front of his shells with his back to her, like Aina, whose hand was now resting on his shoulder, although Jolly assumed he couldn't feel it.

She took a deep breath, then collected herself and moved past the silent couple.

'Come on,' she said hoarsely, and set off without looking round at them.

Not for the world could she have brought herself to look either of them in the eye just now.

FIERY RAIN

The sky above Aelenium was burning.

Beyond the mist, the night sky was already red with the light of the sea battle, and now the defenders of the city themselves were setting the world ablaze as the Ray Guard riders poured flames down on the kobalins.

They had held their positions for many hours, but everyone had known that sooner or later this moment must come, and most were painfully aware of the consequences. Fire was a two-edged sword in the narrow confines of a city like Aelenium, and already it threatened to strike both ways.

From above Griffin saw that parts of the outer rampart were in flames, but so were some of the nearby houses. The coral itself was largely untouched, but the wooden buildings on it and the rooftops offered the fire plenty of nourishment, and it was already taking hold of many homes.

The defenders had retreated, and were waiting beyond

the flames for any kobalins who were driven by blood-lust or fear to leap through the blaze. At one place in the south, a kobalin chieftain was driving troops forward in spite of the wall of flame, and soon the kobalins had put out part of the fire with their own bodies. Black, greasy smoke rose among the buildings, while the advancing kobalins trampled the bodies of their burnt companions into the ashes and stormed the rampart over them.

'See that?' called Griffin's new marksman, a man called Ishmael.

'Yes,' said Griffin, thinking: I almost feel sorry for them. But he didn't say so, for he was afraid Ishmael might not understand his pity. He couldn't even really account for it himself. The kobalins were their adversaries, their mortal enemies, and down below dozens of human beings had already fallen victim to their claws. Yet the fact was that they weren't acting of their own free will. The true enemy was the Maelstrom. And of course the being that it had sent out to win the battle for Aelenium: a creature for which they still had no name, and which for lack of any better term they all called the kobalin commander.

At the same time, they were fairly sure that this creature was not a kobalin itself. The rain of fish suggested a monstrosity like the Acherus that had killed Munk's parents.

However, no one had yet seen the kobalin commander, not even Griffin and Jolly, who had come closer to it than anyone else.

'Damn these fish!' cursed Ishmael, as he whirled one of the fiery globes above his head on a long chain, ready to fling it into the depths below, where the rampart risked being breached. 'Keep your head down, boy!'

Griffin felt the iron vessel full of blazing oil circle above him, and he was almost more afraid of it than of the kobalin lances. Only a few of those were now being thrown. It was amazing that in spite of the flames and heat so close to them, the rays obeyed their riders. The net of chains in which the fiery globes lay dangled about two yards below each animal, fixed to its saddle. D'Artois had hoped he need not use these weapons, so the Ray Guard had made only a few practice flights with them. Griffin himself had been on only one.

Ishmael, a fair-haired, fair-skinned giant, had arms like tree trunks, and he needed them to haul the fiery globes up out of the net on their chains. He said the marksmen had to swing the missiles above their heads to increase their effect. Griffin wasn't so sure; he thought they could just as well simply drop the globes on the kobalins. He had an uneasy feeling that Ishmael was enjoying himself and getting a kick out of it. That was all very well so long as it didn't endanger the lives of Griffin and the ray. So far, however, he hadn't let a drop of the burning oil fall on the animal or its rider as he threw the globes. Ishmael was unusually strong and skilful, and he deeply hated the kobalins. No, thought Griffin, it was surely better not to show any pity for them. Unless he wanted Ishmael to throw him down too, along with one of the globes.

His eyes followed the fiery missile as the marksman let it go. It dropped straight for its target, the chain clinking as it followed, and traced a burning track through the night. Before the globe crashed into the kobalin hordes, Griffin lost sight of it for a moment. But then a flower of flame shot up among the screaming creatures, and he knew that Ishmael had scored another bullseye. He himself felt no triumph, only deep horror.

'That was our last,' shouted Ishmael above the din. 'Let's land and take some more globes on board.'

Griffin shook his head. 'No more fiery globes! Look down there. Most of the places where we could get more supplies are already too crowded for me to land. I'm not going to fly around just wasting time while we can get a few of the brutes equally well with other weapons.'

He sensed Ishmael's eyes on his back, and expected

vigorous contradiction. But after a moment Griffin heard the marksman loading rifles and cocking hammers behind him. Soon Ishmael began firing into the depths below, all guns blazing.

They flew twice more around the besieged city, diving as they raced above the starfish arms, which were swarming with kobalins by now, and then swept through the plumes of smoke from the burning barricades. Griffin couldn't see Walker, Buenaventure or Soledad anywhere.

In all this chaos human beings and kobalins alike had become vague, scurrying figures, looking as small as toys from up here. Griffin felt strangely removed from the fighting, even though he was in the thick of it.

As they kept moving from hot regions of air into the chill of night and back, he thought of Jolly again. What was happening to her down on the sea-bed? Were she and Munk still on their way, or had they reached the Rift?

'Hey, boy! Devil take it all, look at that!'

For the first time Griffin was glad to hear Ishmael's brusque voice. It took his mind off the nightmare images forming spontaneously in his imagination.

But reality was no better. 'The fire over there,' called Ishmael, pointing to one of the arms of the starfish. 'Isn't that building the sea-horse stables?'

Griffin's throat felt as dry as if he had swallowed some of Ishmael's hot oil. For a moment he almost lost control of the ray. Matador and the other hippocamps! They'd all burn to death down there!

He glanced the way Ishmael was pointing, and breathed again: yes, fire was burning on that arm of the starfish, but it hadn't reached the long, low complex of the stables yet. However – and that was almost as bad – the entire starfish arm was in the power of the kobalins.

But then Griffin saw something else: the grooms had opened the gates of the stables before retreating into the city. Beneath the smoke, a stream of sea horses was pouring out into the open sea, shooting past the kobalins in panic and disappearing through the wall of mist. His whole body tensed, until he realised that the kobalins had better things to do than attack the harmless sea horses. Sure enough, he saw not a single hippocamp dragged down into the depths. Obviously the servants of the Maelstrom were letting the herd pass. Griffin looked for Matador, but couldn't make the creature out in the tide of animals beyond the drifting smoke. Silently, he wished his sea horse luck, and blinked back the tears stinging his eyes.

Ishmael fired his rifles and pistols at the kobalins outside the stables, and then they were past the starfish arm, leaving the stables and the escaping herd behind.

'They were lucky!' shouted the marksman above the clamour of the weapons and the wind roaring in their faces. His laughter sounded relieved. Like all the guardsmen of Aelenium, he was deeply fond of the elegant sea horses.

They were halfway around the city when they flew into a shower of dead fish once more. This time Griffin did something that he had carefully avoided so far: ignoring d'Artois' orders, he broke away from the ring formation of the Ray Guard riders and flew his mount out of it at a sharp angle.

Ishmael was shouting in high spirits, as if all this was great fun. At the same time he fired a whole salvo of shots at a kobalin horde about to go on land. The hits he scored in their front ranks drove the creatures back into the water. Ishmael cheered.

'Where are we going, boy?' he asked as he reloaded his guns.

'Would you like a *real* fight?' Griffin asked in return. He felt Ishmael's high spirits infecting him – perhaps because of his own relief at seeing the sea horses get safely away, or perhaps because all this madness had infected him too.

'You bet, boy.' Ishmael clapped him on the shoulder. 'Who are we after, then?'

Griffin pointed through the clouds of dead fish and down

to the water. The light of the fire didn't reach as far as this, but the moonlight showed a dark, indistinct outline beneath the waves, where something large and shapeless was circling the starfish city.

'That thing,' said Griffin grimly. 'We're going to kill the kobalin commander.'

Soledad came back to her senses feeling as if her back would break in two if she moved more than just her head. Her right arm was burning, and when she looked at it she saw that the leather of her diving suit was shredded from the elbow down. However, most of her skin beneath it seemed to be intact.

She felt hopelessly confused as her headache mingled with many bewildering images: the battle with the kobalins for the anchor chain, her flight to the underwater city, then complete darkness – a deep black pressing down on Soledad's eyes like thumbs. She had been trying to find a way out, had slotted her last aerated stone into place and then – as the air grew staler and staler – she had finally found a shaft leading up. The last thing she remembered was the impression of a mighty body gliding into the shaft, filling it and displacing the water, growing longer and longer, coiling more and more intricately. And then nothing more. Just the blackness. A deep, gaping hole in her memory.

In spite of her aching back she tried to raise herself. She was lying on something that felt like a flight of steps – and sure enough, she was right. It *was* a flight of steps.

And she became aware of something else, although curiously with some delay: she was no longer wearing a diving helmet. She could breathe freely without an aerated stone to supply her with air. The reason, of course, even if she was a little late working it out, was that she wasn't under water.

Her surroundings were faintly lit, as if by moonlight falling through thin cloud cover; bluish-white light wavered over the steps. They were obviously part of a long spiral staircase set inside a round shaft. Soledad's legs were still up to the knees in water, but below the ripples lapping against the walls of the shaft the steps went on down into the depths.

The faint light came from countless glowing stones, one on each step in the angle between it and the wall, and this winding ribbon of light continued under the water too.

The shaft must have given guardsmen on earlier diving expeditions access to the underwater city. But how had she herself come here?

With difficulty, Soledad drew her legs up out of the water and tried to straighten her upper body completely. She managed it, although the process put quite a strain on the sore muscles in her back. But the pain was the result of her uncomfortable position on the steps, not of any further injuries. How long had she been lying here? It must be several hours, for her wounds from the battle for the anchor chain had stopped bleeding some time ago. The leather and her encrusted blood were sticking together.

Stand up, she told herself. You must stand up.

She tried – and failed. Groaning, she dropped back on the steps. Another attempt. This time it worked. Unsteadily, but feeling more confident, she pushed off from the wall with her left arm. She didn't want to move her right arm if possible, at least not until she knew how badly injured it was.

She stood there for a while, as breathless as if she had just made a superhuman effort. Yet all she had done was to stand up. Why did it cost her so much of her strength? She must be in a much worse state than she had thought at first.

She looked warily back at the surface of the water. The shaft was almost circular, which meant it had been made by human hands, or at least they had worked the coral. It was about ten paces across. She couldn't see how far down the spiral staircase went, for after a short way the glow of the stones was too faint to come up through the water.

Soledad put her head back – this time, surprisingly, it didn't hurt – and looked up. Above her she saw seven or eight more spirals, although she couldn't say how many for certain. The light from the glowing stones so far up was only a pale suggestion, and the spiral staircase itself might well wind much higher.

Soledad got her breathing under control again. At least she was alive. And as far as she could see there were no kobalins anywhere around.

But the question remained, who had brought her here? Someone or something had shredded her diving suit and brought her to safety. If she really *was* in safety.

She felt dizzy, and for a moment lost any sense of what was above and what was below. Her sense of balance was slow to return, but then she began climbing. Dragging her feet, hurting all over, she made it from step to step. Soon she found that as her body got used to the strain it was easier.

Walker's face appeared before her in the darkness, half memory, half wishful thinking. The thought of him gave her new strength. She *had* to get to the top.

Down in the shaft behind her, the surface of the water exploded.

She flung herself back against the wall and saw a fountain of water shoot up, but she wasn't close enough to the abyss below to see what had come to the surface. Rigid with fright, she heard it lashing about in the water. Waves slapped against the walls of the shaft, and something made the steps quiver beneath her feet.

She stood there for a long time without moving, her back and the palms of her hands pressed against the coral wall. She tried to keep her breathing as calm as possible, but the more she concentrated on it the more breathless she felt. She had no weapon now, and would have to face the creature with nothing but her bare hands if it decided to follow her up the spiral staircase.

And suddenly she felt panic, not just fear but pure horror that left her unable to breathe. She wasn't ashamed of it; she had been through too much in the last few hours to go on acting the part of the proud, fearless pirate princess. It was time to admit to her fears. And with this thought she also gave way to curiosity and stepped forward to the edge of the staircase, which had no handrail.

The water was calm again, but that didn't mean there was nothing there. The creature had stopped lashing back and forth in the narrow space of the coral shaft. Now it was upright like a living tower in the middle of the shaft, its reptilian body reared aloft, motionless and almost hypnotically calm. Droplets of water pearled from its black scales into the depths below. It stayed so still that only when Soledad looked again did she see what it really was: a sea-serpent as black as night, as broad as the trunk of a jungle tree, and with a triangular head almost as large as Soledad herself.

With a sudden lightning movement the serpent darted up some six feet higher. Before Soledad knew it, the creature's eyes were level with her own.

And what eyes they were! Slit like the eyes of a snake, each of them larger than a human skull and the colour of spotless amber, as clear as golden glass and so deep that you could lose yourself in them within seconds.

Soledad didn't have the strength to move. She stood there motionless. The serpent's jaws could reach her anywhere in the shaft. There was no point in running away.

But still the creature made no move to swallow her up. Soledad's ribcage rose and fell, her breathing resounded from the moist walls. Silent and unmoving, they looked into each other's eyes, princess and serpent, for what seemed an eternity – and a moment came when Soledad understood. She read the truth in that amber glance, in the clarity of those eyes, in the depth of that mighty intelligence.

The serpent had saved her, but not for selfless reasons. The underwater city was its domain, its preserve, and if the kobalins won and Aelenium fell, the serpent's own habitat would be destroyed. It had not pulled Soledad out of the water altruistically, of course not; such notions had no place in that ancient mind. It had rescued her to strengthen the city and harm the kobalins. For that reason and no other.

Soledad stood there for a few moments longer, and then slowly bent her head and bowed. 'Thank you,' she said, not sure whether the serpent understood her words. And quickly, before she could stop to think whether it was unseemly or even impertinent, she added, 'If you really want to help us, guard the anchor chain.'

Fighting for calm with difficulty, she turned and went on climbing up. In silence and without any sound at all, the serpent's body rose too. After two more spirals of the staircase it was still level with her. Then it suddenly disappeared, so quickly and silently that Soledad was aware of it only after climbing another step. Down below she heard a loud splash, and then only the sound of turbulent water lapping against the walls.

The serpent had gone.

Soledad made herself climb steadily on. And she felt a strange new power in her, as if the glance of those eyes had cleansed her inwardly and woken her reserves of strength. Deep in her heart, she knew it was not an animal she had just encountered, not a monster from the boundless sea, but something very different.

As she went on, she closed her eyes for a moment. A little smile played around the corners of her mouth. Something had touched her, leaving far more of a mark than the creature's fangs could have done.

How arrogant they had been to assume that all the gods who had survived the ages in Aelenium lived in human form.

Her way came out in the middle of the maze of coral streets and squares, only a stone's throw from the second defensive rampart.

Soledad had stumbled up the last steps and reached a wooden gate. She hammered on it, shouting, until someone on the other side finally pushed back a bolt and cautiously opened it. Two uniformed guards looked at her suspiciously, rifles and lances pointing her way. Only when one of them recognised her, and the other worked out that the young woman in a diving suit couldn't be a kobalin, did they let her through.

Looking over the men's shoulders, she found herself in a small room, dimly lit by a few torches. Some nets were stretched over the walls to dry. The cellar of a perfectly ordinary house, Soledad suspected, camouflaging the entrance to the underwater city.

One of the men tried to take Soledad's arm when she seemed about to fall, but she pushed him away in annoyance, straightened her back and walked proudly past the guards, shaking her head in silence when they offered to tend her wounds. Behind her the gate to the underwater city closed again, and the bolt squealed as it shot home.

The serpent's huge amber eyes still shone in Soledad's memory: bottomless golden pools. More than anything she had witnessed near the anchor chain, that glance filled her with both fear and breathless amazement. Such perfection, such cold calculation. And at the same time, such superiority.

As if dazed, she got the men to show her the way out, climbed steps – yet more steps – and at last she was in the open air.

For a moment it felt as if she had stepped straight into the serpent's eyes. The night sky had turned gold, flooded by the light of countless fires. The deadly gleam of the flames broke on veils of cloud and banks of mist. She knew what that meant, yet she couldn't fight the fascination of the firelight. The death of so many, the destruction of so much, yet the light was immeasurably beautiful. Though she doubted whether anyone else saw it that way.

Soledad shook her head and rubbed her eyes. She seemed to be slowly waking from a dream. The amber eyes faded, merged with the infernal blaze of the sky and the burning city. Only now, with every step she took, did she become herself again.

Ahead of her the street led to a small, deserted square with a broad balustrade on the far side. From there she could look down over the lower slopes of the city, across the sea of rooftops with shadows surging among them like boiling oil. Streams of refugees were running through the streets and up the mountain.

The lower rampart had fallen, she saw that at once. Its defenders were in retreat, already on their way to the second defensive ring above the poets' quarter. Before long the first of them would reach it.

Soledad looked up at the sky above the water. A few Ray Guard riders were circling in front of the wall of mist that now looked more like a wall of fire, but most were flying above the shores of Aelenium, firing missiles at the hordes of kobalins on land.

The night was ablaze beyond the mist too. Soledad wasn't sure if it was the distant red of dawn, reflections from the burning city, or the fury of the sea battle still raging between the Antilles captains and the cannibal king Tyrone.

An idea came to her, and once it had taken root in her mind she couldn't shake it off. She moved away from the balustrade, hurried back across the square, and turned into one of the neighbouring streets.

Soon she had reached the narrow house where the Hexhermetic Shipworm lay dreaming. The guard at the door had been withdrawn, the door itself was closed but not locked. Soledad went in and ran swiftly up the steps to the attic.

The cocoon had grown larger since she was last here. New layers of silk still seemed to be forming, and there were more of the threads holding the bizarre structure in the air. It now filled almost two-thirds of the attic. The finest of silk yarn stretched from rafter to rafter, from floor to sloping ceiling, and drifted like hangings inside the network.

'Worm?' She sketched a nod, though she didn't think he could see it. If he was still alive, as she assumed, his mind was presumably somewhere else, caught in a dream which, she hoped, was more pleasant than the terrible reality of the battle outside.

'I'd give a lot to know what you're seeing now,' she said thoughtfully. The cocoon still seemed to be pulsating slightly, sending slight ripples through the network.

Again and again, fine threads came loose, joined others, and formed new layers within the net. There was a barely audible rustling in the air.

She cautiously put out her hand to feel the silken layers, but withdrew it just before she touched the network. She was afraid of waking something that might not yet be ready to return to them.

'I don't really know why I came,' she said to the Worm. 'But I've seen something down in the underwater city . . . something that wasn't of this world. Jolly said many of the people living here in Aelenium are really ancient gods – or what was left of them after they lost their power. But what I saw down there . . . well, I can't imagine that it was ever *more* powerful than it is now. I sensed that – do you understand? Something in those eyes got to me. There was something . . . well, *really* god-like about it. Sounds crazy, right?' She sought for words, but found none to express what was going through her head. 'I mean, it didn't do anything . . . or at least, not really.' With pain in her eyes, she looked at her forearm and then went on. 'It seems to have saved my life, and I think I know why. It doesn't want Aelenium to fall to the Maelstrom. It loves this place as much as Forefather or the Ghost-Trader. I think they all need Aelenium, perhaps because it's only here they can still live in peace.' She stopped, shaking her head, thought for a while and then said, 'Anyway, I'm wondering what *you* really are, Worm. It wasn't just chance that we brought you here, was it? I mean, the Wisdom of the Worms you talked about is just a load of sea-lion droppings. You're no more of a shipworm really than the serpent down there is a serpent.' She took a firm step towards the silken cocoon, and then didn't know herself what she was trying to say. 'Am I right?' she asked quietly.

The Worm – or whatever was inside the cocoon – gave her no answer. Not that she had seriously expected one.

She snorted softly and then shook her head again. She was tired out, and the thought of having to fight on terrified her.

'Well, nice to have talked it over with you,' she managed to say ironically, and went over to the only window in the attic. From here she could see the upper defensive rampart, which was now surrounded by crowds of people. She took a deep breath and ran back down the stairs, leaving behind the silken network, the cocoon, and whatever was inside it.

She wondered what would happen if kobalins entered the house. If something made them climb to the attic.

What would they see there?

And would they dare to wake it?

Out in the street, dead fish were raining down. A troop

of guardsmen met her on their way to the upper defensive rampart. She joined them, reached the barricade where it ran right across what had once been a marketplace, and looked for anyone she might know.

A hand touched her shoulder. As she spun round she was already in his arms.

'Walker,' she whispered into his shoulder, and then she began shedding tears.

THE WEIGHT OF
DEEP WATER

The mountain at the bottom of the deep sea looked like a termite mound, although a thousand times larger and curiously regular in its proportions. Almost like a fore-finger pointing upwards, warning travellers on the sea-bed against going any further: beyond me only death lies, it seemed to say.

'What's that?' asked Jolly.

Aina lowered her voice as if she feared someone inside the mountain could hear her. 'The nest of the kobalins, as you call them. This is where they were born.'

Jolly and Munk exchanged a glance. '*All* the kobalins?'

The girl from the bottom of the sea shook her head. 'Only the oldest. The fathers of the Deep Tribes, long before they split up and fought each other.' She shifted from foot to foot. 'Until the Maelstrom united them again.'

'We heard that the ancestors of the kobalins came from the Mare Tenebrosum,' said Jolly, remembering what Count Aristotle had told them at the Council meeting. 'And some human beings allied themselves with those ancestors, and it seems that's how the oldest of the kobalins came into being.'

Aina shrugged her bare shoulders. 'I don't know anything about that. But anyway, this,' she said, pointing to the finger-shaped tower of rock, 'is the place where the first of them . . . slipped out. Or were born.'

Jolly took a step towards the edge of the narrow rocky plateau where they were standing. They had only just left the shelter of a collection of round rocks as tall as houses and emerged on this natural platform. From above they must look like ants scurrying out of a heap of pebbles.

Ahead of them a panorama opened up, a view of a deep rocky valley full of jagged crevices, ravines, and sharp-edged ridges that must cut through any sinking ship like a knife blade. The kobalin mountain, a guardian watching over the Rift, a ghostly outline on the limits of what their senses could perceive, rose above this unwelcoming landscape.

They had gone no further downhill since meeting the

albino kobalins. It seemed that Aina was right – they had crossed the outlying regions of the Rift and were now approaching its centre.

Perhaps the kobalin mountain really was something like a last sentry stationed outside the heart of the Rift, the place from which the Maelstrom sprang. The roaring and raging in the darkness were noticeably louder now, but they still couldn't see anything. Their polliwiggle vision didn't reach far enough.

'When I was escaping I swam over the rocks,' said Aina. 'We could walk, but that would take longer and –'

'We'll swim,' Munk interrupted her.

Jolly looked at him askance. 'Oh yes?'

He sighed, as if he was tired of quarrelling with her over everything and everyone, although she had only wanted him at least to ask her opinion. 'We have no time to spare, Jolly. You know that as well as I do.'

'What about those seeking currents?' she asked angrily. 'What's the use of saving a few hours if one of them catches us, and either kills us or washes us back heaven knows how many miles?'

'We could work our way forward bit by bit,' Aina put in. 'From one ridge of rock to the next. And we can rest when we reach the kobalin mountain.'

'Oh, great idea,' replied Jolly. 'We'll just ask if they have a nice warm place by the fire for us, right?'

Aina smiled. 'Long ago, before we set out, we were told about the mountain ourselves. There's no danger we need fear there. Kobalins have never lived in the nest – except for one.' She went over to the edge of the plateau. Her right hand felt for a long strand of hair and rolled it absent-mindedly between her fingers. 'That one was said to be the mother of the kobalins. Even her own children feared her. But she lived there in her pit of silt and bones so long that the rock grew up over her and closed her in. After that she was too huge and fat to squeeze through the crevices and passages, so she couldn't get out again.'

'Huge?' repeated Jolly, with misgivings.

'She probably died long ago.' Aina was silent for a moment, and seemed to be thinking. 'We can go a longer way round the mountain, but it will cost us time.'

Jolly looked across at the peak again. It was difficult to estimate its height in the faint twilight. She suspected the mighty tower of stone must be about a hundred paces high from where it first showed above the rocky labyrinth to its gnarled summit, but it might easily be yet taller.

'Let's get a move on,' said Munk.

Jolly gave up, and nodded. The three of them took off

from the edge of the plateau and began crossing the rocky hills, swimming strongly.

The landscape below was like the one where Munk and Jolly had met the luminous fish at the beginning of their journey, except that it seemed even more rugged and sharp-edged, as if a giant had hammered away on the rocks in the grey mists of time. Here too the bottom of the ravine lay deep below, beyond the reach of polliwiggle vision. Seen from above, wavering rivers of shadow seemed to flow through the cracks in the rock. Pure blackness surged around the cliffs and stone needles.

Jolly's fears were soon confirmed: she had underestimated the distance to the kobalin mountain, and thus presumably its height too.

Soon they had to stop for a rest, for swimming was a greater strain on their strength than walking over the sea-bed. It was ages since they had last slept, and their meals had been irregular and insipid in flavour.

Jolly was just munching a tough piece of salted meat made even saltier by the seawater when Aina let out a warning cry. They swiftly slid down a wall of rock to crouch side by side in a crevice. As soon as they were sheltered a seeking current came rolling across the wilderness, a towering wave of swirling dust moving with a force that made even the rocks shake. This was the fifth of these underwater tidal waves they had seen – the last of them not so long ago – and Jolly feared they must expect to meet them more and more often so close to their destination. Luckily Aina was quick to sense them coming, and usually saw the danger a little earlier than the other two.

The three of them had just left their hiding place and were swimming back up to the top of the rocks when something unexpected happened. This time it took even Aina by surprise.

A second seeking current quickly followed.

They had hardly emerged above the rocks when they thought they heard the roar of the invisible Maelstrom swelling. That immediately turned out to be wrong – for the sound came not from the Maelstrom itself but from a raging, swirling wall of sand and water following the first after only a slight delay. It was not as tall, but so wide that it reached from one side of their polliwiggle vision to the other.

'Jolly!' shouted Munk. 'Get down!'

The warning came too late. She had seen the danger at the same moment, but she had no time to react. She couldn't see what happened to the other two either.

The seeking current caught her, and then it was as if she

had been put in a gigantic barrel full of sand and splinters of rock while the whole thing was vigorously shaken.

Dust and small pebbles got into her mouth and eyes. She couldn't tell which way up she was. All she sensed was that she was being carried away by forces greater and more destructive than any she had thought could possibly exist. Her consciousness was blotted out by pain and panic, and darkness extinguished even her polliwiggle vision.

It's separating us! was the last clear thought to flash through her mind like a fiery blaze.

Then she didn't think any more at all.

At least for a while.

'Jolly!'

I'm unconscious. The thought echoed through her mind like words spoken in someone else's voice. I've never fainted before in my life. But now . . . yes, I'm unconscious.

'Come on, Jolly, wake up!'

She knew that voice. It wasn't Munk's.

'Aina?' The name passed her faltering lips. Her eyelids opened, trembling, her eyes were flooded by grey twilight, and then she saw shapes. She could see more distinctly now. She could recognise things.

Aina's face. Above her.

'There you are, back again,' said the girl with a smile. 'About time too.'

Jolly put out her hand – and it passed through Aina as if she were an image in a dream. In fact, for a moment that was what Jolly took her for, until she remembered. Remembered what Aina was. Remembered Munk. And the underwater tidal wave that had carried her away. Her hand felt stiff as it passed through the girl's body. It was because they were close to the Maelstrom. Aina did indeed gain in substance the further they made their way on towards the heart of the Rift.

'I . . . I feel sick,' she whispered.

Aina nodded. 'The seeking current flung you against the rocks. You were lucky.'

'Lucky?' Groaning, Jolly felt her skull. 'That's not what my head's telling me.' Even touching it hurt. Her scalp was irritated. It felt as if a thousand hands were tugging at every single hair.

With difficulty, she looked around. She was at the bottom of a ravine, or so at least she supposed. There was a wall of rock behind her, and another a few feet ahead of her. Darkness arched high above, not a ceiling of any kind but the limits of polliwiggle vision.

The current must have caught her and flung her into one

of the clefts in the rock. But it could have been worse. As far as she could tell, she had no broken bones, although thick blood was trickling from a few grazes to mingle with the seawater. The salt stung the open wounds.

'Where's Munk?'

Aina pointed to the darkness behind her. 'Looking for you. He was desperate when you suddenly disappeared. We separated.'

'Didn't the current catch you, then?'

Aina shook her head. 'We made it to shelter behind the rocks just in time.'

Jolly nodded, without really listening to her. At least their mission wasn't endangered. Deep inside, she felt guilty at the idea that she was the one whose accident had delayed them.

'How much time have we lost?'

'Not much.' Aina put her head on one side and scrutinised her, as if expecting some particular reaction to this reply.

Her glance made Jolly feel uncomfortable. 'Why are you looking at me like that?'

'You don't need to fear that you're holding Munk up.' Aina's voice was gentle and full of understanding. 'That's what you're thinking, aren't you?'

Was it so easy to see through her? Well, even so – what

business of Aina's was it? She was just taking a deep breath to say something sharp in reply when the girl slowly shook her head.

'There's no reason for you to feel jealous of me,' said Aina quietly.

'I –'

'At least, not yet.'

Jolly stared at her. Then she took her eyes off Aina's enigmatic smile and looked around for Munk. He was nowhere to be seen.

'Don't worry about him. He's behind the rocks, looking for you.' Aina did not move. She knelt down on the ground in front of Jolly, and her dark eyes were shining like polished onyx. 'He's all right and he's looking for you over there, only a couple of ravines further north – far enough away not to hear if you call him.'

Jolly worked her way up the wall behind her until at last she was standing on her own two feet, reasonably steadily, although her sense of balance was playing her up.

'Who are you *really*?' she asked.

Aina stayed kneeling on the ground and looked mildly up at her. 'A polliwiggle like you. Only a few thousand years older.'

'You're lying.'

'No. Everything I've told you is true.' Her smile flickered like firelight. 'I just left a few things out.'

Jolly was about to take off from the ground and swim away, but Aina shook her head and gestured in a way that made her hesitate. 'Don't. You won't manage to warn him, and he wouldn't hear you.' Aina joined her hands into a hollow shape and held them to her right ear. 'He has something better to give him advice now.'

'That damn shell!'

'What I said about it wasn't a lie either. It is more powerful than any shell you two ever had in your hands. Munk realised that at once.'

'You cow!'

Jolly thought of flinging herself on Aina, but she knew that any attack was pointless. Her hands would go straight through the other girl. But then again, how could Aina, in that state, prevent her from getting away? She couldn't even hold on to Jolly.

A shadow passed above her and took shape a moment later. Something was falling over Jolly, and when she put up her hands to fend it off she felt it in her fingers.

A large, wide-meshed net.

White, eyeless figures stepped out of nooks and crannies in the rocks.

One of them had thrown the net, and was still holding a cord fastened to it in one claw. The net was weighted down all round with stones tied into the edge of the mesh, making it much heavier than it had looked at first.

Jolly had no time to avoid it. The strands of plant fibres sank down on her and Aina. But while the net settled around her head and shoulders, it simply passed through Aina as if she wasn't there at all. The girl rose to her feet with a sigh, leaving the outer part of the net on the ground, but Jolly was so hopelessly entangled in it that the albino kobalins had plenty of time to shuffle up, bending low as usual, and seize her.

'Don't struggle,' said Aina calmly. 'They're stronger than you.'

Jolly shouted Munk's name, but she guessed already that Aina was right. He couldn't hear her in the middle of this maze. There was no echo down here because of the water, and the rock swallowed up all other sounds.

Two kobalins took hold of her arms through the net and lifted her off the ground. They might be blind and smaller than she was, but they had greater strength than any human being. Wiry sinews stretched taut under their white skin, and their long claws held on like the claws of gigantic birds. Jolly cursed and swore, but she was simply carried away without the faintest chance of fighting back.

Aina, light of foot, walked along beside her. 'No one's going to hurt you.'

'Oh yes, that's what it looks like!' Jolly got out. The strands of the net cutting painfully into her face made talking difficult. Two of them ran right across her mouth, preventing her from opening her lips wider than just a crack.

'No, believe me,' Aina assured her seriously. 'You and Munk are the last living polliwiggles. You're much too valuable for either of you to be dispensed with. At least as long as there's no alternative.'

'What about those other two polliwiggles? Your friends.' Jolly wasn't sure whether her distorted words could be understood, but Aina replied as naturally as if she had no difficulty in making out what she was saying.

'One of them is dead. You killed him. And the other . . . I don't know that I'd still call him a polliwiggle.'

'We killed . . .' Jolly fell silent. A bitter foreboding awoke deep inside her.

But before she could think any more about the idea that had come to her, the ravine suddenly went round a sharp bend. The ground was rising. When Jolly looked up at its sloping walls, she saw where Aina and the kobalins had brought her.

The kobalin mountain rose high above them. From down here it looked like a gigantic tower, only slightly broader at its foot than up above. If they took her up the zigzag path rising on its outer wall, there was a chance she might be able to see Munk in the distance. A faint hope, admittedly, but for a moment it gave her new courage.

Until she saw a second party of kobalins working on a round slab of rock some way above her. The creatures placed rods under the massive slab to act as levers and rolled it aside. An opening in the rocky wall came into view. A gateway to the kobalin nest, not tall, not broad – just large enough for a human being to be pushed into it.

'What are you going to do to me?'

'You'll stay here until I send for you.' Aina smiled. 'Then it will all be over, and you'll have a chance to make your decision. For or against staying alive. You'll have plenty of time to think about it.'

They reached the opening in the wall, which was well below the level of the other peaks. If Munk was swimming above the ravines in search of her, he'd never be able to see her from up there.

The kobalins pushed her through the opening, net and all. Jolly stumbled and became entangled in its mesh worse than ever. Cursing, she tumbled down a smooth stone slope.

Above her, she heard cries from the two kobalins who had pushed her in. As she lay there dazed for a moment, she saw Aina standing alone in the opening alone.

'You must forgive them,' said the girl, sounding annoyed. 'They are rough creatures. I have punished them for it.'

Jolly couldn't see what Aina had done to the kobalins, but as they had both disappeared she could guess. Once again, she was horrified by Aina's cold-blooded attitude.

She pulled the net off her face so that Aina could see the hatred in her eyes. 'How long am I going to stay here?'

'Oh, not very long. The battle for Aelenium will soon be over. After that we'll overrun all the settlements along the coast, and then . . . well, we'll see.'

'How did it do it? I mean, how did the Maelstrom get you to go over to its side?'

Aina tilted her head, as she often did when she was wondering about something. 'You still don't understand, do you?'

Jolly's stomach muscles tensed. 'Then explain.'

'Not now.' Shaking her head, Aina stepped back and gave her creatures a signal. 'I'll be back, and then we'll talk.'

A crunching sound told her that the levers were in use again. The opening narrowed.

'And Munk?' shouted Jolly. She managed to get the net off her legs, but it was too late to try scrambling up to the opening now. 'What about Munk?'

Aina gestured, and the block of stone stopped moving for a moment or so. 'Munk?' she asked with genuine surprise. 'But I am his friend!'

She didn't laugh, did not even smile as she finally stepped back and away from the opening in the rock. The gravity of her pale features horrified Jolly even more than everything else that had happened in these last few minutes.

She called Aina's name, but it was too late. The round stone rolled across the opening. At the last moment something shining shot through the crack. Then the slab of stone sealed the final gap, falling into place with a hollow rumble, and lay there heavy as lead.

All was quiet. No sounds from outside came through the stone, and nothing around Jolly moved. She blinked away the tears that had sprung to her eyes, tears of rage rather than fear. Then her blurred glance fell on the handful of luminous fish hovering above her like a swarm of glowing insects.

'You?' she asked faintly, but she couldn't even feel glad of their presence. Instead, she looked over her shoulder in the only direction still open to her.

She saw a long cavern stretching on and on. Its end was out of sight.

With her knees shaking, she struggled to her feet and looked up at the closed opening one last time. The little shoal of fish scattered. For a moment they swam frantically about, and then formed a densely concentrated ball of light above Jolly's head.

She wouldn't have needed them to see her way. Polliwiggle vision worked even inside the mountain. First hesitantly, then with an increasingly determined step, she set off, going deeper and deeper into the lifeless silence of the kobalin nest.

TWO GIANTS

The kobalin commander was circling around the city. It slipped through the churning water not far below the surface, just visible from above as a shadow.

Griffin steered the ray after it, about thirty feet above the waves, following the same course. So close to him, the rain of dead fish was disgusting and often painful – quite apart from the fact that it obstructed his view. The scaly bodies glittered, dazzling him in the light of the rising sun.

Behind him, Ishmael was cursing non-stop. Whenever he raised his rifle the corpse of a fish landed on the barrel, forcing it down. It was impossible to take accurate aim in this stinking chaos.

'I really don't know if this was a good idea,' shouted the marksman above the din.

'It's fear of their master that drives the kobalins on.' Griffin's head jerked back to avoid the lashing arms of an octopus falling from the sky right in front of him. With his left hand, he swept the corpse off the body of the ray. 'If we can kill the kobalin commander, then –'

'Then the battle will be over?' Ishmael mocked. 'Do you really believe that?'

'No,' replied Griffin coldly. 'But it would be a first step, wouldn't it? This entire battle is going round in circles. It's time to do something unexpected.'

Hearing himself speak those words, he thought they didn't sound like himself. But that was another consequence of this war. When it was over, and if they were still alive, they'd all be different people. And as Griffin guided the ray on above the foaming, mountainous waves, he wondered seriously if he hadn't already changed when he said he was ready to fight on the side of Aelenium. Or even earlier – when he decided to stay with Jolly.

Dead fish pattered down on the wings of the ray. The animal had difficulty keeping its height in the air. Both riders were shaken back and forth; it was like flying a roller-coaster. Yet Griffin managed to keep the ray on the track of the mighty shadow making its way through the sea.

It was hard to define the creature's physical shape. Its outline seemed to change all the time, sometimes long, sometimes oval, then an indeterminate shape with growths emerging from it. It was the size of four or five rowing boats, and stood out only vaguely from the blue-black depths of the water, which led Griffin to suppose its body must be translucent, like dark-tinted glass.

He had expected a particularly large kobalin, or a kind of twin of the Acherus. But now, at close quarters, the commander of the Deep Tribes resembled neither of those beings. It was completely different, and that frightened Griffin far more than any giant kobalin, or some golem made of body parts of corpses. He'd seen so many terrors in the last few weeks that he feared the unexpected more than any already familiar monstrosity.

'What the devil *is* the creature?' asked Ishmael, who had given up firing at it. Instead, he was now holding on with one hand and defending himself from the falling bodies of fish with the other.

'I haven't the faintest idea.'

'They say you and the polliwiggle met it before.'

'We were close to it, but we didn't see it. If we had we wouldn't have come here at all.'

'That's really encouraging.'

Griffin reined in his ray, for the kobalin commander was slowing down under the water. Had it noticed that they were following its trail up in the air?

Their answer came in the shape of half a dozen lances hissing their way. Through the rain of fish, Griffin had been unable to see the kobalins moving through the waves close to their master. Ishmael cried out when one of the barbed tips grazed his shoulder, but the injury wasn't dangerous. All the other lances missed, for the kobalins themselves couldn't take good aim through this hail of dead fish.

'All right?' asked Griffin with concern. 'Or shall I turn back?'

Ishmael laughed, with some difficulty. 'Not for the world! As long as my head's still on my shoulders we stay airborne.'

'Don't make rash promises.' And Griffin pulled on the reins of the ray, sending the animal into a steep dive until the underside of its belly touched the waves. It was a dangerous manoeuvre, particularly for the ray, but Griffin's calculation worked out. The ray's mighty head rammed two kobalins. Flung out of the water by the force of the impact, they went whirling away. The others swiftly dived down and scattered in all directions.

Griffin brought the ray up again, but stayed just behind the gigantic dark shadow beneath the surface.

'Can you fly this ray?' he shouted to Ishmael through the wind blowing in their faces.

'Sure I can,' replied Ishmael, before his tone of voice changed. 'Hey! Just a minute! You don't mean that seriously?'

Griffin took the long dagger used by the guardsmen out of his belt. 'What do you think? You're never going to get it from up here with bullets.'

'You can't do that! It's madness!'

'Got any better suggestions?'

'They'll tear you to pieces before you even get anywhere near that thing.'

'It's on its own at the moment.'

'That's how it may look from up here. But it's still their supreme commander, or something like that. No general goes into battle without his bodyguard.'

'The battle's not out here, Ishmael. The shore has fallen, the first rampart is down. The fighting's in the streets of Aelenium now. That brute is just watching from a distance. And it really doesn't look as if the sea is teeming with kobalins here.'

'Don't do it!'

But Griffin wasn't listening to the marksman's protests. He half turned in the saddle. 'After I've jumped, you slide forward and take the reins, right?'

'You're crazy!' Ishmael sounded as if he were seriously

considering knocking sense into Griffin with the butt of his rifle. But before the marksman could prevent him, Griffin rose in the saddle. He stood on the shoulders of the ray with his legs apart, the reins still in his hands. The wind blew his many braids backwards, swirling them around his ears like palm fronds in a monsoon.

He looked past the ray's head and down. Any moment they would be right above the kobalin commander. By now Griffin felt sure the lances flung at them had just been chance – if the creature had really noticed them, surely it would have dived down.

Unless . . . unless it was waiting for him. Perhaps it wanted to take part in the battle itself, even if it could only demonstrate its power on a pirate boy.

'Griffin!'

He had been expecting Ishmael to make another attempt to hold him back. He ignored the cry.

The marksman grabbed hold of his trouser leg. 'Griffin, for heaven's sake wait! Look at that!'

For a moment Griffin's determination wavered – and then so did he as he saw what was coming through the water from the left. He had to cling to the taut reins, or in his standing position he would certainly have lost his balance.

A gigantic dark shape was surging through the waves

towards the kobalin commander, many times larger than it was and far more massive. A mighty jet of water shot up from the sea like a triumphant trumpet fanfare.

'Jasconius!' Griffin exclaimed.

'Your friend the whale!' Ishmael's voice cracked. 'By heaven, he looks a better opponent for that brute!'

Griffin was still hesitating. Then he realised that it would have been suicide to plunge into the depths now. He would certainly be crushed when the two giants collided. Quickly slipping back into the saddle, he guided the ray into a close orbit around the scene of the duel.

The whale and the kobalin commander met, too far below the surface for Griffin to make out any details. All he saw was that the monster's translucent form changed again just before they clashed, flowing out into a kind of star shape as if to fling sharp extremities against Jasconius. But its spines were not solid enough to stop the whale, who crashed into the creature violently and with murderous power, and then they both disappeared under a seething carpet of foam and towering waves.

Ishmael cursed again. 'I can't see them any more!'

Griffin couldn't utter a sound. He feared for Jasconius and Ebenezer, and suddenly he realised how crazy it had been to think of attacking the kobalin commander alone, armed with his dagger. An inner voice whispered to him that perhaps even the whale had no chance against one of the Maelstrom's lieutenants. Not even Jasconius.

He would have given anything to be able to join the fight, but there was nothing to be seen through the tossing waves. The sea was boiling. Screams were carried on the wind, and this time they blew not from the city but from everywhere all at once, a screeching and roaring that made Griffin long to drop the reins and put his hands over his ears. His fingers, stiff and pale, clutched the leather, and the euphoria he had felt some minutes ago when Jasconius appeared turned to sheer panic. At the same time he understood how narrowly he had escaped death.

'Jasconius!' he shouted, but he knew the whale couldn't hear him.

Ishmael seemed to come to his senses before Griffin. 'Let's fly back to the city. We can do more there than here. What's going on down there isn't our fight now.'

The surface of the sea broke up. A circular jet of water flowered below them, reaching for the ray and its two riders with glittering, watery fingers. At its centre the back of the whale appeared, and something else, something covering parts of that back, a spreading, viscous mass like jelly. Or a gigantic jellyfish that had fastened on the body of the whale.

'There it is,' exclaimed Griffin.

'What?' Ishmael's voice was trembling. 'That . . . thing?'

'That's its body. That's why it's been changing shape the whole time.'

The silvery jellyfish creature was obviously trying to close around the body of Jasconius and crush him in its hold. But there was something else. Griffin saw it only at second glance. And although it was directly under him now, he could hardly believe his eyes.

'Holy saints!' cried Ishmael. 'Do you see that too?'

'Yes . . . yes, of course.'

'Is it human?'

Griffin patted the back of his ray to steady it in its flight. The jets of water had subsided now, but the whale and his adversary were still on the surface. Jasconius was tossing and shaking himself, beating his great tail-fin about and angrily sending jets of water up from the opening on his back, which was not yet covered by the jelly-like substance, although the edges of the viscous mass were moving together with smacking sounds. Soon they would close around the whale's body.

But what shook Griffin and Ishmael so much was the human figure lying inside the massive jellyfish, naked, arms and legs outstretched, looking upwards. It was pressing the silvery slime down on the whale with its back.

'He's still a child!' cried Ishmael.

'One of us?'

'I've never seen him, anyway.'

For it was a boy, perhaps a little younger than Griffin, although from this distance no one could be sure of that. He had raven-black hair, and his skin was darker than Griffin's or Ishmael's. One of the Caribbean islanders. The translucent mass flowed and pushed itself over him, pressing him against the whale's body, and by every law of nature the boy should have been dead, smothered by the milky substance of the giant jellyfish.

Yet he was alive. His lips were opening and closing as if he were calling out. As he did so the mass of jelly filled his mouth cavity. Not a sound emerged. Normally Griffin would have supposed that the boy had been caught in the sticky substance, perhaps sucked in by it – but the expression on the stranger's face baffled him.

The boy looked angry. His features wore an expression of vicious hatred, and it seemed possible that the words he was calling weren't cries for help at all, but orders.

Was *this* the kobalin commander? A human being, still a child, using the massive jellyfish just as a means of transport, armour for his own weak body?

Did *he* command the Deep Tribes, and was he now urging the giant jellyfish to even greater rage, so as to conquer and kill the whale more quickly?

'Is there any way we can free the lad?' asked Ishmael, who obviously didn't share Griffin's fears. To the marksman, this was only a child in need of their help.

But Griffin guessed that the truth was different. Together, this boy and the jellyfish surrounding him, like a prehistoric insect caught in amber, formed a single being, no longer human but not entirely a monster. Together, they were the kobalin commander, the Maelstrom's representative in this battle between men and half-forgotten gods.

Jasconius plunged down again, taking the jellyfish and the boy with him. Once again the water foamed up, the waves broke against each other, and again the two great creatures both disappeared under grey sea-spray and the firelit reflections on the waves.

'Back to the city!' shouted Ishmael. For the first time there was panic in his voice, mingled with total bewilderment.

'No,' said Griffin. 'I have to see how this fight goes.'

Ishmael's hand came down on his shoulder. His fingers pressed Griffin's muscles painfully. 'There's no point, boy. Whatever happens, we can't do anything about it.'

'But I have to *know*! I owe Jasconius that much at least.'

'At the cost of both our lives?'

Griffin saw what Ishmael meant when the marksman's hand let go of him and pointed to the right. A teeming shoal of kobalins was approaching below the waves. The points of their lances ploughed through the water like shark fins.

Once again he looked at the place where Jasconius and the kobalin commander had sunk. The two giants could not be seen under the surface of foam and seething spray.

'I can't turn back now,' he said firmly.

'Boy!' Ishmael's voice was imploring. 'This isn't your battle.'

'Oh yes, it is. It involves us all. Jasconius . . . the whale, I mean, he's fighting for us. And Ebenezer . . . the Man in the Whale, that's what everyone called him, they hadn't a good word to say for him, they claimed he was a murderer. And now they're both risking their lives for us.' Griffin looked angrily back at Ishmael. 'Are you seriously saying this isn't our battle? Well, it is. Except that someone else is fighting it for us and may die.'

For a moment the man's features worked. Griffin saw that his words had hit home.

'The least we can do is wait to see how it ends,' said Griffin firmly. 'Only the two of us can tell the others about it. We at least owe Jasconius and Ebenezer a *memory*, don't you think?'

Ishmael hesitated, and the expression on his face was slightly guilty. But then he looked down at the depths in alarm. 'We're never going to be able to tell anyone about anything!' he shouted. 'Turn away, boy . . . *turn away*!'

At the sound of Ishmael's voice Griffin acted instinctively. His hands pulled the reins, but the ray was moving much too ponderously. A lance thrust through its right wing from below and came out above it. The animal shook itself, uttering a dull roar. Its wing-beat became irregular, and for a moment it seemed to be trying to throw both its riders off. Ishmael cried out. So did Griffin, but somehow he managed to stay in the saddle. More harpoons came up, their sharpened bone tips bristling with barbs, and one grazed the body of the ray. The animal shook itself again, and this time Griffin lost control. Ishmael roared and cursed, and then suddenly fell silent as a harpoon ploughed a bleeding furrow in his thigh. The shock took his speech away for a moment. Then he uttered a high scream of pain that chilled Griffin to the marrow.

'I can't . . . hold it!' shouted Griffin. Then the reins were torn from his hands, the ray reared, and its body coiled in a way that Griffin would never have expected of such a colossus.

224

'Hold on!' he called to the marksman, and then invisible hands pulled him out of the saddle. He lost his balance – and slipped off the ray.

'Griffin!' Ishmael saw the boy fall, forgot the burning pain in his own leg for a moment, and tried to grab him.

He just managed to catch Griffin's right hand.

Griffin cried out as a fearful jerk went through his arm. Then he realised that he hadn't hit the water but was still in the air, dangling beside the ray and held there only by Ishmael's hand.

'I'll . . . pull you . . . up,' gasped the man grimly, but they both knew it was hopeless.

Down below, the kobalins were jabbering. Harpoons were flung at them. But the ray, staggering through the air, had already moved too far from the horde in the water, and all the lances aimed their way missed. Which didn't alter the fact that the animal was still shaking itself in pain and rearing; it couldn't beat its sound wing and its injured wing in time with each other.

Griffin was shaken back and forth. He hung there helplessly, too weak to pull himself up by Ishmael's arm with only one hand. And the injured marksman's strength was failing him too. They both realised at the same time that their efforts were in vain.

'It's no good!' cried Griffin. Or perhaps he only thought it. He felt his fingers slipping from Ishmael's hand, little by little, with nightmare slowness. Yet there was no stopping it now.

Ishmael's features were distorted into a desperate grimace. He could hardly stay in the saddle. The tormented ray had gone entirely out of control, and was flying in a swerving zigzag that didn't really bring it any closer to the city.

Another panic-stricken turn, and then the animal, still staggering, sailed through the air back the way they had come, towards the screeching kobalins and their sharply barbed harpoons.

Griffin was going to fall. He knew it.

Only seconds now.

Ishmael had tears of grief and rage in his eyes as he looked down at Griffin. Their glances met. They both knew how this wild ride was going to end.

Griffin accepted the truth a moment before his companion.

'No!' shouted Ishmael, as he understood what the boy was going to do.

But Griffin wasn't listening to him. He had a choice: he could let himself drop a good fifty paces from the kobalins

– or he could hang on a couple of seconds longer, and then fall in the middle of their harpoons.

'No!' cried the marksman again, but it was too late.

'Grab the reins,' shouted Griffin as he gasped for air – and let go.

Ishmael's scream was in his ears, filling his whole head as he struck the water hard. The waves seized him with foaming fingers and drew him down into the depths. Darkness with a red glow in it surrounded Griffin as he sank like a stone. Then he began to struggle, first in panic, then regaining some control. He had lost his sense of direction and didn't know if the kobalins were already on their way to him.

He just hoped Ishmael would manage to control the frantic ray. Then he himself wouldn't drown or be torn to pieces by the warriors of the Deep Tribes entirely in vain. Then it would all make some kind of sense.

Kobalin claws seized him. He felt he had to cry out, even though he didn't, even though he was defending himself, doing his best to fight, not to give in.

Not to die. Not now.

Not without seeing Jolly one last time, holding her, hearing her voice.

Then they fell on him, a whole dozen of them, and dragged him away with them. In several directions at once.

THE CANNIBAL FLEET

For a moment Griffin thought the kobalins were going to tear him apart. They hauled and dragged at his arms and legs – until one of them finally uttered a shrill screech, all the others stopped in alarm, and the pain in Griffin's limbs receded.

He immediately began defending himself again, but it was useless. There were too many of them, ten or more, he couldn't say for certain in the wild, turbulent water. There were snapping mouths all around him, long claws and thin, shimmering bodies surrounded by air bubbles swirling on the eddying waves.

They brought him up to the surface to breathe. He gasped avidly for air, even tried to snatch a glimpse of Ishmael and the ray, but he couldn't see them anywhere.

Once again he was being hauled through the water, and a ring of grimacing kobalin faces emerged around him.

Three of them dragged him swiftly in the same direction, so fast that the foam spraying into his face almost took his breath away again. Somehow he managed to fill his lungs at intervals, as they raced towards the wall of mist now glowing with the red-golden light of dawn. Not even the smoke rising from the burning shores of Aelenium could entirely obscure the light of the morning sun.

Only when they plunged into the mist did they leave the light behind. Nothing but the hail of dead fish falling around them could penetrate the vapours; it meant that the kobalin commander must still be somewhere near. Despair came over Griffin, not just for himself but because he feared that the jellyfish creature had killed the whale and Ebenezer. He wondered what would happen to the rooms behind the magic door if Jasconius died. And what about Ebenezer, if he had managed to find shelter in them?

But he had no time to think seriously about the whale's possible defeat, for now he saw where the kobalins had brought him.

Ahead of them a curious mound rose from the water, half veiled in mist. At first sight it looked like a tiny island not ten paces across, rising about six feet above the waves. But as they came closer Griffin saw that it was made up of large half-mussel shells; the structure was rather like a gigantic turtle. Only when they were close to it did he see that each half-shell was held above a kobalin's head – underneath the mound, the water was teeming with kobalin warriors carrying this artificial island on their clawed hands. And on it stood a figure half-hidden by veils of mist.

Two kobalins leaped up on the island, seized Griffin's arms and pulled him out of the water. The shells crunched and scraped against each other under his feet, but held together, leaving no gaps. It wasn't easy to keep his balance on them as the two kobalins led him to the figure waiting for him at the highest point of the shell island.

Griffin held his breath as he looked into the face of the creature opposite him.

It was his own.

Or almost, anyway. For like streaks of ink mixing in water, a second face mingled with the copy of his own features, thinner and more delicate – a feminine face.

Griffin couldn't utter a sound. What he saw before him, in constant movement and as incomplete as a half-made clay bust, was his own double alternating swiftly and repeatedly with the face of a girl.

Jolly's face.

Then he understood. It was the wyvern, the shape-shifter that he and Jolly had met between the worlds. The creature that had appeared to them then in the form of Agostini the bridge-builder. When the bridge went up in flames the wyvern fled, and Griffin had hardly given it a thought since then.

The wyvern smiled – a curious mixture of Jolly's and Griffin's own smiles. Obviously the creature hadn't yet decided whose shape it was ultimately going to take. Not only did their features keep alternating on its face, they seemed far from complete. The nose, for instance, didn't look like either Griffin's or Jolly's, and the wyvern was having great trouble with Jolly's long black hair. But it had even more difficulty with the many rings in her ears, and the silver pin she had put through the skin above her nose.

Back then, when Agostini's double had dissolved before his eyes, Griffin had been able to catch a glimpse of the creature's true nature. And now, in this indeterminate state of transition, you could see what the wyvern really was: not a single being at all, but a swarm of thousands upon thousands of tiny, beetle-like creatures coming together like teeming grains of sand to make a surface similar to skin but that changed colour like a chameleon, and could present the illusion of a human being or any other living thing.

So now it was going to be Griffin. Or Jolly. One or the other. Which it had taken prisoner was probably the deciding factor.

Without a word, the wyvern put a pulsating hand out to him.

Griffin pushed off from the mound with all his strength. He wasn't going to let the wyvern steal in behind the defensive ramparts of Aelenium disguised as him. His own adventures with the polliwiggles gave Griffin access to all the defences and all the dignitaries of the starfish city. The damage the wyvern could do in his likeness didn't bear thinking of.

But for now the last touch seemed to be missing. The creature needed Griffin himself for that, the living, breathing original of the copy.

And Griffin wasn't letting it have him.

He stumbled back, carrying the two kobalins with him, and the sudden movement set the whole shell island swaying. The edges of the shells crunched as they touched again. For a moment a broad gap opened up beside him. Furious jabbering came from the crowd of kobalins under the shield of shells.

The wyvern uttered a long, shrill scream that went right through Griffin like an icy wind. It started after him, but with its body still incomplete it didn't have full control over its movements. It staggered, stopped, and tottered for a moment before getting a new footing and standing upright again.

Griffin rammed his left elbow back, felt the teeth of one of the kobalins splinter as he hit them, and shook it off. Screeching, it slid back into the water. The second kobalin, the one that had dragged Griffin up to the top of the mound, wasn't so easily tricked. Griffin hit out, but the creature bent low to avoid the blow, and tried seizing him round the waist. Griffin was just in time to turn sideways and escape at least one of the kobalin's claws, but the other struck him in the side. The tips of the long, sharp claw-like nails pierced his skin, and the wound made him cry out with rage and pain. Then he managed to grab the kobalin's outstretched arm and fling it over the side of the shell island. Jabbering, the creature splashed into the water.

Something was clinging to the back of his head. A stabbing pain like a jellyfish sting spread over his scalp. Then he felt something crawling on his temples, his throat, his forehead. Griffin roared out loud, shook himself, nauseated, and flung himself aside. The wyvern was dragged to the ground with him while the tiny, beetle-like creatures swarmed over Griffin's face, studying its contours to transfer them to the entire assembly.

Somehow or other Griffin drew the knife from his belt. The blade went through the body of the wyvern as if through butter, but left no injury – it was like thrusting his knife into a heap of sand. When he took it out again, teeming insects closed the opening like dust trickling into it.

The kobalins' heads appeared round the sides of the mound of shells. They had swum around the strange island and now, after a moment's hesitation, hauled themselves up over the edge of the platform. The first of them rose from the water with bared, yellowish-white fangs showing through the misty vapours.

But Griffin ignored them. He knew his fight was hopeless, but he wasn't simply giving up. He passed one hand over his face, driving a broad furrow through the beetles busy closing over his features like a mask. The wyvern bellowed in pain. Griffin realised that the beetles could well be parts of a single organism. If he separated some of them from the rest it was like cutting off a part of the wyvern's body.

Once he had realised that, he made pitiless use of his knowledge. The wyvern screeched and screamed as Griffin did his best to tear whole clumps of beetles from the monster's body and throw them out into the water.

He didn't have much time left. Yet in all this tumult, and while he made a huge effort not to let the beetles cover him entirely, the behaviour of the kobalins puzzled him. They had surrounded him; almost all of them were standing on the shield-like shell structure now. But they didn't attack. It was almost as if they were keeping an eye on him, waiting to see the outcome of his grotesque duel with the wyvern.

The shape-shifter hit out with limbs made of scrabbling, teeming insects. Griffin's strength was slowly failing him. All those hours in the saddle of the ray, the tension, the fear; then his fall into the sea, his hopeless struggle with the warriors of the Deep Tribes; and now, to cap it all, his fight with the wyvern and the never-ending rain of dead fish.

To his right, the waves parted in an eruption of dark salt water, followed by a translucent cone of jelly rising from the waves like a glassy finger pointing up. Twice the height of a man and clear as crystal. And inside it, standing upright, with folded arms and a malicious smile playing around his mouth – the boy.

The boy Griffin had seen from the back of the ray when the jellyfish creature was enveloping Jasconius. Black-haired, dark, delicately built. Younger than Griffin himself. A pretty child – but for that smile, that evil grin on his face.

Griffin and the wyvern were now locked in a grotesque embrace, half standing, half on the ground. Clumps of teeming beetles were drifting on the water everywhere, blindly and frantically trying to get back to the others against the current. The wyvern was suffering terrible pain, but it hadn't yet given up its plan to take Griffin's shape.

But then it saw the boy towering above the shell island inside the jellyfish cone. At the same time the wyvern uttered harsh sounds through a dozen orifices on its body, perhaps orders or appeals for support. However, the boy only watched and smiled.

What's going on here, Griffin wondered, who's fighting whom? What have I got myself into?

The shape-shifter roared again, but the boy inside the jellyfish shook his head, very slightly. He made a brief gesture towards the kobalins. They had all clambered up on the shield of shells and so far had been waiting to fall on Griffin, claws dangling and fangs bared. Now their master gave them a silent order to retreat. In a flash the warriors of the Deep Tribes slipped into the water. A few moments later Griffin and the wyvern were alone on the mound of mussel shells.

Griffin closed his eyes. If the kobalin commander was here, uninjured, it could only mean that the whale was defeated.

He gave vent to his rage and despair in a great cry, and either his anger or a final moment of revolt gave him the strength to break the wyvern's resistance. Griffin struck the shape-shifter with his fist in the middle of its blurred face, felt his fingers go in and find something like a hard kernel at the centre of that teeming head. He couldn't be certain, didn't even have any real indication that this was really the wyvern's brain. He just trusted to luck and his intuition.

His hand closed around the firm substance – and with a savage cry he pulled it out of the swirling chaos of beetles.

At once the swarm collapsed on itself, seemed to spray apart in a firework show of colours as it hit the shield of shells, and poured through the cracks in the island and over its edge in a cascade of tiny beetles.

Seconds later Griffin was alone. Exhausted, he fell to his knees, and with all his remaining strength closed his right hand around the wyvern's brain. The black organ, which looked like a clod of earth, wasn't hard enough to withstand his grasp. Soundlessly, it crumbled in his fingers.

The boy inside the jellyfish laughed.

His mouth opened like the mouth of a portrait coming to life behind glass. His hands twitched excitedly. Only his eyes remained unchanged, wide open and staring at Griffin. He looked like a puppet with too few puppeteers working the strings to make it seem natural – every movement was incomplete, there were details missing from all his features: eyes that didn't smile with his mouth; clenched fists with the thumbs still sticking out as if paralysed; and when he opened his mouth to speak no sound came out.

He's talking to them through his mind, thought Griffin, scrambling up again. For the shells beneath his feet were moving together, closing all the gaps, and the kobalins in the water formed a perfect circle around the mound.

The conical form of the jellyfish still towered upright behind the ranks of kobalins and above the waves. When they lapped against its sides they did not fall back but were absorbed by the jelly-like substance, as if it drew its strength from the ocean itself.

So that was why Jasconius couldn't defeat it, thought Griffin in grim sorrow. Never mind how fiercely the whale attacked the jellyfish monster, as long as it was in the water it had inexhaustible strength in reserve.

'What do you want?' Griffin shouted at the boy. The wounds he had suffered in this and his earlier fights were hurting. He felt dizzy, and his legs threatened to give way. But nothing, no injury, however bad, would make him kneel before this monster.

Some of the kobalins were getting uneasy. Griffin saw them only indistinctly, but he noticed that their jabber sounded more agitated. Some of them were paddling back and forth nervously; others dipped their heads underwater and looked down into the depths.

The boy inside the jellyfish opened his mouth as if to utter a shrill scream.

And the sea exploded.

Griffin saw the surface of the water rear up below the jellyfish. Like black walls, the jaws of the giant whale rose round the kobalin commander, surrounded him entirely – and swallowed him. But Jasconius was still rising from the sea like a black tower, very fast yet as majestically as if time had slowed down so that everyone could see what was emerging from the water.

The kobalins under the shield of shells scattered, screeching. Suddenly Griffin had nothing to stand on. The shells drifted apart, and a huge tidal wave washed over him and the warriors of the Deep Tribes.

The gigantic body of Jasconius went on rising until more than half of it was above the ocean. Then the whale had reached his highest point, seemed to hover in the air for the fraction of a second – and let his whole massive weight fall sideways.

Jasconius dropped back into the sea in a mighty eruption of water, spray, and kobalins flung around at random. His mouth was closed now; the jellyfish and the boy had disappeared inside it. As Griffin struggled desperately to stay on the surface, he saw that the whale's whole body was covered with dead kobalins and countless harpoons. The boy in the jellyfish must have hurled the full power of the Deep Tribes against his opponent. But he hadn't reckoned with the great whale's stamina.

Griffin saw Jasconius sink with his prey, and he guessed – hoped, prayed – that the duel was over: the kobalin commander was now only a gigantic jellyfish in the belly of the whale, with no chance of renewing his strength in the water. Griffin had often seen what happened to a jellyfish washed up on shore: it dried out and finally dissolved.

But for that to happen, no fresh water must get into Jasconius's body. And suddenly Griffin understood why the whale and Ebenezer had taken this step.

Jasconius was already dying. Hundreds of harpoons were sticking into his body. The claws and teeth of the kobalins had ripped deep wounds in his skin. His attack on the kobalin commander was a final defiance, a last, determined effort of the will.

'*No!*' Griffin shouted, so loud that even the mists could hardly mute his voice. Shattered, he drifted in the rough water, forgotten by the fleeing kobalins and unable to follow his dying friend down into the depths. He wanted to be there at the end, wanted to thank Jasconius one last time for all he had done. And Ebenezer . . . the mere thought of him pierced Griffin's heart.

Despairingly, he hit the water with his fist. Then he dived head first, swimming down into the dark as far as he could. The lack of air became unbearable, the water pressure hurt his ears. But he went on down, although he knew it was useless.

He would never see Jasconius again. The whale had taken the kobalin commander with him in death. He cried out, into the water this time, and his rage and grief became a last surge of air bubbles swiftly rising. He couldn't help it, he had to surface. Now.

He let the water pressure take him up without moving his arms and legs to help, for at this moment he didn't mind whether he reached the surface alive or dead. He had lost Jolly, perhaps forever; Aelenium was succumbing to fire and the Deep Tribes; Soledad had probably died in the battle for the anchor chain; and now Jasconius and Ebenezer were gone as well – the two who had been dragged into this business by Griffin himself, and who had joined the battle for his sake.

They had sacrificed themselves. For him. For all the others.

His head broke through the surface in the middle of the mist. He gasped for air in pain, and shouted angrily into the vapours once more. Then his movements weakened. He let himself drift, never mind where. Further into the mist, out to the battlefield again, it made no difference.

But something happened to shake him, suddenly reviving his will to live, and this time it wasn't the thought of Jolly.

A dark outline emerged from the mist not far away. For a wonderful moment he hoped it might be Jasconius, that nothing had happened to him, he was still alive and –

It was the bows of a ship.

Wild shouting came down to him from the deck of the galleon. The sails hung slack from the yards, and the ship herself was moving painfully slowly. It wasn't hard for Griffin to avoid her by swimming a few rapid strokes. Heart thudding, he looked up at the tall wooden side of the vessel.

Heads were dangling from the bowsprit, men's heads, and he recognised at least two of them from his years as a cabin boy. One was Rouquette, the oldest of the council of captains of the Lesser Antilles. Beside him swung the head of his second-in-command, Galliano.

So the battle between the cannibal king and the Antilles captains was decided. Tyrone's fleet had finally set course for Aelenium. The vessel making her way past Griffin through the ring of mist must be the cannibal king's flagship. No one else had the right to adorn his ship's bows with the heads of his fallen enemies.

Griffin glided over to the hull of the ship and let it pass him at a little distance. Then he caught and held a rope, perhaps left over from the last keelhauling, that was dangling down into the sea, drawn along with the ship through the waves. The vessel lay low in the water; she must be filled to bursting with warriors, cannibals and cannon.

Gritting his teeth, Griffin slowly climbed the rope. He had done the same thing a dozen times before, but the wound in his side, which hurt horribly, made it difficult today. He waited just below the rail until the ship made her way into the ring of mist, knowing that all the seamen would be distracted by the sight of the burning starfish city ahead.

Then, without a sound, he hauled himself on board, made quickly for several chests of weapons, and got into cover behind them unnoticed.

'The kobalins are running for it!' shouted someone in the ranks of defenders, and soon many voices were taking up the cry. 'They're in retreat! They're withdrawing!'

Soledad had been fighting beside Walker for the last few hours, in the middle of a throng of injured, ragged, exhausted figures. The stench of fire, blood and sweat hung in the air.

Next moment Buenaventure was beside them, grim and silent; he must have killed more kobalins than anyone else, and the only sound he uttered now and then was when he cursed his blunted sword, then struck down three more with a single blow.

They were standing on the second defensive rampart, above the poets' quarter. Smoke rose to them from far below, but the fires on the shore didn't seem to have spread.

'They're right,' Walker murmured. 'The kobalins are running away. What the devil – who'd have thought it?'

His long hair was sticking together in strands; his face was smeared with kobalin blood and dirt. His shirt and trousers, like all their clothes, had taken on a muddy grey-brown hue; the fabric was torn by kobalin claws in many places, and scratches and grazes showed through.

'Soledad!'

She turned to him, reluctantly and still a little incredulously bringing herself to look away from the hordes of kobalins retreating from the rampart, racing headlong through the streets and back towards the shore. In a stampede of scaly bodies, fangs and scraping claws, the Deep Tribes were tumbling down to the water.

Soledad suppressed an urge to fling her arms round Walker in her relief – she still didn't trust the sudden calm. This unexpected retreat might be a trick, some kind of devilry to lull the defenders into a false sense of security. But then why was it so disorderly? Why were the kobalins trampling each other down in their flight, scratching and biting one another as each tried to be first to plunge back into the sea?

'As if they're afraid of something,' growled Buenaventure. His breath was coming fast. During the fighting Soledad had glanced at the pit bull man a couple of times, and saw him panting with his tongue hanging out of his mouth.

'Looks to me more like the other way around,' said Walker.

Buenaventure glanced enquiringly at him. 'Hm?'

'It's as if they suddenly *aren't* afraid any more – of their chieftains, even of the Maelstrom.'

'You mean,' said Soledad, swallowing, 'they've lost their commander?' She didn't look at him, but her cheek muscles quivered as she gazed at the fleeing army of the Deep Tribes.

'Who knows for sure?' said Walker. 'But without a leader they're following their instinct and plunging back into the water. They hate land and the air.'

'And fire!' said Buenaventure, sniffing the smoke.

Soledad let herself sink down with her back against a beam in the rampart. 'But that would mean that the kobalin commander has been defeated.'

Some of the soldiers were about to follow the kobalins and strike down the stragglers, but the officers of the guard held them back. They still couldn't believe their own eyes, and they certainly didn't believe in what the kobalins were doing.

Soledad turned her eyes from the congested streets to the sky above the water. A handful of rays were circling there; the rest were busy carrying the injured from the rampart up to the halls of refuge. Had one of the Ray Guard riders out there killed the kobalin commanders? And where was Griffin? She couldn't make out individual riders on the rays through the smoke that was now glowing with the light of the morning sun; they were little more than light-coloured dots on the mighty animals' backs. Soledad sent up a prayer to heaven that nothing had happened to the boy.

Uncertainty was gnawing at her, in spite of the huge relief she felt at the sight of the Deep Tribes retreating. But was this really a long-term withdrawal?

The defenders set about binding up each other's wounds. Water bottles passed from hand to hand, and they all greedily quenched their thirst. Those who could only just keep on their feet, at the end of their tether now, were helped down from the wall by their companions.

'Now what?' asked Buenaventure, at a loss. He hadn't even lowered his sword yet, as if he still couldn't believe that the battle had come to an end. Even the deafening shouts of rejoicing from all parts of the rampart weren't enough to convince him.

Walker took a step forward. 'I think,' said the captain, 'we –'

A shout interrupted him. Even before he could finish what he was saying, the general rejoicing turned to chaotic cries of alarm. Somewhere in the streets above them bells were rung, and very close to Soledad a young man burst into heart-rending tears.

She followed the direction of the others' gaze, and saw what had changed their cheerful mood within seconds.

Out of the mist, still hard to distinguish through the drifting smoke, came ships. Black flags flew from their masts, and the wind bore the muffled sound of war cries to the slopes of Aelenium.

'That's Tyrone!' exclaimed Walker. His face was stony. 'Out of the frying pan into the fire, by heaven!'

The sailing vessels emerged from the ring of mist like ghost ships. Their decks were swarming with gaudily

247

painted tribal warriors and pirates brandishing swords.

'Are those the cannibals?' whispered the weeping boy who was standing near Soledad.

No one answered him.

A CONVERSATION
IN THE DEPTHS

The cavern in the kobalin mountain was long, rather narrow, and not very high. But Jolly's hopes that the angular way through the rock might become a tunnel leading somewhere were soon dashed.

After she had gone thirty or forty paces her polliwiggle vision could make out the back wall in the darkness, first only as a faint outline, then as a steep slope consisting of rocks and small stones. Obviously the roof had fallen in at some time in the past. There must be quakes down here, even volcanic eruptions that were never felt on the surface, and this thought made Jolly's sense of isolation intolerable. If she died in this place it wouldn't even make a ripple in the sea above. No one would ever know.

Oddly enough, as she looked up at the rocky roof of the

cavern with glazed eyes she couldn't help thinking of the sky – a bright, clear, blue sky now thirty thousand feet above her, as far out of reach as the moon and the stars. She thought of the wind in the Caribbean that had so often blown in her face and made the flapping sails billow out. She thought of the freedom of the endless ocean. She remembered her old life on the *Maid Maddy* and her foster father Bannon as he used to be before he betrayed her – which was how all this had begun.

Then the memory of a single face went through her like a sharp pain. Griffin's face. It was almost as if some part of him was reaching out to her: a hand waving to her one last time, saying goodbye forever.

Jolly sank to her knees and burst into tears.

It was too much, at last it was just too much. She had borne pain, the sorrow of parting, loneliness and Munk's hostility. She had accepted all that. But now all her resistance gave way and the grief she had suppressed for so long broke over her.

She crouched on the ground for a long time, eyes closed, curled up like a child at its wits' end, and she wept until she didn't know whether she had any tears left, for they flowed straight into the sea, leaving no trace.

Something nuzzled the tip of her nose.

When she opened her eyes she was dazzled by the little fish's luminescence. The rest of the shoal were dancing in front of her face, while their tiny pairs of dark eyes gazed expressionlessly at her.

'Leave me alone,' she whispered, weakly shooing them away with one hand. The shoal scattered, but immediately formed once more. One of them nudged her nose again; two others shot past her cheeks. This time they felt almost like hands gently stroking her face.

In her memory, swirling light and darkness merged to make a picture: three old women joined by their long hair sat at spinning wheels on the sea-bed, spinning the water into translucent, sparkling yarn. The threads, some single, some in several strands, stretched away into the distance from that strange place. Woven together on what looked like a random principle, they formed a glittering web reaching out in all directions: the Weavers sat at the centre of a network of veins that embraced the whole world.

Then the image moved away from what Jolly remembered seeing for herself and took her on a journey. Her gaze raced at breakneck speed along a thick strand of the magic threads, over underwater mountains, through ravines, deserts of dust at the bottom of the sea, forests of bizarre growths. Finally it passed over rugged clefts and crevices, past mighty structures that might be submerged ruins, on again through grey wildernesses until . . . yes, until it reached this cone of rock, the nest of the kobalins. Here the magic yarn crossed countless other strands, and Jolly understood: the mountain rose above a magical crossroads, a place where veins running in from many different directions met, and their power pervaded it.

The luminous fish scattered, swirled around Jolly's head, and came together again in a shimmering cluster that hopped up and down on invisible currents.

The images faded with the end of her journey to the kobalin nest, and Jolly's hand instinctively went to the bag at her belt. She had lost her rucksack and all her food, but the bag around her waist was still there. And so were her shells inside it.

She struggled up and blinked a couple of times, as if it were the only way to make sure her surroundings were real. The fish darted nimbly around each other in a mood of excitement that she couldn't quite understand.

'I suppose you can't help me,' said Jolly, 'so I'll have to help myself, right?' She sniffed one last time, swallowed, and felt new strength flowing through her.

She crouched down, set the shells out in a circle, and waited for them to speak to her. It wasn't long before she felt her hands making movements that were only partly under her own control. Her fingers removed some of the shells, replaced them with others, changed the pattern again and again. Satisfied at last, she stopped moving the shells, examined their arrangement, and slowly nodded.

For a few seconds she closed her eyes, and when she opened them again the magic pearl was there almost of its own accord. She couldn't remember when she had ever found it so easy to conjure up the shell magic. It must be something to do with the power of this place. Jolly couldn't even imagine how dense the network of magic yarn must be in the Rift itself, how interwoven the magic, how concentrated its strength.

The pearl at the centre of the pattern of shells glowed and sparkled. Then it moved away from its position and floated up the steep slope of broken rock, exploring clefts and crevices, diving into hollows and holes. As it did so the luminous fish followed in a curving line like the sparkling tail of a shooting star. Jolly was enchanted by so much beauty in this bleak wilderness.

At last the pearl made for a dark corner where the slope met the roof of the cavern. Still glittering, it disappeared into an opening that was invisible from below. Jolly's heart leaped up. The pearl had found a way through the rubble of the fallen roof.

A little later it came back, shot down to Jolly and placed itself at the centre of the pattern of shells again. Once there it hovered, waiting impatiently to be put back inside one of the shells. Jolly did as it wanted, her eyes closed and her hands outstretched in invocation. When she looked again the pearl was gone, and all the shells were closed.

She had never felt so powerful before. For the first time she understood what went on in Munk when he was working shell magic. It was an invigorating, wonderful sense of euphoria, but you also risked forgetting yourself and everything around you; you were in danger of becoming entirely absorbed in this feeling of release and power.

She liked it, it flattered her, but it frightened her too. Silently, she promised herself never to give way to that temptation. She only hoped she would ultimately be free to make the choice for herself.

Quickly, she gathered up the shells, put them away in the bag at her belt, and climbed the rocky slope. The fish were still dancing around the newly discovered opening, marking the place with their silvery light. Without them, Jolly would probably have lost sight of it again.

The hole was larger than she had expected, and she could easily slip through. On the other side she found another cave, the rest of the blocked tunnel through the rock.

She clambered down to the floor and set off, going still deeper into the quiet caverns of the kobalin nest. The fish followed her, making a very faint murmuring, rustling noise. Perhaps it was the sound of their scales rubbing together, or perhaps their rippling voices. Maybe these tiny creatures were chuckling happily in relief.

After a while she lost count of the number of turns and bends on her way. The floor of the tunnel was leading down all the time, sometimes quite gently, then in a steep descent again, and she felt as if the water around her were gradually warming up. Suppose she stumbled straight into a kobalin settlement? A cavernous city of the Deep Tribes on the sea-bed? However, she had already seen many caves, large and small. If the kobalins had wanted to settle here, then surely it would have been higher up the mountain.

Something else was waiting for her down there. And in view of what Aina had said, there was little doubt what it would be. Or who it would be.

All the same, this was the only way she could go. She hadn't yet seen any path leading up. There had certainly been other tunnels forking off, but they led even more steeply down.

Had Munk and Aina reached the heart of the Rift

already? Don't think of it, she told herself, concentrate on finding a way out of here instead.

The tunnel widened. Its walls finished suddenly, and Jolly found herself in a huge grotto, so vast that the end of it was beyond her polliwiggle vision.

At first sight the cave was empty. The floor fell steeply away at Jolly's feet, but only for a step or two. Then the ground became even darker and more rugged. In the middle of the cave this surface seemed to rise in a gentle mound like a hill.

For a moment Jolly thought the grotto must once have been filled with lava that then solidified. The ground was black and wrinkled, and looked very different from the walls of the cave or the floor of the tunnel along which she had come. She hesitated for a moment, then took a step down over the edge and landed with her legs apart on the lower floor of the cave. To her surprise it gave way and felt springy under her feet. It was soft and elastic, like tar that hasn't cooled yet.

A terrifying screech rose, echoed back from the walls and pierced Jolly's ears like needles. In panic, she pushed off from the floor, shot up to the roof of the grotto and hovered there.

From this vantage point she had a good view of the

bottom of the cave, at least for as far as a polliwiggle could see. And she realised that what she had been standing on wasn't a floor at all.

It was a body.

A doughy, gigantic body filling the whole grotto and . . . yes, stuck in it like a cork in a bottle.

The screech came from a mouth as large as a well-shaft in the middle of a fat, broad, spreading face set on the edge of the monstrous body without any perceptible neck or shoulders. Black folds of skin and half-rotted teeth surrounded this gaping maw, and a little way above it – or perhaps beside it, since the face was lying on the horizontal and staring at the roof – Jolly could make out two slits of eyes surrounded by rolls of flesh.

This dreadful being looked like an enormously fat kobalin smashed flat by a mighty fist and somehow or other stuffed into this grotto. In fact the cave must be a huge and very deep rocky dome, with room for the rest of the giant kobalin down below. What Jolly saw was the upper side of this living, screeching cork. She couldn't imagine what kind of power could have forced the creature into this shaft down through the rock.

'What'ss thiss? What'ss thiss?' the mouth hissed. Oily saliva rose vertically from it in blurred strands, looking like smoky air flickering with heat. 'What ssort of thing are you? Who are you?'

'I'm Jolly,' said Jolly.

She was intent on not moving any lower. Her head was almost touching the roof of the cave, and the soft hill of spongy kobalin flesh was a good fifty paces below her.

The mother of the kobalins – as this creature must be if Aina had been telling the truth – uttered a gurgle that passed straight into what was probably meant to be Jolly's name. 'And what'ss ssomeone like you doing here?' added the monster.

'I've been shut up here,' said Jolly. 'Just like you.'

Once again there was a terrible roar and a screech. The roof of the cave shook slightly, dust trickled out of cracks and crevices in the rock. But the creature did not move from the spot. It was stuck there as fast as if it had been walled up.

'Shut up here, yes. Yes, so I was. By that disgusting brood of mine.' The wrinkled black flesh around the eyes was so swollen that it was impossible to say whether the creature was looking at Jolly. 'My miserable, craven, depraved brood. Craven and depraved, they are.'

Jolly wondered whether to swim closer to the distorted giant face, but decided to stay put. The mother of the kobalins might be stuck, might not have the strength to free herself after so many thousands of years — but Jolly didn't trust this apparent truce. She could see no arms or legs anywhere; they must be jammed under the fat colossus. But the sight of that gigantic mouth was a good enough reason to keep a prudent distance away.

'The kobalins are your children?' she asked.

'Yes, yes, yes!' The gurgling, hissing voice sounded impatient. No wonder, after such a long time. 'Will you free me?'

I can just about resist the temptation, thought Jolly, shivering, but instead she said, 'It's possible.'

'Then do it! Do it, yess!' hissed the creature.

'I told you my name, so it would be only polite for you to tell me yours.'

'Kangusta,' roared the gaping mouth. 'Kangussta the Great!'

'Kangusta . . . And you can't free yourself?'

'No, no, no.'

'How am I to help you?'

'Tear down thiss accurssed mountain! Thiss whole accurssed mountain!'

'I'm too small. And if *you* can't do it . . .'

Kangusta let out a hiss that set up a strong current in the

grotto, scattering the luminous fish, who had been anxiously keeping close to Jolly.

'I'm sstuck!'

'Yes, I can see that.'

'It did it to me. Stirred up my brood against their own mother . . .'

The creature might look ponderous, but Jolly wasn't going to underestimate her. A captive colossus, yes – but there was cunning in her voice, something cruel and sly.

'Is there a way out of here?' That was plain speaking, and perhaps too soon for it, but she couldn't bear the presence of this horrible creature any longer. 'A way we could get out of this place together?'

A rumble emerged from the mouth. It sounded like lava erupting.

She's laughing, thought Jolly in horror. She's laughing at me.

'I can see you, little animal. You're like them. Like what they once were.'

Jolly had already begun looking for another opening in the walls of the grotto. Kangusta's words shook her. 'Who do you mean?' she asked, not quite as firmly as before.

'Them! *Them!* The little animals who came – little animals like you. And then . . . and then . . .' She fell silent, but that mouth was still wide open.

'What happened then?'

'Little animal, why do you ask such questions?' She said *assk ssuch quesstionss*, with a dreadful, lip-smacking sound to the words. 'You should know. You're like them.'

'How many of them came here then?'

'One little animal, two little animals. First one. Then later two.'

There was no doubt about it: she meant Aina and the other two polliwiggles who had come to defeat the Maelstrom so long ago. Perhaps not all the other girl had said was lies.

Kangusta's voice became soft and sly. 'You must help me, little animal. Then perhaps . . . yes, I'll tell you all about it. Perhaps.' *Perhapss*, she said.

'I'm too weak. I can't destroy this mountain.'

'Then find a way to do it.'

'I don't have the power for that.'

'Power?' That rumbling, stony laughter again. 'Oh yes, you have. I saw it, long ago. I saw the animals fight it. Shut it up. I saw it.'

Kangusta must already have been stuck here at the time. So how could she have seen something happening outside?

'I see many things,' said the mother of the kobalins, as if

answering Jolly's unspoken question. 'I can see through rocks, taste it in the water. All that happens. I tasted the way the other little animal shut you in here with me. Oh yes.' Her voice grew lower, deeper. 'And I taste you, little animal. Mmmmm.'

In the grey of polliwiggle vision, Jolly saw it almost too late – something darting out of the gulf of the kobalin mother's mouth, a warty strand of black, muscular flesh.

She just managed to swerve aside from that mighty tongue. The tip came down on the rocks beside her, made its way over them, twitching and trembling, and then withdrew with a sound like the crack of a whip.

A roar of rage rose from Kangusta's body, and then the tongue shot out again, as long as a topmast and not much broader. Presumably this was the only part of her body that the mother of the kobalins could still move freely.

The monster's scream ebbed away; the tongue disappeared.

Jolly had to force herself not to run away in panic. Instead, she stayed where she was, just below the roof of the cave and out of reach of the tongue. 'That's no way to do a deal,' she said huskily. She was trembling all over, and hoped Kangusta didn't notice.

'Nimble, quick little animal!' the mouth thundered. 'Tender, tasty little animal!'

'Tell me how to get out of here, and I'll do what I can for you.' The luminous fish had disappeared from view, and were now hovering anxiously behind her.

'There's only one way. Not the way you came. The other. It leads up, leads outside. They bring me food that way. Live, struggling, fat food.'

Jolly shuddered, and felt her stomach heave. Don't think about it. Just stop thinking about it.

The second tunnel, the one Kangusta meant, must lie on the other side of the grotto, outside her polliwiggle vision. But now Jolly knew just how far Kangusta's tongue could reach, it would be easy for her to get there safely.

However, there was still something else she wanted to know. The mother of the kobalins had mentioned Aina and the others. Jolly had to find out what had happened to the polliwiggles. Why had Aina betrayed them?

'If you tasted me being shut in here by another . . . well, animal, then you know she was no friend of mine.'

'Oh yes, I tasted it. I tasted that.'

'Why does she obey the Maelstrom now? Because she does, doesn't she?'

Kangusta's laughter shook the rocky dome. 'Obey? *Obey?* You know nothing, little animal. You know none of the truth. The Maelstrom is powerful, oh yes. It united my brood in fear of it. If it were dead, destroyed . . . then my children would fight for my favour again. Like they used to. But fear unites them, makes them lose all respect for me. Even makes them leave the water!' These words were followed by an indignant roar. It must seem unthinkable to Kangusta that a kobalin would go on land of its own free will. 'If it were destroyed, yes, then some would think of me again. Would set me free. And others would envy them my love and fight for it. Just as they did in the old days. In the good times. The fat, tasty times.' The mother of the kobalins uttered a groan of self-pity. 'But now it's ruined them. Made them forget their own mother. Yes, indeed.'

The tongue shot out again, whipped around the empty grotto at crazy speed, and finally flapped back, limp, over Kangusta's face. It lay there a long time, and there was no sound but the kobalin mother's snorting.

Jolly waited for the monster to calm down again. Only when the tongue began to move, flicking back into Kangusta's mouth like a dying sea-serpent, did she speak again.

'Well, I want to destroy the Maelstrom and get everything back the way it was.' Hesitantly, she added, 'The way it was in the good old times.'

'The tasty times.'

Jolly cleared her throat. 'Exactly.'

'You're too weak.' Kangusta sounded tired now. 'You said so yourself. And I don't trust you. You'll find the way up; you'll leave this place and forget me.'

How could I possibly do that? Jolly wondered with revulsion. She had no pity for Kangusta, but she could well imagine what was going on in the ancient creature's brain. Once she had been venerated by the Deep Tribes, but now oblivion threatened her.

'I will destroy it.' Jolly was surprised by her own decisive tone. 'I'll put an end to it all.'

Swollen flesh twitched around one of the eyes. 'Will you really do it?'

'Yes, or die in the attempt.'

'A brave little animal. Or a stupid little animal. Perhaps both.'

Without thinking, Jolly answered back, 'Better than being fat and lazy and helpless and stuck in this rock!'

Kangusta did not reply, and Jolly thought she was planning something else nasty to say. But then words rose from the black mouth again, very slowly this time, preceded by something like an echo in advance of what the creature actually said.

'You are right, little animal. There were once times, you must know, when I was strong and powerful. Times when all trembled before me, whether kobalins or animals or the wooden fish on which those like you ride over the waves.'

That sounded as if the islanders must have travelled from one island to another by boat even thousands of years ago, thought Jolly. But why was hardly anything left of their civilisation? She answered herself: presumably they never recovered from the first war with the Maelstrom. Yet they had *won* it. So what was going to be left of the Caribbean this time?

Kangusta went on. 'You think the Maelstrom comes from over there, don't you, from the *other* sea? But that's not true. The Maelstrom comes from this world. It was once a little animal like you. Oh yes, it was.'

'Like me?' asked Jolly, bewildered.

'A little animal with great power. You saw it. The one who shut you in here. The first little animal to come down here.'

'Aina!'

'If that's what you call it . . . yes.'

'But she's a human. A polliwiggle.'

'She was like you.' *Ssshe*, Kangusta hissed.

'And she came to defeat the Maelstrom.'

The monster gave that rumble of laughter. 'There was no Maelstrom when she came here. She became it. She *is* the Maelstrom.'

For a moment Jolly forgot to keep swimming, and almost sank. The luminous fish swirled excitedly around her face, alarming her. With a swing of her arms, Jolly brought herself up to the roof of the cave again.

'How can Aina be the Maelstrom?'

'I do not taste everything in the water,' said Kangusta slowly. 'But at the very beginning, just after she made my children rebel against me, she came into the mountain. She wanted to torment me. To torment me, that's what she wanted.' She fell silent for a moment. 'She told me everything, the little animal. How the other animals rejected her because she was different, more powerful. How she sensed that something was going on in the deeps. That was when the powers of the Other Sea invaded my domain! The little animal came; she fell for their ideas and promises. She tried to open a gateway for them, those others, to *be* a gateway through which they could get into our world.' The longer Kangusta spoke, the clearer her voice became. It was as if with every sentence part of her memory of those days returned – memories of the Maelstrom, of the war against the Mare Tenebrosum, but above all of herself. She remembered what it had been like to talk to another living creature and exchange thoughts. It made her no more human, but it did make her less monstrous.

'And as those others whispered to her, the little animal became the Maelstrom. I could do nothing, I had no magic power then, and I have none today . . . but don't tell anyone.'

'Don't let that bother you,' said Jolly in a hollow voice.

'The Maelstrom took power over my domain and my children.'

Jolly thought about what Kangusta was saying. Incredible as it all sounded, it did make sense. Aina had been rejected by her fellow humans – she had told them so herself. And as for the wiles employed by the masters of the Mare Tenebrosum – Jolly herself had seen them. She remembered her visions on the deck of the *Carfax*. If it hadn't been for Buenaventure . . .

She shook herself, as if to get rid of the images in her head. She had almost forgotten where she was. Thoughtfully, she looked at the gigantic head of the kobalin mother. Perhaps she ought to revise her opinion of Kangusta. She was certainly sly, and a horrible sight, but she wasn't stupid. The pity that Jolly had been fending off all this time entered her mind now – mingled with the fear she still felt for the monster.

Kangusta was going on. 'The little animal you saw . . . the one that brought you here, it wasn't real. Only a copy of its old self, before it became the Maelstrom.'

'So that's why we could reach right through her!'

'Yes.'

'What happened to the other two? You said there were two more like me.'

'They came later, when the Maelstrom was at the height of its power. They fought it to keep it back. And with it the powers from the Other Sea.'

Jolly nodded. 'They were shut up in the shell with it, Aina said. Was that a lie too?'

'No. They sacrificed themselves to keep it captive there. Brave little animals. They were gone for a long, long time, caught in the great shell with it. Until the shell opened again later, much later, and the Maelstrom gained power once more. Then they crawled out into freedom too, but they were not what they had once been. In all those ages it had conquered them, enslaved them. It refashioned one of them out of mud and seaweed, and the pieces of your wooden fish that sink down to us in the depths.'

'The Acherus!'

'I do not know that word,' said Kangusta.

'What happened to the other one?'

The black, bark-like skin of the mother of the kobalins undulated in a fit of anger. 'It took power over my brood. It united the Tribes in the name of the Maelstrom. It too is changed, but not like the first.'

The kobalin commander. In retrospect, it did all make sense. Even the fact that the Ghost-Trader had always spoken of just one Acherus, not several. He had told them that the Acherus had been made by the Maelstrom – although not what it had once been.

He knew, she thought, with tears in her eyes. He knew all along what the Maelstrom and its two mighty servants had once been. And he hadn't told Jolly and Munk anything about it; he'd kept them unaware of the danger that threatened them. A danger much worse than death: very likely they would suffer the same fate as the polliwiggles who had taken Aina captive.

The longer Jolly thought, the clearer it became to her that Munk was already well on the way to such a fate.

That was why Aina had chosen him. She wanted to make him her servant, a substitute for the Acherus that Munk himself had destroyed. And Aina still had plans for Jolly, that was the only reason why she hadn't killed her but had shut her up here: she wanted to make Jolly her slave and misuse her magic for her own purposes.

So far they had been assuming they were fighting a creature from the Mare Tenebrosum. But that was wrong –

their enemy had once been a polliwiggle like themselves. Cast out by her own people, she had gone over to the other side and was now its strongest weapon.

'I must find her,' she said, speaking her thoughts aloud. 'I must set Munk free and stop Aina.'

'You cannot stop the Maelstrom,' said Kangusta, rumbling. 'No one can. I have tried – and look at me. I wasn't always as I am today . . . not always.'

'If I defeat the Maelstrom, will you rule the Deep Tribes again?'

Kangusta hesitated. 'If it is truly destroyed, not just shut up again . . . yes, then a time will come when they will see me as what I once was to them.'

'Then promise me something.'

'Why?'

'Because I'm going to restore your old rule over them.' Or at least I'm going to try, she added silently.

'What kind of a promise do you want, little animal?'

'I want you to promise to keep the Deep Tribes away from us humans. Away from the surface. So that there'll be no more attacks, not on our shi . . . on our wooden fish, and not on the starfish city or the mainland coasts. Down here you can do whatever you want – but there must be no more war between you and us.'

'I could promise that. I could.'

'But would you keep your promise?'

A hollow gurgling and rumbling rose from Kangusta's mouth. 'You don't trust me, do you, little animal?'

'No.'

'Then you won't believe my promise either.'

'Is there anything else I can do?'

The rumbling in the throat of the mother kobalin came again. 'So you want me to let you go. Let you go to destroy it.'

'Well, that's the plan.'

'It will not succeed.'

'Maybe not. But maybe it will.'

Kangusta remained silent for a moment. 'You are brave, little animal.'

Jolly sighed. 'If you want to know, I'm simply terrified of you, and the Maelstrom, and this whole horrible place down here.'

This time Kangusta's rumble sounded almost like human laughter. 'Well, little animal, you needn't fear Kangusta any longer. If you succeed there will be no more war between you and the Deep Tribes. It shall be so.'

Jolly heaved a sigh of relief. The warm water of this cave streamed through her lungs, and for a moment she felt almost comfortable.

272

'Go now,' said Kangusta. 'I will tell you what way they come to bring me prey.' She paused for a moment, her gigantic maw opening and closing with a smacking sound. 'Hurry. I can taste disaster in the water.'

TYRONE

'The rain of fish has stopped,' said the Ghost-Trader, looking down one last time from the balcony of the library. Forefather's eyes were not very good any more, and the Trader had to tell him what was going on. 'The kobalins have gone back into the water, but that won't help us. Tyrone's fleet has the city in its sights.'

The thunder of cannon rose from the sea; gun-smoke mingled with the black smoke from the ruins on the shore. The eyes of both men on the balcony were stinging; Forefather's were red and weeping too. The sight of him made the Ghost-Trader realise, once again, how human he had become over all these ages.

Together, they withdrew into one of the halls of books and closed the outer door behind them. The rumble of the guns was more muted here, but the acrid smell of battle had long ago filled even the high halls of the library.

'Is it possible that this is all the Maelstrom wants?' asked the Trader, while his black parrots settled on stacks of books to the right and left of him. 'To drive us into a corner so that we take the last step ourselves?'

'Not we, my friend. Only you have power now. Mine was gone long ago. But there's still enough of what we once were left in you.' Forefather laughed softly and sadly. 'Compared with me, you're young.'

'You could have stayed young too if you hadn't preferred to crawl away to this place. The people in the world outside have almost forgotten you. They worship what they call God, but they don't even give him a name. If you had stayed with them, had shown yourself to them . . . then perhaps you'd still have all your powers.'

'I didn't want that any more, as you know. All that time ago, after the fall of the first starfish city . . . oh, sometimes I would have been glad if memory too had left me when my powers went.'

The Ghost-Trader leaned against a tower of leather-bound folio volumes. 'If I do as you ask, it will bring the Maelstrom even closer to its aim.'

'It has only the mind of a small girl, my friend, don't forget that. A child's hatred drives it. I'd call it defiance if there were not so much at stake. You are the only one who still has the power to stop it.'

'You are asking me to raise the ghosts of the other gods. But they wouldn't obey me for long,' said the Ghost-Trader. 'They are not like humans, whose souls I can bring up from the abyss at will. They are gods! They're like *us*!'

Forefather's bony fingers closed around his staff. 'Yet they would decide the battle in our favour! Oh, if only I could do it myself . . .'

The Ghost-Trader went up to the old man, this time with a gentle smile, and took his hand. 'You used your powers for something better, my friend. You made a whole world.'

'And now I'm to see it destroyed by one girl's fury! Do you call that worthy of a god?'

'It's a long time since Aina was a girl. The masters of the Mare Tenebrosum made her into the Maelstrom, and that's what she has been for thousands of years.'

'But she still acts like a child. All that time ago she felt betrayed by those who had cast her out because of her abilities. It was only because they knew no better. And today she feels betrayed by the masters of the Mare because they didn't stand by her when the first polliwiggles defeated her.' Forefather heaved a despairing sigh. 'She can't annihilate the Mare Tenebrosum, but she can destroy what its masters want most of all for their own: my creation. This world! Aina will leave it in rubble and ashes, only because a few foolish people drove her out of her village, and then she met powers too great for her.'

The Trader nodded thoughtfully. 'She will destroy us.'

'If you don't stop her.' Forefather groaned, and began limping up and down the aisles between the walls of books, leaning on his stick. 'We've been going round in circles for days.' He stopped and met the Trader's eyes. 'We've become like them, don't you see that? Here we are quarrelling like two children who never tire of tugging at both ends of a rope. Back and forth.' Shaking his head, he dropped his voice to a whisper. 'Back and forth, again and again.'

The Ghost-Trader took his silver circlet from under his dark robe. He gently stroked the cool metal. 'I could wake the gods,' he said. 'I could throw them into battle against Tyrone and his vassals. Even against the Maelstrom itself. But who will send them back into the shadows after their victory? I can't do it. The powers I should be rousing would be too strong for me. They'd fall on each other and tear what's left of the world to pieces . . . out of hatred for the creatures who once forgot them, or just because it pleases them. The least of them knows about creation, as you are aware.' Wearily, the Trader leaned against the edge of a table and propped himself on it with both hands.

'Whatever way we choose, it leads to downfall.'

'But they are gods!' protested Forefather. 'They have the right to destroy. The Maelstrom does not. It is only a . . . a monstrosity of Nature. An ulcer, and we have the Water Weavers to thank for it.'

'The Weavers?' The Ghost-Trader's voice was sharper now. 'They were made by this world, and you had nothing to do with it. They don't need the belief of human beings because the world itself believes in them, every stone and every blade of grass. That's the only reason why you despise them.'

'They are –'

The Trader took a step towards Forefather. His one eye seemed to be blazing. 'When the Mare Tenebrosum stirred for the first time, the Weavers did only what seemed to them right in view of the danger. They made the polliwiggles to fight off the masters of the Mare. Do you blame them for that?'

'Yet the first of those polliwiggles was Aina, and she became the Maelstrom! Perhaps the greatest failure this world has ever seen.'

'But a human failure, not the Weavers' doing. You are unjust to those three, my friend. They tried to protect the world.'

Forefather lowered his eyes. 'Because the one who made the world could not,' he said, with guilt in his voice.

Side by side Soledad, Walker and Buenaventure hurried over the coral bridges, up the steps and along the streets of the devastated city. They had joined a troop of guards acting as scouts to discover what morale was like in the cannibal king's army. How badly had they suffered in the long sea battle? What held this motley army of savage tribal warriors and the scum of the Old World together?

By now the cannibals' fleet had stopped firing on the city, presumably because the cannon on the ships couldn't aim high enough to hit targets further up the steep slopes of Aelenium. None of the cannonballs had reached beyond the shore, which was already laid waste anyway.

The scouts made their way downhill, and the lower they went the denser was the smoke of the smouldering fires. Soon they came to the first ruins. Nothing remained of many of the houses and villas but their walls standing against the sky like charred skeletons.

None of them said a word, and it wasn't just the fire and smoke that kept them silent. Soledad had been in many sea battles, but in those you seldom saw more than a few bodies in the water. Often your dead enemies went to the bottom in their sinking ships. But walking through a city that was a single huge battlefield was a nightmare.

She cast a surreptitious glance at Walker, and was surprised to see how much the sight of all the destruction and suffering affected him too. Without a word, she took his hand as they went along.

'Look!'

The cry startled them. They stopped. One of the soldiers had reached a coral balustrade around a small square looking south. From there they had a view of the shore through clouds of smoke. Soledad and the others hurried to the man's side.

The first attackers were just coming ashore on the piers of the starfish arms, leaping out of their boats with wild war-cries, storming in disorder towards the streets.

One of the guards, a man with a white, neatly trimmed beard now spattered with kobalin blood, made a derisive face. 'Pirates and savages are no soldiers. They understand looting but not war.'

Walker was going to contradict him vehemently, but then he noticed that neither Soledad nor Buenaventure protested.

'Is that an advantage for us?' asked Soledad.

The soldier shook his head. 'With such numbers of

opponents? Before the first of them reach the rampart they'll be swarming all over the place down here. No doubt they'll simply continue what the kobalins began.'

Buenaventure growled his assent. 'They'll overrun us.'

Soledad thoughtfully massaged her wrists. 'Hardly. Tyrone must have had some two hundred ships. There's not more than half that number down there.'

'A quarter at the most,' said Walker. 'Assuming there are no more waiting in the mist.'

'I wouldn't think so. Tyrone will throw everything he has left into battle.' Soledad smiled, a cold smile. 'The Antilles captains did him a lot of damage.'

The white-bearded soldier spoke up impatiently. 'That's all very well, but the fact remains that they far outnumber us. I suggest we get back to the rampart. They'll soon need every man they can get there.' And sketching a formal nod in Soledad's direction, he added, 'And every woman.'

'You go ahead with your men,' said Soledad. 'Walker, Buenaventure and I will try to reach Tyrone.'

Walker raised one eyebrow. 'We will?'

'Soledad is right.' Buenaventure backed her up. 'At least it sounds like a plan, and that's better than waiting up on the rampart for them to come and get us.'

The soldier turned pale, but he held the pit bull man's

gaze. Then he nodded. Perhaps he was glad to be rid of the three pirates.

Soledad turned to Walker. 'Let's try it, at least.'

He sighed slightly and then shrugged. 'A beautiful woman is always right, so my father used to say.'

Soledad flashed him a smile. 'I thought you never knew your father.'

The white-bearded soldier, annoyed, cleared his throat. 'Very well,' he said firmly, 'my men and I will go back. I wish you three luck – and I mean it.'

The soldiers' footsteps were soon drowned out by the crackling of fires and the screaming on the shore. A few moments later the others were on their way again. Soledad and Walker went ahead, with Buenaventure right behind them.

Fire had made some of the streets so hot that they had to look for another way. And some alleys were so full of dense smoke that it was almost impossible to breathe. Finally they crossed a narrow coral bridge with no handrail leading over one of the broader main thoroughfares. Below them a horde of pirates and cannibals in traditional war-paint was storming uphill, followed by a troop moving in more orderly formation, looking warily at the openings of the burnt-out windows on both sides of the road. Some of them also glanced up at the bridge, and Soledad, Walker and Buenaventure were only just in time to throw themselves down and avoid being seen.

A black figure strode along in the middle of the pirate troop. The cannibal king's head was shaved except for the long black ponytail hanging down the back of his neck. Unlike the other pirates, Tyrone sported the war-paint of the savages whose leader he had made himself years ago. He wore the black, flowing garments of a nobleman, with knee-high, broad-topped boots and a wide cloak, which made it look as if he were pulling a dark trail of smoke along after him. From up here the three of them couldn't see his teeth, filed to sharp points, but just knowing about them made Soledad feel sick.

She feared him: there was no reason not to admit it. Tyrone was cruel, utterly unscrupulous, and an excellent fighter too. Even when he was still a pirate sailing the Caribbean, his exploits had been legendary. After his disappearance into the Orinoco jungle, and later when he returned as leader of the cannibal tribes, there had been many rumours. There was no cruelty, no act of barbarism that he hadn't outdone long ago.

His officers hurried with him through the smoke-filled streets, tall men with hard, scarred faces. They were followed by another horde of pirates, ragged cut-throats protecting their master's back.

Among them there was one who looked like –

'Griffin!' Soledad's jaw dropped. 'Look! Down there! Isn't that Griffin?'

'Can't be,' growled Buenaventure.

'It is! You're right!' Walker's voice rose in excitement, and even as he spoke he tried to lower it again. He didn't like to show how fond he had grown of the pirate boy during the weeks they had been sailing together.

Griffin was walking along with the pirates, weaning a dirty shirt, red-and-white striped trousers, and a black scarf round his head. He was carrying a sword with a notched blade over his shoulder like a stick.

Soledad put her head a little too far over the side of the bridge; for a moment she must be clearly visible from below. But only one of the pirates raised his eyes, as if he had sensed that she was there.

Griffin hid his surprise, trying hard not to show his excitement. But the strain of being in the middle of his enemies was clearly telling on his nerves. His face quivered.

'A devil of a fellow, young Griffin!' growled Buenaventure.

'And he'll end up with the devil himself if he doesn't look round this minute!' Walker sounded alarmed now, and the other two saw what he meant at once. Soledad suppressed a cry of horror.

Two pirates walking just behind Griffin had obviously noticed that one of their number didn't belong there. Now one of them drew his dagger, while the other reached out as he walked along to seize the boy's shoulders.

In the fraction of a second Soledad was on her feet. She took off from the bridge and jumped. Still in the air, she knocked the weapon out of one of the pirates' hands, and struck with her own. Walker and Buenaventure landed to right and left of her and instantly went on the attack. They had jumped into the middle of Tyrone's bodyguard, almost ten paces from where Griffin was just falling to the ground.

Soledad had no time to look for the boy. She had her hands full striking down as many pirates and cannibals as she could, before their adversaries realised that they were facing not an army but only three desperate fighters.

Buenaventure fought like the others, with the difference that the force of his great serrated sword was several times that of Soledad's blade. He leaped to the side of the narrow street over screaming men who fell to the ground, wounded, and with his left hand snatched up a beam that had come adrift in last night's fires. The top rafter of a shed that had once been built against one of the coral houses was still burning. 'Walker! Soledad! Watch out!' cried Buenaventure – and then the shed tipped over in an eruption of flames and blazing wood before collapsing on the pirate horde in a rain of fire. Suddenly most of Tyrone's men were fending off not blades but burning boards. Several bits of wood fell on Buenaventure himself, and he howled with fury. Walker was hit a glancing blow, and only Soledad escaped unhurt from the fiery inferno. Her immediate opponent was also spared, and they went on fighting amidst the flames, the screaming pirates, and the smoke that quickly enveloped everything. Spinning round, she struck the man down with her sword. In sudden panic, she looked for Walker, and saw him with his hair smoking, fighting a cannibal. Buenaventure too was on his feet again, an ugly burn on his left arm, but otherwise more or less uninjured.

But Griffin? Where was the boy?

Most of the pirates had retreated from the fire in the street to the nearby ruins. Some had gone on up the mountain. There was no sense in letting themselves be killed down here when the main fighting force of defenders was waiting on the upper rampart. Tyrone had disappeared as well.

Soledad stumbled out of the wall of smoke towards a man with fair, curly hair, who coughed wildly, suddenly recognised her, and immediately attacked.

'Bannon!' she cried as their blades struck sparks. 'It should never have come to this.'

He did not reply, but struck harder than ever, driving her several paces through the acrid vapours towards the shore.

The smoke was getting thicker and thicker. The stench burned their throats and took their breath away. But Soledad had no choice: she had to defend herself, and she was almost glad Fate had brought her face to face with Bannon. She despised him for his treachery and his willingness to hand Jolly over to Tyrone and the Maelstrom.

Bannon fought grimly and in silence. Their blades clashed again and again. He was physically stronger, but she wielded her blade faster and more skilfully. However, when he managed to parry her sword and attack his strokes were all the more brutal. Once she thought her blade would break under the weight of them, but the steel held. However, the vibration of the weapon passed up to her shoulder, so that for a moment she couldn't raise her arm.

Bannon prepared to deal the death-blow. It had once been said he smiled when he faced a defeated enemy, but not this time, and he refrained from mockery. Obviously he just wanted to bring this fight to an end as fast as he could.

Soledad groaned as she tried to raise her numb arm again and parry his stroke.

Something swished through the air. Bannon twitched, stopped for a moment, glanced down at himself and looked in bewilderment at the blade sticking out of his chest. His eyes slowly widened, his mouth opened. 'A hundred thousand hounds of hell!' he whispered. Then he collapsed as silently as he had fought, fell on his face and lay there, with an old, notched sword sticking in his back.

A figure in red-and-white trousers leaped over the body, crashed into Soledad and hugged her.

'Griffin!'

'Princess!' They were in each other's arms as if years, not just a few hours, had passed since they last met. It felt good to know he was with her again, thought Soledad.

When she let go of him he swayed. Next moment his legs gave way under him.

'Griffin?' She quickly bent over him. 'What's the matter? Are you hurt?'

He tried to smile, which made him look even wearier and more worn out. None of them had had any sleep in a long, long time, but it wasn't just exhaustion robbing him of the last of his strength.

'You're bleeding!' She carefully moved his arm aside and

looked at the dark red patch in horror. The dirty pirate shirt was drenched with blood.

'It's not deep,' he murmured. 'Not dangerous.'

Soledad wasn't listening to him. She raised her head. 'Walker! Buenaventure!' she called into the smoke. Her eyes stung, breathing was more and more difficult, but just now her thoughts were all for Griffin. 'I need one of you here!'

A shout rang through the smoke in answer, and Buenaventure came striding swiftly up, followed by Walker in disarray and covered with scratches. He had a hole burned in his shirt, but didn't seem to be seriously wounded.

'Most of them marched on,' Walker said hoarsely, coughing. 'But this smoke will kill us if we —' He stopped short when he saw the blood on Griffin's side. 'God curse it!'

The corners of Griffin's mouth twitched again, but this time it was hardly even the ghost of a smile. 'It's not bad. Just . . . hurts a little . . .'

'Here, lad.' Buenaventure moved Soledad aside and lifted Griffin off the ground very carefully, as if he weighed no more than a fly, to avoid hurting him even more.

'We must get behind the rampart,' said Soledad. 'He needs help.'

'No, I don't.'

She took no notice. 'Do you think we can make it?'

'No.' said Walker, frank as ever. 'We're behind the enemy lines here. I wouldn't be surprised if they're already fighting up on the rampart. And there are more of Tyrone's men down on the shore. As soon as the smoke's dispersed they'll be coming this way.' He looked with concern at Griffin lying in Buenaventure's muscular arms like a child. 'I'd say we should look for a place to hide and wait till our chances of getting back to the others look better. So far we've just been lucky.'

He's right, thought Soledad. Their skirmish with Tyrone's men would have gone differently if Buenaventure hadn't pulled the shed down.

'I can walk,' gasped Griffin unconvincingly.

'I'm sure you can.' Buenaventure strode away without putting him down on the ground. He carried Griffin uphill through the smoke until it was a little less thick and they could see more clearly. Soledad and Walker stopped beside him.

There was no one on the flight of steps ahead of them. From above, however, the noise of battle came to their ears. Fighting for the defensive rampart had broken out again, but this time it was between humans fighting other humans.

'Looks as if we're right between two waves of attackers,' said Buenaventure. 'The other crews from the ships will soon be following. We'd better hurry.'

They raced up the steps, climbed breathlessly over kobalin bodies and fallen defenders, and a little later they reached the poets' quarter.

The sound of shouting and marching feet swelled behind them.

'They'll be here very soon now!' whispered Walker, with an impressive curse.

'Let's get inside one of the houses.' Buenaventure was about to make for one and kick the door in, but Soledad held him back.

'Wait! A little further on.'

Walker cast a doubtful look over his shoulder. The smoke at the foot of the flight of steps was swirling strangely, swathes of it moving fast. Human figures swarmed behind it. Any moment now the first of them would break through the vapours and see the fugitives.

'Turn left!' Soledad ran on ahead. The two men could only follow her. Lying in Buenaventure's arms, Griffin gritted his teeth. In spite of his pain, and the way he was being shaken about, his eyelids were almost closing.

Soledad ran down a narrow alley, reached a crossroads, and turned uphill again. Any moment this place too would be teeming with Tyrone's men.

'Soledad! We *must* go inside somewhere!' Walker's call

almost made her change her mind, but she ran on, turned aside again, and finally stopped, breathless, outside the door of a particular house. At the end of the alley she saw some of the cannibal king's men coming.

Breathing hard, Walker came up beside her. They were outside a narrow coral facade. He knew what house it was immediately.

Panting, Buenaventure came up too and didn't even stop. 'They're right behind us!' He kicked in the door with a great crash before Soledad could point out that it wasn't locked.

The two of them followed him, but once inside Walker took Soledad's arm and held her back. 'Any special reason why you brought us here, of all places?'

She slammed the door behind them. It sprang back because the broken latch wouldn't connect. 'Tell you in a minute – help me first!'

Together, they dragged a wooden chest up against the inside of the door. If the four of them had been seen it wouldn't hold their enemies back for long, but if not then it wasn't obvious from the outside that anyone had just run into this house.

'Well?' asked Walker.

'For a start, this is taller than any of the other buildings,' said Soledad. 'You can see right down to the outer rampart

292

from the attic. I know. I was here not long ago.'

'Visiting the Worm?' Walker raised one eyebrow, but Soledad wasn't sure whether that meant he disapproved or just didn't understand.

'It's hard to explain.' She avoided his eyes. 'I saw something in the underwater city. And then I had an idea it might be something very like –'

'Quick!' growled Buenaventure. 'Come up here!'

They hadn't even noticed him running up the steps to the room at the top of the house.

Even on her way, before she could see into the attic room, Soledad noticed something wrong. But only at the top of the stairs did she realise what it was: the place was too bright.

Far too much light fell through the doorway, as if up above –

'Where's the roof?' asked Walker, as they all stumbled into the attic together.

A blue-grey void yawned above them, with plumes of smoke bathed in gold by the sunlight moving over it. The two gable walls were still standing, but apart from a few jagged remnants the sloping roof had gone.

'And where the devil is the Worm?' asked Buenaventure. He stared up at the sky for a moment longer, and then remembered Griffin in his arms. Carefully, he laid the boy down. The floor was covered with fragments of the web-like tissue in which the Hexhermetic Shipworm had been pupating. White and grey scraps were blowing around, collecting into fibrous heaps in corners or hanging like sea-spray from what remained of the roof. Buenaventure gathered up some of it with both hands and put it behind Griffin's head as a pillow.

'I'm not . . . I'm all right . . .' Griffin's voice grew fainter and fainter, and then died away entirely.

Soledad anxiously bent over the boy. 'What's the matter with him?'

'Gone to sleep, that's all,' said the pit bull man. 'Let him rest. It will relieve the pain a little at least.'

While Walker inspected the wrecked roof and searched the remnants of the silken network in vain for the Shipworm, Soledad cautiously undid Griffin's shirt and examined the wound in his side. It didn't look too bad: a row of short cuts, not deep enough to injure him seriously. He had bled freely, but not enough to kill him. The worst of it was probably the pain. The wounds were on his side above the ribs, and might well have reached the bone.

She dabbed the sleeping boy's forehead with her sleeve, and left him in the care of the pit bull man.

'Here,' said Walker, who was crouching in the far corner

of the attic looking at something on the floor in front of him. 'Look at this.'

Her eyes narrowed. 'Is that the cocoon?'

'What's left of it. There are more bits of it lying around. The wind's probably blown the rest out into the courtyard or heaven knows where.'

They were fibrous fragments of white tissue, looking rather like broken eggshell with ragged edges.

Walker prodded one of the fragments with his finger. It swayed back and forth, rustling. 'Those don't look like cut edges, do they?'

'No,' Soledad agreed. 'Looks as if the thing broke open and he slipped out by himself.'

She looked at the walls outlined against the void. It appeared as if there had been an explosion here. The pressure wave must have flung all the broken parts of the walls out, and they were probably scattered over half the surrounding area, or there would have been more remnants down in the street. The force of the blast had pulverised the roof.

'What did you mean just now?' asked Walker. 'When you said you'd had an idea about the Worm?'

With a shudder, she remembered the serpent in the underwater city, and how the sight of that strange being had convinced her that she was facing not an animal but one of the old gods of Aelenium. Even now, amidst all this destruction, she still felt that when she had looked at the dreaming Worm in his cocoon she'd sensed something very similar.

'The Worm,' she said, 'isn't a Worm. At least, that's what I think.'

'What, then?'

'A god.'

Walker looked at her without any expression at all. If he laughs, she thought, I'm going to hit him.

But Walker remained motionless, just looking at her. 'A god?' he repeated, in a hollow voice. 'Our *Shipworm*?'

'The ancient Egyptians worshipped beetles. The Indians prayed to toads. And the Indios in the jungle even venerated –'

He silenced her with a gesture. 'But he . . . I mean, he's a pain in the neck. A pest. He nearly ate my ship!'

'Other gods are supposed to have eaten *people*.' She smiled without any humour. 'Would you rather he'd done that?'

'Well, then at least I might believe you.' He quickly added, 'I mean, I do believe you . . . in a way . . . but that . . . that thing! Good heavens above!'

'Doubt is the privilege of believers,' said a voice behind them at that moment – a voice that seemed curiously familiar, and yet very different from before. 'Without belief there can be no doubt.'

Soledad and Walker spun round at the same time. Buenaventure was still holding Griffin's right hand in his huge paw, but now he raised his eyes from the boy and looked at what was hovering outside the broken roof. It rose majestically from the back yard down below, where perhaps it had been waiting, or sleeping, or shaking off the last of its dreams.

Light flooded the ruins of the attic. The four pirates were bathed in radiance. For a moment its brightness overlaid the shimmering rays of morning sunlight coming through the smoke.

'Have no fear,' said the new-born god solemnly from its aureole of bright flame. And more quietly, almost apologetically, 'Oh, striped and spotted rock-newts, I'm so hungry I could eat an entire ship.'

THE RIFT

Jolly had left the mother of the kobalins and her nest behind in the darkness beyond polliwiggle vision. As the rock disappeared into the dark, she did her best to blot it out of her memory too.

She was approaching the heart of the Rift, swimming fast and closely followed by the luminous fish, who copied every movement she made.

Kangusta had told her the way out, and Jolly had lost no time in escaping from the kobalin nest. She had left the mountain high up, through a jagged crevice near the peak, just wide enough for her shoulders to squeeze through. Yet again she realised that Kangusta must have been imprisoned down there before the rock was piled up above her. That was the extent of the power Jolly faced.

Strangely enough, the thought of it hardly alarmed her. Her mind had passed beyond intimidation long ago, and she had made her decision. She would never have thought she could reach a point where courage, despair and resignation were united. Now she felt as if other forces were finally moving her to the last square on a chessboard. The place where it would all be decided.

She hovered over the labyrinth of clefts and ravines surrounding the kobalin mountain. Deep-sea particles floated all around. The shoal of luminous fish followed her at a little distance, and she wondered rather anxiously whether the tiny creatures might attract the Maelstrom's attention. She saw none of the blind albino kobalins, although most of the crevices below her went too deep for polliwiggle vision, and she couldn't know what might be far down there. Nor did she see any trace of Munk and Aina. Presumably they had reached the source of the Maelstrom long ago.

The rocks ahead of her seemed be lower now. Perhaps the sea-bed sank further down for this last part of the way. Finally the limestone rock came to an end, giving her a view of a wide sandy plain.

Somewhere there, she sensed it, was her journey's end. It was still beyond polliwiggle vision, but she already thought she felt the current coming from it. It couldn't be the current of the whirlpool itself, or she would have been

299

crushed by its force by now. It was more of a compulsion inside her: time for this to end one way or another.

She felt she was at the peak of her powers, and for the first time sensed a faint throbbing when she put her hand on the bag of shells at her belt. Almost as if they wanted to be let out and open up to the forces of magic.

Jolly came down low over the plain. Behind her the rocks receded into darkness. There was dead grey sand around her now, stretching in all directions, smoothed out as if by a titanic hand, no doubt by the seeking currents that swept the bottom of the sea at irregular intervals.

Very gradually, something emerged from the darkness ahead. At first sight it looked like a mighty tower rotating on its own axis at incredible speed. It sprang from a structure that she recognised, though only when she looked more closely, as a gigantic white shell half buried in the ground: its two fan-shaped halves were wide open, with only their undulating edges showing above the sand. They reached from one end of polliwiggle vision to the other.

The giant shell was surrounded by a wide expanse of smaller shells, more and more of them the closer Jolly came to the centre of the Rift. Soon she was hovering over thousands of fist-sized shells, a carpet entirely hiding the sand below.

The foot of the Maelstrom, that column of raging water, was no broader than the defensive towers of the cliff-top fortresses built by the Spanish, British and French on the Caribbean islands. But facing a solid stone tower was very different from confronting one made of swirling, racing water. At its base, in the centre of the huge open shell, surged clouds of churned-up sand, the only indication that the powers of the Maelstrom were exerted on its immediate surroundings at all. Jolly could still feel no physical current, only the pull on her thoughts, as if the sight of the Maelstrom had set off an almost irresistible urge to swim closer to it.

Although the foot of the funnel-shaped Maelstrom might be narrow compared to the miles-wide whirlpool where it came to the surface of the sea, the sight of this swirling column of water was enough to arouse boundless awe in Jolly. On her way through the depths she had often imagined what it would be like to see the Maelstrom. Now at last she knew: the sight took her breath away, making her feel tiny and powerless, and the impatient throbbing in the bag at her belt made no difference.

Her shells were clamouring to be set free at last. The magic inside them was protesting wildly, and Jolly wondered uneasily whether, in view of the giant shell before her, their powers might not turn against her. The sea of shells down below made her doubt her own abilities. Did the Maelstrom suck the magic out of all those thousands upon thousands of shells to increase its own strength?

She saw no kobalins anywhere, no fortifications or other defences. This was not a fortress where Aina lived as if in an enchanted castle. How many magic pearls had risen from these shells, and what power did they give their new owner? Well, for one thing the force needed to subdue the ocean itself, shaping it into a consuming whirlpool. For another, power over the structure of worlds and strength to open a portal between them.

Yet, and Jolly was convinced of this, the real Aina had ceased to exist thousands of years in the past. The powers that the girl had once conjured up had consumed her long ago. Like a snake biting its own tail. All that was left was the head: her mind, a mixture of hopes, memories and thoughts of revenge. Out of them, the Maelstrom had made that bodiless copy of Aina, sending it to meet them and beguile Munk.

A figure emerged from the tall clouds of dust at the centre of the shell, where the two halves joined and the funnel of the Maelstrom spiralled upwards. The figure was so vanishingly small against its breathtaking background that Jolly almost failed to see it.

She hovered where she was. She had come here to . . . well, to do what? Unpack her shells, lay them out in a small circle, and hope that the faint trace of magic at her command would work down here?

The figure was floating towards her only a few feet above the carpet of shells. Now Jolly saw that it was Munk, untouched by the suction of the Maelstrom behind him.

'Have you come to fight me?' she called. Her voice was shaking, but there was no point in trying to hide her uncertainty. He knew her far too well not to be aware of what she was feeling.

'I'm sorry to see you like this,' he said as he came closer, hardly moving, as if he were carried by a current.

'See me like what?'

'Alone. And so vulnerable.'

'Hurt, Munk – not vulnerable.'

He put his head slightly on one side – almost as Aina had done – while his fingertips danced around one another, playing a casual game. 'Hurt because Aina shut you up?'

'Hurt because betrayal is far worse than defeat,' she replied.

She had fully expected to find that he had fallen victim to the influence of the Maelstrom by the time she got here, and it confused her to see that he still looked the same as before. Not pale or sickly, no glowing eyes or any of the marks of possession that she had imagined. Far from it – Jolly had to admit that it was more painful to see him happy and full of strength than to face a tired, distressed boy who had been unable to defend himself when Aina took him over.

He was here of his own accord. What he said, what he was going to do – it was all done of his own free will and from his own convictions.

Jolly was so upset that she almost forgot to swim, and for a moment dropped to the bottom of the sea. Shells shattered under her feet. She quickly pushed off, and struggled to come to rest floating in the water again.

'Don't be frightened,' said Munk. 'If she had wanted to kill you she'd have done it by now. She's told me so. She wants you as an ally, Jolly, not an enemy.'

'What did she promise you to make you fall into her trap?'

'Promise?' For a moment he looked genuinely surprised. 'Do you really think she had to promise me anything? She just explained how necessary all this is. The inevitability of the whole thing, never mind what you or I could do about it.'

'Then it's much worse than I feared,' she said

contemptuously. 'You haven't simply given up – you've gone over to her side! To *its* side, the side of the Maelstrom.'

'You still see this as a war, don't you? Good on one side and evil on the other.'

'No.' She had learned from the words of the Water Weavers, and she knew by now that it wasn't as simple as that. 'But killing or enslaving others can't be good, Munk. You know it. Or has the Maelstrom blotted out your memory along with your conscience? It murdered your parents. Have you really forgotten that?'

She saw that her words had gone home. Good: she'd meant them to. He floated closer. Now there were thirty paces between them.

'That was a mistake,' he said, with an obvious effort. Or was she just imagining it? 'An accident,' he added.

She stared at him, open-mouthed, and couldn't reply for several seconds. An accident? The murder of his parents? She shook her head, and put her right hand to her shells in the bag. There was hardly enough room for them in the narrow leather container, and she had to be careful not to harm any of the fragile little things. A pleasant warmth rose through her arm and reached her ribcage.

'You're not yourself any more,' she said, bemused. 'What makes you think it could be a good idea to bring the masters of the Mare Tenebrosum into our world? For heaven's sake, what seems to you right about that?'

Munk said nothing for some time. His features were twitching. 'The Mare Tenebrosum doesn't have much to do with all this any more,' he said at last. 'It began with the Mare, but it won't end with it.'

He stopped not ten paces away from her. They were at the same level above the sea of shells now. The column of water that was the Maelstrom was rotating endlessly on its axis behind Munk, a tireless spinning-top that refused to run down. It rumbled and seethed, but the roaring sound wasn't loud enough to drown out their words. Down here the laws of nature hadn't just slipped askew, they had been suspended entirely.

'Aina has explained it all,' said Munk. He looked nervously around. 'The masters of the Mare Tenebrosum made her into the Maelstrom so that she could act as a gateway into our world for them. But when the Maelstrom of that time was defeated by the other polliwiggles, the masters didn't lift a finger to help her. Instead they stood by and watched her being imprisoned. Time means nothing to such beings, not even a few thousand years, and they decided to wait. They didn't have to endure the torments being suffered by the Maelstrom – or rather Aina.'

For heaven's sake, thought Jolly, that little cow has completely turned his head.

He went on. 'Then, when the Maelstrom gained power again and broke out of prison, the masters of the Mare commanded it to serve them. But it decided to make itself ruler of this world – instead of being useful to those who made it and then betrayed it.' He gestured to her. 'Aina was only acting in self-defence, Jolly. And the same thing nearly happened to you too. Remember how you and Griffin were stranded on the shape-shifter's island? That wasn't just coincidence. The shape-shifter was obeying the Mare. And its bridge was made solely to take you to its masters. With you they'd have been able to make a new Maelstrom, a new gateway, this time to their own world.' He lowered his voice. 'You were lucky. Aina sent you the kobalins to destroy the bridge just in time. That was all that saved you.'

Jolly stared at him. She could see the bridge in her mind's eye – and with it the indescribable view of that sea of darkness. What had the shape-shifter said to her at the time, on the island? *You're expected.*

Now its words made sense. She shuddered. Suppose the kobalins hadn't attacked? Would she have been the one to open the gate to the masters then? Would she have brought disaster on the world? Munk was right: ultimately, the kobalins had saved her from that fate.

She instinctively retreated slightly. Munk did the same.

Jolly's eyes flashed at him. 'Don't you understand what's going on here, Munk? Don't you see what the Maelstrom is doing to us? We're going to suffer the fate of the first polliwiggles! It turned one of them into the Acherus – the monster that killed your parents!' She thrust the words at him like a blade. 'It was once like us. So was the creature commanding the kobalin armies. The Maelstrom wants to do the same to you and me. We're to help it, but not as equals – as slaves with no will of our own.' In her anger she could almost have clenched her hand into a fist round the shells in their bag. 'Do you want to be like the Acherus? Do you really?'

Munk was silent for a moment, as if mentally listening to new whispers, to an answer that someone else was giving him.

'I . . .' he began, and then fell silent again as a second figure appeared behind him, emerging from the turbulent column of the Maelstrom as if born from the water itself. At first Aina's body was transparent, but as she came closer it gained colour and substance.

Jolly felt as if the sea around her were freezing, she was

suddenly so cold. Yet she had expected that sooner or later someone . . . *something* like the figure of the girl would appear.

Aina's likeness floated out of the Maelstrom, and the swirling wall of water opened like a curtain for a split second. Through the gap, Jolly caught a brief glance inside the column, straight to the soul of the Maelstrom.

There was nothing there but darkness, an empty chasm as black as night.

'Munk!' cried Jolly in pleading tones, before Aina was close enough to stop her. The sea of shells on the sea-bed below seemed to be vibrating as if an earthquake were beginning to stir beneath them. 'She'll make us both her slaves. You can't want that.'

The girl who was the Maelstrom was only a stone's throw away now. She didn't have to swim to come closer; she was riding a current that the turbulent column of water had sent out like a gust of wind.

With a single stroke, Jolly swam across to Munk. At first he looked as if he might retreat before her, but then he went on hovering where he was, meeting her gaze with obvious difficulty. There was a pleading look in his eyes, but she wouldn't acknowledge it. She didn't understand it, didn't understand *him*.

She took his arm. 'Munk, please . . . she'll make

something like the Acherus out of you. Out of us both.'

'She's shown me that I belong here,' he said in subdued tones. 'We're polliwiggles. The sea made us. And more veins of magic meet here than anywhere else.'

No, thought Jolly, that's not true. She had seen the place that the veins came from with her own eyes, and it wasn't here. Nowhere could so many strands of magic come together as among the looms of the three old women at the bottom of the sea. But how could she make him understand that? He hadn't been there with her; he didn't know the Water Weavers. When she looked at the dreadful spectacle behind him, it seemed impossible to explain that even greater powers held sway in another part of the ocean, and it was the polliwiggles' true place of origin.

Aina stopped beside them. Her lips opened, and Jolly could see a mouth cavity, teeth and a tongue forming behind them. She made them when she needed them and not a moment sooner.

Why was the Maelstrom using its power so sparingly? Didn't it have enough? Or had it exhausted much of its strength in the battle for Aelenium? Was that why it was so anxious to make use of their polliwiggle gifts? Taking a deep breath, Jolly drew water into her lungs. She might still be alive solely because the Maelstrom needed her.

310

Jolly was getting more and more worked up, but she tried not to show it.

'Why do you resist?' asked Aina, and even her voice became really her own only as she was speaking, when the syllables turned from something vague and blurred into a girl's voice. Was that carelessness because there was no more need to deceive Jolly? Or did Aina really lack the power to do it?

A fascinating idea, but it scared Jolly too. If her enemy was in a hurry to win her over, it would strike suddenly and brutally, without waiting for her to defend herself.

Aina's features moved into a smile. 'Munk has realised that his place is here at my side. So why resist? Humans don't want polliwiggles like us. They hate us.'

'You say that because they threw you out all that time ago.'

'And what about all the other polliwiggles they killed? Why are you two the last left? Don't you see how stupid human beings are? They never look far enough; their minds are closed to the unknown. They fear what they don't understand. They whisper about you behind your back; they point at you and wonder how to get rid of you when you've served your purpose. You may try not to notice it, but secretly you know the truth.'

Jolly shook her head. 'They took Munk and me in and treated us as people like themselves.'

'You're wrong,' said Aina, and looked at Munk as if expecting confirmation.

After a moment's hesitation, he nodded. 'They always told us we were different. They stared at us in the streets of Aelenium and whispered when we passed.'

Jolly's eyes grew cold. 'And you *enjoyed* it, if I remember correctly. For heaven's sake, Munk! You even tried to keep me in Aelenium when I wanted to go looking for Bannon.'

'Because . . .' His voice dropped. 'Because I didn't want to stay there on my own.'

'Because he was afraid. Wasn't that it, Munk?'

He hesitantly nodded. 'Yes.'

'You need never be alone again here in the Rift. You'll be with your own kind.'

Jolly kicked in the water to take herself a little way from Aina and Munk. 'Munk,' she said pleadingly. 'She's lying! She made the other two polliwiggles who followed her into her own creatures. Monsters!'

He did not reply, just bit his lower lip in silence.

Aina changed her strategy, and now her features became harsher. A note of command came into her voice, warning Jolly that the time for talking had nearly run out. The

Maelstrom was in a hurry, for reasons at which she could still only guess.

'Aelenium has fallen,' said Aina. 'There's not much left for you up there now.'

'If that was so you wouldn't need us,' replied Jolly, suppressing a tremor in her voice. Suppose Aina were telling the truth? It just couldn't be true. 'Aelenium is still fighting. I know it is.'

'You saw what happened to the first starfish city. It was ruined; it broke into a thousand pieces. Many lost their lives, and it will be the same again. Long ago they tried to hold me captive for the first time, and they almost failed – but I destroyed the city.' Aina put out her hand as if to touch Munk. 'Show her whose side you are on, Munk.'

Jolly pushed her fingers in among the shells in the bag at her belt, a handful of little shells rubbing against each other, and at the moment useless. She'd have had to lay them out and then conjure up a pearl – and all that would take far too long.

'Don't do it,' she said to Munk.

'He wants you to stay with him,' said Aina. 'Don't you, Munk?'

'Yes,' he said.

'You can make her,' Aina told him. 'You only have to want to.'

'You tried that once before,' said Jolly. 'You tried to make me stay, remember?' Perhaps it was a mistake to remind him of his defeat on board the *Carfax*. But who cared? It hurt her to see him like this. In spite of all their quarrels he was still Munk. The farmer's boy who had fished her out of the water and saved her life. Her friend.

Aina lost patience. 'Do it!' she hissed at Munk. 'Or I'll do it myself!'

Jolly looked around. The shoal of luminous fish was darting about behind her against the grey of the deep sea. She couldn't expect any help from them this time. She'd have to think of something for herself. She looked down at the endless carpet of shells on the sea-bed. Her thoughts went to the depths, down under the empty shells.

What she sensed there shook her. There was no magic left in those shells at all, no sign of any life of their own, no remains of their former strength. The Maelstrom had sucked the magic out of them, taken all their power and misused it for its own diabolical purposes. What Jolly had thought was an immense collection of magical shells was really a graveyard. All these shells had lost their magic forever. Grief clutched at her heart. She felt as if she herself had been cheated of the most valuable thing she owned, gnawed to the bone. And she realised that this was what faced her and Munk: the Maelstrom would consume their gifts and their strength, leaving nothing behind. It wasn't they themselves who would take the place of the Acherus and the kobalin commander, but their empty husks. That was why the servants of the Maelstrom relied on new bodies. Their own strength wasn't even enough for them to move around.

And what was hovering in front of Jolly wasn't Aina herself any more, only a likeness spewed out by the Maelstrom to deceive and mock them.

Jolly let her thoughts go deeper, below the layer of shells, to the real bottom of the Rift. And there at last she found what she was looking for.

The magic strands. The ancient, powerful network of magic veins made by the Water Weavers. Branching a thousand times, it passed through the Rift, intertwining and interweaving over and over again.

When the *Carfax* sank the Weavers had brought Jolly to them through a tunnel of water that carried her as swiftly as a stormy wind to the place where they sat beneath the sea. Could they do it again? Even if it was only to save her from the Maelstrom – and from Munk?

She tried to pick up one of the magic veins in her mind,

but then she was suddenly seized herself and torn away from the strands. Her link to the Weavers' yarn tore like a rope stretched too taut, shot up as fast as a whiplash from the depths, and faded in the twilight of the Rift. Jolly shook herself. Then her view cleared.

She saw Munk sitting cross-legged on the ground in the middle of the burnt-out sea of shells. He had closed his eyes and was concentrating hard.

And she saw something else.

She had been wrong to assume that all the shells beneath her were dead. There were still some, just a few, that were seething with power. Munk's shells! And among them, the largest and most beautiful of all – the shell that Aina had given him.

Munk must have set them out in a pattern on the ground before Jolly ever arrived at the foot of the Maelstrom. He and Aina had enticed Jolly into the middle of the circle. A glowing pearl had formed beneath her feet, just above the ground, hissing and crackling with power – and brighter than any pearl Jolly had yet seen. Only with the help of Aina's ancient shell could Munk conjure up something so powerful.

Aina smiled, and now at last all innocence had left her face. Her features distorted, twisted and turned, formed a whirlpool leading straight inside her skull. Jolly stared at her, and at the same time tried to tear her eyes away from the sight. But Munk's powers held her as fast as if he had enveloped her in a coat of ice that paralysed her. The glowing pearl below her grew larger and larger. Now it was touching her feet, and as it swelled around Jolly it climbed up her body.

It's swallowing me! Jolly thought. But not even her panic gave her the strength she'd have needed to resist.

She wanted to say something, but her mouth wouldn't obey her. Her jaws and tongue were numb. Her eyes could look only straight ahead, into the rotating throat made from Aina's features.

Bright sparks of light appeared to the left and right of Jolly's field of vision and were drawn past her. The Water Weavers' luminous fish had been caught in the current of the whirlpool that was Aina's skull, rushed helplessly towards it – and were swallowed up. Their light went out in the depths of that grey whirlpool, and Jolly felt a sharp pain as if someone had stuck a needle between her ribs. Then the light of the pearl reached her face and enveloped it. Now Jolly was caught at the centre of the glowing globe.

She cried out desperately, with blazing anger and hatred for the Maelstrom, with infinite fury against Munk, who was too weak or too stupid or just too offended by her love for Griffin to listen to her any more.

He didn't even seem to notice the change that had come over Aina. Nothing was left of the girl's body but a swirling spiral of currents racing around itself. At its far end this whirlpool became a lashing, worm-like, watery shape that wound its way towards the mighty column of the Maelstrom and merged with it. Soon the huge pearl in which Jolly crouched, caught there, would reach the column too. She watched helplessly as she was drawn towards the whirlpool and straight into the Maelstrom itself.

WHEN GODS WEEP

The flood of light pouring over the ruined roof of the house dazzled them all. Even as the Worm – or what he had turned into – spoke to them, Soledad still couldn't make out what their friend had really become. Only slowly, as whatever the being they now saw went on cursing and complaining of hunger, asking plaintively if there wasn't a good stout tree trunk anywhere here for a god on the point of starvation, did her eyes get used to the brilliance and the blaze, and she saw what was hovering at the centre of the light.

On emerging from the cocoon, the Worm had become a winged snake, its mighty body coiling constantly in the air, borne up by wings broad enough to cover the whole attic. Their beating sent moist, warm air over the ruins of the house, swirling remnants of the silken cocoon up like snowflakes. The creature's scales gleamed dark purple, almost black, and its wings were the same colour. They were densely feathered, like the wings of a bird of prey, and grew from the upper part of the snake's body, which must measure some twenty paces from end to end, although the creature's coiling and lashing out in the air made an accurate estimate difficult.

Walker cried out, and Buenaventure moved before the defenceless Griffin to protect him. But Soledad kept calm. She was in as much turmoil as her friends, but she had one advantage over them: she had met a being like this before. It had not been winged, but it was just as gigantic. Even the triangular reptilian head was like the head of the sea-serpent from the underwater city. If she hadn't known better she would have thought that the creature in the depths below Aelenium had grown wings to carry it to the surface.

But for all the snake's size and elegance, it was obviously still the Hexhermetic Shipworm speaking to them. God or no god, the creature's cursing and swearing reminded Soledad of a naughty child. 'By Tetzcatlipoca's tell-tale breath, isn't there *anyone* here to bring a new-born snake god a good helping of wood?' The snake fell silent, seemed to think about it, and then heaved a sigh of self-pity. 'I ate everything I could find down in the yard, but that wouldn't have been enough even for a worm, let alone a –' It broke off again, for now its slit-like snake's eyes had seen Griffin. The pointed head shot forward over Soledad, easily dodged past Buenaventure, and bent solicitously over the boy. At first the pit bull man looked as if he were going to lay into the snake god with both fists, but then he took a deep breath and left the snake to do as it wished.

'Boy!' exclaimed the creature in concern. Its voice had a slight lisp, and was remarkably like the Shipworm's, although much stronger. 'What's the matter with you?' The body of the snake moved in a curve, automatically looping around Buenaventure. The narrow pupils turned on Soledad again. 'Not dead, is he?'

'No,' she said. 'He's not dead. Just exhausted and wounded.'

The reptilian head jerked back, and then the amber eyes were looking down at Griffin again. The light undulating around the mighty body of the snake now embraced Buenaventure and the motionless boy too. Soledad almost expected the radiance to heal Griffin, but when the snake uncoiled itself, undoing the loop around the pit bull man (who was cursing freely), Griffin hadn't woken up. The cuts in his side where the blood had congealed were still dark red.

'Where's the girl?' asked the snake. 'Where is Jolly?'

'Still in the Rift,' said Soledad. At least, so she hoped.

'The Rift . . . of course.' The creature's voice sounded thoughtful now, as if it could retrieve only fragmentary memories of what had happened before it pupated.

Soledad saw Walker frowning. 'By Morgan's beard, what's that supposed to be?' he asked, not very tactfully, pointing to the winged snake. The question was meant for no one in particular, but then he planted himself in front of the creature, chin raised, put his hands on his hips and looked up at the gigantic head. 'What's this you've turned into, Worm? Looks to me like something I'd expect to find under a stone.'

'Walker,' Soledad gently reproved him.

'Zzzzsssss,' hissed the snake. The forked tongue shot out, flicked through the empty air and disappeared between the scaly jaws again. 'It would take a bigger stone than you could lift – I wouldn't like you to do yourself an injury, my friend.'

Was that a warning? No, thought Soledad, hardly. In his old shape the Hexhermetic Shipworm had been greedy, deceitful and thoroughly self-centred, but a good heart used to beat in his . . . well, for want of a better word, his breast.

'I am the Great Snake,' said the creature, and sounded almost awe-inspiring now. 'I fly on the winds between the worlds. I consume the enemies of the Ancient People.'

322

Soledad knew the myths of the Indio snake god told by the Caribbean islanders. And she had seen drawings and reliefs of the winged snake in the ruins of the jungle temple of Yucatan, where her father had once taken her with him many years ago. Now she was wondering whether the islanders' mythical deity really was the same as the creature facing them. That seemed incredible. But having to accept that the god and the Shipworm were one and the same was outlandish anyway.

'Consume their enemies.' Walker repeated the snake's words. 'Sounds a good idea to me.'

The head of the snake moved up and down, but it was hard to say whether that was meant to be a nod.

'Can you get Griffin behind the rampart?' asked Soledad.

A strong wind caught her and sent her hair dancing around her face. But this time it wasn't the snake's wings stirring up the air on the roof of the house.

'We'll do that,' d'Artois called down from his ray. The creature's angular silhouette darkened the sky above them, but cast no shadow because the attic was bathed in the light of the snake. No one had noticed the ray coming down from above, they were all so spellbound by the being that had emerged from the cocoon.

Two more flying rays followed the captain, manned by

riders and marksmen. The brightness of the snake god was reflected in the coral and shell studs adorning their black leather uniforms. The soldiers stared in alarm at the creature in the middle of the light. One of the marksmen was aiming a rifle at the snake, but d'Artois quickly raised a hand and he lowered his weapon again.

'I've seen stranger things in this city than a winged snake,' he said. Soledad shuddered to think what creatures the captain might have met during his years in Aelenium. Beings even older and larger than the sea-serpent in the underwater city?

She had an idea. 'You knew what the Worm was going to turn into!' She was speaking to d'Artois, but as she spoke she pointed to the flying snake.

'Not when he arrived,' the captain replied. 'But when he began pupating . . . well, let's say Aelenium can have a remarkable effect on its inhabitants. It brings out qualities in some of us that might have remained hidden anywhere else.'

This was such an accurate observation that they all dropped the subject, and even Walker refrained from saying any more. For what d'Artois had said applied not just to the Worm, but in a way to every one of them.

Noise rose from the street below the riders of the flying rays. The encounter in the air above the house had attracted the enemy's attention by now, and Tyrone's troops launched a second wave of attack. Shots rang out, and one of the rays shook itself as a bullet hit it from underneath. In an animal of such a size a single hit wasn't necessarily fatal, but several of them would send the gigantic beast falling out of the air.

D'Artois shouted orders, and the three rays fanned out at once. As always, their movements were ponderous, their reactions leisurely. The marksmen opened fire – yet it was not they who averted the immediate danger.

Like lightning, the winged snake shot forward, turning past the rays in flight as they drifted apart, raced over the edge of the ruined attic and dived steeply down.

Terrifying screams rose from many throats in the street below. But when Soledad overcame her paralysis, ran to the edge of the roof with the others and looked down, the fight was already over – if what had happened could be called a fight at all. The snake had mowed down the army of pirates and cannibals in a matter of seconds. Soledad had gooseflesh when she saw the remains of a body falling to the depths from both sides of the snake's mouth.

There was no second attack from below. If other men from Tyrone's fleet had seen what happened, they were keeping their distance. However, Soledad doubted whether there had been many witnesses. The snake's attack had been swift and devastating, and from a distance smoke still hid the view.

Noticeably paler all of a sudden, d'Artois gave a brief order to one of his men, who brought his ray down. Buenaventure helped to get Griffin securely in the saddle between the soldiers. The boy was muttering but still not fully conscious. The ray took off again and carried him away, up the mountain and towards the fighting on the rampart. Soledad, Walker and Buenaventure mounted the other two rays, and soon they were all flying over the coral gables of Aelenium, making for the upper defensive wall.

The winged snake followed a little way behind them. It had not spoken again since its attack on Tyrone's men. The light hovering around the snake was gradually fading, as if it too was a part of the magical rebirth.

It seemed that the Worm's transformation was not yet complete.

The Ghost-Trader did not see the companions setting out from the rampart. He had gone on to the library balcony to watch the course of the battle when the smoke briefly cleared. The attackers swarmed through the streets of the starfish city like termites, and it was this sight that finally brought him to his decision.

'It is wrong,' said the Ghost-Trader, 'perhaps even stupid and irresponsible. But I will do what must be done.' He had spoken aloud, for his next step was too weighty and fateful for him to confide it to the silent grave of his thoughts.

He stood out there alone, with flakes of ash blowing round him on the winds while the noise of battle raged on far, far below. He was in despair, and now he could no longer manage to hide it.

Forefather was still in the library with the books, the thousands upon thousands of them that had long been much closer to his heart than the human race he once created. His mind had suffered over all these years, beginning after the fall of the first starfish city. Or was it even earlier? It was not an obvious decline, nothing that showed in the old man's words or actions; he had been passive for the last few thousand years, and that had hardly changed. Instead, it was a vague aura of downfall and death pervading the halls of books. And as there was nothing else here that could die, there could be no doubt who that aura came from.

One way or another, everything was making towards its end.

The Maelstrom was about to consume the world. And if it did not, then the risen gods would do it. The Ghost-Trader had made up his mind to wake the spirits of those deities that had once withdrawn to Aelenium and perished there, forgotten by mankind. He could think of no other option than to set disaster against disaster. Jolly and Munk must have reached the Rift by now, but there was no sign that they had overcome the Maelstrom. The defenders of Aelenium had paid a high price to gain time for the polliwiggles.

But now that respite had run out. Aelenium would fall to the cannibal king, and with him the Maelstrom would achieve its aim. It was a very long time since the masters of the Mare Tenebrosum had been the threat, as the Trader once assumed. The Maelstrom had used them to extend its power, but it had no intention of acting as their gateway. This world belonged to the Maelstrom now, and it would shape it as it liked.

That meant a world without human beings. The girl Aina would be revenged on her own race.

The Ghost-Trader had not decided to take this step because he shared Forefather's weariness and indifference. The fate of mankind wasn't a game. He had lived among human beings too long to believe anything else. And if he was now going to do the only thing he still could, it was because he was desperate and helpless – perhaps for the first time in his immeasurably long existence.

He breathed in the stench of war once more, like a warning that he must not weaken. Then he went back into the library. His black parrots were fluttering somewhere high in the coral dome, but not even they could comfort him now.

'Have you decided?' asked Forefather, looking up from a book in which the writing had faded long ago. He knew the words that once covered its pages by heart.

'I'll do it,' said the Ghost-Trader.

Forefather closed the book and rose. The sound echoed in the hall like a cannon shot. 'I won't go with you,' he said wearily. And he paused for a moment before he spoke again. 'This is where my way ends.'

The Ghost-Trader nodded. 'I know. You can't help me.'

Forefather shook his head. 'That's not what I mean,' he said.

The Ghost-Trader was alarmed, but Forefather gestured to him to be quiet. 'I am like the writing on this paper.' He pointed to the book of blank pages that he had just closed. 'I faded away a long time ago, without even noticing. It seems as if the writing were still there because we know the words by heart, you and I and a few of the human beings in this city. But the fact is,' he said, and took a deep breath, 'the fact is that no one can read this book or me any more.'

The Ghost-Trader was about to protest, but Forefather stopped him with another gesture. 'Mind you don't say I'm still needed here.' Vehement as the words sounded, the old man was smiling gently. 'I made this world, that's true, but I was never able to protect it – not against itself or dangers from outside. My place is no longer here. Let me go, old friend, before I have to see the end with my own eyes.'

'You want me to –'

'I am asking you to do it.'

The Ghost-Trader stepped back and held the edge of a table with one hand. His elbow knocked against a stack of books and sent it tumbling. Neither of the two men even looked at the heavy volumes as they crashed to the floor in a cloud of dust, to lie there like dead doves with their wings spread.

'Only you can do me this last favour,' said Forefather urgently. 'If I could once have done it myself, that time is long over – I can't remember it now. But you, my friend, you can do it.'

Forefather might seem to be speaking in riddles, but the Ghost-Trader understood every word. His friend's meaning was as clear to him as if someone had cut it into glass with a diamond. And the sound was equally painful in his ears.

'You're asking a lot.'

'No,' said Forefather. 'Only determination.'

'More than that. You are –'

'Old.'

'So are we all.'

'Old and faded. And as good as forgotten. They like to venerate something that they believe is me. The nameless creator, the father of all, the word at the beginning of time. But that is not really me. They have forgotten the truth, and soon I shall be like all the other forgotten gods that I once made myself. I shall dwindle.'

'You want me to turn you into a story? Do what I did for Munk's mother?' asked the Ghost-Trader in a voice that shook. 'But that's like killing you!'

'No. You'll be giving me a future, if this world still holds such a thing. Do it, my friend.'

'But it's wrong.'

Forefather smiled and shook his head. 'How could stories be wrong? You know better than that. I'm asking you. And afterwards –'

'You will live on as a story,' said the Ghost-Trader in hollow tones. Perhaps Forefather was right. What were they in human minds, what were the gods but stories?

Forefather read his thoughts. 'I knew you would understand.' Without waiting for an answer, he sat back in his chair and placed his right hand on the cover of the book, as if he felt closer than ever to the empty pages inside it. 'Go round behind me,' he said, and closed his eyes.

The Ghost-Trader still hesitated. Then he mastered his feelings, stepped back behind Forefather and put both hands on his friend's shoulders. Tears gathered in his one eye, and before long they were pouring down his face. It was the second time he had wept within a few minutes. Hundreds of years had gone by, and he had never shed a tear, but now his tears fell freely on Forefather's shoulder and were soaked up by his robe.

'I make you into a story,' he said gently. 'You will be a story in which light comes out of darkness. In which nations are born and die. In which there are suffering and injustice, but happiness and great joy as well. A story of birth and death, of rise and fall, of the constant hope of a new beginning. Of fathers and sons, spirits and eternal life. And of those you made, who will tell each other this story, for they are a part of it and one with it forever.'

The frail body did not collapse or even move. But when the Ghost-Trader carefully raised his hands from Forefather's shoulders and came round in front of him, he saw that life had gone out of the old man's body like a young bird leaving its nest. And with it the story of Forefather flew out into the world, to be told and heard and told again.

'Goodbye, my friend,' whispered the Trader, leaning forward to kiss the old man's forehead. 'Yours was a hard way, but it is easier now, for it goes on elsewhere without burdens and guilt and grief.' And he buried his face in his hands and wept until his tears were exhausted.

Then he climbed to the highest point of the city, the place where Aelenium almost met the sky. As he climbed, he brought the silver circlet out from under his robe. His fingertips passed over the metal, feeling the invisible currents of power.

He did not look back at Forefather when he left the library. He thought he could hear a thousand voices in the distance, all telling the same story, and with that it came true.

THE OLD RAY

Like a distant rumbling, the sound of battle made its way
into Griffin's consciousness. First it was a hollow rushing
and roaring, like wind blowing against the sides of a ship by
night and making the sails flap as if they were ghosts. Then
he made out voices, shouts, the clash of blades, the sound of
pistols and rifle fire.

Griffin woke with a start. He was lying on the hard
floor of a building among the groans of the wounded, who
had been laid side by side here, as if in a field hospital,
most of them on blankets, some, like him, on the hard,
polished floor.

Someone had put some old clothes under his head. The
air was humid and heavy; the mingled odours of blood,
sweat and mortal fear gave off a rancid stench.

Griffin hauled himself up and staggered to his feet, still
dazed. As if bemused, he moved towards the door. He had

to be careful not to stumble over the other men – and a few women too – lying on the floor. A doctor bending over a wounded man in blood-soaked bandages just cast Griffin an exhausted glance, and then turned back to the patient, who needed his help more.

The wound in Griffin's side hurt, mainly because he had stood up too suddenly. He told himself he wasn't seriously injured, and felt ashamed of himself, being brought here for a scratch like that.

Had he been so badly weakened? He could hardly remember. In his mind's eye, he saw Soledad leaping down from a coral bridge into the middle of Tyrone's bodyguard. Buenaventure and Walker had been there too. But then what? A desperate battle. Acrid smoke. And a bright light with something moving in it. Something that looked like a gigantic snake.

Yes, he remembered the snake. And the plumage of its wings.

Very vaguely, he also remembered men holding him steady on the back of a ray while the turmoil of a battle passed by below. Then nothing. That hadn't been sleep, it had been unconsciousness.

As he staggered out of the door into the open air, more pictures surfaced in his mind. The kobalins in the water.

The shape-shifter falling apart before him into thousands of tiny beetles. And then Jasconius rising from the deep with his mouth open to swallow the jellyfish boy.

Jasconius, who had sacrificed himself for Griffin and defeated the kobalin commander.

He went out into the street, and was immediately in the middle of the tumult that reigns behind the lines in a battle: figures scurrying about like ants; the wounded being carried away from the fighting, many silent, others screaming. A few men had lost their nerve and were running frantically back and forth, muttering disjointedly or bursting into tears.

He looked in vain for his friends. One of the larger city squares lay ahead of him. Dealers had once sold their wares here on stalls or in tents, goods brought by sea from Haiti or the islands of the Antilles. Even in those last tense days before the invasion there had been bustling crowds here, and a pleasant aroma of spices and exotic foodstuffs.

Today it was full of wounded or exhausted combatants snatching a moment's rest. The real fighting was going on quite close, where three wide streets led into the square.

Griffin turned and looked up at the peak of the mountain, and could see no smoke rising there. In that case, at least the upper third of the city was still intact.

Suddenly the dust on the ground around him swirled up,

and a mighty shadow landed in the square beside him.

'Griffin!' cried d'Artois from the saddle of his ray. 'On your feet again, I see.'

'Yes, captain. How bad is it?'

D'Artois looked as tired as everyone else fighting in this battle, but a touch of what Griffin was alarmed to recognise as resignation showed in his face too. 'Not good,' said the captain. Behind him, his marksman was using the brief pause to reload his guns.

When he woke up, in those strange, hazy moments where thoughts have a life of their own, one question had gone through Griffin's mind again and again. Now he put it into words. 'Why isn't the Ghost-Trader helping us?'

'What could he do, boy?'

'He could raise the ghosts of all the fallen to go on fighting on our side!'

D'Artois uttered a sound like a cross between a laugh and a bark, more likely to have come from Buenaventure. 'If it were only so simple . . . how would the ghosts be able to tell friend from foe? Believe me, there's been discussion of that notion more than once, but it's pointless. The Trader would have to tell every individual ghost who to fight. If we had a whole army of people able to conjure up ghosts and control them . . . but the Ghost-Trader on his own? Impossible.'

'Is there a ray I can ride anywhere?' Griffin looked up at the sky, where no more than a handful of the mighty creatures were flying now. Their marksmen were firing at the attackers from above.

'Most of us are fighting round on the other side of the city,' said d'Artois. 'They've breached the rampart there. Count Aristotle has fallen, and many good men with him. But we're barring Tyrone's way to the upper part of the city from the air as best we can. We've kept him off so far.' Looking over his shoulder, he saw that his marksman had finished reloading. 'Climb up, Griffin! I can drop you at one of the landing places.'

Griffin didn't wait to be asked twice. He hurried over to the ray's spread wings and climbed into the saddle between d'Artois and the marksman. 'Thanks,' he said. 'I think I can be more useful riding a ray than on the rampart.'

'We may be in desperate trouble,' said d'Artois as he guided the ray into the air, 'but we won't be defeated unless we give up hope. You're a brave fellow, Griffin. A number of us heard what you did for us out there. Perhaps there's more than a miracle behind your survival. If you can infect us all with your courage and your luck, boy, we may yet have a chance.'

Griffin had reddened at the captain's words, and now he

was glad that neither d'Artois nor his marksman could see his face.

The ray carried them a little further up the mountain, away from the square and the fighting on the rampart. Then it began to fly round the coral cone. Griffin saw that the battle was raging around the whole city like a ring of turbulent foam. On the other side, the teeming throng fighting with swords and guns had moved a little way uphill, but a number of the rays and their riders were keeping the attackers at bay. The rampart was breached, but Tyrone's men had little chance against concentrated fire from the air. As long as the defences held elsewhere and the riders of the rays did not have to scatter, the damage down there was limited.

'Captain?' asked Griffin.

'We're nearly there. The square below us . . . you should find a ray there.'

'While I was gone, did you hear anything about Jolly?'

The soldier shook his head. 'I'm sorry.'

'No sign of her? No weakening of the Maelstrom? Or . . . oh, I don't know . . .'

D'Artois shrugged, and brought the ray down. 'We have no scouts out there now. I've no idea what would happen if the Maelstrom suddenly closed. If the mission of the polliwiggles succeeds and there are any immediate consequences for us, I should think we'd notice one way or another, wouldn't you?'

Griffin nodded, but his thoughts were elsewhere: out over the sea, above a roaring abyss full of swirling, foaming masses of water. And with a girl who faced all that on her own.

The captain let him get down into the square, and then took his ray straight up in the air again. Griffin waved to him, and then turned to the few rays lying on the north side of the little square with their wings spread. Their riders were dead or wounded, and quite a number of the rays had been wounded themselves by kobalin lances or pistol shots. He chose a ray that had suffered only a few scratches, patted its flat head, and climbed into the saddle.

'Here, catch!' called one of the grooms tending the animals. He threw Griffin a sword. 'We have no marksmen left down here. You'll have to manage on your own.'

Griffin pushed the sword into a sheath beside the saddle. With a whistle and a whispered command, he brought the ray up into the air in a tight curve. Dust swirled below him as the wide wings whipped up air above the ground.

Minutes later he was on his way to the other side of the city. From above, he took a last look back at the rampart where his friends were fighting. Then he turned the ray, flew out over the water, and rode over the ring of mist where it unravelled at the top as if it were a meadow of white grass. Below him lay the open sea.

In the distance, vapours veiled the horizon like a grey mountain range with its peaks constantly moving, rising and then falling, flowing apart and then gaining shape once more. The outlying parts of the Maelstrom would soon reach Aelenium.

'Fly as fast as you can,' he called to the ray, but it was more himself that he was urging on. 'Take me to the Maelstrom.'

Soledad ran a pirate through with her sword as he clambered up on the rampart, brandishing his own blade and sure of victory.

What a fool, she thought bitterly. We're going to be beaten by an army of fools. That made defeat yet more painful, even if the end result was the same.

Walker and Buenaventure were fighting on top of the rampart as if they had only just gone into battle with all their strength intact. But they were as exhausted as Soledad, and whatever opposition they put up to their enemies was only a last-ditch effort.

Many of the defenders had fallen, first fighting the kobalins and now in the battle against the pirates and cannibals. Word went round that parts of the rampart were already overrun on the other side of the city. Count Aristotle, who had led the defence there, had been killed, and several members of the Council with him. It was only a question of time before the first of the enemy climbed to the mountain peak and stormed the halls of refuge. What was the sense of fighting for victory on the rampart if those you were fighting for were killed by the barbaric hordes?

It was very different from the tales Soledad had heard of glorious battles when she was a girl. None of this had anything to do with honour or pride, let alone heroism.

Soledad didn't feel like a heroine when she struck an opponent down, only like someone who had gained another minute or two, and she suspected that her enemies felt the same. The cannibals, formerly stripped of humanity by rumour and legend, turned out in the end to be ordinary men fighting and dying for their cause. They were certainly an awesome sight with their war-paint and the dreadful trophies dangling from their shoulders and waists. But in a way they were like the kobalins, for they too had been driven into the battle by others.

Tyrone had mustered the support of the tribal chiefs, had joined in their rituals, respected their customs, and finally made himself their king. Now his subjects were dying in battle for him, dazzled by his promises, deluded, exploited. Victory might be theirs in the end, but at what price? The Maelstrom wouldn't distinguish between them and any other human beings. It would kill them all before they even realised how badly they had been deceived.

Meanwhile the winged snake god was wreaking havoc among them, terrifying friend and foe alike. It was due to that strange creature that the rampart still stood on this side of Aelenium. Many arrows were sticking in its scaly body, but its pointed tail, and even worse its terrible mouth, brought death to the attackers again and again.

Soledad had expected the cannibals to panic at the sight of the snake, but she had hoped too soon. When the first arrows pierced its skin, the tribal warriors lost their sense of awe and flung themselves against the creature in desperate waves. Many wounded it, some even came away with a purple feather from its wings as a trophy. But they none of them had time to enjoy their triumph.

Soledad's arm was beginning to tire, and the pain of her injuries loomed larger in her mind. Her whole body hurt, and her vision was blurring even as she fenced with an opponent. Her reserves of strength were running low.

Something must happen. Soon. Or more than just her own life would end today.

*

The stables of the flying rays in the peak of the coral mountain were deserted when the Ghost-Trader came through the great gate. Even the young rays were taking part in the battle, and all the grooms had gone down into the city with their charges, to tend wounded rays in the squares and streets. There was nothing left up here but a moist and slightly fishy smell.

It was late afternoon outside and the sun stood low in the sky. It lit up only the edge of the fifty-foot circular opening in the roof, tracing a golden ring that was reflected in the pools of water on the floor. The Ghost-Trader strode through the empty hall over to the staircase running round the vaulted walls and up to the opening. He had just climbed the first steps when his eye fell on one of the pits set around the walls.

He had been wrong when he thought they were all empty. A single animal was still there, in a pit just below the stairs, and even from the steps the Trader could tell from its leathery skin and noisy breathing that it was a very old ray, obviously too weak to fly with the others.

The Ghost-Trader hesitated for a moment, then climbed down the stairs again, went over to the pit and crouched down beside it. His knees ached; his whole

344

skeleton seemed to be creaking and groaning.

The animal lay there in the comfortable moisture, wings spread, with a gently rippling movement passing through them each time it took one of its hoarse breaths.

'Well, old fellow,' said the Trader, catching himself out, he felt, in the act of talking to himself. 'I expect you'd like to be out there with the others, wouldn't you? That's the trouble with knowing where you belong – you can't shake off the knowledge whether you want to or not.' He smiled sadly. 'I feel just the same.'

Glancing away, he looked up the stairway to the opening in the roof, which was surrounded by a plateau, the highest point in the starfish city. If he was to conjure up the ghosts of all the dead gods he must be able to see the entire city spread out beneath him, with a view of every nook and cranny where one of them had ever died.

The animal was breathing even more noisily now that it had noticed him. The Ghost-Trader didn't know whether the ray guessed who he was; hardly, he thought, for he was a god of men and not animals, and in this he and all the other gods of Aelenium were different from the three Water Weavers, who had not imposed themselves on this world but had sprung from it: from every plant, every stone, every living thing. They had been born of the dreams, wishes and needs of every fibre of the world itself – things over which Forefather had never had any real influence. He might have created the world; he had not understood it. The Ghost-Trader knew that Forefather had envied the Weavers, who were the first step the world had taken towards independence from its creator: the child breaking with the father to go its own way.

He was straightening up, with a sigh, when he saw that the ray at the bottom of the pit was moving. It beat its wings several times, with difficulty, but after several failed attempts they raised it from the ground. Water dripped from its body into the puddles as it rose from the pit until its head was level with the Trader's hand.

'Are you trying to tell me something, friend?' The Trader saw the look in the creature's black eyes. Compared to him it was still young, but for a ray it must be ancient. It was strange to think of this animal rising above its frail condition.

The ray was beating its wings very slowly, just enough to keep its heavy body in the air above the pit. Now it came a little lower down and turned its left wing towards the Ghost-Trader.

'You want me to climb on?' He thought for a moment, and then nodded. 'Why not? If you can take me up to the plateau, then please do.'

He sat on the bare back of the old ray, with no saddle, and felt once again how alike he and this animal were. He too rebelled against fate and nature, and so did the ray beneath him. A wave of emotion went through him at the thought, something almost like a bond of friendship for this brave animal.

They rose into the air through the opening in the roof. The late afternoon sunlight caught them and cast them in bronze as the ray flew forward and put the Trader down on the broad ledge of the plateau. Then, with its breath rattling, the creature lay down on the ground.

A few moments later it was dead, not from the effort but by its own wish: it had been useful one last time and then fell asleep, happy and at peace.

The Ghost-Trader crouched down again, caressed the motionless body and said a silent goodbye to it. If this encounter was a sign, it could hardly have been clearer.

Time to say goodbye to all of them here.

He stood up and looked north, towards the broad band of swirling vapour that spoke of the Maelstrom's vast extent. Ahead of it, a dark dot was moving through the air: a ray swiftly flying away from the starfish city and making for the Maelstrom, with someone on its back.

The Ghost-Trader guessed who the rider was. Griffin

must have felt that matters were approaching an end in Aelenium and couldn't bear to wait any longer, doing nothing, while Jolly wrestled with the power of the Maelstrom and had no one to rely on but herself.

If she was still alive.

With the silver circlet in his hand, he went to the outer rim of the plateau and walked once all around it. As he did so, he looked past the plumes of smoke, the flocks of gulls and the ray riders, so that he could see every part of Aelenium, its rooftops and its twisting streets.

Murmuring, he began his incantation.

WHERE ALL MAGIC FADES

Jolly was hovering inside the glowing pearl, which was now just large enough to take a human being. She was curled up like a child still unborn, eyes closed, lips firmly pressed together. Warmth surrounded her, a pleasant feeling of security. She was where she had always wanted to be, in a welcoming place that filled her with happiness and peace and a sense of safety.

The magic pearl had broken through the roaring wall of the column of water and was now at the very heart of the Maelstrom, in a black abyss that no longer frightened Jolly, for the darkness only intensified the light and beauty of the pearl.

Jolly dreamed all the dreams she had had in her life over again. They were condensed into a storm of millions of images pressed into a single moment, a mighty explosion of colours, scents and sounds. Voices in her head, faces surrounding her like mosquitoes around a blazing fire. And yes, she felt she was blazing too, burning with power, caught in the storm of feelings that she had once known and were now surfacing in her again, happiness and grief and suffering and –

So much suffering.

Blinking, Jolly opened her eyes, and the light that had been dim as it shone through her eyelids blinded her like a red-hot knife. Instead of brightness, all was suddenly dark. And in that moment of blindness, when she saw absolutely nothing, she knew the truth.

She was caught. The Maelstrom had swallowed her.

The dreams turned to nightmares, no longer images but the concentrated force of all sorrows and anxieties breaking over her. Memories tormented her, not long-forgotten dream pictures but the thought of the recent past: the likeness of Aina dissolving into a rotating whirlpool and sucking her in along with the pearl. And Munk, who had conjured up the pearl, was himself blinded not by magical light but by the Maelstrom's enticements. It wasn't power he was looking for, but – and here he was like everyone else in the world, including Jolly – his place in the world and a little security.

Jolly opened her mouth and screamed, a shrill, long-drawn-out scream. It broke through the cramped surroundings of the pearl and echoed in the dense darkness.

She kicked and hit out, but it was no good. She couldn't see which way was up and which was down; there was nothing but emptiness around her. She guessed what that meant, and realised that there was still a little of the Mare Tenebrosum in the Maelstrom whether or not the whirlpool had broken away from the masters of that world. Where did the water that it sucked in go? Not to the bottom of the sea, certainly, or she couldn't have come within many miles of it. So there was still a link to the Mare, and indeed the Maelstrom itself was that link. It might live, think, plan the downfall of a whole world – but it been made as a passageway, a transition, a portal for the masters of the Mare Tenebrosum. There was something of them here, and the darkness was part of their world.

Although she couldn't be sure of it, Jolly imagined herself hovering between the worlds in the middle of a turbulent tunnel connecting the two levels of existence.

Suddenly she saw a point of light appear in the darkness, grow larger, unfold. Caught in the pearl, she had to watch as it raced towards her.

It was Munk. The burning brightness around him came

from the shell he was holding in his right hand – the shell that Aina had given him, the beautiful, dangerous thing that whispered to him when he held it to his ear.

'Don't be afraid, Jolly,' said a voice. It took her a moment to recognise it as his. He came to a halt just an arm's length away from the pearl, hovering in the middle of the darkness. His lips were moving, but not another word came out; it was as if she heard what he was saying *before* he said it, and after a while she realised that the pearl was the reason. The glowing globe holding her captive broke and distorted time; what she heard might be spoken at exactly the same moment, but what she saw was actually happening a little earlier. In her present situation that seemed an insignificant detail, but it added to her sense of being in a dream.

'I'd never hurt you,' Munk's voice said, ringing in her ears, and only then did his mouth move outside the pearl.

'Where are we?' she asked, once she had bitten back the torrent of angry words that sprang instantly to her mind.

'Inside the Maelstrom.'

'I know that.' Did she really? Well, at least that had been her first assumption. 'But what's this darkness?'

His voice sounded as if he were smiling while he spoke, but the corners of his mouth didn't move until she had heard his words. 'You've got too used to polliwiggle vision, that's all. We're not in the water any more – or at least not in any seawater of our world. Polliwiggle vision doesn't work here. It's so dark because . . . well, just because it's dark. Out in the Rift it was the same – except for us.'

That sounded plausible, but wasn't important enough now for her to waste more than a thought on it. He might be right or he might not. It made no difference.

'I want to get out of here, Munk. You must help me.'

'Try it for yourself,' he said, to her surprise.

'What?'

'You can destroy it.' Once again it was a moment before she saw his smile. Then he added, 'Trust me.'

She thought that an odd thing to say, but she didn't wait to be asked twice. She struck the inside of the pearl with her fist and found, to her surprise, that it went through the light. She tried moving her fingers, and it confused her that although she felt herself moving them she couldn't see the movement until a little later. Her hand was now outside the pearl itself, on another level of time.

She wondered whether it was the same for Munk. Did he too see her movements inside the pearl only a few seconds after she had actually made them? If so, she must certainly look strange from outside – as he saw it, her hand

and body must be moving independently of each other.

She put her other hand through the pearl.

'Tear it,' she heard Munk say.

With a quick movement she tore the wall of the pearl apart so fast that the darkness rushed to meet her like a gust of wind. Then she pushed herself through the gap and out to join Munk. The light of the shell in his hand distorted his features into a strange pattern of light and shade.

Jolly brought her second leg through the gap. Like Munk, she was now hovering in the void. This wasn't water around her. It felt thicker and oilier, and moving was a little more difficult out here. Or perhaps this strange slowness was only another effect of the distortion of time here.

'Don't be afraid,' Munk said again. She saw now how exhausted he looked. Pale and drained. 'Aina can't come here.'

Jolly couldn't see what he expected this change of attitude to achieve, but she understood at least one thing: Aina couldn't appear here because they were in Aina – in the middle of the Maelstrom.

'But why –' she began.

Munk pointed to the pearl glowing as it hovered behind Jolly's back. The gap in it had closed up again. 'In spite of everything, Aina's is still polliwiggle magic. A thousand times greater, and distorted, but certain rules apply to it.'

Bewildered, Jolly shook her head. She was furious with Munk, but at the same time badly confused. What kind of a game was he playing? Whose side was he really on?

'Polliwiggle magic works only in the sea or very close to it,' he said. 'On the waves, on the beach, sometimes a little way inland. But this isn't the sea any more. Not here inside the Maelstrom.'

It was beginning to dawn on her, very slowly. This was a place between worlds. She imagined it again as a tunnel, as the tail of the Maelstrom reaching back to the Mare Tenebrosum. If that was right, polliwiggle magic gradually lost all its force here. That was why Jolly had been able to free herself.

'But you shut me up in the pearl,' she said, although the indignation had gone out of her voice.

He nodded. 'Because Aina's magic can't harm you here.'

'Was it a trick, then?' she asked, not really convinced.

Munk tried to grin, but he didn't have the strength left even for that. 'I did it first so that she'd trust me. Then to protect you from her.' He looked past Jolly, straight into the brightness behind her. 'But most of all to smuggle *that* in here.'

Jolly spun round. The pearl was glowing like a moon in the darkness. Jolly reached her hand out and gently touched it with her forefinger. The envelope of light gave way like a soft bag drifting in water, and now Jolly noticed its radiance decreasing. Of course – it too had been made by polliwiggle magic.

She frowned as she turned back to Munk. 'You shut me up in the pearl so that Aina would suck it and me into her?'

He nodded, but his eyes were still on the wavering shape of light. 'I knew she was lying to us. At least, I thought so. I didn't really know until she said all her shells except one had broken under the stone where she hid them. Do you remember how I stopped for a moment while you and Aina went on ahead? I went to look under the stone. And there was nothing there at all. Not a single splinter of a shell.'

'You knew all the time? And you didn't tell me?'

'I didn't want her to notice. I wanted her to think I was on her side,' said Munk. But he didn't sound arrogant any more. This was the old Munk again, even if he was infinitely tired and exhausted. 'Otherwise she wouldn't have let us get this far. Her kobalins could have torn us to pieces at any time.' He hesitated for a moment, and seemed to be listening for any sound in the darkness. 'It all very nearly failed when she shut you up in the kobalin mountain.' He fell silent, and looked at Aina's shell as if gazing at a priceless treasure. 'She gave me her most dangerous weapon herself, to convince me of her goodwill and because this shell whispers things in your ear – if you'll listen to it. But I needed an excuse to use it against her – something to keep her from noticing what I was doing. And for that I needed you. If you hadn't managed to free yourself . . .' He shrugged his shoulders and left the rest unsaid.

She still didn't understand what he was getting at, what his plan really was, but perhaps she was just too bewildered. He had shut her up in the pearl because he had known, or at least hoped, that the Maelstrom would swallow her. But how far did he mean to harm Aina that way?

She waited for him to go on, or do something, but then his features suddenly darkened. He turned right round on the spot once and let his eyes wander through the darkness. There was a deep line on his forehead that made him look older. 'Do you feel it too?'

She was far too worked up to think of anything but all her unanswered questions. She just shrugged her shoulders.

'Out there,' he said softly.

A lump in her throat made speaking difficult. 'What do you mean?'

'There's something there.'

Jolly took a deep breath. 'Aina after all?'

He slowly shook his head without looking at her. 'No, not Aina.'

'Who, then?'

'I don't know.' He drifted backwards, closer to Jolly, but the current that suddenly passed her didn't come from him.

'There's something circling us,' he whispered.

Jolly tried to reply, but she couldn't get a sound out.

Behind her, the light of the pearl was dimming.

'What is it?' Jolly managed to say at last, while her eyes were still trying in vain to find something to fix on in the blackness.

'Then you do feel it?' In the fading light of the giant pearl Munk looked like a low relief in sandstone; his body had lost all appearance of depth. Yellowish-brown light now surrounded them both.

'I can feel it, but I can't see it,' Jolly replied. 'You really don't know what it is?'

She still had to get used to believing she could trust him again, and it wasn't easy. 'What do we do now?'

He did not reply. Suddenly his eyes widened, staring as if spellbound into the darkness outside the dwindling light from the pearl.

She spun round and followed his gaze, but now there was

nothing there. 'Did you see something?' she asked urgently.

He nodded stiffly. 'Yes.'

'What?' She was still straining her eyes to make something out herself.

'It was big.'

'How big?'

He was going to answer when once more, for the fraction of a second, something glided past on the very limit of the light. This time Jolly saw it too. It disappeared again at once, in a fluid, shadowy movement suggesting that this was only a tiny part of a very much more gigantic body.

'By Morgan's beard!' Munk swore. It was a long time since she'd heard him say that. In spite of all that had happened in the Rift it brought back pleasant memories.

'Is that one of the masters of the Mare Tenebrosum?' Her voice was no more than a whisper now. She wasn't sure whether Munk could hear her, but then he nodded.

'Could be. Originally the Maelstrom was its gateway.'

For a second or two Jolly closed her eyes. Almost the same thought had already occurred to her. If this place was an in-between region, a kind of tunnel between their world and the Mare Tenebrosum, and if one of the masters of the Mare was already inside that tunnel – or several of them – then the Maelstrom wasn't as powerful as Aina had claimed.

Kangusta had said the Maelstrom didn't intend to serve the masters as a doorway. But if some of them had slipped through all the same, it must mean that the Maelstrom had lost power. However, what was weakening it? It wasn't joining the attack on Aelenium itself, so it must be something else.

Think! she told herself.

Perhaps when Munk killed the Acherus he had given the Maelstrom a deeper wound than any of them suspected. The Maelstrom ultimately used the magic power of its polliwiggle servants. As the Acherus was dead, only the last polliwiggle from that faraway time was left, the kobalin commander. Suppose it too had been destroyed in the battle for Aelenium? Wouldn't the Maelstrom have lost two-thirds of its power?

'Jolly!'

She started, expecting something huge to fall on her. But there was no one there but Munk.

'The light of the pearl is getting weaker and weaker!' he said excitedly. 'It's burning out. Do you understand?'

'Of course. And when it's gone right out, that thing will snap us up and –'

'That's not what I mean!'

She looked blankly at him. 'Then what?'

'That pearl was the most concentrated magic I've ever conjured up,' he said. 'I mean, it was . . . *powerful*. And if the light is still there, it means that the magic can't have disappeared entirely.'

'But we've already found out that in here polliwiggle magic doesn't –'

'Well, perhaps not. But the pearl is still glowing, which means its magic is alive.'

'So?' She guessed that all this was part of his original plan when he manoeuvred to get her and the pearl in here. But what was that plan? He looked past her into the darkness, but the being out there was keeping its distance, still circling them outside the glow of the pearl, almost as if it feared the faint light.

'Do you remember what I told you back on my parents' island?' he asked. He was speaking hastily now, his words tumbling out. 'About the first time, when I didn't shut a magic pearl up in a shell again at the end of the magic?'

'Yes, the palm trees on your island had red leaves. And once the roof of your farm burned down. But what does that –'

He nodded excitedly. 'And when you kept me from shutting the pearl up again on the *Carfax*, the magic went out of control and hurt my back.'

She was beginning to understand.

'What do you think,' said Munk, 'is going to happen if the biggest, most powerful pearl I ever created isn't put back in its shell?' He swallowed, and in the dying light she saw his Adam's apple bobbing up and down.

'The other shells are lying somewhere out there in the Rift,' Munk went on. 'This is the only one where the magic can go.' He indicated Aina's shell in his hand.

'If such a powerful pearl isn't shut up in its shell,' said Jolly in growing excitement, 'then there'd probably be . . . something very *bad*, right? A catastrophe.'

He nodded sadly.

'And,' Jolly went on, her voice shaking, 'it would look for the nearest shell, so as to disappear into it – and it would have to be a very *large* shell to capture so much magic on the loose.'

'The Maelstrom's own shell,' said Munk. 'Its root.'

Jolly glanced at the shrinking pearl, which now looked something like a shapeless pig's bladder. The light was very faint now. It would fail entirely any moment.

Munk started. 'There it went again!' He pointed at the approaching darkness.

There was no doubt that the being out there would fall on them as soon as the magic light went out. But Jolly had eyes only for the dying pearl. 'It'll explode like a thousand barrels of gunpowder. Or . . . or do something else crazy!'

Munk looked down, dejected. 'If it's only half as strong as I think, it will blow everything for many miles around to pieces.'

'Us too?' She knew the answer. But the thought of her own death suddenly hardly hurt. It was as if she had been aware from the first that she would never get away from this place alive. As she sought for the truth in her heart, she realised that she had known or at least guessed it all along.

She felt strangely peaceful. It was almost a feeling of . . . yes, contentment.

She nodded to him, and he raised the hand holding Aina's shell, took a last look at it – and brought his other fist down on it so hard that the shell burst into a cloud of tiny splinters. A sound like a scream carried on a stormy wind came from far away.

Jolly put out her arm and took Munk's hand.

At that moment his face looked as if it were being sucked backwards into the darkness. But he wasn't moving away – instead the darkness suddenly came closer, closing around them like a tide of black ink.

The pearl faded.

'Jolly?' she heard him call. Then she was caught in a powerful current and their hands were torn apart.

Something huge was racing towards them.

And the magic pearl, barely visible now, exploded.

Within a second, absolute blackness turned to its opposite. The magic, now released, flared up like a spark reaching the end of a fuse.

Silence.

And then –

The ray carried Griffin over the outlying parts of the Maelstrom as if they were passing above a mountain range made of water. From this great height, the churning masses resembled a constantly changing landscape. Tides moved in broad channels, washing over and into each other, mingling in countless smaller whirlpools, although even these were large enough to swallow up a whole fleet. Hills rose, with foaming crests, and flowed apart again. Gigantic hands of spray and salt water reached up from the sea and seemed about to pluck the ray and its rider out of the sky.

Griffin was flying over a thousand feet above the ocean. He had never climbed so high on the back of a ray. Since leaving Aelenium he had flown not only forwards but also upwards, reaching a great enough height to get a view of at least part of the swirling, raging brute that was the Maelstrom.

But he had been wrong in thinking he could get even a faint idea of the sheer size of it from up here. The masses of water shooting past already filled his entire field of vision, and still he couldn't see the real centre of the whirlpool, the eye of the monster.

After a while, however, he noticed that the world seemed to be dipping away in a downward curve in the distance, as if the globe had suddenly become much smaller and its curvature was visible. So that was where it went down into the abyss, straight into the heart of this inconceivable, monumental monstrosity.

He had long ago stopped perceiving the noise as sounds. His ears surrendered before the task of filtering out details or even fluctuations from the chaos. It was all one, a constant roaring and droning that filled and almost burst his head.

The ray was afraid of what lay below. Now and then it bucked and jerked so violently that Griffin was afraid he might slip out of the saddle, in spite of the straps holding him. On Tortuga he had once heard a one-legged priest preach a sermon about the Apocalypse, the end of the world and the infernal beast that would rise from the sea on the

Day of Judgement. How wrong that picture of the Last Day had been! Now it turned out that the sea itself was rising, and could be more terrible and cruel than any creature of flesh and blood.

The crests of the Maelstrom's waves reached out in all directions, and now the slope of the boiling surface was steeper too. It would soon be going vertically down below him, and again he had some idea of the great powers that must be at work to curve the ocean itself like the back of a gigantic living creature.

Pulling on the reins, he signalled to the ray to rise yet higher. The animal willingly agreed. It would probably have flown to the moon if Griffin had wanted, just so long as they were out of reach of the great mouth opening mile after mile below them.

The slope had become a steep wall, clouds of boiling vapour and foam stretched beneath him, but at last Griffin could just see the opposite side of the abyss in the distance. He was right above the central point of the Maelstrom now. Treacherous eddies of wind tugged at the ray's wings; dangerous air currents threatened to suck it down. It was difficult to estimate the diameter of this titanic funnel, but from side to side of the curved rim it must be many miles across. It was too much for Griffin's imagination to think that this great maw opening up in the structure of the world went all of thirty thousand feet down, growing narrower and narrower until its lowest point could disappear into a shell on the sea-bed.

Jolly was somewhere down there.

If she ever got that far, a voice at the back of his mind whispered. He did his best to suppress the thought, but he didn't entirely succeed. Jolly had ventured into regions beyond all human experience, accompanied only by someone who at one point had been almost her worst enemy.

There was no point in pretending to himself. Her chances weren't good. Yet he was glad to be here now, in a place closer to Jolly than any other in the world. He could only hope and perhaps even pray that she was still alive.

For a moment he actually considered plunging into the depths on the back of the ray, just to see how far he got. How deep could he go inside the Maelstrom without being caught by the rotating walls of water? But he thought better of it; what was the point of inviting his own death? That wouldn't help either Jolly or his friends in Aelenium.

In a curious way, and in spite of everything, he was almost relieved. At last he could see what they had been talking about for so long with his own eyes. He saw the

Maelstrom lying below him, heard its roar, felt its terrible attraction. He sensed that the enemy was close, and his hatred flared up again. If he managed to get back safely to Aelenium, he thought grimly, he would fight for the freedom of humanity until there were only two possible alternatives – survival or absolute downfall.

But before he turned away and set off on the homeward flight, he couldn't resist the temptation to go a little lower. It was as if the current of the Maelstrom were working on his mind, pulling like a magnet to entice him into the depths.

Come closer, the mouth of the Maelstrom hissed up at him. *You can't escape me.*

While he was still wrestling with himself, trying to resist the temptation, something suddenly and instantly brought him back to his senses.

Deep below, beyond the layer of water vapour and the rising, curving jets that formed over the abyss now and then like bridges, radiant brightness flared.

For a moment he thought it was another cloud of water-drops, white as snow and denser than the others. But then he saw that the whole of the cloud-cover was glowing as if lightning had struck and, in the fraction of a second, had set the whole world alight.

A fountain of light shot up from the depths, standing at the centre of the Maelstrom only a stone's throw from Griffin like a column of flickering, blazing fire.

The ray reared as if it had flown into an invisible wall. Griffin let out a yell of terror, slumped in the straps that held him, and fought for several seconds to keep from falling out of the saddle. The wounds in his side were burning. When the animal was flying level and Griffin, heart thudding, had managed to pull himself up and retrieve his balance in spite of the pain, the column of light was scattering before his eyes in a cascade of glittering, fiery sparks.

From deep, deep below rose a monstrous roar, drowning out even the raging masses of water. It seemed to be rotating with the walls of the Maelstrom, moving from side to side. The ray panicked, but instead of shaking itself again shot forward, beating its wings strongly, going faster than Griffin had ever known one of its kind to fly before. It was looking for the shortest way to the rim of the Maelstrom, to escape the central point and the swarms of tiny lights still dancing and sparkling there.

The roar grew louder, and suddenly it seemed to Griffin as if the rim of the funnel were moving away from them, further and further into the distance, to prevent the ray and its rider from ever reaching it. And while this strange race between the ray and the curve of the Maelstrom went on, Griffin looked over the animal's wings and down into the depths.

The clouds of vapour moved apart, and with them the masses of water around that gaping mouth in the sea. The funnel grew wider, broader, while the bestial roar still filled the world. It was quite different from the mere sound of stormy water.

The ray's wings beat faster and faster now, as if the animal still hadn't reached the limits of its strength. Gradually the rim of the abyss came closer, a swirling slope that at some point would flow into the level surface of the ocean.

But before they reached that point Griffin saw something else.

There was no water vapour beneath him now. The clouds had drawn apart, and the walls of the funnel were glowing as if the water had turned to white-hot lava.

Far below a shaft gaped open in the water, going all the way down to the bottom of the sea.

He felt dizzy and then sick, but when he retched he brought up nothing but bile. No wonder; it was an eternity since he last ate anything.

Below him lay the Rift.

The abyss yawned six miles deep and at least two miles wide. There was a patch of something white at the bottom of it, presumably sand, like an area of desert in the middle of the sea. At its centre something shimmered, a dot that might be almost anything. Much too large for a human being. Perhaps a shipwreck.

Or a closed shell.

The ray uttered a strange cry, a muttered sound of alarm, and a moment later Griffin knew why.

The abyss was closing too. The rotating walls of the Maelstrom rushed together from all sides at once. The bottom of the sea was already invisible again, and waves circled faster and faster, closing in, filling the void with the ocean tides.

'Faster!' cried Griffin in panic. 'Faster!'

The ray was now going almost as fast as a sea horse. Its wings beat at an extraordinary tempo, and its heart was pumping so hard that Griffin bounced up and down in the saddle.

They made it.

Somehow or other they made it.

When the Maelstrom closed behind them, and a colossal column of water rose to the sky, they were just far enough away not to be caught by the surging tides.

Griffin closed his eyes and shouted out loud as crystal curtains of water, thrown up from below, fell around him from the sky.

Beneath him the surface of the sea was rising in a tidal wave several hundred feet high. For a moment it seemed almost to freeze. Then, as monstrous forces erupted, it rolled away in all directions at once to submerge the shores of the whole world.

The voices of countless gods were eddying through the Ghost-Trader's mind when he saw the light on the horizon. A finger of blazing brightness, it shot up and pierced the blue-grey sky like a glowing dagger.

The Trader was distracted, just for a moment, and his link to the forgotten gods was broken. An angry roar came from the places where they were waiting impatiently to be reborn – and was suddenly cut off.

An invisible fist struck the Ghost-Trader and flung him to the ground. The silver circlet slipped from his hand to the ledge. He was lucky to stumble only a few paces backwards, or the force of the blow might have taken him over the side of the plateau and down to the pens of the rays below. As it was, he lay there, groaning, but then raised his head and stared at the horizon.

The light faded in the middle of surging walls of vapour. The world seemed to be holding its breath. Silence sealed the Trader's ears like liquid wax, and all he heard was the blood beating in his temples. Even the noise of the battle seemed to stop, perhaps because the combatants too felt that something entirely unexpected was happening.

The door through which the ghosts of the dead gods had been about to enter this world was closed. It would take great strength and assurance to reopen it and begin the incantation again.

But perhaps that wasn't necessary any more.

A grey tower of water spiralled up from the heart of the Maelstrom so many miles away, clearly visible even at this distance. Its top touched the sky, unfolded like the cup of a flower, and finally fell in an explosion of cascading water.

The Ghost-Trader saw all this, and understood at the same moment that a tidal wave was on its way. He knew it before he finally saw it, a wall of seawater. The ocean reared under it, bucking like an unruly animal and shaking the air.

The two parrots flew up above the Ghost-Trader, rising until they were only two dark dots in the sky.

He struggled to his feet, looked around for support, and found the body of the old ray. Never taking his eyes off the tidal wave thundering towards Aelenium, he went over to the dead animal, leaned his back against it, and closed his eyes in anxious expectation.

Silent and motionless, he waited for the end.

DOWNFALL

A few minutes before the mysterious light tore the Maelstrom apart, before the Ghost-Trader broke off his incantation and before Griffin's ray, with the very last of its strength, reached the safe heights above the tidal wave, the defensive rampart in the upper third of Aelenium was breached for the second time.

After the fall of the southern side, the attackers succeeded in driving their way past the desperate defence put up by the guard. Ragged figures who had spent days in the dark holds of Tyrone's fleet, awaiting the outcome of the sea battle against the captains of the Lesser Antilles, now poured over the rampart. Several guns brought on land and rolled up the streets had breached the fortifications. Many of the people of Aelenium would have died if those in command hadn't seen the situation in time to get them to safety in the neighbouring streets.

Pirates and cannibals streamed through the dense gun-smoke, stumbled over splintered coral and pieces of wood, and marched, yelling and brandishing their swords, across squares where children once used to play and men and women sat singing over their wine in the evenings.

The first wave of attackers came to a halt when the guards at the street corners and behind a few makeshift barricades opened fire. But the next to advance used the pause when rifles and pistols had to be reloaded to engage the defenders in fierce hand-to-hand skirmishing.

Riders of the Ray Guard saw what had happened from the air, and soon d'Artois found himself forced to divide his mounted rays, sending a troop from the embattled south of the rampart to the new breach in the west. The attackers there were halted, but those in the south now met less resistance, and were gradually gaining the upper hand.

'It's hopeless,' the captain told his marksman. As commander, he ought not to have shown his despair openly, but he had known his men for years, and they had no secrets from each other. 'They'll take the city before the sun sets,' he said, downcast.

The marksman fired a salvo into the depths from several rifles. When the smoke of his weapons dispersed, his eyes fell on the mist in the north.

'Look at that!' he cried, clapping d'Artois on the shoulder.

The captain glanced the way he was pointing, and saw what he meant. Beyond the ring of mist, high above its fraying vapours, the sky turned radiantly white for a split second, as if a second sun had risen above the Atlantic. The light was followed by first a moment's dark twilight, and then a primeval roar like the eruption of a volcano.

Something tall and grey cut through the captain's field of vision, like an axe splitting the horizon. It was as if the world had been turned on its head as the waters of the ocean rose roaring into the sky.

Soledad had stopped counting the arrows in the body of the flying snake long ago. The creature that had once been the Hexhermetic Shipworm was still fighting as recklessly as any beast of prey, but gradually its many injuries were sapping even its great power. The snake was certainly large, and a bite or a blow from the end of its tail was deadly, but it was also an easy target for the arrows of the cannibals and the pirates' bullets.

From the place behind the rampart where Soledad had retreated for a moment's rest, she could see clearly that the winged reptile was bleeding from many wounds, even where no arrows were stuck between its scales. And however great the panic it inspired in the attackers, the cries of triumph when another arrow met its mark were equally loud, rekindling the invaders' determination.

Soledad was about to leap up and go into battle once more when she suddenly found Buenaventure beside her, his tongue hanging out of his dog's face as he breathed hard. The sword he carried had more notches by now than its original serrations.

'Walker's wounded!' he called to her.

Her heart almost stopped beating.

'I carried him down from the rampart,' the pit bull man went on. 'Left him in an empty house at the side of the square. The one over there with the little windows.'

'How bad is it?'

'Not too bad. A wound in his side and a deep knife-cut in his upper arm. Nothing to kill a man like him. But he's lost a lot of blood and can't go on fighting.'

'Take my place up here, will you? I'll be right back.' She pointed to one of the houses. 'That one?'

Buenaventure growled assent, and then, with a wild war-cry, flung himself into the battle.

Soledad ran up the steep slope of the square as fast as she could go. Several times she had to swerve to avoid the wounded being carried from the rampart to the makeshift field hospital. At first reinforcements had kept coming up across the square, but not any more. Anyone who could hold a weapon was already in the front line.

She reached the entrance of the house, raced into a corridor and looked through the open doors to the left and right.

'Walker?'

'Soledad?' His voice came from the first floor. 'Up here! That hairy, stinking brute of a friend of mine dumped me here like an old cripple. Help me get back to –'

He stopped short as she came flying through the door of a first-floor room, anxiety plain to read in her face.

'Well, damn it all,' he said with a grimace of pain, 'you were worried about me!' He was lying on some blankets with a single pillow under his head. The rest of the room was empty. All the furniture had been taken out to reinforce the rampart.

'Oh, not for a moment,' she replied, running to him and hugging him hard. 'When he said you were wounded, I thought . . .'

He tried to raise himself from where he lay. 'I'm all right. It just makes me sick to be lying around here useless, while –'

The rest of his words were drowned in the terrible roaring that came through both windows, even drowning out the noise of battle.

Soledad leaped up. 'What the devil . . . ?' She couldn't hear her own voice, the noise outside was suddenly so loud. The ground was shaking, and then she was torn off her feet by a strong blast of air and tumbled right across the room.

As chance would have it, she landed with a crash by one of the windows and against the wall. Groaning, she was about to struggle up again, but for some reason or other her sense of balance wouldn't obey her. Only then did she realise that the floor wasn't flat any more. The entire house was keeling over like a ship in a storm.

The wooden shutters over the windows had been smashed by a shot ricocheting off them, probably hours ago, so she had a clear view of the square outside.

At first she couldn't believe what she was seeing.

It was as if a hurricane had fallen on the city. There was water everywhere outside, spray, grey foam, people in panic. But that was just a foretaste of what was coming.

A grey wall.

The Maelstrom, she thought objectively. It's here. It will sweep us all away.

But it was not the Maelstrom. It was the ocean itself rising against them.

And then, in the endless, unreal seconds before the tidal wave itself struck Aelenium, she saw something else.

The defensive rampart had disappeared, torn away by the first surging masses of water, and with it everyone on it. Where Soledad herself had been fighting only a few moments ago, there was nothing.

Buenaventure and all the others had gone.

The tidal wave looked like water, acted like water, and to those who were drowning it tasted like water in their last desperate moments. But in those few seconds when it struck Aelenium it seemed to be carved from solid stone, crushing human beings, coral and the ships on the shore alike.

The greatest miracle in the midst of all this misfortune, in the middle of death and the coming end, was that the anchor chain held.

There were a number of other miracles, lesser by comparison but equally great and merciful to the lucky few.

There was the little girl who had stolen out of the halls of refuge in the heart of the mountain with her brother to watch the battle from above. She was caught at the very last moment by a ray's wing when a jet of water washed her off the roof of a house.

There was the cannibal who took refuge from the incoming floods on a statue, and seized hold of a guardsman who was being torn away by the tidal current. The savage hauled the man up to the statue's shoulders too, and there they sat side by side in silence, deadly enemies only a moment or so ago but now gazing at their common, unimaginable adversary together.

There was the cabin boy of a pirate ship who survived only because he tumbled head first into a half-empty apple barrel at the last minute. And while the hull of the sailing vessel broke up under him, in some mysterious way he remained uninjured and was found later unconscious but alive, drifting in his barrel and still head down. He never went to sea again, and he never ate another apple in his life.

There was the small troop of guardsmen who made for the roof of the only house still standing in the poets' quarter. And the old woman who, despite her great age, limped over to the rampart and faced the first waves with her stick raised aloft like a soldier brandishing his sword at enemies who outnumber him. She too survived, half drowned but strong enough to recover. And there the doctor who, in desperation, braced his back against the door of the field hospital to protect the wounded patients from the water with his body. The waves actually did flow around the building, perhaps because some god was watching over it, or perhaps the house was built a very little higher than its neighbours.

There were many such episodes, but far, far more ended in death, and the disappearance of many without trace.

Hardest hit were the attackers. The tidal wave was high enough to devastate the lower two-thirds of Aelenium, and by now there was no one there but cannibals and pirates making for the upper rampart. They were all swept away. Of the dozens of ships by the shore, not one was left, and all but a handful of the few crew members who had stayed on board during the battle drowned miserably.

The defensive rampart itself was destroyed, and both attackers and defenders died on it. Only those above the rampart were almost all spared: many wounded guardsmen and citizens of the starfish city, but also people who fled uphill in the nick of time just as the water came in.

No one ever knew how many lost their lives that day. A head-count was taken in the starfish city later, but it was never certain how many pirates and cannibals had died.

Tyrone's fleet had been destroyed at a single blow.

*

As the tidal wave raced on towards the Lesser Antilles and finally the mainland, where it slowly lost force and ebbed away, Soledad and Walker sat close together in the bedroom of the house to which Buenaventure had brought the captain.

They were huddling in a corner without speaking, keeping their eyes closed, each listening to the other's breathing and the noise gradually dying down outside.

At last they moved apart, and Soledad helped Walker over to the window.

'I'm going out to look for him,' said the princess tonelessly. 'I'll find him. He must be somewhere.'

'I'll come with you,' said Walker.

'No!'

'He's my friend.'

'I'll find him for you,' she said gently. 'You're too badly injured to go chasing about.'

'My right arm is still sound. I can use a sword, and shoot a gun, and –'

She placed a finger on his lips. 'With that wound in your side? Let me go and see what it's really like outside. Then I'll come back for you.'

She got to her feet and quickly took a couple of steps back, so that he couldn't stop her. It hurt to see him hauling himself painfully up. He tried to follow, but had to abandon the attempt, his face twisting with the pain.

'Please,' she said, 'stay here. I couldn't bear to lose you.'

Their eyes met again. He gave up and leaned back against the wall, exhausted. 'I'm sure he's still out there somewhere.'

She smiled encouragingly, then ran downstairs and out of the house. Torrents of water were still flowing through the streets, and the whole city was rocking like a galleon that has jettisoned its cargo in strong seas. Soledad wasn't sure what the tidal wave had done, but she doubted now whether it had been a weapon of the Maelstrom. Tyrone's men had been on the point of victory. Why would the Maelstrom risk their death?

Because human life means nothing to it, she thought icily. And because the attack wasn't going fast enough.

But what had the Maelstrom gained? Aelenium itself had not been submerged. In all probability, thought Soledad, that was thanks to the anchor chain. And its protector. She remembered their meeting in the underwater city and the sea-serpent's sparkling eyes, and now felt nothing but gratitude at the thought of that encounter.

Out in the square most of the wounded were still lying where they had been before the tidal wave came. Some had been flung about, a few probably washed away – Soledad couldn't be sure. The first to bring aid were slowly venturing down from the streets above, many of them distressed and with tentative, uncertain steps. They were almost all looking to the north, where the sky was now bright blue. If there was going to be a second wave there was no sign of it.

Soledad hurried over to the confused and injured men in the square. Soon she reached the three streets across which the rampart had been built. A few ruins lay there, but the rampart itself had almost entirely disappeared.

She went to the mouth of the central street and looked down it. After a few dozen paces it wasn't a street any more. The tidal wave had destroyed many of the buildings in the middle of Aelenium, tearing walls down, lifting roofs off, leaving only ruins behind. Water ran down all the streets to form branching rivulets below.

But it was even worse further down.

The buildings in the lower part of Aelenium as far as the water must have been wiped away in an instant. Where hundreds of houses had stood a little while ago, there was nothing but a void. Only smooth white slopes were left, looking as if they had been covered with shattered ice floes – all that was left of the intricate coral formations that used to stand here. From where she stood, Soledad could make out one arm of the starfish, and it too was entirely empty, as if swept clean.

Tyrone's army had disappeared without trace. Gooseflesh rose on Soledad's skin; tears stung her eyes as she wept for the beauty of Aelenium and so many deaths.

'Princess?' A question, and then a jubilant cry. 'Soledad, it's you!'

She spun round and saw no one in front of her, but immediately spotted the shape above her, like a dark hole torn in the sky. The winged snake was hovering there, its feathers ruffled, the broken shafts of arrows sticking out of its scaly body.

'Have you seen Buenaventure?' Soledad burst out. 'My God, you look terrible,' she added. 'We must get those arrows out of you somehow or –'

'Never mind that,' the snake interrupted her. 'They're only scratches. And no, I haven't seen him.' It lowered its voice. 'He was up on the rampart when . . . when it happened, wasn't he?'

'I must find him!' Soledad tried to shake off her horror at the sight of the destruction in the city, but she couldn't forget all the dead. Once again she turned to the flattened rows of houses. 'The worst of it is that they've all simply disappeared. As if they were still alive but somewhere else.'

The snake's dark eyes blinked at her, and then it rose a little higher, beating its wings powerfully. 'I'll help you search,' it said, moving off at once over the rooftops above the rampart to the east, while Soledad went west.

She soon came upon the first of the injured, who had been flung through windows and doorways, into back yards and against walls by the incoming tidal wave. Many had taken refuge in the winding streets, washed up there like flotsam. It was possible, she thought, that something similar had happened to Buenaventure.

But hard as she searched, she couldn't find him. She asked many people if they had seen him, but seldom got an answer, for most of them were in too bad a state of shock to understand what she was saying. Soledad helped several of the injured, and waited impatiently with them until more help arrived. Only then did she go on again.

All in vain.

She found no trace of Buenaventure. Discouraged and dejected, she went back to the large square where she had last seen him. There she met the snake again, back from searching the east of the city.

'Nothing,' the creature cried out to her between two wing-beats. 'What about you?'

In silence, Soledad shook her head, and wondered how

she was going to give Walker the bad news. What words could she find to tell him that his best friend had been washed into the sea and drowned? That he'd never see Buenaventure again?

She murmured hoarse thanks to the snake, and then crossed the square again, walking with a heavy tread towards the house where she had left Walker.

The square was full of people now. Most of them had laid down their weapons and were doing their best to help others. A few cannibals were being led away by guardsmen. No one seemed to be in any mood to fight now, as if the reason for the battle had suddenly become indistinct and blurred in their minds. Soledad herself felt the same. It all seemed so long ago, although hardly an hour or two had passed since the last of the skirmishing.

The scene looked unreal. This city, the wind now blowing, the people – none of it was the same as before the disaster. Soledad couldn't bring herself to look up at the blue sky; she felt as if its clear, pure beauty were mocking her.

Reaching the door of the house, she wondered whether she had really left it open. No, she was sure she had closed both halves of it behind her as she went out. Had Walker followed her after all? She quickened her pace, running up the stairs. Was Buenaventure alive, and had he been the first to find his way to his wounded friend?

But then another idea came to her. Or more of a presentiment, a vague foreboding of danger. Her hand was on the hilt of her sword as she approached the bedroom door, and her heart was beating fast when she entered the room. 'Walker?'

A man stood at the far end of the room, broad-shouldered, clothed in black. He held a drawn sword in his right hand and in his left a cocked pistol. His frock-coat was encrusted with dirt and blood, but he himself seemed to be uninjured. The long black ponytail hanging from the shaven back of his head was untidy, and looked as if it had been too close to a fire. But the most terrifying thing about this figure was the war-paint. It had run on his face in the water, and he looked as if his features had melted and then solidified into bizarre new shapes.

Walker was lying lifeless on the floor in front of him. Tyrone had planted his right foot on the captain's ribcage, like a military commander posing for a statue of victory.

'I was expecting you, princess,' said the cannibal king, and he bared his sharply filed teeth in a grin.

WHERE IS JOLLY?

Griffin felt the ray tiring under him. The animal beat its wings more and more slowly now, and it was having difficulty in maintaining height as it hovered above the ocean.

The cascades of water cast through the air in the eruption had almost torn Griffin from his saddle. Although the ray was already well away from the centre of the Maelstrom, even the outlying areas of the titanic explosion had sent tons of water raining down around them. But now that the great column of water had collapsed on itself and the tidal waves had rolled away, the sea below them was gradually growing calmer. From up here – six or seven hundred feet above the waves – it looked almost as if nothing had happened, although the stormy waves were a strange sight when there were no clouds in the sky, and it wasn't even particularly windy.

The most remarkable thing of all, however, far more

extraordinary than rough seas without any wind, was the disappearance of the Maelstrom.

At first Griffin had thought the tidal wave was a weapon employed by their enemies to devastate Aelenium and the islands of the Caribbean. But now, considerably later, he was coming to understand that the Maelstrom didn't even exist any longer. It had been destroyed. Their greatest adversary had simply vanished.

Deep within the whirlpool, something seemed to have exploded. It had brought the blazing light shooting up from the heart of the swirling water. Then the same force had expanded the Maelstrom like an empty envelope and finally made it fall in on itself. The raging walls of the shaft of water had fallen together from a height of thirty thousand feet, and their violence had set off the tidal wave.

Where was Jolly in all this chaos? And what had become of Aelenium and his friends?

The wave had rolled away towards the starfish city like a mountain range on the move. Griffin had been at sea long enough to know how hard water could strike. When it hit the city it must have felt like a diamond wall, an irresistible power. There would have been no escaping it, no defence against such a colossal force so close to the centre of the detonation. It must have crushed everything in its path.

When he looked south the horizon was blurred and grey. At least the ring of mist around Aelenium still seemed to be there. But what lay beyond it? He dared not imagine the extent of the destruction.

He felt very much alone up here on his ray. Suppose he was the sole survivor of the starfish city? Suppose all the others had been crushed or drowned?

His hands clenched on the reins; his fingernails dug into his palms. The wounds inflicted by the wyvern were hurting horribly again. His left side blazed alternately with hot and cold fire.

And then he saw the lonely dark dot down on the water.

A piece of flotsam – or a human being?

'Lower!' he called to the ray.

The animal lost height, moving in a wide curve towards the blue-grey surface of the water. White crests of foam covered the sea with fine lines that from above looked like a fishing net.

A figure was drifting on the waves in the middle of this net.

No, it was *running* over the waves, though it had difficulty in keeping a footing. The sea below rocked so violently that every step was a challenge. As he circled in the air, bringing the ray down, Griffin saw the figure fall several times, scramble to its feet after a few attempts, and lose its balance again on the hills and valleys of the sea.

He called Jolly's name, but the wind blew his cry from his lips. The polliwiggle down there hadn't noticed him yet, but was fully occupied in trying to make progress over the churning ocean.

'Jolly!' he shouted again.

But then he fell silent. It wasn't Jolly down there, even though the figure wore the oiled leather clothing in which the two polliwiggles had left the starfish city.

Munk raised his head and blinked at the sky. He must have seen the gigantic dark shape of the ray, and he stopped. A wave rose beneath his feet but did not throw him over. His lips formed Griffin's name.

'Munk!' cried Griffin, too upset to ask anything but the essential question, for a dreadful suspicion was rising in his mind. Hands shaking, he brought the ray into orbit around the boy on the water. 'Where's Jolly?'

Munk looked at him as if it took him a moment to grasp the meaning of those words. 'Jolly?' he asked, as if dazed.

'Where is she?' cried Griffin again. He could hardly control himself. All at once he saw his fears confirmed. He had warned Jolly of Munk, but she wouldn't listen. 'What have you done with her?'

'What have I . . . ? Nothing. She . . . she's not here.'

'Is she still down there, then?'

'I . . . I don't know.' Munk had to turn on his own axis on the water to follow the flight of the ray with his eyes. He swayed, and nearly fell again.

'You don't *know*?' Griffin could no longer keep back his anger. Something in him boiled over. The despair of the last few hours, all the suffering and losses, his pain, and now this – it was just too much. 'What have you done, Munk? God damn it, I knew you'd betray her!'

Munk stared at him, eyes wide. He was pale and looked ill. Perhaps he was just too exhausted to defend himself.

Grief and rage blinded Griffin. His wounds were burning worse than ever, and the blood roared in his ears like a cascade. A single thought possessed him: Munk had come back – leaving Jolly down below. She was dead. And it was Munk's fault.

Griffin tore at the reins and sent the ray racing towards the other boy only just above the surface of the sea. Munk flung himself aside at the last moment, before the animal could ram him. He fell flat on a wave, and groaned in pain.

Griffin uttered a curse, brought the ray to a halt much too abruptly, and was almost flung out of the saddle. All his wounds opened again, but he ignored them.

He turned and made for Munk again, even closer to the water. This time he was going to get him.

Soledad stared at the motionless body before her. Tyrone did not move from the spot. From where she stood, she couldn't see whether Walker was dead, but why would Tyrone have left him alive?

Shouting furiously, she brought up her sword and raced forward. For a moment Tyrone seemed surprised by the vehemence of her reaction, then he brandished his pistol. But that didn't deter Soledad. She wasted no thought on the danger as she swiftly ran in. Her blade thrust at Tyrone, but the cannibal king leaped back, parrying it with his own weapon.

Sparks flew as the swords clashed. Soledad was right in front of her enemy now. Walker's body lay between her feet and Tyrone's, perfectly still. Was there fresh blood anywhere? Was he still breathing? The cannibal king gave her no time to find answers to those questions. Instead, he launched into an attack meant to send the sword flying from her hand.

Soledad retreated, leaping back, and was relieved to see Tyrone following her. With his left hand, he stowed his pistol away in his belt. Didn't he want to kill her? At least

Walker was forgotten, left behind, and that had been the main reason for her retreat: to entice her enemy away from him. Either Tyrone had lost interest in the captain, or Walker was already dead.

With another cry, she parried the next onslaught of Tyrone's sword. She was very close to the door now, moving backwards out into the corridor.

'I saw the dog man carrying your friend Walker into this house,' said Tyrone, between two thrusts. 'And when the water had gone down I came back. I thought I'd find you here sooner or later, princess.'

The swords clashed with massive force. Both blades were deeply notched.

'Guess how disappointed I was to find only this scum. And already so badly wounded that he didn't even make a passable opponent.'

Soledad's next lunge took him by surprise, but he recovered quickly and answered her attack. They were almost out of the bedroom by now. Tyrone was forcing Soledad back to the staircase, perhaps hoping she would be easy prey if she had to retreat down the stairs.

'Is he dead?' she got out grimly.

His grin was so cold that even the sight of his sharply filed teeth could make it no more terrible. She thrust, wounding his shoulder. With a gasp of surprise, he leaped back. She had been able to see the two points of his tongue, split and dyed black in a ritual of the Orinoco tribes. Soledad sent up a prayer to heaven that she would get the chance to cut it out.

He smiled again. The wound in his shoulder was bleeding, but didn't seem to trouble him much. 'I don't want to kill you, princess. I just need a hostage so that I can get out of this city. Don't you think they'd let me have a flying ray if I threaten to cut your pretty face to ribbons?'

She snorted scornfully. 'I'd rather die here and now.'

He shrugged. 'Well, if you leave me no choice.' His hand moved towards his belt, but for now only as a threat. Soledad looked at the pistol again. It was still cocked.

How very careless, she thought, lunging again. As she did so she dived under his sideways swipe at her and pointed the tip of her sword at the pistol.

The blade brushed against the gun and touched the trigger.

Tyrone let out a yell as the pistol went off. The gunpowder exploded with a green flame, and a puff of smoke ran down his left leg. The cannibal king's knee almost gave way, and then there was blood on the floor. The bullet had lodged deep in his thigh.

'You . . . witch!' he uttered, gasping with pain, but with amazing will-power he kept on his feet. Leaning back against the wall of the corridor, he succeeded in parrying her next thrust.

'Give up, Tyrone,' she demanded, between heavy breaths. 'You're going nowhere with that wound.'

His blurred features distorted into a demonic grimace. Only his eyes were still human in that devil's mask. 'I have the power of the shamans,' he said in cutting tones. 'I have met the Maelstrom in a dream. In *its* dream. No one has ever been there before. That is why it chose me. And it is still . . . even now . . . my master.' He pressed his left hand to his wound. The smoke had dispersed, and now Soledad could see what the bullet had done on its way down his leg. 'It will . . . stand by me,' he gasped as he slid down by the wall.

Soledad went to disarm him, but he struck out with his sword so violently that he nearly caught her in the stomach. She flinched back, but soon saw that he was helpless. All the same, he was barring the corridor between her and the room where Walker lay.

'What have you done to him?' she asked coldly.

Tyrone did not reply but just laughed, louder and louder.

'What have you done to Walker?' she asked again, but

when she ventured another step in his direction he struck out with his sword once more, driving her back.

Losing the last of her patience, she feinted, jumped over his blade as it struck, and landed with her right foot on his injured leg. Tyrone's scream was so loud that it must be audible in the square outside.

Good, she thought, perhaps someone will come and finish this dirty job for me.

With her left foot, she finally kicked the sword out of his hand, leaned forward and put the tip of her own blade to his chest. 'One false movement . . .' she warned him.

And Tyrone laughed again.

Laughed and laughed, until his laughter turned to hoarse coughing.

Soledad swept back her arm – and thought better of it at the last moment. Instead of killing him, she brought the hilt of her sword down on his skull with all her might. His coughing stopped; his features finally seemed to flow into each other, and his chin fell on his chest. He collapsed unconscious.

Soledad climbed over him and dragged herself weakly to the door of the room. Tyrone's laughter seemed to follow her, a ghostly echo, as she entered it and bent over the lifeless Walker.

*

Munk shouted something as he flung himself aside again, dodging the deadly weight of the ray by a hair's breadth. Griffin couldn't make out what he was saying, and merely cursed because he had missed his adversary.

Munk had Jolly on his conscience, he was sure of that. All the helplessness he had felt these last few days and hours, even the emptiness after his victory over the wyvern, came over him again. He couldn't blame Munk for everything, he somehow dimly realised, but that didn't matter now either. What Griffin had suffered during the battle he had suffered for Jolly, just to see her smile again. Munk's treachery had made more than that reunion impossible. It seemed to Griffin as if everything else was unimportant.

Whether the wyvern was dead or alive, whether the kobalin commander had survived or not, whether Aelenium still existed or was lying at the bottom of the sea – suddenly none of it was of any significance. He simply had no power to find out more about it, or time to stop and think of it for so much as a couple of seconds.

He wanted to pay Munk back for what he had done. At the moment, that seemed to him more important than anything else, and even he was surprised to find himself so vengeful and desperate.

You're going crazy, a voice in him whispered. You're losing your mind.

Well, what if he was?

For the third time he turned the ray. Munk disappeared behind a mountainous wave, but that wouldn't save him.

Walker's eyelids began to flutter when Soledad shook him. She could only hold him and stare at him, as if she were seeing something impossible.

She had been convinced that Tyrone had killed him.

But he was alive.

Walker was alive!

'My head hurts,' he croaked, dazed.

Her jaw dropped. 'Your . . . your head hurts?' Then she pulled him to her, making him groan in pain again, but that didn't bother her. She held him close and wept as she had last wept when her father, Scarab, died, and somewhere deep inside she wondered why you shed the same tears whether someone dies or whether he comes back to you.

After a while he took her head very gently between both his hands and kissed her. She couldn't help thinking how strange it was for her to feel so much for this uncouth, unshaven pirate, but then she gave up trying to find an answer to that riddle.

'I thought you were dead,' she whispered a moment later, very close to his ear.

He hesitated before gradually remembering what had happened. 'Tyrone . . . he was here. Where is he?'

'Lying out there in the corridor.'

He stroked her hair with his sound hand. 'You fought him?'

She nodded. 'He's wounded. And unconscious.'

Walker smiled. 'I saw you out on the rampart . . . you left a lot of those cut-throats alive. Found your soft heart, eh?'

For a moment she avoided his eyes almost as if she were slightly ashamed, but then she looked him in the face and kissed him again, smiling.

When she drew away, she saw that his expression had changed. His face was ashen, but without a word he flung his arm out and pushed her violently away from him. Utterly confused, she flew to one side and crashed against the wall, began to protest – and saw the figure that had been standing behind her, sword raised, about to split her skull with a single blow.

Tyrone's eyes were clouded; his mouth slightly open. He turned to her. His arrogant smile was gone, and there was nothing but hatred in his features now. The smudged war-paint looked as if someone's fingers had drawn deep furrows over a face made of mud.

'*No,*' roared Walker, as he realised that Tyrone was about to throw his sword at Soledad like a spear.

'Go to hell!' whispered the cannibal king.

She was just going to roll aside when a movement distracted her attention, making her hesitate for a second.

Something thundered through the door like an angry bull. Steel flashed.

Tyrone threw his sword. At the last moment she turned away, but not far enough. The blade went into her right shoulder, flinging her upper body to the floor.

The mighty figure racing up behind Tyrone struck even as he ran, and his serrated sword blade cut through Tyrone's black ponytail. There was a double crash as the cannibal king fell to the floor, dead.

The pain in her shoulder was making Soledad feel faint. She groaned softly, raised her head once more, and looked at the steel blade sticking into her.

'Oh, damn it all,' she whispered tonelessly.

Walker crawled over the floor to her, and was just in time to catch the back of her head as she lost consciousness. Before everything went black before her eyes, she saw him bending over her, alarmed and full of concern.

There was another face beside his too.

Surprisingly enough, it was the face of a dog.

'Griffin!' Munk staggered to his feet again. 'Stop this nonsense!'

Nonsense was too mild a term for what Griffin had in mind. But as he sent the ray sweeping close above Munk yet again, serious doubts entered his mind for the first time. Was he still, in his thoughts, in the middle of a battle in which you struck out blindly in all directions, without stopping to think about guilt or innocence? What had become of principles like fairness and justice?

In short, had he lost his wits entirely?

Horrified at himself, he reined in the ray and turned it again, but this time much more slowly. He flew to within a few paces of Munk, who was crouching between the waves on all fours, out of breath and looking up at him.

Griffin cleared his throat. He felt a little of the tension and aggression fall away from him, but none of his terror on Jolly's behalf.

'Where is she?' he shouted down to the boy.

'I don't know, damn it.' Munk looked as if he were on the point of bursting into tears, but he still had himself under control. 'When everything suddenly . . . went bright like that . . . we were separated. It was all so fast. Water came from everywhere, and at the same moment . . . oh, I don't know, it was as if something was reaching for me –

like a tunnel through the sea – and it pulled me away . . . to somewhere. Then I was on the surface all at once, and . . . and I don't know where she is, Griffin. I just don't know.'

'You were together down there?' asked Griffin. 'In the Maelstrom?'

'In the middle of it.' Munk's face now reflected his despair and anger. 'And damn it all, I didn't get up here alive just to be run down by a flying ray! I didn't do anything to Jolly. The pearl . . . the magic . . . oh, I don't know, it exploded, and then there was all that light, and then . . . and then . . .' He swallowed, and fell silent.

Griffin's guilty conscience stirred powerfully, and he suddenly felt wretched. Had he really meant to kill Munk? Heavens above, what had this dirty war done to them all to make friends fight each other?

'If I come far enough down to the water, can you climb on?' asked Griffin.

'I think so.'

Griffin turned the ray through several degrees, bringing it so low that the crests of the waves slapped against its belly. Munk managed to catch the edge of one wing and pulled himself up by it. Breathless and visibly weakened, he climbed into the saddle behind Griffin.

'I'm sorry,' said Griffin, and he meant it. 'I . . . I don't know what got into me.'

'You were doing it for Jolly,' said Munk faintly. It sounded like an observation, not a complaint.

'Yes,' said Griffin uncomfortably.

Munk put a hand on his shoulder. 'Then let's get going,' he said. 'We have to find her!'

MAGIC YARN

Somewhere in the depths of the ocean Jolly was racing along a tunnel made of water, not a whirlpool like the Maelstrom but leading horizontally through the sea. Darkness and light swept past her, sometimes a few flecks of colour, perhaps shoals of fish or coral reefs, or even creatures that no human being had ever seen before. At first she panicked and tried to slow down in self-defence, but without success. Then she remembered that she had already been this way before, it had been the same then, and she realised that yes, she was racing through the sea, or maybe through something that only looked like it.

She still wasn't sure whether the place where the Water Weavers sat really lay on the bed of an ordinary ocean. In the same way, the Mount Olympus of the Greek gods had certainly been no normal mountain, and the Asgard of the Nordic peoples wasn't at the end of a real rainbow.

After a while she just let herself drift rapidly on, closed her eyes, and concentrated on not feeling sick at such speed. She didn't want to meet the Weavers looking green in the face and with bloodshot eyes.

The last few minutes – or hours? – had passed in a strange and frenzied way, as if she herself were standing outside events. The last thing she could remember clearly was the pearl fading in the darkness of the Maelstrom. Or no, there was more: the light had been extinguished, the pearl drowned in darkness. Then came an enormous movement, one that she felt but did not see. Something had come towards her at vast speed, something so large that the water around her was pressed back and tore her away to somewhere else, far from the pearl and, she supposed, from Munk too.

Munk! What had become of him? The thought of him hurt as if . . . yes, as if she might never see him again.

Then there had been the light, far away, because the displaced water was carrying her on. And in front of the light, just for the fraction of a second, she had seen a gigantic shape – the outline of something that first circled around her and then, when the light went out, moved towards her. But it had all happened too fast for her to make out any details. Nothing was left but the impression of monstrous size and strangeness – and something like a touch of amazement at the power being unleashed.

After that the light turned to darkness, probably not in fact but as she remembered it. She suspected that she had lost consciousness for a moment. But perhaps what was happening before her eyes was just too strange and forceful for her senses to grasp. It was as if her mind had simply closed down the hatches, refusing to take in any more, in the same way that only a certain amount of cargo will fit into the hold of a galleon. Her ability to understand was brimming over like a full water butt. No more would fit in.

And now the Water Weavers too.

It was strange how naturally she expected to meet the three of them. She had reached the end of her journey. She didn't know whether the magic liberated by the pearl had destroyed the Maelstrom or not, but one way or another this was the end.

Perhaps she was dead.

'Not dead,' said a woman's voice in her mind, and when she opened her eyes she was sinking the very last of the way down to the sand of a plain beneath the sea.

Three shell-encrusted spinning wheels were set at the points of a triangle in front of her. Sitting at them with their backs to each other and their ancient faces looking out were the three Water Weavers. As on the first occasion when they had summoned Jolly, they were joined together by their long white hair, which stretched between them like fine cobwebs.

'You are not dead,' the voice repeated. Even that first time, it had irritated her to be unable to make out which of the three was speaking when. None of them raised her head or stopped working as their fingers tirelessly turned the wheels, spinning pure water into the yarn from which they wove the magic net. The strands of yarn, finger-thick and as clear as crystal, stretched in all directions over the plain and far beyond, through all the deeps and shallows of the oceans.

'You are back,' observed one of the old women.

'That is good,' said another.

'Very good,' said the third.

'It means that the Maelstrom is destroyed.'

'The way to the Mare Tenebrosum closed.'

'The threat of the masters averted.'

'For the time being.'

'Yes, for the time being.'

'Not for ever.'

'Hardly that.'

Jolly's head was spinning with the speed at which the Weavers fired off their comments. Her legs gave way and she sank to her knees on the sea-bed. Sand swirled up and settled again. She felt dizzy, and now she felt sick too.

'It will soon wear off,' said one of the old women.

'Don't be afraid.'

Jolly raised her head and defiantly scrambled up again. 'I'm not. Not of you.'

The three of them said nothing. Their fingers danced around their spindles as they sorted out their watery yarn, and they kept their eyes lowered.

'May I ask you something?'

'Whatever you like,' replied one of the women.

Jolly thought for a moment. 'Aina became the Maelstrom because she went over to the side of the powers of the Mare Tenebrosum, didn't she?'

'They gave her the power to become the Maelstrom.'

There was a difference, but it meant little now. Jolly went on. 'And then she . . . then the Maelstrom refused to obey the masters of the Mare. It wanted to have its revenge on the human race alone. Aina's revenge. Right?'

'That is one explanation, yes.'

'But what part did the shape-shifter play?' asked Jolly.

'It was a creature of the masters. They conjured it up, crossing the barrier between the worlds, and they did it with the magic of the Maelstrom.'

Another of the Weavers took up the tale. 'When the Maelstrom understood that, it was almost too late. The wyvern had built the bridge over which you were to cross to the Mare Tenebrosum.'

'That was why the Maelstrom sent the kobalins,' said the third woman.

'But one thing it could not do: it could not kill the wyvern. The shape-shifter was made from part of itself. The Maelstrom would have had to turn its magic against itself to destroy the creature.'

'But the wyvern was destroyed all the same.'

'Your friend the boy killed it.'

'My friend?' said Jolly excitedly. 'You mean . . . *Griffin*? . . . How is he?'

'He is alive.'

She was so relieved that her knees almost gave way for the second time.

'He destroyed the wyvern,' said one of the Weavers, unmoved, 'and so he did what the Maelstrom itself could not.'

Jolly protested. 'He certainly didn't do it to help the Maelstrom.'

'Of course not.'

'But nonetheless the wyvern's death suited the Maelstrom.

For now the masters of the Mare Tenebrosum could not influence the battle for Aelenium.'

'What's happened to Aelenium? Are they all right there?' It was a faint hope, and she knew it. It couldn't be as easy as that.

'Aelenium will be rebuilt.'

'What about my friends?' asked Jolly hesitantly. She was terribly afraid of the answer.

'Many of them survived the battle.'

'But . . . that means some are dead, doesn't it?' she asked reluctantly, although the relief at hearing that Griffin was alive still outweighed all other feelings.

'Yes.'

She swallowed a lump in her throat. 'What about Munk?'

'The second polliwiggle is alive.'

She drew a deep breath.

'Others are dead,' said one of the Weavers.

'The One has gone.'

The One? Jolly thought. Then she understood. 'Forefather is dead?'

'The creator has gone away.'

'Leaving the world behind.'

'In our care.'

Thoughts were whirling around in Jolly's mind like a

swarm of mosquitoes. She guessed that she was forgetting things – things she ought to be asking now, for this could well be her last chance. But she could think of only one question. 'Why didn't you help me when I was in the Rift?'

'We did.'

'As well as we could.'

'We sent you the luminous fish.'

Jolly nodded slowly. 'The Maelstrom swallowed them up.'

'Yes, that is sad.'

'But when everything looked so bad, why didn't you bring me out of there?' asked Jolly. 'The way you did before.'

'We could not.'

'Not so close to the Maelstrom.'

'Not while it was alive.'

'It would have sucked in our powers, and they would have made it even stronger.'

'And even if we could have done it, why should we have brought you out?'

All Jolly's limbs ached, and the dizziness wasn't dying down. She went slowly towards one of the Weavers. 'Why?' she repeated. 'Because I almost died. That's why.'

'But then who would have destroyed the Maelstrom?' asked one of the old women disarmingly.

Jolly lowered her voice. 'I didn't destroy it. That was Munk. It was his idea and his magic.'

'He would not have done it if you hadn't been with him. You brought him to his senses.'

'It was all a part of your destiny.'

'You were the trigger.'

'Which is more important?' asked one Weaver. 'The cannon or the gunner who lights the fuse?'

'The sword or the soldier who draws it?'

'The soldier or the general who leads him into battle?'

Everything seemed to Jolly to be going round and round, including the old women's words: they appeared to take vague shape, a swirling cloud of syllables and sounds, lulling her and making her sleepy.

'We want to thank you, Jolly.'

'You are exhausted. You must rest now.'

She nodded, dazed. 'I'd like to do that with my friends.'

'Goodbye, Jolly. You have done much more than you think.'

'Very much more.'

She was about to protest when she felt herself caught again by an invisible current. Something carried her up from the sea-bed and away from the Weavers until the three women were only dots fading in the distance, the blurred and mysterious origin of the yarn. It occurred to Jolly that *yarn* was also another word for *story*. And hadn't this story begun with the Water Weavers? They had created the polliwiggles, including Aina, and thus in a certain way the Maelstrom itself. It seemed to Jolly as if she had come upon the trail of an even greater truth. But as so often when you realise you are very close to something important, it eludes you before you can grasp it. And so Jolly forgot her idea, and did not think of it again.

All around her the water was becoming a narrow tunnel again, she was chasing through it, and for the first time she realised that she was moving through the veins of magic themselves. Straight along the yarn to one of its ends.

Griffin and Munk did not exchange a word as the flying ray, moving its weary wings up and down, brought them back to Aelenium.

They had spent hours circling above the sea, first where the Maelstrom had been, then in a wider and wider orbit. A time came when Munk pointed out that they were moving in the shape of a spiral or a whirlpool, as if the Maelstrom still had them under its spell. This idea made Griffin so uneasy that for the rest of their search he made the ray fly a random zigzag course, and he was almost relieved to feel no supernatural current hauling them back into spiral flight again.

And it had all been in vain. They hadn't found Jolly. Darkness fell quickly, but they had gone on searching while the moon turned the sea into a landscape of grey peaks and deep black valleys of shadow.

They would probably have gone on flying until daybreak and even beyond, but soon it became obvious that the exhausted ray couldn't carry them much longer. It had spent many hours in the turmoil of battle, with hardly any time to rest before Griffin flew it out to the Maelstrom. Now it had reached the limits of its strength.

'It will fall into the sea if we don't turn back,' Griffin had said, and without a word Munk agreed. There was no point in it. They weren't going to find Jolly.

Now, some time later, they were approaching the ring of mist. At first sight it looked as if nothing there had changed – if it hadn't been for the countless items of flotsam from wrecks drifting on the sea. After a while they saw dead bodies in the water too, and steeled themselves for the images of horror that might well be awaiting them beyond the mist.

As the vapours thinned, their worst expectations were exceeded. The sight of the devastated coral slopes was terrible: a grey-white landscape of ruins reminding Griffin of the fissured slabs of lava on the slopes of the volcanoes that rose on some of the Caribbean islands. Most terrible of all, however, was the absence of any human beings in this wilderness. He had expected to see some wandering through the ruins, alone or in groups, looking for survivors or anything that could still be useful. But the slopes were empty, completely lifeless.

Only on coming closer did he see by moonlight that the upper third of the city had been spared. Houses, towers and palaces stood there intact; streets and squares were still linked by filigree bridges crossing them; and the points of light flickering in many places turned out to be camp fires with people crowding around them.

Munk still said nothing, and when Griffin spoke to him the only answer to pass his lips came as a few disconnected words. He had been hoping that the destruction of the Maelstrom would preserve Aelenium from the worst, but now he learned the painful truth.

Yet for all the horror and pain, they had good reason to be thankful that the city still lay steadily at anchor, and there were people left to rebuild what the war and the tidal wave had destroyed.

Staggering slightly in the air, the ray flew over the rooftops of the intact quarter, and with one last effort rose to the refuge of its stables.

Two people were standing on the ledge around the opening through which it flew. One was the Ghost-Trader. His voluminous cloak hid the second figure. They both seemed to turn to the new arrivals, but the ray was too exhausted to slow down again or hover on the spot so close to home. With no strength left in it, it came down over the opening and landed abruptly on the floor of the rays' hall.

Grooms came hurrying up to tend the animal. Griffin and Munk helped each other out of their straps before the men reached them. Both of them were as drained as the ray, and Griffin's wounds were throbbing painfully as if they were inflamed. He had not lost much blood, but his shirt was sticking to him where his injuries were encrusted, and he felt twinges of stinging pain as he tried, with difficulty, to keep on his feet.

Munk saw him stumble and tried to catch him, but then they both collapsed and stayed wearily sitting on the ground. Griffin buried his face in his hands.

'Griffin, my boy.' The Ghost-Trader's voice penetrated the mist of self-reproach and grief that had settled around him. 'I'm so glad to see you back with us.'

Griffin raised his face and looked at the one-eyed man. The two parrots were perching on his shoulders, heads on one side. Bemused, he wondered why the Trader was smiling.

A hand was laid on Griffin's shoulder. It belonged to Munk.

Slowly, as if in a dream, Griffin turned his head to him. And now Munk was smiling too. What in the world . . . ?

'Griffin,' said the Trader, stepping aside. 'Look who's here.'

Behind him, the figure who had been standing on the ledge with him came into sight.

Griffin burst into tears.

Jolly knelt down beside him and kissed him.

THE NEW WORLD

The sea horses returned two days later.

Jolly was standing on a balcony with Griffin, looking down over the devastated slopes to the water. The Caribbean sun blazed in a clear sky, making the crests of the waves below shimmer hazily. Amidst all the glowing and glittering the hippocamps came into sight as tiny dots, first singly, then breaking through the ring of mist in a mighty shoal to approach the desolate starfish city where their stables had once stood. The first of them had already arrived, and were gathering at the cuttings in the starfish arm where they once came ashore.

'So d'Artois was right,' said Griffin. 'He was sure they'd find their way back.'

Jolly had difficulty taking her eyes off the majestic shoal of hippocamps. But she glanced sideways at Griffin and smiled. 'Why aren't you on your way down yet?' she asked, laughing. 'You know you can hardly wait!'

'I just want to see if Matador's with them.'

'I'm sure of it.'

'Yes . . . well, I hope so.' With that he turned, gave her a quick grin over his shoulder, and disappeared into the palace. Considering that his ribs were bandaged under his clothes, he moved very quickly.

Jolly watched him go. His many blond braids flew out behind him like the tail of a comet. She had told him more than once since their return how glad she was to be with him again, but somehow she hadn't managed to express anything like her real feelings.

Sighing softly, she turned to look at the water again. Down on the shore, some of the leading sea horses had been caught. A few saddles from workshops in the upper parts of the city had been quickly buckled on their backs, and now the first riders were setting out to bring the chaotic hippocamp formation into order. More and more kept coming through the mist. The animals had stayed together over the last few days, and must have dived to depths where the tidal wave couldn't hurt them.

'Jolly?' Soledad's voice came from inside the building. She sounded anxious. 'What's going on? Griffin just ran past as if a thousand kobalins were after him.'

Jolly went in. Soledad was lying in the bed of her guest room with her left arm and right shoulder bandaged, looking impatient enough to rip the covers to pieces. A deep line of concern divided her forehead.

'Heavens!' she groaned. 'I'm so tired of lying around here while –'

Jolly silenced her with a soothing gesture and sat down on the edge of the bed. Over the past two days she and Griffin had spent a great deal of time with the princess; the three of them had told each other their experiences, talking excitedly, marvelling, and realising that it did them good to talk about all these things, almost as if it made them into wild adventure stories thought up by someone else. Now and then Munk had looked in, but usually he soon went back to the libraries, where the Ghost-Trader was doing his best to initiate him into the secrets of Forefather's book-room. Munk had asked to be allowed to stay in Aelenium and devote his time to the books. Soledad had said he probably just wanted to get out of helping with the work of clearing the devastated lower parts of the city, but Jolly knew better: Munk was fascinated by books and ancient knowledge, and Forefather's death and the end of the Maelstrom didn't change that.

The polliwiggles avoided talking about their journey at

the bottom of the sea. A time would come when they could speak of it, but now at least the memories of what they had been through were still too fresh.

'Well,' said Soledad seriously, when Jolly was sitting beside her, 'what's happened? I hope you're not silly enough to quarrel with Griffin when the two of you have only just –'

Jolly took Soledad's hand and shook her head, laughing. 'Don't worry. Not everyone around here shows how much she likes someone else by quarrelling with him from morning to night.'

'If you're referring to that little spat between Walker and me this morning, let me tell you, people can be fond of each other even if . . . well, even if their opinions happen to differ.'

'Buenaventure said the two of you were snapping at each other like two dogs fighting for a bone.'

'Well, he should know.' Soledad smiled. 'Anyway, it wasn't a quarrel. But lying about in bed doing nothing sends me crazy – and I suppose I take it out on poor Walker now and then. All the same, about you and Griffin –'

'Everything's fine, don't worry.' Now Jolly told her about the return of the sea horses, and the princess's face brightened.

'Thank God. The people here have lost enough already. It's good that at least they still have the hippocamps.'

Jolly was going to say something when her glance fell on the open doorway to the balcony. The sky above was darkened by a flight of rays diving steeply through the air beyond the balustrade. At the same time distant cries came up from below.

'What's going on now?' Jolly jumped up and ran out.

'Well?' cried Soledad impatiently before Jolly was even out of the room. 'Can you see anything?'

'Just a moment. I – oh no!'

A moment later Jolly was running past Soledad's bed to the door, the same way as Griffin had just gone and moving at least as fast.

With difficulty, Soledad raised herself. 'Could someone please tell me what on earth –'

Jolly stopped, a shaking hand on the doorknob. Her face was ashen. 'It's the whale. His body has surfaced from the sea.'

She did not catch up with Griffin on her way down, and when she reached the water she saw him standing at the front of the crowd. She made her way through to him. His features were set and grey.

She followed his glance to the corpse of the giant whale. Like an island that has only just emerged from the tides, the body rose above the waves not a stone's throw from the shore. Several mounted rays were circling in the sky, and a number of sea-horse riders had left the hippocamp herd and made their way over to Jasconius.

The whale was drifting on his side. From here she could see one of his eyes looking dully up at the sky. For a moment Jolly thought she saw life and movement in it, but then she realised that it was only the reflection of the sunlight on its gigantic black pupil.

She put her arm round Griffin and felt the tension of his body. At first he didn't move, but after a moment or so he responded to her embrace.

'I'm so sorry,' Jolly whispered.

'I knew he was dead,' he said huskily, gently releasing himself from her and calling one of the sea-horse riders over. At the first attempt his grief-stricken voice failed him, but when he tried again the rider heard him and came to the pier. After a moment's hesitation, the man climbed out of the saddle and handed the animal over to Griffin.

The crowd that had gathered by the shore did not make a sound. Everyone was watching the boy, spellbound, as he moved over the massive corpse, first on all fours and then on his feet, leaning slightly forward.

Jolly leaped from the shore on to the waves. Striding out,

she ran across the water, reached the whale, and clambered up the smooth skin until she had reached Griffin.

He was crouching down beside Jasconius's eye. His face was streaming with water anyway, and she couldn't tell if he was shedding tears. She knelt down beside him without a word, took his hand and held it, giving him the time he needed to say goodbye to Jasconius. No one disturbed him, neither the people on the shore now sadly dispersing nor the riders of the rays, who turned away after a while and flew back up to their hall.

'He was my friend, you know,' said Griffin quietly after a while, without looking away from the great dark eye.

'I know,' she said, swallowing. 'And I'm sure he knew it too.'

Griffin slowly nodded. 'He saved my life. He saved the whole city. Without him the kobalins wouldn't have . . .' He stopped, and lowered his head.

Jolly wondered whether to put an arm round his shoulders and hold him close, but then decided not to. He would come to her when he needed her. But this was his own moment, something private between him and Jasconius.

A sea horse was reined in not far from the whale. Captain d'Artois had one arm in a sling. He looked sympathetically at Griffin. 'No one here will forget him,' he said, so quietly that his voice hardly rose above the sound of the surf breaking around the dead whale, almost as if he were afraid of rousing the boy from his grief.

Griffin raised his head. The water on his face had dried, but his eyes were still reddened. 'Jasconius was very old. And very lonely until Ebenezer joined him.' He was silent for a moment, and then said, 'He knew what he was sacrificing himself for. Ebenezer had shown him that some human beings are different.'

Suddenly they heard a splashing in the whale's half-open mouth, and then a series of loud, gasping breaths. Griffin started, and in excitement he slid down the curve of the great head to the corner of the huge mouth.

Jolly followed him when she saw how his expression had cleared.

'Ebenezer!' he called, and then he slipped halfway over the opening and reached in. 'Ebenezer! Thank God . . . !'

Jolly slid down beside him and took the old man's other arm as he came up from the whale's throat, coughing and panting. Together they pulled him past the mighty teeth and out. D'Artois was having difficulty in keeping his sea horse calm. It seemed as excited as its rider.

Ebenezer stared at them in astonishment. Then Griffin flung his arms around the old man with a cry of delight. The monk laughed. 'Take it easy, boy!' He returned the hug warmly, although he still looked weak.

Griffin was reluctant to let him go. 'We thought you were dead . . .'

'I was behind the magic door,' said Ebenezer, still panting. 'And then I . . . dived, when I realised we were coming up . . . I saw the dead boy, and the . . . the remains of the jellyfish . . . and then I swam after the light . . .'

Griffin hugged him again, so hard that he made the old man gasp for breath. But next moment his glance fell on the whale's lifeless eye, and his features darkened again.

Feeling helpless, Jolly met d'Artois' eye. With a slight gesture, he told her it was best not to do anything, just sit there and wait.

Leave the two of them alone for a moment, his glance seemed to say. Let them mourn a friend together.

And so they crouched side by side, high up on the body of Jasconius, while the waves lapped around the whale and the wind swept over the devastated arm of the starfish city. The soft sound of hammer blows came from the slopes; a voice called something out. The mist formed ghostly swathes, and up in the sky flying rays shone in the sunlight.

*

It was Munk who thought of the book.

Jasconius was given a funeral with all the honours Aelenium could show and sent to the bottom of the sea for the last time, weighted heavily down. Next day Ebenezer asked permission to visit the libraries of Aelenium, and Munk offered to show him round. In the course of that afternoon, Ebenezer told him about the research work he had done on the coast over thirty years ago: his writings on the insects of the Orinoco and the drawings he had done. Of course, he added, he was very sorry it had all been lost when he was assumed drowned.

Munk remembered what Jolly had told him about her search for the poisonous spiders of the *Maid Maddy*. She had come upon a book in the library written by a missionary about three decades ago, but taken to Europe and printed there only after he was supposed to have perished in a shipwreck.

After showing Ebenezer round, Munk had found the book in a corner of the library and took it to Jolly. She and Griffin were beside themselves with delight when they found the author's name on the title page. Griffin in particular was so happy with his find that he went straight to Soledad, who was just taking her first shaky walk with Walker on the outside balconies of the palace. He told her all about it; she too was delighted, and even Walker murmured a few appreciative words.

It was not until that evening, when they were all eating together with the winged snake comfortably coiled up under the window, letting the moon shine in on its feathers, that Griffin suddenly stood up, called for silence, and asked them all to drink a toast to the dead Jasconius and to Ebenezer. Then he ceremoniously handed the monk the book Munk found in the library.

After spending thirty years in the belly of the whale, Ebenezer opened the leather-bound cover and saw his name. He was so moved that he sat down and leafed excitedly through the pages, while Jolly and Griffin held hands under the table, and Buenaventure went round behind Munk, clapped him on the shoulder, and whispered in his growl of a voice that there were great heroic deeds like defeating a Maelstrom, and smaller ones like making an old man wonderfully happy, and there wasn't much to choose between them.

They all sat together for a long time that evening, enjoying each other's company, telling tales, making plans, and dreaming of the future here in Aelenium and elsewhere. All the time, Ebenezer held the book clasped to his breast like a lost child, and whenever he thought no one was looking he stroked it and wiped a tear from the corner of his eye.

Several weeks after the battle for the starfish city and the end of the Maelstrom, Soledad put on one of the diving suits again, fitted an aerated stone into it, and went down into the depths with Jolly. Her shoulder still gave her some pain, and she moved her left arm more stiffly than her right arm, but on the whole she was surprised to find how easy it was.

For a while they sat on one of the steel links of the anchor chain, legs dangling over the dark blue abyss. Jolly could hear what Soledad was saying behind her mask, and although she already knew the story of her encounter in the underwater city she was happy to listen to it again, for now Soledad described all the details and told her about her request to the giant serpent. Jolly remembered the feeling that had come over her and Munk when they explored the underwater city together during their first days in Aelenium, a sense of panic and the knowledge that something was there behind them, just out of the field of polliwiggle vision. All at once it made sense, and she knew that what had been following them had not necessarily meant them any ill.

She looked out at the slanting, fissured coral walls of the

underwater city where they fell to be lost from sight somewhere below. Their hollows and clefts and the beauty of their intricate forms moved her, if not in the same way as the first time.

Finally she nodded to Soledad, and they set out together. The princess led Jolly to a cavern, and through it they entered the underwater city. Now it was Jolly's turn to swim ahead; her polliwiggle vision made it easy for her to take her bearings in the dark caves and tunnels. Soledad had some of the glowing stones with her, and used them to mark the way they must go back.

It wasn't long before they reached a deep vertical shaft. Jolly felt almost sure it was the one through which she had once come up with Munk.

Soledad changed the aerated stone under her diving helmet and then looked down into the darkness. Jolly tried to imagine how terrifying that bottomless black must be without polliwiggle vision – even she felt uneasy, although she could see a hundred times further than Soledad.

She was all the more surprised when the princess suddenly said, 'It's coming.'

Jolly wanted to ask what made her so sure, but at that moment she saw it herself.

Below them, where the shaft dissolved into darkness at

the edge of polliwiggle vision, something was moving. The darkness rippled, and then something emerged from it: a mighty reptilian head, triangular, with slits for eyes, followed by an enormously long serpentine body. The creature shot towards them straight as an arrow, displacing such quantities of water that the pressure sent the two intruders shooting some way further up.

Soledad kept calm, while Jolly had to struggle with herself not to flee before the swift approach of the sea-serpent. The gap in the wall through which they had slipped into the shaft now seemed impossibly far away.

The serpent's climb slowed down; the currents ebbed away. The head rose before them and stopped level with their faces.

'We came to thank you,' said Soledad, under her helmet.

The serpent looked at her for a long time without any noticeable reaction, and then its eyes turned to Jolly. The mouth opened very slightly, and the tips of a fine, forked tongue licked out straight towards her.

'Don't worry, it won't hurt you.' Soledad's voice sounded so hollow inside the helmet that it wasn't clear how convinced she was by her own words.

But then something strange happened. At first Jolly was about to flinch away from the tongue – and the next moment, very suddenly, all her fears left her. This happened just as the two tips of the tongue touched her cheek, moved over it with velvety softness, went on down her chin to her neck and then to a place above her heart. It lingered there for a second or so, and then moved fast as lightning back into the serpent's mouth.

Jolly didn't even breathe a sigh of relief. All her fear was gone. Now she understood what Soledad had felt when she faced this being for the first time. It was an emotion in such overwhelming contrast to the giant reptile's terrifying appearance that it made her quite dizzy.

'Soledad says you protected the anchor chain from the kobalins,' said Jolly to the serpent. Was she wrong, or did understanding flash in those cold snake eyes? 'Without you the city would have been destroyed by the tidal wave.' She thought briefly, but nothing else occurred to her except to bow low in the water. 'Thank you,' she said.

The serpent's head moved up and down several times, which might have been a nod or just the result of a chance current. At last the tongue flickered out a second time, touched Jolly and then Soledad, and vanished back into the serpent's mouth. The serpentine body turned in a narrow curve before their eyes, rushed endlessly past them, and shot back into the depths.

436

Jolly and Soledad hovered there in the shaft for a long time, looking into the darkness below their feet in silence. At last the princess said, 'I wanted you to see it. So that I'd know I didn't dream the whole thing up.'

'It's beautiful,' said Jolly. 'And very old, I think.' She remembered Jasconius, now resting somewhere at the bottom of the sea, and wondered how many such beings might still survive in the darkness down there. Creatures of terrifying appearance that were not what they seemed. A shudder ran down her back, but this time it was a pleasant feeling, born of the certainty that even her meetings with gods and Water Weavers were merely a sparkling foretaste of all the marvels still waiting out there.

They turned, went back through the underwater city along the route they had marked, and were soon swimming through a curtain of sunbeams reaching down into the water, refracted a million times and sparkling.

'Do you think the Worm can dive in that new body?' asked Soledad just before they broke through the surface. 'If so, there's someone down there a snake should meet. They could date each other.'

Smiling, Jolly reached for the rungs of the iron ladder and climbed up it to the arm of the starfish.

Griffin was waiting for them on the pier. Walker and

Buenaventure were with him, and all three were waiting expectantly to hear what they had to say. Later, they had to repeat it all for Munk and the former Hexhermetic Shipworm, and a third time for the Ghost-Trader, who nodded thoughtfully when he heard them and then wandered back to the library in silence, leaning on Forefather's staff, as if all these events had robbed him of the strength of many years.

The parrots were sitting on his shoulders, one with red and one with yellow eyes, and they still remained motionless when he went on to Forefather's balcony alone, looked out over the nocturnal sea, and breathed in deeply and deliberately. He gazed down at the coral slopes, where new buildings were already being carved out, then up to the plateau at the peak. Several flying rays circled it, like shadows swallowing up the stars.

Last of all he looked down to the shore, the water between the starfish city and the ring of mist, and his gaze went on into the depths of the ocean, where he saw many beings, both mighty and very small. He saw Jasconius dreaming in the dark, and he saw the veins of magic, newly woven where they had been torn before.

Hugh and Moe chattered quietly close to his ears. The Ghost-Trader turned and went inside. His staff clicked with every step, the sound of it following him like an invisible companion.

He quietly closed the door to the balcony behind him, and went back into the labyrinth of books. Munk and Ebenezer were waiting for him with a thousand questions – questions which had ten thousand answers.

Soon the three of them were sitting there in the middle of all the stories in these books: a boy, a monk and a god. When that thought struck the Ghost-Trader he laughed out loud, and on being asked why he murmured something about destiny, and old age, and knowledge, and made himself out mysterious and mystical so that they wouldn't understand what had moved him. But the truth was that he enjoyed their company, and for the first time in many long ages he even enjoyed his own.

Far away, beyond coral walls, corridors and halls, Jolly and Griffin kissed, watched Soledad and Walker arguing, listened to the winged snake preening its feathers with a rasping tongue under the tall arched window, and finally looked over Buenaventure's shoulder as, working by candlelight on a large sheet of paper, he put the finishing touches to his designs for a new ship, a three-master like the *Carfax*, but a vessel that he hoped would be slimmer and faster.

Later they went out into the moonlight, wandered along a pillared arcade of the palace, breathed in the salt tang of the sea, and looked at the workers' camp fires down on the slopes.

And that night, at last, Griffin finished the coral tattoo on Jolly's back.